THE BLOOD THAT BINDS US

THE BOUND BY BLOOD SERIES

ERIN MAINORD

First published in the United States of America May 2023 by Lake Country Press & Reviews.

Cataloging-in-Publication Data is on file with the Library of Congress.

ISBN: Paperback: 979-8-9877391-0-5

Ebook: 979-8-9877391-1-2

Author website: https://www.erinmainord.com

Publisher website: https://www.lakecountrypress.com

Editor: Borbala Branch

Cover: Emily's World of Design

Formatting: Dawn Lucous of Yours Truly Book Services

Author photo: Kaitlyn Hull Photography

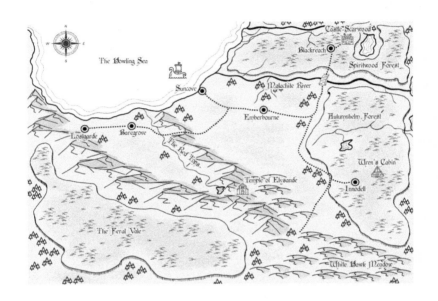

Dear Reader:

I am thrilled you have picked up my book. Your support means far more to me than this writer could ever put into words. That being said, mental health is so important and for that reason, I will always include content warnings for each of my books. If you read any of my stories and find that I missed something, please reach out and let me know so I may adjust my list appropriately.

The following is a list of **content warnings** for what you will find inside The Blood That Binds Us.

Please note this list contains spoilers:

Alcohol consumption, death, descriptions of blood, explicit language, explicit sexual content, mention of child abuse, sexual assault (including attempted rape on-page and mention of it occurring in the past,) sexual kinks (blood and knife play,) talk and threats of genocide of fantasy peoples, and violence.

This book ends on a cliffhanger.

Mental health matters.

You matter.

For Ian.
Much like my heart, this book has always belonged to you.

PLAYLIST

The following is a list of the songs I had playing on repeat while writing this story.

Animal: Caroline Rose
Desire: Meg Myers
Howl: Florence + the Machine
(I Just) Died In Your Arms: Hidden Citizens
Middle of the Night: Elley Duhé
No Light, No Light: Florence + the Machine
Power Over Me: Dermot Kennedy
Simmer: Hayley Williams
Snow White Queen: Evanescence
You're Breaking Me: Topic & A7S

CHAPTER 1

I imagine the taste of their blood on my teeth.

My throat burns with the thought of it dripping over the swells of my lips and rushing down my neck like cardinal veins. One tiny kill is all it would take, and I would be free.

She tugs on the chains secured to my throat, and I jerk from the sharp sting of the iron collar. I glare at the back of the head in front of me—a woman with a long brown braid resting against her light, improvised armor. Her leather skins don't stand a chance against kingdom steel; foolish to attempt this, even for them. I hiss at the iron shackles binding my wrists— the metal searing my skin, reacting to the chaos simmering just beneath my flesh. If only I could yank her head by that pretty braid.

"We're closing in. Stay alert. Stay alive," Cathal calls from up ahead. There are many of us, maybe a few hundred, maybe more. Not nearly enough, not even with me as leverage.

"Ya hear that, witch?" brown braid smirks over her shoulder. "Almost there."

Leaves crunch beneath my naked feet like snapping bones. I could dislocate my thumbs, slip my hands through the cuffs of the toxic metal and flee, but they'd come after me.

They always come.

I glimpse Cathal's head bobbing towards us, his silhouette dark against the backdrop of moonlit alders and the midnight sky. He stops when he reaches brown braid and spins to walk alongside us. A dark beard hugs his squared-off jaw, and his blue eyes rake over my body in disgust. I ball my fists at the sight of their leader, my nails digging in deep enough to coax blood from my palms.

"Attack with vigor. Get them on you and *that one*," Cathal spits with a nod in my direction.

"Understood, Your Grace." *Your Grace?*

"I can't cast while in iron," I interject. *They know this, so why—*

"Margalo will take care of that," he says, shooting her a knowing look before continuing up ahead. Cathal disappears into the horde of Legion soldiers—men and women armored in thick animal skins. Leather that will do little to protect them from swords forged from the highest quality steel.

I almost smile at the mental images of them being slaughtered like cattle. *Almost*, because even that is too merciful an end for these monsters. A rebellion that dwells in darkened forests and preys on those unfortunate enough to cross their camps.

I trip on a loose rock and stumble forward, my hands sinking into the mud to break my fall. Margalo shoots me a warning glare and yanks me upright with a quick tug of my chains.

"I'm gonna let 'em wound ya first, witch. Make sure you're fired up for 'em," she says.

Cathal's words replay in my ears, and their plan clicks in my head. I assumed they were intending on using me as a bargaining chip—exchanging me for leniency—but I realize they're even more feeble-minded than I gave them credit for.

When we near Castle Scarwood, brown braid—*Margalo*—is going to push us into the front lines, guaranteeing physical combat between them and us and triggering my survival instinct. And for someone like me, survival means bloodshed. A sure win for Legion, the rebellion that captured me a fortnight ago.

One flick.

One little flick of my wrist and her head would explode. My palms rub against each other with eagerness, but even if the iron wasn't suffocating my ability to cast, the consequences would be many more head explosions than just brown braid Margalo's. Because one is never enough. Not for someone like me. When my kind decides to kill, there is no washing the cherry red stain from our palms, no wiping the cardinal splatter from our chins.

The turrets draw a jagged line through the darkened sky, and judging from the height of them, we are less than half the hour from castle borders. My brain racks itself for a plan. When Margalo releases me from these chains, I cannot begin casting. One body is all it would take. One person's blood in my fingernails, and it would mean the extinction of my humanity.

I could attempt to flee. If I didn't hesitate and bolted the second my chains hit the ground, maybe, *just maybe,* I would be fast enough to make it through the fighting before a kingdom arrow finds my spine.

Shouts from ahead snap me back to focus. Margalo plants her feet in the dirt, and I stumble to a halt behind her as Legion battle cries carry the others charging forward, the metallic clashing of swords clattering in my ears. Fire claims the ground around us, no doubt ignited from the kingdom's flaming arrows. My lungs warm with an intake of the wispy gray perfume, and the smoke stings my eyes like burning mugwort. And then we're moving again as Margalo races ahead, my body betraying me by following behind, the chains of my iron collar attached to her waist.

Margalo draws the sword from her hip. I pull furiously against my chains, but it is futile. With a rapid lunge, a kingdom soldier slaps his sword against Margalo's, and they begin to dance, me stumbling behind like a broken marionette. I focus on Margalo's movements and mirror my steps to hers—left, right, down, left again—but when she suddenly dodges a blow I don't see coming, I am too late, and my right shoulder is pierced by the needle-like tip of his blade. I don't stifle my scream and half double over, now really being rocked in all directions by Margalo's erratic movements. The rusty scent of my own blood flares my nostrils, and my lips curl into a snarl.

"Now!" I screech. My vision blurs—from the smoke, loss of blood, or my own fury, I am unsure—but I hear as she slices our attacker with a final blow, his body slumping to the ground as she withdraws her weapon from his gut. She spins on her heels to face me, ripping a cord from her neck. Attached to the end of it is a key she jams it into the lock binding my collar together, and again at my wrists. I grind my teeth when the iron falls from me, the metal leaving a nasty purple singe everywhere it tasted my skin.

Free. I am free.

"Sic 'em, girl!" Margalo shouts to me.

Power rushes to my arms, my palms, flushing out the frozen pockets left behind from the stifling metal and heating it to a dangerous warmth. A heat I could unleash onto all of them. I could slaughter this entire Legion brigade in a blink before having to stop and lap the blood from their oozing wounds.

But I can't. I haven't come this far, endured this much to throw my humanity away. And certainly not because brown braid Margalo is ordering me to.

I don't think—there is no time to think. I throw my left hand above my head and charge towards the silhouetted line of kingdom soldiers, hollering to their armed shadows.

"Stop! Help me—I'm a prisoner! I'm their prisoner!"

Arms wrap around my chest from behind, and I howl from the pressure against my punctured shoulder. My back presses against smooth plated armor—a kingdom soldier then. My mouth goes dry as my vision tunnels in and out. A soldier charges towards us, waving his hands frantically as he yells to the one holding me, but his words are lost in the pounding of blood in my ears. Everything is black, then a sudden splash of color as my eyes fly open again, fighting to remain alert, to remain in control.

Is it happening? Am I still me? Or have I lost my own war against *her*, the monster that has hidden deep in my flesh since I was born?

The pain in my shoulder dulls, and the soldier vanishes from view. *Shame.* I wanted to try to read the words on his lips —to see if they believed my plight. Everything gently fades away—no trace the kingdom ever existed; no sign Legion ever dared to challenge them. Maybe she isn't so evil then, if she washes away the pain of reality so effortlessly. And with that comfort—the thought of not even existing flickering in the remains of my consciousness—everything goes silent, and I bury myself in her.

CHAPTER 2

Smack. Smack. Smack.

Someone is using my forehead as a drum pad. I turn my head to brush off the musician, but the chilled emptiness against my cheek is enough to stir me fully from sleep. An unforgiving pole juts into the flesh between my shoulder blades, my hands bound behind it. A dry dressing adorns my shoulder where the sword plunged into me—someone patched me up.

The room is narrow and vacant aside from a single chair across from me, the walls a nasty shade of cream, almost yellow in the faded glow of the torchlight. The room smells stale and musty like a bed of stinking iris. There is no drum player here—just the thudding of my brain against my skull—a horrible headache. A quick rattle of my chains confirms they are secure, but the magical itch crawling on my skin tells me they are not of iron. They don't think they are holding a witch then, let alone what I am. Best not to alert them of that—yet.

"Hello?" I shout into the empty room. "I'm awake! Somebody get in here!"

A moment passes, I hear a key snuggle into the lock, and the pale yellow door groans as it swings inward. A man dressed in typical kingdom garb walks into the room, followed by a shorter man wearing the same formal, black uniform. They position themselves diagonally from me on opposite sides. I stare at the tall one, then the short one. Easy enough targets to disable if I need to.

"You took quite the nap there," the tall one says. "Must have been a nasty gash on that shoulder." He nods towards my bandaged arm. The sleeve to my tunic has been ripped off completely; whomever bandaged me clearly didn't take the time to do so thoughtfully.

"Where am I?"

"I think the more appropriate question is, *who* are you?" the shorter one chimes in.

"A lady of Aegidale, and I wish to know where I am being held, and why I am chained up like a dog," I snap.

Their laughter reverberates through the dismal room.

"You hear that, Wyeth? She's a *lady*," short one mocks.

"Fetch His Grace," Wyeth orders. "This will be most entertaining."

Short one nods and leaves the room, leaving Wyeth staring at me inquisitively. "Might you tell me, what exactly was a *lady* doing with the rebellion?"

"I'm not a lady by title, but I am still a *woman* protected under kingdom law. Do you think they bound me in chains to chat and exchange pleasantries with them? I was taken." I spit the words at him, narrowing my eyes to imply I found his question moronic.

He snorts once in disbelief, and neither of us speaks again until the door behind Wyeth pushes open, revealing the shorter guard and, behind him and a foot taller, a young man. I recognize him instantly.

Singard Kilbreth. The Black Art of Aegidale.

Our neighbors across the sea are ruled by kings—mundane lands governed by human leaders. But Aegidale has always been headed by a mage—one selected and blessed by the goddess of the arcane herself: the Black Art.

My spine stiffens in his presence. Singard visited Innodell once, soon after he took the throne a year ago. I haven't seen him since, and I hoped I never would again.

"Your Grace," Wyeth dips his head upon his entrance.

Singard nods to them both, a silent dismissal, prompting them to mirror a quick bow and echo the appropriate farewell. Their absence leaves only one sound in the room: the clacking of the Black Art's polished shoes as he crosses the room and sits in the only chair. He wears a black surcoat made of soft leather, adorned with a gold threaded design along the turned-up neck. His hair is as dark as the leather, unbound and long down his back, and he looks at me for the first time, revealing green, downturned eyes. His inky hair bends at the cheekbones set sharp within his warm, copper skin.

"Your Grace," I say, my tone muddling his title with conde-scension.

He leans forward so his forearms rest on the tops of his thighs. "Miss," he replies, surprisingly polite. When I don't continue, he does. "What is your name?"

I consider lying, but I don't see the advantage. Not many know my name anyway. "Wren," I answer truthfully.

He nods once. "My soldiers tell me you were dragged here with chains on your neck. Upon being released from your collar at the hands of your accused captors, you surrendered as a prisoner. Now, Wren, some things here aren't making a lot of sense to me, and I don't like when things don't make sense. So, why don't you begin by telling me who you are, why you were associating with Legion, and every other detail that comes into your head." His tone sounds almost disinterested, but the sharpness of his stare pins me in place.

I swallow hard but muster forth a hardened glower of my

own. "They came for me in the night. My father is a well-to-do trader who recently came into good fortune. I can only assume I was taken to be used for ransom." It's only a partial lie. I *was* captured, but not because of who my father is. Because of who I am.

"They did not treat you kindly," he nods at my throat which I'm sure is a deep shade of amethyst now. "Now tell me, why would they bring you along on their ridiculous attempt to siege and risk losing their ransom in the fight? Surely they didn't expect us to bargain for a *trader's daughter*." He draws out the last two words as if he's testing them on his tongue, seeing if they taste like lies.

"I think they were hoping your men would hesitate if they saw a prisoner. The woman who was dragging me along— Margalo was her name, I heard her talking with the one in charge about getting me to the front lines." I don't dare mention Cathal's name. I don't think the Black Art would take kindly to me being on first name terms with the Legion commander. "Perhaps I was to be used as a distraction or something. There were others like me, women that were taken, but why they would expect Castle Scarwood's armies to be so merciful, well... I don't read minds, Your Grace."

Singard leans farther forward in his chair, his eyes flickering between both of mine, trying to read the expression I keep blank on my face. He won't be able to gather anything from my blanketed stare, but he can't hide his thoughts from me as easily. I focus on the spot behind my eye—the center of my collective—and grab it with my mind's will, flexing it with my mental fingertips.

The collective is the life force that surrounds us all, but each person has a small portion of it to call their own. A private void to store one's thoughts, dreams, needs, and desires. Mages possess the ability to bend their collective—to tap into its energy and manipulate the world around them. And then there is my kind, the only kind, that can reach out and pry into someone else's to know what feelings linger within their hearts, and taste the motivations hidden behind smooth words. I project my collective towards him, completely undetectable to anyone but myself, and scratch the surface of his consciousness.

I immediately wish I hadn't.

A hundred phantom blisters burst all over my body, and my chest threatens to cave in on me, to collapse under the weight of the shame and sorrow that presses on my breast. I'm immobilized, my lungs not wanting to fill with air, but I continue to breathe anyway, not able to stop my chest from rising and falling, even as each breath buries the pain further into me. I drop my hold on his collective and let mine snap back into place, back to the safe spot behind my eye, and I let out a tiny gasp when the invisible blisters disappear as quickly as I felt them emerge.

What was that?

"Are you alright?" he asks, appearing confused at my sudden sharp inhale.

"My shoulder," I mumble nonchalantly, certainly not willing to tell him the real reason for my faltered breath—that I had pried into his collective and nearly doubled over from the crashing wave of pain.

"What is your father's name? I can have my emissary locate him, and if your story checks out, we can coordinate a safe return."

I shake my head. "I'd rather my father not know I was ever taken. He has a temper and would surely get himself killed trying to go after the men that took me. If I return alone, I can dismiss my absence as something else, running off with a gentleman caller perhaps, but certainly nothing to do with Legion."

"Your father must be a smart man."

He's not. I haven't seen my father in over a decade, not since he and my mother discovered what I was and decided I was no longer a child worthy of love.

"I'll make you a deal, Miss Wren."

My eyes narrow. I don't like deals.

"Legion cannot possibly have many more resources. They need coin, I'm sure of it. If they went to the trouble of locating you for their gain, well, they certainly aren't going to be content to let you stay here with me." His eyes sparkle as if *he* finds the thought tempting. "You will stay at Castle Scarwood for the time being. Let them come back to collect their prize, which they will because they're dumb enough and desperate enough. When they do, confirming what you say is true, you may leave on your own accord."

"I beg your pardon? I can't stay here."

"You can. And you will." His tone is level, calm, but drips with suggestion that this is not a choice.

"My father will be worried sick. I need to return home." Another partial lie. I do need to return home, but home isn't with my father.

"And if you aren't lying to me, you will."

"Am I to be kept here?" I ask incredulously, motioning with my chin to the room around me.

"I will have a room arranged for you. But understand, if you attempt to flee or harm me or anyone in this castle, I won't be so merciful again." The promise rolls off his tongue with ease, not a sliver of toxicity, but with a gentle coolness that sends a shudder skittering down my back.

If agreeing gets me out of this room and access to the

castle, it is the best option. Eyes on the castle's surroundings will be necessary for me to coordinate a successful escape.

Not wanting to agree too quickly and reveal my eagerness, I ask, "And if I don't agree? To remain here for as long as you see fit?"

A predatory smile raises one side of his mouth. "Then I can only assume you truly are one of Legion's play-things, and I *could* end this right now, but I think I might wish to keep you around for a bit longer." He leans forward in his chair, his eyes dropping to the mouth I hold tight. "However, I don't think you'd find your conditions as agreeable as I would." The smile vanishes from his lips, and he raises one dark eyebrow in silent question, his green eyes daring me to reject his offer to stay here.

I don't let him intimidate me. I stare back at him, hard, but I dip my chin in a quick nod.

He rises from his chair and walks to the door, pausing before leaving to speak over his shoulder. "I'll send River to collect you. I look forward to our time together, Wren." My name slides off his tongue like soft velvet, worn in and comfortable. And I don't like it at all.

Not much time passes before there are two taps on the door, and an older woman with hair like sunset enters. She wears a pale servant's smock, her face aged but gentle, with light brown eyes framed by vibrant red-orange locks.

"Hello dear," she greets, and then looks at my hands disap-provingly. "Let's get you out of this nonsense." River reaches into a pocket of her linen apron, pulls out a key, and promptly undoes my binding.

I breathe a sigh of relief as the blood flows back into my forearms, and I go to stand up but stumble forward, my hands catching my fall on the hard floor beneath me.

"Easy, dear. Here, let me help you." River extends her arm, and I use her as support, ascending to my feet fully this time.

I mutter a thank you, and she instructs me to follow her, promising food and clean clothes. River guides me out of the room and down a dimly lit hallway, the mounted flames casting shadows along the sickly yellow walls. We round a corner, and the hall widens into a larger tunnel, the corn silk paint replaced with empty barred cells on either side of us.

I follow River up a stairwell tucked behind the final cell, to a wooden door she opens to what I presume is the ground level of the castle. She guides me down another corridor, the pale gray walls broken up by large arched windows inlaid in intervals. I glance out each window casually, not wanting to seem too ambitious to scout my surroundings—not that my every move won't be watched by the Black Art and his servants. He doesn't believe me, only a fool would be dumb enough to, but he knows a Legion spy isn't getting out of this keep unnoticed. He is laying a trap, a cat waiting for the mouse to corner itself, but he hasn't accounted for the unexpected.

I am the falcon.

My view is obstructed by shelters spread across the lawn, likely barracks and bathhouses, and I can't get a clear view of how far we are from the keep or how heavily guarded it is. But given Legion's presence last evening, I can assume it is guarded with men armed to the teeth. The corridor dumps into a large, open room with magnificent archway columns dividing the space. The stone floor is a deep charcoal gray with specks of white ridden throughout, and two long burgundy rugs span the length of the room on both sides of the columns. To our right is another stone stairwell—this one much wider than the one we climbed in the dungeon, that spirals clockwise to floors above us. I follow River up the grand staircase and down another hallway with wooden doors lining both sides. She stops, unlocks the third one on the left, and ushers me in before her.

The room is marvelous, from the gray walls with a silvery ornate design swirled in, to the several white rugs thrown about the floor. A pair of wooden armoires sit against opposite walls, and at the back of the room, a bed certainly sized for more than one. A towering headboard looms over the golden bedding, inviting and warm. A room clearly designed for more welcomed and respected guests, and nothing like my cot at home. Next to the bed is a set of doors that open to a balcony, perfect for surveying the castle's exterior grounds. I have no doubt it was Singard who selected this room for me, baiting me with a view and access to the outside, even if it *is* on the second story.

"You should find this space comfortable, I hope," River says. "Settle in, and I'll bring you a hot meal and fresh clothes. But please do not leave the room. I'm afraid His Grace has instructed for you to remain here for the remainder of the night. See you in a bit." River closes the door, and I hear her secure the lock behind her.

I listen for her footsteps to fade and then focus on the knob, willing my collective to grab the lock and wiggle it gently. It obeys. I nod once to myself—undoing that lock will take but a second of magic. I waste no time throwing open the doors to the balcony and beholding the grounds beneath me. The tops of the watchtowers are visible from my room, so I am facing the castle's entrance then. The gardens, a living mural against the lawn, span the space between the castle and the northern courtyard. Rounding the east side of the grounds, within the keep's borders, is a thicket that appears to continue along the perimeter out of view. Ideal camouflage to get closer to the gate, but also the most obvious. I need to find an exit that offers me cover, but not so obvious that Singard will have guards stationed there, expecting me to try to blend in. I will need to get outside for a closer look—it is far too dangerous to attempt anything without a thorough plan.

Dusk tints the sky a deep lavender. They must have sedated me with herbs after tending to my shoulder if almost a full day has passed. Tended to, but didn't heal. Surely the kingdom has healers on site, but Singard isn't going to authorize treatment so long as he suspects I am working with Legion. I resist the urge to close the wound myself, knowing if they saw me tomorrow with a repaired shoulder, it would be a giveaway I had used magic to do so. Perhaps it is still the mystery herbs in my system, or merely the stress from the past weeks of being held in a Legion camp, but my eyelids become heavy and begin to strain. I wait for River to return and devour the meal she brings—roast mutton with currant jelly and stewed vegetables. I didn't bother sniffing it for poison. If his reputation precedes him, Singard prefers a more hands-on approach to silencing his enemies.

I pull on the night dress River brought and slip into the golden bedding, not caring if the crusted blood and dirt on my feet stains the silken sheets. In fact, I hope it does.

CHAPTER 3

S leep hadn't come easily, despite the eerie stillness of the castle after dark. I am almost surprised to wake naturally and not by someone forcing their way into the room. With no weapons at my disposal, I am left to rely on my power, something I have no intention of revealing to these people. Had someone tried to attack me overnight, I would have been left without alternatives, but I suppose if they are intent on killing me anyway, hiding my power would be senseless.

I climb out of the too-large bed and reach my good arm above my head, lengthening my spine from the night of restless sleep and wincing at the pain in my other shoulder. My soiled bandage needs to be swapped for a clean one, and I need herbs to fight infection if *he* still won't allow a healer to mend the wound. A tea tray sits on the small end table by the door, and next to it, a stack of clean clothes. River must have brought them in this morning, and a rush of dread caresses my back at the realization that her entrance didn't wake me. I must have finally fallen asleep early this morning, my mind and body too exhausted to have reacted to the lock clicking over. On the tray is a small breakfast spread of bread, cheese, and nuts, and next to it, a folded note telling me to come downstairs when I am ready.

I test the doorknob—unlocked. *Only locking me in during nightfall, Your Grace? I would think you experienced enough to know that violence has never hidden from daylight.*

Tossing a handful of the nuts in my mouth, I thumb over the pile of clothes. No pants or tunics—only a stack of neatly folded dresses. It's likely that dresses are the only women's clothing the kingdom has in its reserves given the stature of ladies that would be staying here, but something tells me there may have been consideration that pants and a tunic would be much easier to flee in. I put on a cerulean blue, floor length dress from the stack and secure my hair, the color of dandelion fuzz, into its usual thick braid that runs from my forehead to the center of my back.

I must act with haste and return home before my sister comes looking for me. Cosmina isn't my sister by blood, which is good for her sake so she didn't have to endure the heavy hand of my mother, but I couldn't love her more if she was. It has been two weeks since my capture. She will wait a short while knowing I wouldn't want her coming anywhere near Cathal and his rats, but she is sick with worry, I'm sure. I have no doubt she is driving the others we share our home with to insanity talking about it, knowing it was Legion who took me. They've been after me for years, and her patience won't last forever. She *will* come looking.

I pat the dress smooth along my sides, the clingy fabric bunching a little too much around my hips. With a final glance in the mirror to ensure I am decent, I leave my room.

The hallway continues to my left with an assortment of parallel doors on both sides. I head right, back towards the stone staircase that continues climbing to an unknown number of stories above me. I'm not past the first downward spiral when a tall man rounds onto the steps in front of me.

My chest tightens as if all the air is sucked from my lungs. I recognize him from the same visit I had seen Singard once, when he visited Aegidale's cities as its new ruler.

Dusaro. Singard's father and previous Black Hand to Ephraim.

Ephraim was the Black Art before Singard. His reign lasted my entire lifetime, only ending when Legion managed to outwit the kingdom in a sneak attack that ended his life. When a Black Art's reign concludes, either due to illness, being overthrown, or death, the Black Rite is held to determine who ascends as the next supreme leader.

The potential ruler presents an offering to Adelphia, the goddess of the arcane, to ask for her blessing. If Adelphia accepts the offer, she binds a fragment of her power to theirs, ensuring their magic is superior to other mages. Black Arts have always been mages, as it would be too simple to take the title from someone mundane.

After Ephraim's death, Dusaro participated in the Rite, expecting the throne to pass to him given his long servitude as Black Hand. Adelphia denied his offering, causing the Rite to continue to the Black Hand's only son. Singard participated in the ceremony and was blessed by the goddess, and as such, crowned.

The law prevents the Black Art from selecting someone of kin to serve as their Black Hand, the emissary to the throne, forcing Dusaro to resign from his position—and prompting Singard to select a new trusted adviser. I have not heard if he has chosen yet.

Dusaro climbs to the step I am on and peers down at me with dark brown eyes as if studying something that disgusts him. His hair, the color of a crow's wing, hangs long and straight down his back, even longer than his son's. Twin braids are loosely woven onto either side of his head.

"You must be the rebellion scum my son is chewing on," he drawls, sweeping his eyes over me from head to toe. He presses his lips into a thin line.

"I beg your pardon," I scoff, taken aback by his immediate hostility. I have heard stories of his father's unbalanced temperament, but the coldness in his stare was not mentioned in village gossip.

"Yes, you do look the type," he mutters more to himself than me. "I trust my son knows what he is doing by allowing you to walk amidst my home. It isn't often we allow a traitor such... amicable... conditions."

"His Grace and I have negotiated terms, my Lord," I say, coating his title with distaste. "Shame on you for arriving at such an outrageous conclusion so quickly."

He chuckles once without humor. "Terms be damned girl, I catch you taking a wrong *breath,* and it'll be your head on a spike." He pushes past me and continues climbing the stairs, and I waste no time descending them.

Two women dressed in servant linens are washing the towering archways dividing the room. I ask them where I can find River, and head in the direction they point, down the hallway that begins past the base of the stairs. River is preparing breakfast in the oversized kitchen, her scarlet hair a braided rope down her back. She pauses chopping the bunch of fennel in front of her and peers over her shoulder at me.

"Wren dear, good morning. Oh, don't you look lovely. I hope you found the clothes to fit alright."

"They are fine. Thank you."

"Did you sleep alright, dear?"

"Not exactly," I mumble.

"It's hard getting comfortable in a bed you aren't used to. But that's a fine room you're in, you have Sin to thank for that."

Sin? A fitting nickname.

"Don't mention it," Sin says from behind me.

I spin around, startled I didn't hear him approach. He leans with his shoulder hugging the kitchen threshold, dressed in a burgundy leather tunic and brown trousers. In the morning light, I notice just how strongly he resembles Dusaro with his long, black hair and copper skin, but Sin's green eyes are in stark contrast to his father's dark ones.

"I trust Ms. River has taken exceptional care of you thus far." He saunters over to the wide-stretched counter and leans down to kiss her on the forehead.

I wipe the surprise from my face before either of them notices. "Exceptional indeed, Your Grace."

River reaches up to pat the side of his arm. "Breakfast will be ready within the hour," she says in her sing-song voice.

"Miss Wren, would you care to join me for a walk? Since you are to be here for the foreseeable future, I thought you might want to see the grounds."

I would be a fool to believe him. He wants more information from me, unconvinced I am who I say I am. Smart man. I would question me too.

I pull my shoulders back. "Certainly, Your Grace."

A walk means visibility of the keep. Perhaps he wants to see how much I assess his security, baiting me with a walk to study my attentions outside the castle. He offers a polite smile and motions with his chin for me to follow him.

I've never been to Blackreach before, Aegidale's leading city and home to the land's most elite estates. I was born in Innodell, a modest city southeast of Blackreach, across the bridge that separates the capital from the rest of Aegidale. After my parents disowned me and Cosmina found me starving on the quaint city streets, she brought me to Morrinne and her chosen family that homesteaded out in Autumnhelm, the dense woods north of my hometown. Cosmina worked at the local inn and was one of Morrinne's few friends, often setting aside supplies left behind from travelers to give to her when she would make a trip into Innodell for resources.

Morrinne and her family were like me, outcasted by a society too dangerous to live in. They are transcendents, born of magic, but a different kind than mine. Shifters of physical form, they can shed their human skin and manifest again in the shape of something else, something more animal. No two transcendents share identical second skins, but they are all beautiful—and terrifying if you are not privy to the knowledge they maintained their sense of self, despite their altered physical forms.

Ephraim's reign brought more and more prejudices against them, instilling fear in the cities that they were something to be frightened of, abominations of nature. He went as far as to enforce curfews on their kind, ensuring they were not out prowling after dark, and encouraged the execution of any who broke that unforgivable law. Legion claims it is transcendents they fight for, but Cathal's army has as many mundane soldiers as they do shifters, probably more. I never met a person with more disdain for authority than Cathal. He merely exploits his transcendent ancestry as a means to recruit other shifters, to supplement his lack of soldiers with brawn. But I know better—Cathal just really hates anyone that tries to tell him what to do.

Legion's harsh strategies include recruiting others by force, coercing children into their ranks, and an ends-justify-the-means mentality. Morrinne and her family—*my* family— wouldn't dream of joining such a malicious group. They instead keep to themselves, venturing into Innodell for work and resources but always returning to the cabin in Autumn-helm at night, away from those that would try to provoke them. It is not uncommon for the prejudiced to try and bait them into shifting, to give them a reason to report them to kingdom guards and light their pyres.

Sometimes I wish I was a transcendent so I could shed this skin, even for just a few minutes. The transcendents are at least tolerated so long as they follow their rules, but I am something worse, more feared, and irrevocably forbidden to live by kingdom law.

Sin guides us to the large courtyard spanning the front side of the castle. He walks next to me as we stroll past the neatly groomed hedges and manicured bushes, offering details every few steps about the general layout of the surrounding sides of the castle not visible from the path we walk. Budding flowers of pink, purple, and pearl poke through the greenery, preparing for spring's renewal. The potent colors of the grounds are sharp against the stone gray of the castle's exterior.

"What are your impressions of Castle Scarwood?" he asks.

I choke down a laugh. "Do you want my honest answer to that?"

Sin motions with both his hands for me to proceed.

"I think the castle is beautiful. The grounds are clearly well cared for," I say, waving to a freshly clipped hedge near us. "Your handmaid is arguably one of the nicest people I've ever met. But you must forgive me if my impressions are a bit clouded. I didn't exactly plan on being captured and now being held so far from my home."

"Fair enough," he says with a shrug of his wide-set shoulders. "But you should know River isn't a handmaid. She's the housekeeper, and this place would fall apart without her running it, doing everything at once, delegating the chores to the servants." The admiration in his tone suggests he views her as more than just head servant too.

"Fair enough," I echo his response.

"So, tell me, how did Legion manage to get their thieving hands on you anyway?"

There it is, the subtle questioning I expected. It is why I rehearsed my story several times before falling asleep, and again while getting dressed this morning.

"I was running an errand for my father. He had a delivery that needed to get to Baregrove and also business to attend to in Innodell, so I offered to transport the goods for him. I should have stopped to camp when the sun was setting, but I wasn't far and wanted to get there in one day, so I kept riding. They rode up on me so fast, I didn't really understand what was happening until they were pulling me off my horse and onto one of theirs."

Sin nods, but his face remains expressionless, giving no indication of whether he believes me or not. I don't dare slip into his collective right now and risk that same rush of pain I felt last night, if that strange, intense emotion still lingers in his body. Not when there aren't others to distract from my reaction in case I slip up and reveal it on my face. I can only blame it on my shoulder for so long.

"I will need my shoulder tended to today. The bandage is beginning to soak through, and I will need something to ward off infection. Unless you would allow a healer to see me."

He glances over to me and at the stained bandage peeking out from the boxy neckline of my dress. His jaw tics once, and he quickly averts his eyes. "I'll let River know you need herbs."

I laugh once without humor. "I suppose I don't blame you for not trusting me."

We approach the gate separating the castle from Black-reach, and two armored soldiers bow to Sin as they call to the guardroom above to raise the portcullis. We head through the small tunnel opening where a second portcullis is raised for us, and we step into Aegidale's wealthiest city. I take note of the two flanking towers positioned high above the gate and lower my eyes quickly, not wanting to be caught staring at any given post too thoroughly. Leaving through this entrance unscathed will be near impossible. I have to keep looking.

"Do you keep work in Innodell? Aside from helping your father," he asks.

I nod. "I help run an inn."

Cosmina's parents owned the inn, and as a partial owner herself, she allowed me to work there to earn my keep, but I also know she wanted to keep a watchful eye on me during the day. Returning to the cabin in the woods with me every night wasn't necessary, but she always did. Cosmina uprooted her life for me, and when asked about it, she dismisses it as she simply felt that she should. She is only a handful of years older than me, but she was like a mother to me. And as I got older, our relationship blossomed into a sisterly bond stronger than any iron chains.

"How are you liking your position? I understand it was assumed your father would be next to serve," I ask him, wanting to switch the topic off of me.

"Do you want *my* honest answer to that?" He throws my earlier question back at me.

I mimic the hand gesture he had given in return, and a tight smile pulls at his mouth.

"It's bloody tiring."

"I am sure Legion has been keeping you busy," I say in an attempt to sound understanding, but he snickers at my response.

"Those pissants are annoying at best, but they're certainly not difficult to squash."

If there is one thing the Black Art and I agree on, it is that Cathal and his followers *are* a bunch of pissants.

"I agree they need to be stopped, even if I can understand some of their motives."

Sin shoots me a sideways glare as we step through the first trees of the Spiritwood forest, the woods that run along the east border of Blackreach. I only know of its name because once the forest meets the Malachite River, it becomes the Autumnhelm woods on the other side of the bridge. The nestling of trees I noticed inside the castle's borders must have once been connected to Spiritwood before the kingdom built part of its keep through it.

"I don't agree with the transcendent laws. I think it's ludicrous to impose restrictions on them," I continue.

"The restrictions are there to protect the people of Aegidale."

"Protect them from what?"

He exhales sharply. "From those that would rather see this isle crumble and fall before they bowed to a Black Art."

I shake my head. "You're describing Legion soldiers, not transcendents. You cannot judge an entire race by the actions of a few radicals."

"They are *all* abominations."

"Abominations? You can throw magic from your hands, but because they were blessed with another skin, they are abominations?"

"They are *thieves*," he spits.

I plant my feet and turn to look at him. He mirrors so that we stand chest to chest.

"Have you considered they have resorted to thievery because no one will allow them to earn an honest living? Because everyone is too frightened of them, because of the prejudices Ephraim and your father modeled, and that *you* seem content to continue."

He leans forward so his head towers over me, the tips of his long hair almost touching my shoulders. "They are unfit for society. *Animals* that cannot control their own impulses."

"That is not true," I whisper. I don't need to brush his collective to feel the explosive energy rolling off him, and to know I have crossed a line with him.

"Bold of you to question my authority to my face." The venom dripping from his words tells me he is not impressed by it.

I feel the arrow before I see it.

It is laced with magic—stirring my own as it whirls towards us. Towards him.

Closer.

I throw out my hand, and the arrow halts in its path, hovering in the air about three feet from plunging into the back of the Black Art's heart. He whirls around and slinks into a defensive crouch as I flick my wrist to the right and send the magic-dipped arrow hurtling into the brush.

Sin conjures a destructive wake and thrusts it away from him—magic that will send a crippling wave towards anyone in his power radius. A symphony of cries unleashes as his magic finds the assailants hidden in the trees. I detect at least a few different screams—a small group of them, then. I look over to him, and when his eyes find mine, I know there is no going back. How could I have been so stupid to reveal to him I am a mage? I didn't think—it happened so fast, and I couldn't risk assuming he'd stop the arrow on his own quickly enough. Not when he was so distracted.

Distracted by me. And nearly killed by Legion because of it.

I run. I run like hell.

Surely I will be executed for treason. I know how this must

look to him. Baiting the Black Art into a vulnerable position while Legion uses the distraction to attack. He already had his suspicions about me, and I just confirmed them.

"Stop!" he orders from behind me. I feel the magic racing towards me, and I dive to the right, causing his blow to spiral into a tree instead. I push my legs faster, willing them to carry me quicker and farther into the woods, farther from him.

"Stop!" he calls out again, and I dodge another blast of his magic, this one shearing the bark off a tree to my left.

I won't be able to put enough distance between us quickly enough, not before his magic can chase me down. It is now or never. Digging my heels into the dirt, I skid to a stop and whirl around, the magic flying from my palms before I'm even turned completely. My collective rams into him before he can react, sweeping his feet from the ground and launching him back and out of view. I hear his body collide with the grass and dirt, and I mutter a prayer to an unnamed goddess that it buys me enough time to get the lead I need. I take off in a sprint again, wishing I had transcendent legs to carry me faster.

CHAPTER 4

He doesn't know.

He saw me do magic, but nothing a casual mage can't do. He has no reason to assume I am anything more than that, not that I'm sure it matters. Casual mage or not, I assaulted the Black Art.

Punishable by death, and as if he needed another crime to stack on my piling record, I didn't confess I was a mage when asked about myself. It will be seen as a lie by omission, given the nature of why I was being held. And the worst part isn't that I will be executed, likely publicly, but that I will die being accused of working with Cathal. I would rather die a thousand painful deaths than ever be associated with his name again.

It was freezing the night he came into the inn, needing a bed and a warm drink. I stayed well past my shift that evening, caught up talking with him about anything and everything. Cathal was funny... kind... and I was vulnerable. He was the first man to show that kind of interest in me, and I fell for him so quickly. I think that was the worst part of it all—how damn easily I gave my heart to him.

My head whips towards the sound of running water, and I follow the gentle roar, sighing deeply when I find its source. I kneel next to the steam and make a cup with my hands, scooping up a handful, and slurp it from my palms.

Cathal was the only other person to whom I confessed what I was outside of my adoptive family. I knew he was involved with some kind of group, had listened to his ramblings about the corruption of the kingdom, but I didn't understand the extent of it back then. He was a transcendent, someone who could understand the struggle of being ashamed of what you are, or so I had thought.

They came for me that night. He brought friends, other members of his group that would soon be known as Legion, and together, they held me down and chained me in iron. They brought me to their hideout in the woods where they took turns kicking me, beating me, violating me—punishment for what I was, they said. Cathal demanded I use my power to aid their cause and overthrow Ephraim and his crooked reign. If I didn't give myself over willingly, they threatened to kill Cosmina and our other pack members. Trusting Cathal was the biggest mistake I've ever made. All he saw was a ticket to victory, a Legion asset, a *trophy*.

Back then, I was too afraid to fight back, too worried I would accidentally kill one of them and become the monster depicted in the legends of my kind—legends mothers warned their children about on crisp autumn nights. If I had offered *myself* a fraction of the trust I threw at Cathal when I told him what I was, they never would have stood a chance.

I kick off my sandals and hike up the skirts of my dress, easing into the stream. I wince as the cold water rushes over the tops of my bloodied feet, crashing against my ankles and carrying the dried dirt from my blistered toes. If I ever make it home, the first thing I'm doing is demanding my bear-of-a-friend, Eldridge, give me a foot rub.

I haven't risked healing my shoulder and draining my

energy further, not until I have covered more distance and can rest. If I can find some yarrow, the leaves are great for warding off infection. Or there should be some witch hazel around here somewhere... if I could just find some wormwood, I can make a tea and—

Branches snap behind me.

Goddess above.

I slowly lift one foot out of the water, then the other, and slip them back into their leather sandals. Hoisting my skirts up, I tiptoe back into the brush, careful to not rustle a single leaf or kick a loose rock.

"Up ahead—I think I see something!" a man's voice calls from way too close for comfort.

I dive into a sprint. Hurtling into the trees, I run as fast as I can without colliding into their thick trunks. Faster. *Faster.* Adrenaline rushes to my calves, compelling them to not quit, to not feel the burn as my muscles tighten, weaken.

Running is surviving. I run.

I don't register the pain as a low-hanging branch thumps against my stomach, sending me falling to the unforgiving ground. My palms catch most of my weight, breaking my impact before my face slams into the dusty, red-tinged soil.

They're on me immediately, their footsteps quickening in tune to the thrumming of the blood pulsing in my veins, willing me to get up, to keep running. I don't have time, not enough time.

Flipping onto my back, I chuck a shard of magic from my palm, throwing a man about to tackle me backwards into the brush. Another guard dives to the side, nearly being thwacked by the body I sent flying. I flip back over and tuck my knees to my chest, ready to break into another sprint when a heavy set of hands slam onto my back. A strangled breath rips from my chest as I hit the ground, a jagged rock scraping my mouth where my jaw connects with the muddied floor. My blood sweetens my lips, and I go deadly still, not daring to breathe. I wait for the attacker's weight to shift again, priming my core to buck him off when he does, but the assailant matches me with a primal stillness of his own.

And then his familiar voice whispers against my neck, sending every hair on my body snapping to attention. "I wouldn't try that again."

Sin slides down so his knees jut into my sides, pinning me between muscular thighs. I jerk under him, prompting his legs to squeeze me harder as he wrestles my wrists from under my stomach and wraps them with the all too recognizable sting of cold iron. He isn't gentle as he pulls the chains snug against my skin and tests them for durability. I swallow the urge to scream as the metal reacts to my magic, singeing my flesh as if trying to burn the chaos out of me.

He grabs my elbow and yanks me to my feet. There are four others with him—three men and a woman, all dressed in soldier uniforms except the woman who wears a long black tunic under a dark, hooded robe. I bare my teeth at them, inciting a chuckle from a couple of the men.

"Easy there, little witch," Sin sneers.

He glances up at the sky that has darkened into a muted purple. I evaded them for more than half the day; a valiant effort, but I wasn't quick enough. "Set up camp. We'll head back at sunrise," he orders the other four.

He must have sent for his guards before coming after me, or maybe he only returned to the castle to fetch the iron, knowing it was now a *little witch* he was hunting, as he called me. The kingdom prides themselves on having a council of royal mages but looks down on any not born from a noble bloodline. *Witch* is a derogatory term, synonymous with dirty-blooded. A mage whose power wasn't inherited.

He smacks the dirt from his pants and meets my glare with one of his own. "I suggest you settle in—we have a long night ahead of us."

I barely hear the threat in his words over my pounding heart.

I should have let that arrow fly.

CHAPTER 5

S in hasn't spoken since the others left to hunt supper. I sit with my back against a tree and watch as he creates a tinder nest and coaxes a fire to life—the smell of burning wood enough to emit a low rumble from my stomach, though I doubt I will be fed.

"As entertaining as it is to watch you pretend to be normal, why didn't you just start a fire with magic?" I finally ask.

He pulls the dagger tucked against his hip and sits next to the fire, propping his elbow on his raised knee and stretching out his other leg. Sin ignores my question and begins shaving off strips of wood from the bundle of twigs he collected earlier. His eyes don't leave his work, his hands moving quickly and efficiently to create the extra kindling. I steel my spine, my eyes tracking his dagger every time he expertly slides his blade across the dry wood. The scraping of metal on lumber pricks my ear—a warning he is practiced enough to land his blade dead center in my throat with a casual toss.

I shuffle against the tree and bite my lip as the chains rattle with my movement, the iron burning the delicate skin of my wrists. Iron stifles a mage's ability to manipulate their surroundings—a purifying element—but it does nothing to stop me from flexing my collective and *tasting* the energy around me. Bracing for the mental impact I felt the last time I explored his collective, I silently stroke his energy with my own, an ability only my kind possesses.

Curiosity. Ripe and blatant, likely him internally questioning who I really am and what I'm after. I press in further, spreading apart the layers of his mind with my own, scanning them quickly and undetectably. I dig deeper—and there— hidden somewhere in the center is... *fear*. My hold almost slips off its icy surface, but I dig in with mental talons and chip away at it for a closer look.

Heat consumes me. Not from the fire now climbing steadily before me, but from *inside* him. A surge of molten heat floods my core and coils through me—anger. Anger and... *shame*.

I sheathe my claws and let my collective spring back to its home behind my eye. He glances behind us, hearing something I don't, and a few seconds later, the guards return carrying a few small game animals they rush to get roasting over the fire. They converse amongst themselves, but Sin remains quiet, busying himself with adjusting the spits above the fire before he crosses the camp and slumps to the ground next to me, pressing his back against the other side of my tree. I try not to straighten too much as his closeness teases the hair on my skin.

Keeping my posture as casual as I can muster, I say, "I suppose I am to starve since you intend on killing me anyway."

He shoots me a sideways glance. "If I had decided on killing you, you'd already be dead."

"Surely you can understand my hesitation in informing you of my abilities, Your Grace."

"We have no fight with witches."

I laugh once without humor and drop my eyes to where my wrists disappear behind my back.

"That isn't because you're a witch. That's because you're a

witch working with the rebellion," he says, a muscle feathering in his burnt umber cheek.

"I would rather you fillet and hang me from my feet to drip to death before I ever work with Legion. Do not insult my honor, Your Grace."

He raises an eyebrow at me, and something like a smile twitches on his lips.

I turn to angle my body towards him. "Also, you can cut the witch speech. Just because I wasn't born into a home of silken sheets and fine brandy does not mean my skill set is any less than. I study the art as much as any other *mage*. My bloodline is irrelevant."

He leans closer and drops his gaze to slowly rake over my body as if he could assess my worth through my appearance. "Does that term bother you... *witch*?" he asks, flicking his tongue across his top lip as if the thought amuses him.

I swallow the urge to spit at him. "This *witch* saved your life."

The mischievous glint vanishes from his eyes, and he moves closer, flattening his palm against the tree, inches from my head. "I keep asking myself why a Legion witch would have stopped that arrow. Tell me why."

"Reflex. It isn't in my nature to stand by idly while someone is attacked. You wouldn't be familiar with the concept, Your Grace."

His lips curl up into a wicked smile, and his green irises burn with fevered heat. "No. You want to know what *I* think happened? I think you knew they'd be out there, just waiting for the opportunity to plant an arrow in my back, but when it came down to it, you didn't have the spine to *watch*."

"Your Grace," one of the guards calls, standing awkwardly between the fire and where we sit against the tree, holding a cooked slab of rabbit. Sin takes the skewered meat and doesn't hesitate tearing off a chunk with his teeth.

I take a steadying breath. "Don't blame me because you allowed yourself to become distracted, not even a day after they assaulted your outpost and—"

"*Failed* to assault," he interjects.

"Regardless, it was foolish to leave the keep with them lurking about, all to make some show that your gates are well-armed. Had I not stopped it, we wouldn't be having this conversation. But for once, I think I would have preferred if I *had* been more like you, Singard, so I could have stood by and let that arrow pierce your frigid heart. It goes without saying, I regret my choice." I look pointedly at my chains.

Sin grabs my chin and tilts my head back so I'm forced to meet his hardened stare. "Do not *ever* use my name again. Something that nice doesn't deserve to be inside a witch's mouth." He holds my jaw for an extended beat, his breath hot and rattled against my face, before loosening his grip.

I jerk my chin out of his hand and wait for him to relax his posture. "Seems I'm not the only one that gets ticked off from being called the wrong thing. Which do you prefer then— Your Grace, or *o'chosen one*—or is there another title that warms your black heart? Oh! I think I like that." I smile sweetly at him and cross my legs. "You are my Black Art after all—how about if I just call you something a little more fitting... *Blackheart.*"

Sin exhales sharply and moves to sit next to me again. "I suggest you stop talking before I *make* you stop, witch." He holds the spit still smoldering with the scent of fresh game in front of my mouth. "Eat."

I will my stomach not to rumble. "I am not a pet—I do not eat from dirty hands."

He sighs. "As soon as the sun rises, we're heading back, and you'll slow us down if you're weak with hunger. Eat," he grumbles again.

"I will not be fed like a dog. You want me to eat so badly, unchain me. I'm clearly not escaping so long as I have *o'Blackheart* for company," I muse, pressing my lips into a firm line and blinking sweetly at him.

Wrath shadows his face. "You don't like chains? Fine. Then let's have it your way," Sin growls.

Suddenly he is on me, straddling me with his knees on either side of my hips and reaching behind me to grab my forearms.

"Let go of me!" I twist under him, and he tightens his hold on me. I yank against my chains knowing it is useless—iron is strong and unforgiving—but I pull against them with all my might anyway.

He mutters something to himself, but I don't decipher his words over the obscenities I begin shouting at him.

And then I feel it.

His magic enters through my arms and snakes up to my chest, its slimy coolness slithering behind my sternum, entwining itself through each of my ribs. His weight bears into me as he leans closer, his nails digging into my arms, and I flail beneath him, ignoring the searing pain in my shoulder as I try to knock him back. I writhe and twist as his magic flows deeper, but go deadly still as it creeps up my throat, taking its time exploring me, marking me. And then with the same rapidity it entered me, it rushes from my mouth and back into him.

But not all of it. I still feel him in the pit of my stomach—a stain left behind from where his magic twisted and settled inside of me.

"What have you done?" I whisper, unable to muster an ounce of ferocity in my voice.

He drops my arms and hunkers in front of me, devouring the shock and realization from my face with a covetous grin, knowing I don't ask the question in earnest.

A tethering spell.

Wherever I go, no matter the distance, the stain will link us, allowing him to track me—a magical brand. I want to be furious, to shout in his face how much I loathe him and his power and his stupid kingdom, but the words stay frozen and unspoken in my chest.

Running is no longer an option.

Sin's eyes strip me bare as he reaches around me and breaks my binding—tossing the iron chains away from us. His unspoken statement couldn't be louder if he screamed it in my ear—he doesn't need iron chains to control me.

He bound me to him against my will, snatched away my final thread of independence as if it were nothing more than an afterthought. Warmth rushes to my hands as my magic pulses freely through me once more. Sin kneels in front of me, and I bare my teeth at him—a warning.

"You don't own me," I whisper, my voice a hushed fury.

He reaches out and cups my jaw in his hand, leveling his eyes with mine when he says in a voice as cold as winter's wind, "You couldn't behave on your own, now we'll see how you behave for *me*, little witch." He reaches for the spitted rabbit once more and holds it to my mouth, his long hair almost grazing my chest. "Now eat."

I hold his stare as I tear into it, imagining the red juice splattering my cheeks was his.

CHAPTER 6

"**G**et up, it's our turn." Sin nudges me with his boot. The others had taken turns going off in pairs to wash in a nearby river, and the robed woman and her partner just returned, signaling we are next. I stand, straighten my dress, and follow Sin into the woods as he heads towards the running water that will serve as our bathing quarters. He never glances over his shoulder to make sure I'm still following. He doesn't need to.

He would know if I ran—courtesy of his magical brand.

I could kill him. End his life without so much as a whisper and flee before enough time passed for the others to grow wary and come looking for us. I shake away the thought. There is no hiding from her—the dark hunger stirring inside me, always watching, always listening. It wouldn't matter how silent I was —*she* would hear. And she would come.

Neither of us speaks as we hike through the dense woods, the moon our only lantern through the maze of overgrown brush. I take the opportunity to study Sin while he's focused on pushing the low-hanging branches aside for us. He's tall—easily a head above me—and his shoulders are wide-set and bulky inside his leather tunic. His hair is as black as the night, swaying gently past his shoulder blades as he trudges forward.

I steal a glance at his long legs, hidden behind loose-fitting trousers, but remembering how tightly he pinned me between them earlier, I needn't guess how muscular they are.

The trees part, and we approach the river bank populated with cattails and tall grasses. Morrinne often gathered cattails and hung them around the inside of our cabin. Once dried, she would use them to make salves great for treating insect bites and sell them at the market. It wasn't much, but a way to earn a little extra coin for the pack. I frown at their brown spikes as the thought of never feeling another of her motherly hugs punches me in the gut.

Sin reaches for the buttons on his tunic.

I clear my throat. "Are you going to undress in front of me?"

He makes a spinning motion with two of his fingers, signaling for me to turn around. "You don't have to watch. Unless you want to."

I sneer at his lazy grin and turn my back to him, sitting in the blanket of tall grass. Water splashes softly behind me as he wades in and begins to wash himself. I pull one of the cigar-shaped flowers to my nose and inhale its marshy aroma, the earthy smell a reminder of home. A home I may never see again thanks to Sin, his kingdom, and the godsforsaken Legion that spiraled me into this mess.

"What are you going to do with me when we return?" I ask.

"Despite my attempt to be fair with you, witch, you lied to me and *assaulted* me."

"You would have arrested me on the spot—you cannot fault me for defending myself."

"I have *killed* men for less."

"Then why am I still breathing, Blackheart?" I should probably stop antagonizing him, but his superiority complex coats my tongue with bile.

"You're of better use to me alive—for now. I can *smell* them on you—filthy, rebellion trash. You're harboring their secrets. You can either share them willingly, or I can rip them from your tongue myself. It's your choice, witch."

"I. Told. You—I'm not working with them," I say through gritted teeth.

"Then who?"

I whirl around to bark my response, but the sight of the Black Art, water dripping from the ends of his coal black hair and trailing down the hard planes of his chest, leaves the words swollen in my throat. Despite the vulnerability that comes with being exposed, he is more intimidating without his clothes. Sin may possess superior magic, but he isn't underestimating the power of a physical fight either. His bare chest is broad and defined, his stomach sculpted by years of swordsmanship all the way down to where the water ripples above his groin.

Being Dusaro's son, he would have fought in the war with Baelliarah, slitting men's throats in battle before most boys could properly slit a deer's for supper. During Ephraim's reign, transcendents fled to our closest neighbor in an attempt to escape the prejudices thrust upon them. Baelliarah welcomed them with grace, but when Ephraim learned what they were doing, Aegidale invaded and fought for the return of the shifters, unwilling to risk that Baelliarah was using them to pad their own armies in preparation to attack our island. One glance at Sin's arms confirms he could easily overpower me in physical combat should he decide to get friendly with the iron again.

I raise my eyes to meet his, his irises the same shade as the lush carpet of algae growing on the river rocks and appearing almost reflective in the moonlight. "I. Work. For. No. One."

His stare hardens. "My father will never believe that."

"Then I guess it's a good thing your father isn't the Black

Art," I snap.

"Remind me of *your* father's name again," he challenges, calling me on my lie from earlier. I don't answer but hold his stare as he searches both my eyes. "I thought so."

"I saved your life."

"And that's the *only* reason I haven't killed you yet. Now unless you want to be plagued with filthy thoughts about me, witch, I suggest you turn around so I can dress. It's your turn to bathe—you stink."

My eyes hurt from how far back I roll them, but I turn and listen as the rushing water makes way around him as he wades to land and dresses. I don't comment on the detail he let slip— my possible knowledge of Legion secrets is not the only reason he let me live. Stopping that arrow from penetrating his cold, brutal heart must have plucked a string on it after all.

He tells me when he's clothed, and I gather the skirts of my dress in my hands. Peering over my shoulder to make sure he is looking away, I slip it over my head and toss it on the bank before dipping a toe in the water. Gooseflesh erupts on my arms and legs like an infectious blight as I step in deeper, the gelid water wringing the warmth from my veins. Being a head shorter than Sin, the water clothes me to the tops of my breasts. I shake my braid loose and lean back so it unravels into the rushing water, letting the river cleanse it of dirt and debris.

I use the silence to rack my thoughts for a plan. Now that I am tethered to him, if I make the decision to run, it is a lifetime sentence. How long will Cosmina and the others wait for me to return before they come looking, risking themselves for the sake of my freedom? If I manage to slip away from Sin, I could send word to my family to keep them from looking for me— maybe leave a note at the inn for Cosmina—but spending the remainder of my life fleeing from dark corners to abandoned alleys doesn't seem like a life worth living. I need more time.

With a final wring of my hair, I deem I'm as clean as I'm going to get and glance back to Sin before turning around, finding his near reflective eyes burning a hole into my back.

I slap the water like one might smack a horse's behind, sending a wave of bitingly cold spray towards him. "Don't watch!"

He sidesteps the assaulting water with ease and crosses his arms against his chest. "The last time I lost sight of you, you made me chase you half the day. I'm not in the hunting mood tonight, witch."

"I also wasn't tethered to you with your dirty spell," I hiss. "And unless *you* want to be tested with less than pious thoughts about me, I suggest you turn around."

Not so much as a flicker of amusement crosses his face before he spins on his heels and stares out into the darkened woods. Careful of the loose river rocks beneath my bruised and swollen feet, I trudge towards the bank and step onto dry land. I pluck my dress from the ground and bunch the fabric together to step into the skirts and—*what is that?*

Inked into the skin along my left hip bone is a small black heart. I press my fingers against the design—its lines too elegant and delicate to symbolize something so cruel, but there it sits, unassuming on my body as if it has been there forever—Blackheart's black heart.

"YOU BRANDED ME!" I knew the tethering spell bound us together by magic, but to physically *mark* me—my fingers curl at my sides, and not caring that I'm naked, I shove my hands against his back.

Faster than I can track the movement, he spins and grabs my hands, holding them too tightly in both of his. His lips curl into a grin as if a facetious thought crosses his mind, unfazed by my attempted assault.

"I told you—*you're mine.* That," he looks at the dainty heart inked into my skin, "is to make sure you don't forget." His eyes flash back to mine, not trailing to look at any other part of me besides my hip, and I can't hold it back—I spit at the Black Art's feet.

"Go to Hell, Your Grace." I yank my hands free from his, and he doesn't fight me.

"I thought you'd enjoy the symbolism. You seemed to think the nickname was so clever, I thought you may wish to enjoy it a little more... permanently."

I snatch my dress from the ground, and Sin turns around again without my order. Forcing the dress to wiggle down my wet body, I shove my arms into the sleeves and swear as my shoulder strains to lift above my head. I place my hand against the bandage, now sodden from the bath and blood, and reach for my collective to heal the wound.

His hand slams down on the back of mine. "Leave it," he growls, baring his teeth. "You don't use magic unless I give you *explicit* permission to do so. Otherwise, you can have your chains back to match your new ink."

I let my hand fall to my side, and his eyes flare with perverse amusement.

If you only knew what kind of magic I am capable of, Blackheart.

I may be trapped with the Black Art through his invisible tether, but a wicked smile tugs at my lips as I imagine the shock enveloping his face when I show him what I really am —*who* I really am. He raises an eyebrow at my sudden change of expression, to which I simply shrug and push past him in the direction of camp.

His quiet footsteps fall in line behind me, and I can almost hear the devious grin stretch across his face. I want to whirl around and punch him square in his stupid muscular chest, but I don't, knowing my shoulder couldn't tolerate it, and neither would the Black Art. He let my earlier assault pass without punishment, but I don't doubt trying that again would flare his temper beyond whatever semblance of control he has left.

The walk back to camp feels longer than when we left it. Maybe it's the burning in my spine where I feel Sin's stare burrowing into my flesh, or maybe it's the desire to sneak a peek at the black heart weighing on my hip like the heaviest of swords. Either way, my calves beg for mercy as we crunch through the remnants of winter's dead leaves, my feet tired and heavy in my too-thin leather sandals.

I am almost relieved when we spill through the last of the trees and into the small clearing that is our camp. Lying against the tree from earlier, I find the most comfortable position I can manage in the grass with my back to the lot of their miserable faces. The fire crackles and pops behind me, the dry branches gasping for their final breaths, when I hear one of them address Sin, a maniacal chuckle in his voice.

"You willing to share her, Your Grace? We wouldn't mind a turn if you're done with her."

My blood turns to ice in my veins as I wait for his response, magic flooding to my forearms. I will melt the skin from their flesh before I let one of them even get close.

Try me.

A broken gasp like he was grabbed by the collar erupts from the guard who asked the lewd question.

His tone promising something lethal, Sin warns in a voice like sharpened steel, "The witch is *mine*."

The guard stammers an apology, and I let loose a shaky breath. While I would be shortsighted to trust any of these men, I *do* trust they won't cross Sin. Nonetheless, I turn so I am facing them before I pretend to sleep.

CHAPTER 7

A plethora of guards peer down at us from the towering stone walls of the castle's stronghold. They *are* preparing for Legion to return then—to reclaim their stolen witch. I don't doubt they will come. Cathal won't risk allowing someone with my power to remain behind his enemy's walls, even if that means foolishly ordering his threadbare army to rush into the kingdom storm that will surely consume them whole, bones and all.

Swallowing hard, I toss my hair, still tangled and free from its braid, over my shoulder, and step into the dim tunnel as the grated gates of the portcullis are raised for us. Sin thinks I am a Legion spy, that I surrendered to his army as some sort of elaborate ruse to infiltrate his borders. He is treating me as a prisoner of war. He has no idea I was Legion's prisoner long before I was his, and he certainly doesn't know why Cathal would go to such lengths to snatch me back.

A tussle of burnt steel and smoke assaults my nose as we emerge from the tunnel. The castle rears up in the distance, its spiked turrets a serrated knife threatening to tear through the tender wisps of clouds. Sin dismisses the others, and they head towards the barracks to my right, the tight rows of buildings with sloped roofs and burly men chortling outside them. Sin motions for me to follow him, and we head towards the castle, the shadows of its magnificent towers hovering over us. The last rays of afternoon light stretch from either side of the looming stone walls, as if the setting sun was embracing it in a warm hug.

The cobblestone feeds into a lush green carpet as we step into the same gardens visible from the balcony of my room last night. Spring is upon us, the weather already much warmer than the bone-chilling nights I spent in a Legion camp. It was winter both times they captured me—the night I confessed my secret to Cathal many years before, and a few weeks ago when I made a foolish mistake—one that resulted in me hitched over a horse's backside like freshly killed game.

"Your Grace," a man with short, dark hair approaches us, stopping to bow to Sin when he is near. He is clad in a suit of blackened steel, a blue-gray cape billowing out behind him as a squall rips through the keep, its icy kiss on my neck a violent reminder of the nights I spent huffing into my hands and rubbing my arms vigorously while Legion soldiers draped their shoulders with sun-dried hides.

Sin nods in greeting. "Aldred."

"The council is waiting in the war room, Your Grace—your father requests your presence at once. What are the arrangements for this one?" Aldred asks with a nod in my direction.

Sin's downward eyes sweep to mine with a look that could melt glaciers to rivulets. "Lock her up."

A wry smile twists my lips as I meet his stare with a threat of my own—a promise to incinerate his soul should we find our positions reversed one day.

"At once, Your Grace. I will send Anika to follow up on her wound." Aldred glances at the rotting two-day old bandage peeking out from my dress.

"Don't. Maybe she'll start remembering some things once the infection sets in."

I hate him.

Aldred snaps his fingers at me and waves me forward. "With me, then."

Restraining the urge to scream a combustion spell in his face, I follow Aldred the rest of the way to the castle. He leads us down the stairs at the end of the long ornate hallway, down to the sickly yellow dungeon where I spent my first night chained to a post. Barred cells stretch along both sides of the hall, the stench of death hovering around us like a sentient host welcoming us to its rotting, forgotten home. With no iron bracelets on my wrists, Aldred unknowingly walks with a predator at his back.

Sin believes my power to be that of a garden witch and nothing more—he doesn't know every throb of his pulse beckons to me like a virgin begging to be touched. I wonder what his goddess-blessed blood would taste like if I slashed open his chest and drank from his bleeding heart.

Aldred pulls open one of the cell doors with a metallic clang that rattles the room and motions for me to hurry inside. I fix him with a hardened stare as I step into the too-small space, and he—*he turns his back to me*—to pick up a bundle of chains from the dark corner under the stairs. If I wasn't so godsdamned determined to not be the monster my mother was sure I'd become, I could have ended his life a hundred times over now, each time more painful than the last. I'll escape from this castle, one way or another, but I won't shed blood to do so. And right now, there's no chance I'm slipping through this keep unnoticed—not yet anyway.

Flexing the chain between his hands, Aldred returns to find me standing with my arms already outstretched in front of me. I will my face to erase all expression, knowing it is best to keep the uncertainties of my current predicament to myself. He slaps the iron on my wrists and binds them together with just enough slack I can keep my hands from touching. I don't so much as blink when he slams the cell closed with an ear-splitting clatter.

I perk up at the smell of food before I take note of who's carrying it. River slides a dinner tray through the small opening under the bars—a bowl containing some kind of meaty stew with vegetables, a chunk of soft bread, and a few cubes of cheese. Unable to satisfy the rumbling in my stomach quickly enough, I scarf it all down immediately.

"I'm sorry, dear. Singard... he gets into these *moods*."

"Does he force you to serve him?"

"Gods, no," she chuckles, and I discover I adore her laugh—a warmness amidst the algid emptiness of the dungeon. Her face falls as she realizes my question was genuine. "I don't find myself agreeing with every decision that boy or his father makes, but I do love him like a son. Raised him as one too. His mother isn't around, you know."

I didn't know, but I suppose I have never seen the Lady of Castle Scarwood before.

"Where is his mother?"

"Now that is venturing into territory I don't think I'm fit to discuss. These walls have ears, best to remember that. Eat up, dear—I'll be damned if you reduce to skin and bones on my watch."

Her faint laughter fades as she climbs back up the stairs, and it isn't until the heavy door closes behind her that I realize how much I yearn to hear the soft creaking of those steps again, indicating her return. Hopefully with more food.

Alone with intrusive thoughts of traipsing through a sea of bodies adorned in kingdom uniforms, I stare into the flames flickering softly from inside metal sconces. I envy the fire, so unbothered and content to burn as it strives to reach greater heights. If it were to climb a little too high and reduce the castle to ash and dust, no one would blame the torch for the destruction—for doing what it was simply created to do. If only I were as lucky.

CHAPTER 8

The ceiling rumbles above my head with what sounds like frenzied footsteps, and I almost puke at the lurching in my stomach, as if someone was pulling on the invisible rope connecting me to the Black Art. I peer through the bars as the dungeon door flies open, the stairs squeaking as someone barrels down them.

I suck in a breath but let it loose when a different dark headed male than I was expecting drops into view and hustles towards me, fumbling with a ring of keys.

"What is happening upstairs?" I ask as the pounding of frantic feet continues above us.

The guard thrusts one of the many keys on his ring into the cell's lock and hauls open the door, ignoring my question. He grabs me by the elbow and drags me towards the stairs, not slowing his steps as I stumble behind him, my legs weakened from the iron.

"Are you taking me to him? Has His Grace decided on my punishment?" Or is he simply ready to act on his promise to rip the truth from my tongue as he threatened at the river? I struggle to plant myself, to force us to halt, but he yanks me harder, scrambling my feet like a startled goat. "Listen to me—

you sneak me out of here, and I will reward you with whatever you want. I have coin. Plenty of it. Let me go and it's yours."

He pulls me up the stairs, not so much as glancing behind him with my offer. Hurtling us through the door, the guard escorts me down the long stretch of hall and into the foyer with the towering archways. The room is packed with bodies, but it is Dusaro that rushes towards us, his tight-lipped expression nothing shy of furious.

Dusaro grabs me by the crook of my arm and jerks me around his body, slamming my back against his chest. He grabs a fistful of my unbound hair and rips my head back, exposing my neck to the kingdom steel he presses against it. Blood turns to ice in my veins, and I go still, lowering just my eyes to survey my surroundings. Several guards stand in a semicircle around the room, hands on the swords at their hips, ready for the order to draw. With Dusaro now at my rear, I behold the backs of Sin and a woman at the far end of the room. She is tall with a petite, slender frame, loose midnight curls coiling around her waist. She angles towards me and—

Goddess above.

Ileana.

Legion hadn't held onto Ileana for her arcane talent—she was as mundane as they came—but she helped orchestrate an attack against the rebellion that ended in her capture. This was during my first stint with Legion, several years ago when I confessed my secret to their leader. It wasn't that Ileana was a die-hard kingdom supporter; she simply hated the destruction Legion wreaked in the cities and heard the rumors they were recruiting soldiers by force. She and a few others managed to take out a quarter of the camp with arrows before they were on them. Cathal killed her friends but insisted they keep her alive —that death was too merciful for a woman with a tongue as spiteful as hers. They chained her up and delighted in her suffering as they dragged out her punishment. Not going back for her the night Cosmina snuck into the camp and freed me has not ceased to be my biggest regret. I cowered in the moment I needed to find my strength the most, and she continued to suffer because of it.

How in the gods' names did she end up here?

A muscle feathers in her brown cheek, and I follow her menacing stare to the man slumped on his knees before her, twin swords at his neck courtesy of the two guards hovering above him.

The sight of him flares my chaos, and the iron colors my wrists with matching amethyst bracelets, reacting to the magic bubbling there, antagonized by the mere image of him breathing in my presence. *Our* presence. Because kneeling before her, an arrow protruding from his makeshift armor, is the man who tortured us both.

Given Cathal's human form, the arrow must be iron tipped, preventing him from shifting. He rolls his head back to look at Sin with those glaring blue eyes—eyes that watched as his friends kicked me into submission, beat me into misery, and violated me into nothingness.

"I only knew it was a matter of time before you'd grace us with your presence again," Sin smirks at the Legion commander.

They attacked. While I've been rotting in a cell beneath our feet, Legion stormed the stronghold—again. And clearly were unsuccessful given their leader now kneels in a crimson pool before the Black Art.

"That eager for another beating, Singard?"

Sin shakes loose a gravelly laugh. "Admit it, Cathal—you're out of resources, out of bodies, out of time." He clicks his tongue, crossing his arms as he stares down at the man that defiled my body. "You're almost making it too easy to win. I rather enjoy a good fight. But I'll bite—tell me, Cathal—why are your men outside my keep, starting a fight they cannot win? *Please*, enlighten me."

"You have something of mine," Cathal's eyes flash to mine, "and I want it back."

"Ah... yes. I suppose there is the matter of the witch. What *can* we do about that?" Sin begins to pace, his footsteps clacking against the stone floor with each measured step.

My blood pounds in my ears, my breathing turning ragged despite my attempt to remain calm, to not show a flicker of emotion in a room full of enemies. Even an apex predator knows when it is outnumbered.

"Give her to us and we'll leave," Cathal muses, his mouth twisting with dark amusement as if he knows his proposal will stoke the Black Art's pride. The kingdom does not negotiate.

Sin's footsteps come to a halt, the sudden silence in the foyer deafening as he stares at his feet, deliberating his next words. My heart races under Dusaro's arm, exposing my panic under my mask of collectedness. I would rather throw my neck into Dusaro's eager dagger than leave as Cathal's bartered pet.

"Sure... I could hand her over... be rid of her and your miserable men out there." His green eyes, now glistening with verdant wickedness, dart to mine. A smile equally as nefarious settles on his lips, and he takes a casual step towards me. "But I have a better idea."

Suddenly his hands are on me—wresting me from his father's grip—and he whirls me around his body, fitting one large hand around the base of my throat and wrapping the other across my chest like a steel band. A shaky yelp spills from my mouth before I can swallow it. I regret it instantly, but I swear his grip on my neck relaxes slightly.

Sin angles his head towards me, his breath a torrid caress along my nape. Gently, he drags the tip of his nose up my neck, all the way to the underside of my chin. I stop breathing, my palms sweating, every nerve in my body ordering for my magic to surge, and every one being struck down by the iron at my wrists. He holds us here, his mouth hovering inches above where my pulse pounds wildly in my throat, when he says in a voice soft as sodden roses, "You surrender... or I rip her throat out."

My lips mash together, heat nearly radiating from my body as my power claws against its iron shackling. From my periphery, I glimpse as Sin parts his lips slightly, his teeth admiring the soft skin of my jugular.

"You won't kill her," Cathal calls his bluff, deviousness twinkling in his dark blue eyes like vicious stars. Goddess above, I hope he *is* bluffing, but my nostrils flare as the scent coming from Sin shifts into virile hunger.

"I swear on my life if you don't surrender right now, I'll rip her throat out with my own teeth," he snarls, jerking me tighter against him.

Cathal lets out a low laugh, seemingly unaware of his own blood pooling around him. "You really think I'd call off my men to save that bitch's life? You're even dumber than I thought, Kilbreth."

"Last chance, Cathal. I would love nothing more than to sit here and bear witness as you watch your love bleed out."

"My love? Oh, now that *is* good," he cackles, his words transitioning into a boisterous, manic laughter. "I wouldn't love her if she was the last living thing to fuck. Kill her." Cathal shifts his focus to me. "Don't worry about your friends, Wren. We'll take real good care of them," he says with a wink.

My hands ball so tightly into fists, my nails prick my palms. "Don't you fucking go near them," I choke out under Sin's grasp.

"That dark-haired sister of yours—wonder if her snatch is as tight as yours."

My blood turns to lead, and I strain to look at Sin, the back of my head still forced against his shoulder. "Kill him. If you kill me, you fucking kill him too."

Cathal grins, his lapis blue eyes sparkling as he licks his lips and laughs quietly to himself. He shifts his attention back to Sin. "It doesn't surprise me the kingdom has resorted to using bloodwitches now."

I stop breathing. His words echo in my head, each one promising swift death.

Bloodwitch.

With one final breath, I close my eyes—I refuse to let Cathal be the last thing I see before Sin delivers my fate. The kingdom does not spare bloodwitches—mages whose collectives are rooted so deep in bloodshed they cannot trust themselves to remain in control once they take a life. We absorb the energy of those we kill whether we want to or not, amplifying our power and making us stronger and harder to stop with each body that falls limp from our blood-stained palms.

"You let a bloodwitch into our home?" Dusaro asks with chilling calmness. "Such stupidity."

Sin's grip on my throat tightens slightly at his father's comment, and heat ignites into a vicious necklace along my neck. I flinch from the sudden onset of pain, and the burning simmers out a moment later. *And here I thought my father and I were the epitome of troubled relationships.* Seconds tick by as I wait for him to banish Dusaro for his insult, to order for him to be taken to the dungeon or worse, but Sin remains a bronzed statue behind me.

There is no use in pleading for my life—there has never been bargaining with the kingdom, and even if there was, I'm not sure my life is one worth begging for. Not when it puts my sister, who will surely risk her own neck to save mine, in danger. My chest hardens to granite beneath him, but I can't slow my pulse thudding against his hand, my body fighting for life even if my mind has accepted its demise. Seconds feel like minutes. My chest rising and falling in rhythmic breaths, a pendulum ticking down my final moments. Sweats beads along my nape, shoulders, lower back—*just get it over with already*.

"You wanted to weaponize her against us?" Sin breaks the thunderous silence.

"Had she cooperated a little more, it would have worked. Was a stellar plan, actually. But she's a resistant bitch. She's too big a liability anyway—better for both of us that she doesn't remain alive." Cathal's too-casual tone sends a heap of red-hot coals tumbling through my core.

I grit my teeth as I wait for Sin's dagger to send me to the next realm. Or maybe he wasn't exaggerating when he threatened to rip my throat out. Is that how I'll jump from this life into the next? Slipping from his grasp as I fall into a ruby puddle, thoughts of Cosmina and Eldridge and Morrinne pirouetting behind my eyelids as my heart gives out. It's better than the alternative, I suppose. As much as I hate the kingdom for their prejudices against my family, I'd rather die by the Black Art's blade than bleed under a Legion knife. With a steadying breath, I relax my shoulders and wait for death's sweet, promising kiss.

"Lock them both up."

My eyes fly open, and Sin thrusts me away from him, into the hands of two uniformed guards. Another two pull Cathal to his feet and steer him behind us, our footsteps echoing in singular purpose as we head back towards the dungeon stairwell. Cathal yells something back to Sin, but I don't register his words, my mind spinning as I try to make sense of what just happened.

I'm alive.

My knees take the brunt of the fall as one of the guards shoves me back into my cell, and I barely take notice as they lead Cathal, still muttering to either himself or his own escorts, around the corner that continues out of sight. At least he is being kept far away from me, far enough I can't see that diabolicalness in his eyes, or hear that maniacal laughter in my ears.

I touch the chilled stone beneath me. *Real.* I run my hands over my arms, my face, through my hair. *Real.*

I am real.

I don't allow myself to remember how his blue eyes had looked in the dark.

CHAPTER 9

Twenty-one. My cell door has twenty-one bars. I don't know how many times I've counted them, only that it is a lot. I eat. I sleep. I count. River has not come to see me again, and a guard has been bringing me meals twice a day instead. Based on my food intervals, it is the third day I've been locked down here.

The fever set in yesterday. My skin gleams with perspiration despite the chill nipping my bones like hungry sparrows. If Sin doesn't come down here and kill me, the infection will.

We'll take real good care of them.

Cathal's threat on my family hasn't left my mind since it left his ugly mouth. They need protection. The mother who accepted me as her own... Cosmina who showed me compassion when no one else did... my brothers and sisters who welcomed me into their home, even when I wasn't one of them.

I should have never gone hunting alone. It was a rule we didn't break—no one ventured off by themselves. Morrinne and I had the watch the afternoon I was captured, while the others were away at the jobs they kept in the nearby city. Our food supply was dwindling, and Morrinne had been so preoccupied with knitting a scarf for my other chosen sister, Zorina, I didn't want to disturb her. Winters are harsh in Autumnhelm, and Zorina never sat still for long. She was a wanderer, always taking to the woods and venturing the outskirts of Innodell. Morrinne always pestered her about keeping warm. It didn't matter that transcendents naturally keep warmer body temps—Morrinne wanted her to have a scarf to keep the chill off her neck, and she insisted Zorina would wear it despite her efforts to convince Morrinne she would simply shift when she caught cold.

Legion had been quiet for a while and naively, I forgot the deadliest predators are often the stealthiest. It wasn't until they looped the iron chain over my head and across my chest that I even knew they were there. My family would return to learn from our panicked mother that I was missing—and the worst part—Morrinne would blame herself, even though it was my mistake, and mine alone.

The slow, rhythmic clacking of leather shoes against the ground announces his arrival. I scramble to sit up straighter before he reaches my cell, not wanting him to see how weak the infection and iron has already made me.

Sin stares down at me through the bars, scanning my face —first one eye then the other, before dragging his gaze over my cheeks, the curvature of my mouth, the slump of my shoulders. What he is looking for, I don't know, nor do I have the energy to care at this point. He leans back slightly while studying me, his hands shoved deep into his black trouser pockets. Keeping my expression fixed, I poke mental fingertips into his mind. My core clenches as a tempest of wrath and pride and shame spirals into my gut like a fisted punch. I press against it harder, forcing his collective to flatten against mine so I can read him easier.

"Stop," he snaps.

Startled, I drop my hold, and my collective springs back into place.

"I can feel you in there—in my head. I thought I was going mad before."

"You could feel me in there?"

"Barely, but yes. If I'm focused, I can feel... *everything*." A perk of Adelphia's blessing I'm sure, though his disgruntled tone suggests he does not appreciate it. "I never felt anything like it before. I brushed it off as nothing, but when Cathal told me what you were, it made sense. How does it work?" His stare flattens me against the wall, demanding, cold.

"I can read feelings, intentions. I don't know your thoughts —don't waste the energy trying to block them."

"Isn't that exactly what you would say if you could read them?"

"Does it even matter?"

Sin stares at me a few seconds longer before moving to lean against the cell, slipping his hands in to loosely hold the bars. "Answer a few questions for me. Honestly," he adds in warning.

I wave my hand for him to continue.

"You're a bloodwitch."

Not a question, but I nod anyway. "Mhmm."

"Tell me who you really are and how you ended up here."

A cold wind sweeps across my neck, maybe from the thought of revealing anything about myself that could later be used against me, or maybe from the fever that now bedevils my body. I wait a few breaths before answering him, musing over how much detail I want to spill to my enemy. The answer is none, but I can't spin another lie and risk getting caught in it.

Pausing to make sure my breath is steady, I answer him. "I have been hiding from Cathal for a long time. Years. Legion is under the impression if they have a bloodwitch fighting on their side, they can bring the entire kingdom down. They captured me several years ago when Cathal tried seizing Scarwood during Ephraim's reign. He threatened my family—detailing the despicable things he would do to them if I didn't use my power to aid them. Cos—my sister—she found me before we made it to Blackreach. I didn't think they would come for me again without the element of surprise, and they didn't for a long time. But as soon as I let my guard down, for a split second, they struck like the dirty snakes they are, and I found myself their prisoner once more. That was a month ago—I think." Time has blurred with recent events—maybe a month passed, maybe six of them.

"And what did they plan on doing with you afterwards? Surely they anticipated you turning on them as soon as you saw to our destruction."

"They overestimate their ability. And underestimate mine."

"How did Cathal find out what you are?"

"I told him," I answer sheepishly. "We were... we were together... for a short time."

"He betrayed you," he states knowingly.

I nod. "I thought I could trust him. He and his men came for me that same night and took me to their camp. That's where I met Ileana, which brings me to a question of my own: what the hell is she doing here?"

"Ileana is my Black Hand."

I choke on a laugh, one entirely void of humor. "She's serving the kingdom? You must be joking." Ileana hates Legion more than anyone I know, and after the torture they put her through, I'm sure that loathing is as much a part of her as her blood and bones. But working for the kingdom? That is as much Ileana's style as outerwear is on Zorina. "How did she even get here? She was still in that camp the last I saw her." *When I left and didn't go back for her.*

"She's here now, and you will respect her as the Hand to the throne. The how and why isn't of your concern."

Curiosity pecks into my brain like a chickadee gobbling up seeds, but I push it aside. I need to speak to Ileana herself if I want the real truth anyway—*her* truth.

"When you ran from me the other day, where were you heading?"

"Home." I look at him cautiously before continuing. "I have a family."

"Is your family also—?" he trails off as if *bloodwitches* was too dirty a word for his mouth.

"No. My parents disowned me when I was young, when they discovered what I am. They didn't have the guts to kill me themselves, so they thought they'd let starvation or illness do it for them. I was very lucky. Someone found me and took me in. I live remotely with her and a few others, away from unnecessary risks."

"What kind of risks?"

I study him closely when I answer. "They are transcendents."

He arches a dark eyebrow. "You were raised by shifters?"

"Yes. Ephraim and your father's reign made it too dangerous to live in the cities, so they kept to themselves. Me being what I am, I also preferred to sleep away from prying eyes. Our arrangement worked."

"Apart from where Cathal found you?" he asks with a glimmer of sarcasm.

"I made an egregious error," I grumble through clenched teeth.

Sin folds his arms across his chest and begins to pace in front of the cell. "Why haven't you escaped? Legend says when a bloodwitch makes their first kill, the power they gain makes them crazy, consumed with bloodlust and power and sex. You could have killed all of us by now."

I will my cheeks not to flush at the mention of the caster's high. Magic is an aphrodisiac for most mages—the more power they expel, the stronger the urge. When a bloodwitch kills and consumes that kind of power, it's rumored to unleash a desire that trumps all other feelings, except maybe the need to keep killing. Since I've never taken a life, I haven't experienced it, but I have felt twinges of a... heat... when I would spar with Eldridge or find myself occupied with violent thoughts. Judging from the flutters of warmth I've felt when merely flexing my magic, I don't doubt the rumors are riddled in truth.

I feign a yawn as if his questions are boring me. "Because if I had killed you or anyone else, Blackheart, I don't know what the magic would do to me. I would prefer I didn't turn into a murdering lunatic."

He stops pacing and peers down at me, his eyes widening slightly. "I was *seconds* away from ending your life and that was before I knew what you were. You slit your own throat by not escaping."

I lean my head against the wall behind me. "I'm aware."

"How did your parents learn what you are?"

I keep my gaze fixed on the opposite wall when I answer. "The smell of blood... it appeals to me. But I've never killed anyone, and I've only ever hurt those that hurt me first."

The image of my mother's face when she learned what I was flashes in my mind. When I scratched her arm deep enough to draw blood, the disgust and disbelief that twisted her mouth as she saw the *want* on mine.

He loops his arms through the bars again and leans forward. "There is a gala being held here tomorrow. There will be some families in attendance whose support I count on very much. I would like you to attend and listen in on them."

"Listen in on them?"

"I need to know who I can trust and who I cannot. I have reason to believe an ally is aiding Legion—smuggling resources to them. They should have collapsed in on themselves by now, and yet, they continue to come back time and time again, throwing bodies at my keep. Tell me, Wren, how does a rebellion that's hated by half the isle continue to show up healed from injury and wielding new weapons? Attend my gala and mingle, get a read on people. Tell me if I need to divert my *attentions* to certain individuals."

"You want me to spy for you?"

His eyes sweep over me, taking in my disheveled appearance, and I wonder if it is obvious how weak the infection has made me. "It would be a mutually beneficial agreement."

"Enlighten me." I smile with feigned interest.

"You heard Cathal, same as I. This family of yours, he sounded rather determined to take his resentment towards you out on them. One in particular—something about a dark-haired sister with... qualities I won't repeat." He shakes his head, as if even he didn't appreciate Cathal's vulgarity when describing Cosmina. "Legion can't hurt your family if they're dead in the sea. We eliminate their supplier, we eliminate Legion. No Legion, no Cathal running around making predatory comments."

"Did you kill him?"

Sin shakes his head. "I want him *alive*."

He doesn't elaborate, and I don't ask. "If I help you, what's in it for me?"

"I'll consider not killing you," he answers, not a sliver of amusement on his face.

"I want my freedom. If I help you, I go free."

"You help me, and your *family* remains free."

I push my collective against his again and shred at it with phantom fingernails, searching for any trace of deception. Hatred burns through me instead—his hatred for Legion, I presume.

"Think about it, Wren. Every minute Legion remains alive is a minute you risk them hurting your family. Help me cut off their supply chain, and the rebellion is one less threat in their lives."

"Your entire kingdom threatens their lives," I spit. He must think even lower of me now knowing I was brought up by transcendents. Bloodwitch by birth, transcendent sympathizer by choice. I wonder if it rivals how low I think of him.

"It's your choice. How's that shoulder healing up on you?" the Black Art smirks, his eyes honing in on the rotting flesh now oozing a sickly yellow pus.

I glare up at him and scoff at the green irises now beaming with wicked amusement. "You're willing to heal me and remove the iron so I may dance with some strangers at a ball?" My tone implies the severity of the risk he would be taking.

"You've already shown me you aren't willing to do what it takes to escape."

His words punch me in the gut. I want to hate him for his remark, but the anger now surging through my core is reserved for me. He is right. I don't know if I'm making it out of Scarwood alive, but if helping the Black Art ensures my family's safety, I owe them that.

I blow out a breath. "Alright, Your Grace. I agree to do your bidding and pry the secrets from your enemies' minds since you and your council have failed to do so."

"Careful, witch."

I extend my arms in front of me, the chains dangling from my wrists like metal serpents. He throws open the cell with magic and breaks my iron bindings in the same cast. Storming into the dank cage, he reaches for my wounded arm.

His predatory grin widens as I scream with the stretching of tissue.

CHAPTER 10

Honey steeped in a piping cup of jasmine tea. The deep golden fabric of the gown River cinches tight around my waist is familiar, and an image of the warm beverage that never left Morrinne's side flashes in my mind, followed by a pang of homesickness. If she saw me standing here now, adorned in a dress that likely costs more than the entire value of everything we own, tears would drip from her eyes. But they wouldn't be tears of joy as she beheld her daughter in the finest fabric money could buy—she would cry out in horror and beg Sin to show mercy, knowing the elaborate dress was merely his way of sprucing up his next meal before cutting into me like I was nothing more than a tender roast.

"I can hardly breathe," I say as River gives an exceptionally aggressive tug of the corset strings at my back.

"Good. That means I'm doing it right." River meets my eyes in the mirror and smiles apologetically.

Sin arranged for me to return to the ornate room I slept in my first night, before he knew I was the very monster his kingdom was hell-bent on eradicating from existence. The room—more like a small suite—is exactly as I left it, except the large armoire now holds an array of finely tailored dresses, most of them able to be stepped into without the need of an assistant to secure the bodices. While I may have glowered at the fancy attire before, I find small comfort in knowing it was unlikely the Black Art would have ordered for my closet to be stocked if he intended on killing me. Or at least not in my immediate future.

I frown at my own reflection. The rich golden gown drips from my shoulders and fans out at the elbows, leaving my forearms and shoulders exposed. Deep bronze piping in a crisscross pattern garnishes the bodice, and flowers of the same matching golden-brown thread are woven through the skirts in a brocade style masterpiece. I may be the only mage in the room, but it is River who has the real magical hands. She painted my lips a warm shade of pink, the color reminiscent of the rose petal jam I made for holidays and special occasions. The hue is bright against the light brown of my eyes and snowy hair River pinned back with an elegant crystal hair piece. The rest cascades down my back like hilly, snowcapped peaks, all the way to the small of my waist.

Sin lifted the fever from me when he closed my wound, and after a cold wash in the bathhouse and a hearty meal of roast mutton and crusty bread, the blush tint returned to my cheeks. The bruised purple marks left behind from the iron faded from my wrists sometime overnight, and if it wasn't for the Black Art's bidding I must do tonight, I might even be feeling sprightful.

If he told River what I was, she didn't mention it, and I didn't ask. With my fever gone and all traces of iron vanished from my skin, there is nothing stopping me from fighting my way out of here. Nothing except my own stubborn will to not stoop to the devilish legends whispered about my kind.

You've already shown me you aren't willing to do what it takes.

I hate him for being right. I hate myself for *allowing* him to be right. If I was sure I could remain in control, that I wouldn't fade away as the bloodwitch crawled out from the ruinous depths of my collective, I would have never been taken by Legion, and certainly never rotting away in a subterranean cell beneath Sin's feet.

River pulls the final strings tight, and with a quick fluff of the dress's skirts, she steps aside and clasps her hands together under her chin, admiring her work.

"How in the gods' names did you make this happen?" The annoyance in my voice isn't because her work is poor quality, but rather, the opposite. *I look like one of them.*

"You and Sin aren't the only ones with magic up your sleeves," she says with a wink. "Now that my most important job is done, I need to get downstairs and make sure the girls didn't let any details slip through the cracks. These balls are quite important to His Grace." River tucks the cosmetics and hair styling tools she brought with her into her basket and leaves, sucking all the comfort from the room when she does. River may be mundane, but her ability to make others feel at ease, even one of Sin's prisoners, is a skill not even the most advanced of mages could replicate.

With a final look in the mirror, I pull my shoulders back and sharpen my gaze. Violence may be my least preferred means of escape, but I need to look the opposite in front of Sin. Lifting my chin and molding my features into marble, I appear strong. Fierce. And definitely capable of punching a dagger through his eye. I run my hands over my waist, admiring how the corset River tightened draws attention to other parts of me that are inherently feminine. And with that final touch of confidence, I drop my hands to my side and march out of the room.

The foyer that was brimming with violence just a few nights ago now bubbles with ladies dressed in lavish gowns and men tailored in fine coats. Decorative cloths of deep burgundy run along the wide-stretched tables, almost hidden under the silver platters offering assorted cheeses and fruits, and others adorned with glasses of spiced wine. Wrapped around the towering archways are flowers of vermilion red, their vibrant petals the only reminder of the Legion blood that coated the floor beneath them just days before. I follow the beckoning of stringed instruments that leads me to a set of already propped open doors, and beyond them, the castle's ballroom.

The room is a storm of color and dance. Women's skirts, sewn from the fabrics only available at elite modiste shops, whirl around the room as the musicians signal the next partner dance is about to begin. A glorious gold chandelier dripping with crystal accents hovers above the center floor, where men are lining up on one side, and women the other. I recognize no one in the sea of cosmetic painted faces. These are the lords and ladies from high-ranking families—families that live in Blackreach—and ultimately serve the kingdom. More tables presenting an array of foods—meat tarts, mushroom pastries, and flaky pies overflowing with a brilliant pink-red filling resembling rhubarb stretch across the perimeter of the room.

I move through the throng of bodies, some swaying to the music, others gathered in small groups. The indistinct chatter of politics and potential marriages and dowries nests in my ears until the clinking of silver against glass calls my attention to the far side of the room.

There, Dusaro stands on top of the dais, holding his glass of mead above his head as if saluting the gods. The crowd quiets as he begins to address the room. "Our beloved guests— nothing brings me greater joy than to be here, amongst the greatest and mightiest families of Aegidale. To celebrate together the great fortunes to grace our land under the fine leadership of my son and his beautiful Hand."

His beautiful Hand.

I offer up a silent thanks to whichever god or goddess is looking out for my old friend, though I'm certain *she* doesn't consider us friends anymore. The mass of lords and ladies to my right steps backwards and bow in synchronized unison as Sin and Ileana walk with rehearsed grace to replace Dusaro on the dais.

Despite Ileana's mundane nature, she looks equally as powerful standing next to the Black Art. Her warm sepia skin is as clear and bright as daybreak, her angular face framed by a long mane of thick raven curls that hang to her waist. Her deli- cate brown shoulders peek through her thin-strapped dress, the color like melted steel with deep blue beading along the neckline. The beaded accents glimmer like tumbled gemstones, and I instinctively run a hand along my neck as the image of Cosmina's sapphire necklace that was a staple to every outfit she wore prances through my mind.

Ileana smiles at the crowd, warmth and softness replacing the daggers she once stowed in those dark brown eyes. At her side, Sin wears a long-sleeved burgundy surcoat with gold threadwork along the shoulders and neckline, and fitted black pants. His usual unbound hair is tied loosely at the nape of his neck, and he mirrors her smile, his emerald eyes bright with excitement. Looking at him now, fitted in his formal wear and his militant paws not wrapped around my throat, he looks... *good.*

Sin takes a step forward, and the last of the excited whispers fall silent. "Tonight... isn't about negotiations. It isn't about war or winning or sacrifice. Tonight, is for your families and mine, honoring those we love and will protect at all costs. Now, raise your glasses with me to a better and safer tomorrow."

A mural of goblets fly into the air with shouts of 'to a better and safer tomorrow' as the noble men and women bid their toasts and drink their wine. It takes all my self-restraint to not knock the glass away from the lord pulling a deep sip of his mead at my side. While transcendents dip their heads as they hurry from one dimly lit alley to the next, lords wear their fancy coats and make toasts in fortified castles promising their extinction. Disgusting.

Sin and Ileana step down from the platform and are instantly swallowed in a circle of eager townsmen intent on bending their ears, probably pitching more ideas on how to eradicate the shifter *problem*. I uncurl my fingers, not having realized my hands balled into fists, and move to a less crowded part of the room, near one of the striking white pillars.

With a steadying breath, I force my face to relax and fix it with one of casual interest as I scan the room, flexing my collective away from me. A chorus of emotions invade me. Scattered notes of intention and feeling—pride and joy and lust—dance through me as the hymn of their collective energies prod at me with their melodic songs. Gluttonous desires that fill my mind with thoughts of balmy summer nights and tangled sheets tear through me like a violent wind. My eyes sting with greed, images of crown jewels and golden trinkets prance before my eyes, invisible to all but me. Something sweet like gardenias laced in vanilla beckons to my nose as thoughts of corseted gowns and ripe bosoms wrestle for my focus. Tilting my head to the side, I casually press two fingers to my temple, steering my collective through the room, listening for anything reminiscent of betrayal. I continue to scan, to *read...* beauty, coin, the tranquility of rainy evenings spent indoors—

"Evening," says a male who sidled up next to me.

I jump, my collective snapping back to its place behind my eye, and my hand smacks against my chest with an audible thwack. A young man with wavy chestnut hair and a matching well-groomed beard grins widely at me. A second too long passes before I remember to force a smile back.

"Bennett Langston. My apologies, my Lady—I didn't mean to startle you."

"Wren. Lovely to meet you, my Lord," I say, extending my hand.

He grasps it firmly in both of his and raises it to his lips. "Bennett," he corrects and kisses the backs of my knuckles.

If I wasn't so determined to play my part well, I may have vomited on his leather shoes which have been shined to a mirror finish. But like the good lady I am, I offer a polite smile and drop my hand back to my side.

"Why don't I recognize you?" Bennett asks.

"I'm only visiting Blackreach, so I'm afraid I don't know many faces. His Grace and I are old friends."

"Well, our mutual friend sure knows how to host a ball." He leans in closer and extends his hand, eagerness sparkling in his deep blue eyes. "May I have the next dance?"

"Oh, I don't know. I think I'd embarrass myself and you," I lie. My father was an excellent musician and taught me most of the partner dances when I was a girl. Dancing is one of my favorite pastimes. Or so, it used to be.

"Spare me one whirl on the floor, and if you deem me bloody incompetent on my feet, I'll never ask for another one again." He waves me forward, dipping his head slightly to meet my eyes.

I bite my lip as I fail to come up with an excuse quickly

enough, and after an awkward number of seconds later, I slip my hand into his. Fine. *I already put on the damn dress.* His smile stretches too wide for his face, and he leads me towards the center of the floor. We separate so we face each other from opposite sides as the musicians play an opening piece, a warning the number is about to begin, sending the last of the ladies scurrying to take their places.

The dance is simple. Bennett and I step towards each other, and placing our palms together, we move in a slow circle. First one direction, then the other, before dropping our hands and switching sides. As we step around each other, I notice Bennett is rather handsome, if you are attracted to noble men who look the part. And judging from his wandering eyes sweeping from my neck to the ties of my bodice, I am willing to wager he finds me attractive too. We join hands again, and he spins me away from him, his hand finding the small of my back as I twirl back. Nervous laughter spills from my lips, and I regret the awful sound immediately. As we sidestep, my feet perfectly in line with the ladies who have undoubtedly danced at dozens of balls, Bennett angles his head towards me.

"You look as delicious as the feast, Lady Wren."

I smile with forced sweetness. "Do you always charm ladies by comparing them to beef pies, Mr. Langston?"

He laughs quietly and presses his lips against my ear. I stiffen at the contact. "Only the ones I'd love to taste."

Oh, royal men, how they take my breath away with their scintillating compliments.

Saving me from *that* uncomfortable exchange, the music slows to a close, and we bow to one another. Bennett reaches for my hand and kisses the back of my knuckles again.

"Mr. Langston."

I never thought the sound of the Black Art's voice would bring me relief.

"Your Grace," Bennett says, his attention snapping behind me as he dips into a deep bow.

"I see you've met my friend." Sin's mouth twitches into a slight smile as he steps up next to us, and I'd be surprised if the forcedness of it didn't cause him pain. *Is my presence truly that disgusting to you, Your Grace?*

"She was just doing this fool the honor of dancing with him." Bennett shoots a coy wink in my direction.

"I was visiting with your father. He appears to be keeping sound health, as do you, Mr. Langston."

"Thank you, Your Grace. We are keeping well indeed."

"May I steal a dance with our lovely friend?" Sin asks, as if Bennett could refuse if he wanted to.

Bennett leans at the waist once more and glances my way. "My Lady," he says in farewell before turning and leaving us.

I hold in the smirk. I have spent my life pretending to be something I'm not, but never once have I pretended to be a lady. While grateful for the distance between Bennett and myself, I swallow hard before turning back to face Sin, who has already assumed his place on the gentlemen's side of the floor. Taking my spot opposite him, I lift my chin and set my feet in the proper position to begin.

The weight of the room presses in on me as heads turn and stares burn into my back. No one here recognizes me, and they are no doubt wondering who the mystery woman is, and why the Black Art has asked her to dance. I share in their curiosity.

Slowly, he drags his stare up my body and back down again, and I swear layers of my skin begin to melt away everywhere his eyes peruse over me, lingering on the fit of my dress and the lines of my neck. *Sad you didn't get to rip my throat out, Your Grace?* I fix him with a molten leer of my own.

His black hair, secured at his neck with a leather tie, falls down the back of his reddish-brown coat. His jacket fits snuggly in the shoulders and arms, showing off the swells of muscle beneath, and his black pants are tighter than the baggy ones I'd seen him in before. If Bennett is handsome, Sin is something darker, wilder, and infinitely more dangerous. He raises a dark eyebrow at me, and I can almost hear his question in that stupid, low voice of his—*like what you see, witch?*

The wailing of violins fills the space, and I step towards him, the skirts of my gown sliding across the stone floor behind me. He exposes his palms and I don't hesitate pressing mine against them. Something reminiscent of a static charge pulses between our hands, as if the magic in mine is reacting to the power in his. I'm not certain he feels it too, but I swear his narrow eyes widen slightly as if he does. Or maybe he is just repulsed by the thought of brushing skin with a bloodwitch.

"Do you know who the Langstons are?" Sin asks.

"I don't know who anyone here is."

"They manage Aegidale's trade, domestically and with our neighbors across the sea. Their support—particularly Bennett's father, Sterling Langston—is very important to my father and I."

"You want me to get a read on this Sterling?"

He shakes his head. "I want you to stay very close to *Bennett* for the evening. If the Langstons are up to something, he's privy to it. Find me immediately if there is anything indicative he is conspiring with..." he cuts himself off, glancing at the dancing couples on either side of us. "Conspiring with *them*," he finishes.

"Do you think he might know anything about my family? If... *they*... have come for them?"

He spins me away from him, and when I whirl back, he slips one hand to my waist and pulls me closer to him. "Unlikely he does, but I might," he purrs, his voice too low for anyone but me to hear.

"What do you know?"

"There isn't a lot I don't know, Wren." His voice sounds almost disinterested, but in the few encounters I've had the displeasure of sharing with the Black Art, I've come to recognize the forced levelness of his tone right before he proposes a one-sided bargain.

I stare up at him, trying to force him to meet my gaze, but he looks over my head at the couples dancing around us, plastering a casual expression on his face and not one of a man about to deliver an ultimatum. "Can we skip the foreplay and jump straight to the point, Blackheart?"

His lips widen, and he runs his tongue across his top set of teeth in a movement that is pure animal. "I think that's the first time a woman has ever asked me that."

I may be dressed like a lady, but the look I shoot him is anything but ladylike. "Hm, I suppose they didn't want to be disappointed so soon."

The hand at my waist grips me a little tighter, and he curls his fingers between mine where our palms remain pressed together. Still looking away from me, he inclines his head slightly, steering his words towards my ears and mine alone. "Careful, little witch."

Before I can respond, Sin spins me away from him again, and I perform the solo steps with proficiency. I smile to myself at the thought of Sin's curious expression at my back, wondering where a *little witch* learned to dance. Grabbing my skirts, I whirl back towards him, and if he was questioning where the knowledge came from, he doesn't ask. We join at the palm again.

"So, are you going to continue to exploit my gifts in exchange for the safety of my family, or are you ready to negotiate like a big boy?"

The smirk on his mouth has me instantly regretting my

word choice. "Contrarily, that is *not* the first time a woman has called me that." His eyes flash to mine, and he wipes the grin from his face in the same motion. "But that is precisely what I'm going to do."

"And should I grow tired of being your personal spy, Your Grace, then what? Are you going to kill me and lose the one secret weapon you have at your disposal?"

The melodious violin-led number mellows to a close, and we bow once to each other. Around us, the couples scatter and return to their conversations, while the Black Art and I remain planted here, chest to chest, as if seeing which of our fiery stares will melt the other first.

"Do not mistake my affinity for strategic advantages as anything but that. You are merely one power play in a sea of many. The second your existence ceases to benefit me—you said it yourself—you are at my *disposal*."

"If you care about this Sterling so much, why don't you send me to read him instead?"

"Because the Langston boy is attracted to you," he says, his expression reserved. "And I imagine it is easier to read a man's underlying intentions if his thoughts aren't scrambled, but rather fixed on one emotion." His gaze slips to my collarbones and then a little lower, before he jerks his attention back to my face, making his point.

My hands clench so hard, my knuckle joints nearly tear through the skin. I keep them balled up at my sides so I don't reach out and yank his tongue straight from his mouth. For him to infer Bennett was indeed interested in continuing our evening together, Sin must have been watching us. Unease trails an icy finger across my neck at the thought of the Black Art having eyes on me without my knowledge. "You are a rotten person."

His attention darts to something behind me.

"When I heard there was a Legion witch named Wren in our home, I knew it had to be you," Ileana coos, seemingly unconcerned with any guests that may be lingering in earshot.

I spin on my heels and shut my mouth at once, realizing it had fallen open slightly at the sound of her voice.

"Surprised to see I didn't rot and die after you and your sister left me for dead?"

Shame floods my cheeks, and I take a step towards her before halting, remembering her new title. I clasp my hands against the front of my skirts and slip into a curtsy. "I have been worried about you, Ileana—my Lady," I correct. "I'm so... that night—"

"Save it," she snaps, cutting me off. "Do what you've been brought here to do, and when this is over, don't expect my help when Singard realizes how worthless you are to the kingdom." She gives me a pointed stare, unsheathing the daggers she has mastered hiding in her tawny brown eyes, and walks away, her tall, slender frame bleeding into the crowd.

Her words plunge a sword into my gut, even if they were expected. I don't blame Ileana for hating me, not when she knew Cosmina and I fled to safety in the shadowed woods while she remained bound in rope and starved. She doesn't know how that decision has haunted me every day since, in both my waking hours and nighttime ones. But it doesn't matter.

I left. And I didn't go back.

"I suggest you find Bennett," Sin says from behind me.

I wait for his footsteps to fade into the joint noise of the gala before relaxing my posture. A group of women to my right snicker amongst themselves, straining their necks to watch as Sin catches up with Ileana and they make their way through the crowd together.

"Do you think they are betrothed yet?" one asks.

"Gods, I hope not," another whines, pretending to fan herself.

"Ladies please, don't speak about my future husband that way," a third one giggles, causing all of them to erupt in maniacal laughter.

The thought hadn't crossed my mind before, but that could explain why Sin chose someone mundane as his emissary. I shake off the thought. Ileana is smart. She wouldn't escape a group of predators just to marry one in a different uniform. I swallow the worry, scan the room for Bennett, and find him sampling some kind of stewed meat encrusted in a flaky pastry shell.

He looks up at the clacking of my heeled shoes approaching him and smiles when he sees I am their wearer. "I guess my dancing didn't scare you too much."

"I thought you were a lovely dancer, actually," I say, pulling my right shoulder in front of my face and peering over it at him in an attempt at flirting. As soon as I do it, I regret the action, imagining how silly I must look, but Bennett's sudden grin tells me otherwise.

"Care to take a walk with me?" He extends a hand outward.

I'd rather light myself on fire. "That would be great."

I slip my hand into his, and we hurry from the castle's grand ballroom and head outside to the courtyard. A gust of wind whips through the keep, gooseflesh blooming along my arms. Bennett shrugs out of his jacket and drapes it across my shoulders. Normally, I'd refuse it, but the wind's unforgiving bite has me clutching his jacket closed around my body.

"Thank you. So how long have you known His Grace?" I ask.

"Since we were kids," he says, one side of his mouth raising as if remembering their boyish faces in his mind. "My father served Ephraim since before I was born. Sin and I used to entertain ourselves together while our fathers worked. Once we were old enough and expected to participate in the meetings, we still found ways to sneak around and goof off, but we got better at hiding it. Neither of our fathers were particularly fond of us playing when there were decisions to be made and wars to plan. But, once we were old enough that our opinions began carrying weight, there wasn't much time for play anymore."

"It's hard to imagine such fine men were once boys." I shoot a sidelong glance in his direction. "Sin says your family manages trade?"

"My father is the director of trade and overseas alliance. It's all quite boring, really."

We round the corner of the castle, heading down the east side which I hadn't seen before tonight. The dark contours of the Spiritwood trees stretch across the eastern perimeter, their shadows promising illusions of shelter and safety, though nothing within this keep is safe. Not since *he* learned what I am. Under different circumstances, I would love to venture beyond the tree line and explore what herbs and flowers bloom within. Not everything grows in Autumnhelm, but being a little farther north, some of the more reclusive plants may thrive here. Though even if I collected some, I doubt I'm making it back home to dry and pestle them into seasonings.

"I hope Legion hasn't been stirring up too much of a problem for you and your father." I watch his expression carefully, but if the mention of the rebellion fazes him at all, it doesn't show on his face.

"Legion is nothing more than a nuisance. Hardly a problem."

"I've heard reports of people going missing. Legion soldiers raiding homes and forcing them to fight against the kingdom. Promising horrid things if they refuse. Have you heard anything about that?" I latch my collective onto his and am almost surprised to find it entirely mundane.

"I've heard the rumors, yes. But honestly, if there are people with wills weak enough to be persuaded to fight for Legion, threat or no threat, they deserve what's waiting for them."

Fire licks at my heart, and I resist the urge to send him spiraling face first into the ground. "If they are out there threatening to kill these peoples' families if they refuse to fight with them, I can't exactly fault them for protecting their own. Legion soldiers are vicious. You don't think this should be a priority for the kingdom?"

"The kingdom is slowly cutting them down, battle by battle. They're hidden in the woods all around Aegidale, never settling in one place for long. It isn't efficient for Sin to send soldiers out to hunt them down when they're scattered everywhere, and risk leaving the castle with fewer numbers in the process. Not when they're dumb enough to keep showing up and throwing corpses at the front gates. They'll run out of supplies eventually. They can keep recruiting by force, but they can't intimidate the banks out of their coin."

I keep my face expressionless as I hold his collective with my own, scanning it as he speaks. No ounce of care for those lost to the rebellion, no flicker of deceit as he mentions Legion's inevitable downfall. Bennett Langston isn't manipulating the kingdom, but I certainly wouldn't deem him trustworthy.

I feign a yawn and shrug out of his jacket, handing it back to him. "I must have had one glass of wine too many—I've grown quite tired." *I can't stand to look at your face one more second.*

He punches his arms back into his jacket. "I'd love to see you again, Lady Wren."

"I'm not sure how much longer I'll be staying with His Grace."

Bennett clearly doesn't have information on the whereabouts of my family, and even if he did, I don't think it's possible for him to care any less about them. He's not the rat Sin's looking to trap, though I don't doubt Bennett is vermin, nonetheless.

"Please, I implore you. Meet me in the market tomorrow evening before sundown. I know these events are supposed to be free of political chatter, but it always seems to find its way inside them. Let's get to know each other on neutral ground, away from the whispers of war and alliances."

"I'm not sure..." I say, trailing off as I rack my brain for an excuse. *If I'm being honest, I'd rather take the heel of my shoe to my eyeball than spend another minute with you.*

"Please. Tomorrow evening. Market center. If you don't show, I'll take the hint. Just think about it." He raises his hands and steps back in an attempt to show he isn't trying to force me.

"I'll think on it, my Lord." *Go to Hell.* "I should be getting back inside." My knees dip in a quick curtsy, and I turn to leave.

"Wren," he calls after me. "I sure hope you come."

I brush my chin over my shoulder but don't stop walking. "Goodnight, Mr. Langston."

CHAPTER 11

My soiled clothing clings to my rain-slicked skin. My hair, likely resembling a goldfinch's nest, drips down my face, and I don't bother shoving the wet strands from my eyes. What's the point? There is nothing to see. Nothing to feel.

I am nothing.

A whisper pulls at my ear, and I roll my head towards the sound. Two sky blue eyes lock on mine from within the tree line. Cosmina! She makes a circling motion with her hand, silently asking if anyone else is nearby. I shake my head. Remaining crouched, she creeps towards me, and not even the leaves dare to crunch under her feet. She breaks my binding with magic, and I slip my wrists out, rejoicing in the instant relief as the toxic metal falls from my hands. Cosmina hoists me to my feet and drapes my arm over her shoulder.

"Quickly now," she urges, steering me towards the thicker part of the woods. I plant my feet.

"Ileana," I mumble.

"What?"

"Ileana... my friend. We have to get her first." My words slur, the exhaustion from being near starved and bound in iron turning my brain to sludge. "She's that way." I lazily point in the direction of their makeshift shelter, not visible from where we stand, but is about *a quarter mile from the tip of my finger. It is where the higher-ranking men sleep, and where Ileana is often forced to be their nighttime guest.*

"There isn't time, Wren. We need to leave now before someone sees us."

"Ileana," I call louder, not thinking clearly, hunger making me delirious.

Cosmina clamps a hand down on my mouth and yanks us both forward, faster now. I know she is right. Going anywhere near that shelter is too risky— surely someone has the night watch and would hear us. If we are caught, none of us will leave here alive. Reluctantly, my feet give way and obey, and I let my sister steer me towards the darkened woods.

Goddess, help her. Protect my friend.

The sound of my own heart thrumming wildly in my ears is overshadowed by rapid tapping on my door, and I realize someone has been knocking.

"Yes?" I call from where I lie in a heap of sweat-drenched sheets.

"I'm coming in."

I blow out a breath at the sound of his voice. *Of course.* The energy in the room shifts as soon as Sin throws open the door and closes it behind him. It becomes heavier, thicker, like the molasses I sometimes used for marinating when Eldridge occasionally brought home a bottle of whiskey. I'd mix it with the liquor and use it to glaze our game, and after we indulged in the sweetened meat, we'd polish off the bottle together next to a spitting fire, spinning tales and laughing drunkenly, even if just to forget the horrors facing us for a few blissful hours.

Eldridge was great like that. Despite all the shit we were forced to deal with, I could always count on him for a few moments of... something else. Comfort, maybe. Warmth. Security. If I ever leave the cabin, I'm not sure I'll find another place I'd be comfortable calling *home,* but if I did, it would feel a lot like Eldridge.

Sin's eyes widen slightly as he takes in the sight of me still tangled in the damp sheets. "You look terrible."

"Bad dream. What do you want?"

"I guess the lady doesn't look forward to my company—ouch." He feigns a wince. "You disappeared last night after you left with Bennett." He dips his head slightly, prodding me to continue.

"You told me to stay close to him."

"And was our little plan successful?"

"He is a slimy individual. I don't like him. Maybe even more than I don't like you." I kick off the sheets and climb out of the bed, pulling on the silky lilac robe I laid out last night.

"Don't go replacing me that easily. I rather like being the highest on your hit list." Sin crosses the room and leans against the wooden armoire, next to the propped-up mirror.

"He thinks Legion is a lost cause and that they'll burn themselves out soon enough. Oh, and let me not forget to mention, he feels the innocent men and women they are stealing, violating, and raping deserve it because they got caught in the first place. But I guess you don't care about that, either."

"You do understand I am working *against* them, little witch?"

I grab the brush from the bedside table and yank it through my knotted hair. "I do."

"Did you detect anything suspicious with your—?" He draws a circle around his head to reference my ability. "Anything that indicates the Langstons may be supplying the rebellion in secret?"

"No. Bennett isn't betraying you. In fact, if I thought you capable of any semblance of affection, I'd say his admiration runs deep enough to court you."

"Are you jealous he may like me more than you, love?" he asks, the gleam in his eyes downright sinful.

I pull open the armoire doors and run my hand across the dresses, an assortment of colors and patterns. Some are sewn from airy, pastel fabrics, and others look as though they were made from liquid metal, silvers and blacks shimmering on a satin backdrop. I don't doubt which side of the closet was stocked according to Sin's tastes, so I hover my hand over some rosy pink and yellow ones, internally cringing at their hideous design.

"What is on the agenda so I know how to dress? Are we fine dining or murdering kittens today, Your Grace?"

"What else did he say?"

"Nothing else relevant to your interests. Unless you care to know he finds me as scrumptious as the beef tarts at your ball, because my," I smack my hand to my chest, "did that compliment make a girl's knees buckle."

"I see the rumors of bloodwitches and their dramatics are true."

I fix him with a heavy glare. "You're welcome. I've upheld my end of the deal, and I did it without arousing suspicion. He even asked me to meet him in the market tonight, so he obviously doesn't know it was a set up."

He purses his lips. "So you're going."

I move to the armoire and reach around him to snatch the ties for my braid from the inner shelf.

"Why would I go? He has no information for me. For *us*," I correct.

"Did you mistake that as a question?"

I move so I stand in front of him, close enough my chest almost brushes against his.

"What information do you have regarding my family? You said you knew something."

"Yes, information for *me* to know and *you* to work for." Sin runs a hand through his unbound hair, and I watch in the mirror as it falls down his back like spilled ink.

"I could have devastated this place when they brought me here. All of you. I *chose* to hand myself over, to ask for protection from the kingdom, risking my *life* rather than kill your people. But you are no better than them, no better than Cathal, trying to use me for your own gains. I am not your puppet," I spit the last word at him, jabbing a finger into his chest.

He grabs my arm and pins it between us, my chest rising and falling faster now. "I am your Black Art." The snarl in his voice is unmistakably a warning, but I've never been good at heeding the cautions of men.

"No leader of mine would condone the extinction of my kind or my family's. You are *nothing* to me."

Sin's downward eyes narrow even farther, reducing to feral slits, and he drops my arm, his hands balling into fists. I prepare to duck if he swings at me. "You forget yourself, Wren." His tone is low, restrained, like he is attempting to leash the fire I stoked. Sin backs away from me, hands still clenched, as if needing to put distance between us. "Put some clothes on. I'll send Aldred to escort you."

"Escort me where?"

"To breakfast. You'll be joining the council this morning."

"I assume it isn't optional."

"We need to discuss strategy for your meeting with Langston tonight." He backs up a few steps but doesn't divert his stare. "Don't fuck it up, Wren. It won't pain me to punish you."

I almost respond, but a flicker of self-preservation halts the words before they spew from my mouth. He turns and leaves, closing the door behind him a little too forcefully.

Grimacing at the closet, I yank out a bright yellow-orange dress, its color rivaling the sun for vibrancy, and slip it over my head now sporting its top-heavy braid. The Black Art's words repeat in my head, and I don't allow myself to consider what *punishments* he had in mind. His Grace has a reputation for being cruel, but I'm not sure just how far that cruelty extends. Would he have me locked in the dungeon again, or would he go as far as to maim or physically harm me? *It won't pain me to punish you.* Punish, not kill. I suppose there is comfort to be found in that.

Aldred arrives and escorts me from my room minutes later. We climb the baronial stone staircase to the story above us, and I follow Aldred down the corridor, the gentle flickering from the wall sconces the only light in the windowless hallway. Paintings of scenic landscapes, sprawling forests and bodies of water adorn the walls, fitted inside gold leaf frames. I eye the sweeping strokes of blues and greens, the terrain reminiscent of the woods I grew up in, and make a mental note to come back here alone to further appreciate the artwork.

The hallway veers into two wings, and Aldred leads us into the left one. My eyes drift to the shadowy vastness of the right wing, and I wonder what curiosities lie within that expanse. Perhaps tools to aid in the Black Art's *punishments.* My thoughts drift to a dark room with an obsidian spike ridden cabinet and a wall lined with sting delivering whips, but I dissolve the image. If Sin was intending on torturing me for information, he would have done so the day he dragged me back here, convinced I was a Legion spy. But he didn't... *something* made him hesitate.

"Where are we going?" I had assumed we would be served our breakfast in the dining hall.

"The war room. His Grace prefers all planning to happen there."

So secretive, Your Grace? Though, I suppose if I was conspiring against my closest allies, I would prioritize subtly as well.

We stop in front of a wooden door with a blackened horse head mounted on it, the circular knocker a ring through the steed's nose. I would think it forged from iron if not for the burn it would incite on the Black Art's hands and his council's, assuming His Grace keeps mages in his close circle. Crafted from a different metal then.

Aldred pounds the heavy accent against the door once and swings it open without waiting for a response. He motions for me to enter before him, and I step into the castle's war room. The space is small, mostly occupied by a long rectangular table in the center. The wall behind the table is filled with a series of matching wooden bookcases stretching all the way to the ceiling, the spines of countless leather-bound volumes facing outward.

Five sets of eyes glue onto mine. Sin sits at the head of the table, flanked by Ileana and his father on either side. Aldred moves to sit next to Dusaro, and the commander motions for me to take a seat in the high-backed chair next to himself. Across from Aldred is the robed woman I recognize from the small group Sin brought with him before coming after me. When I ran from him and he hunted me down like I was no more than a rabbit, existing only to fill the stomachs of wolves. His Grace may have bound me to him in more ways than one that night, but a magical tether does not mean he owns my will. *A rabbit-hearted girl I am not, Your Grace.*

The chair across from me belongs to a balding man I don't recognize, dressed in the same onyx robes the woman wears. He gives me a disapproving once over as I take my seat, and I shift my eyes to take turns meeting each set still adhered to mine. With her hood down, the woman's short auburn hair is visible, along with a silver amulet at her neck, an upside-down triangle etched into its surface. The points represent life, death, and rebirth—the insignia royal mages tend to gatekeep. They don't like sharing the symbol with those of mixed blood—hell, they won't even share the term *mage*. Since I was born to mundane parents, the kingdom will never refer to me as anything other than *witch*.

A large window overlooks the grounds at my left, and a stone fireplace crackles softly at my right. Two servants, each carrying a tray with covered platters, enter the room and place heaping dinner plates in front of us. My decorative plate is loaded with generous portions of eggs, ham, and bread with a deep reddish-purple jam that smells of figs cut with a hint of citrus. I force myself to eat slowly, to not let them see how much that time I spent locked in the cell has stoked my hunger. One of the servants begins filling the mugs at our place settings with a steaming amber tea. Sin takes a deep sip of his tea and clicks his tongue against the roof of his mouth before addressing the council.

"This last stint of theirs has left them vulnerable. We have Cathal now, and without that prick handing out death sentences to his men like candies, I doubt they'll be as forward. Scouts found what remains of them held up in Spiritwood and Autumnhelm. They're splitting up and hanging low, but they won't be able to sustain much longer."

I swallow hard at the mention of Autumnhelm. The woods

are vast, but the thought of Legion sniffing anywhere near our cabin turns my stomach to lead. My chest aches thinking of how many innocent lives will be lost—stolen by the rebellion who brings in more mouths than they can feed. I steal a glance at Ileana and wonder if it bothers her to hear Sin speak of them. Does it pain her to know the heart of the man who hurt her in so many ways continues to beat beneath her feet? I wonder if she has the nightmares too.

"They'll either die from their injuries, or better, be picked off by those *things* they're so hell-bent on defending," Dusaro snickers.

Ileana's eyes sweep over to mine as if Dusaro's remark reminded her of what I had shared with her of my adoptive transcendent family.

"Still, we can't be certain they're not having supplies smuggled to them. They've proven to be resilient bastards, but that's where my Wren may be able to benefit us. She caught the eye of Bennett Langston last evening, and he has graciously invited her to join him again tonight. We are all aware of Wren's... abilities... and I think we will find it in our favor if we use her to our advantage. I don't like to suspect the Langstons anymore than any of you, but the facts remain. They have coin and resources, and the reclusiveness to deliver it to Legion unnoticed. And while I generally find the Langstons to be tolerable, should I learn they've crossed me, I will deliver a brutal death to each of them myself."

I don't flinch from Sin's violent promise. Actually, I find the fact he referred to me as *my Wren* to be more disturbing than the bitter threat he made towards the Langstons.

"Forgive my ignorance, but how does your power work exactly, Wren?" Aldred asks.

I blink innocently. "Which one?"

"Your ability to interpret intentions."

"Mages are closely connected with their collectives, as you know. I can manipulate mine to sort of latch onto others and meld them into my own. It allows me to feel someone's most inner, truest feelings." I glance back to Sin to find him watching me intently as if he can't fully mask his curiosity about my magic. Or maybe he is remembering the times he caught me reading him before and is uncomfortable with my knowledge of the raging emotional storm wreaking havoc inside him.

"Fascinating," Aldred breathes.

Dusaro clears his throat. "More like an abomination."

"The only abomination in this room is your manners." I turn my attention to Dusaro but swear I see a smirk on Sin's face in my periphery.

"You forget who you're talking to, bloodwitch."

"And you forget I could explode your heart without breaking a sweat, my Lord."

"Enough." Sin silences both of us with a heavy glare.

Finished with my food, I fold my arms across my chest and remain quiet for the remainder of the meeting, only nodding and answering curtly when directly spoken to. I learn Aldred is the commander of the kingdom's armies, which explains the heavy armor he was wearing the last time I saw him. The robed woman and the balding man—Anika and Cassius—are, in fact, part of the royal mage council.

I shake my head when Sin asks if I have any questions about the role I am to play tonight. Like the good little lady I am, I will strengthen Bennett's affection for me and exploit that vulnerability as a catalyst to search deeper into his collective, looking for any signs of distrust I may have missed. Anything that may suggest the Langstons are responsible for the weapons and medicines Legion seems to continue getting their hands on.

On that note, Sin dismisses the council, prompting them to quickly stand and file from the room. I push my chair in and turn to leave, not bothering to bid farewell to Sin whose smoldering gaze still watches me intently.

He clears his throat. "I'll send River to dress you this afternoon."

"I am perfectly capable of getting myself ready, Your Grace. There is no need to bother her."

The grin that appears on his face is utterly indecent, and his eyes slowly trace down the lines of my neck and linger on the ties of my bodice for a second too long. "I want you done up like you were last night."

And with that statement, whatever rebuttal I was about to make gets stuck in my throat as the weight of his words sinks in. So instead, I feign a smile and dip my knees in an exaggerated curtsy. "As you command it, my Blackheart."

CHAPTER 12

I spend the afternoon meandering through the castle gardens, the splashes of white and violet petals a welcome distraction from the thoughts insistent on plaguing me. Various scenarios of how my meeting with Bennett will play out turn over in my mind, again and again.

And then it dawns on me—I will be alone tonight.

Slipping away from Bennett would be easy. Countless excuses take shape on my tongue—each providing a reason for us to separate, giving me just enough time to put some distance between myself and Scarwood before he alerted the kingdom of my disappearance. If I acted fast and clung to the woods, I would be gone before they caught my trail. The trees are too dense for guards to chase me on horseback and with a head start, I may be able to pull it off. The thought seduces me like a roguish enchantress, but freedom—though sweet and enticing—is not a dream I can afford to entertain.

Because *he* would track me with the tethering spell. Hunt me down himself like some sort of rabid beast, and I the last living thing to eat. If I fled for home, I might as well draw a map and hand it to Sin, courtesy of the magical rope binding us.

I do not doubt Sin's strength. The bloodwitch within me

could overpower him if I were to spill blood and unleash her, but so long as I keep her caged, Sin's magic is boosted with Adelphia's blessing, and therefore, more powerful than mine.

I haven't forgotten the horrid sensation that washed over me each time I reached out and touched his collective. Like standing at the edge of the Howling Sea as a tsunami-sized wave reared up and crashed into me. Except if the sea was on fire, and the water ignited everything brave enough or stupid enough to step into its path. That amount of pain and shame and guilt isn't merely the product of being the Black Art, responsible for an entire kingdom of people. It is the result of something more, something darker, and a small part of me wants to know more about it.

The part of me that is riddled with darkness—an anger I've grown as accustomed to sharing my body with as the bones in my flesh. Anger at my parents for not loving me. Anger at Cathal for his betrayal, and for the violation he bestowed upon my body. And anger at myself. Fury rises in my throat as I acknowledge that part of me that hates myself more than all the others who have wronged me. For not being strong enough to fight back against those that have hurt me. Only a coward would have walked away and left her friend to rot in a Legion camp. It is that part of me, the part that knows shame and wrath and guilt, that would like to know more about what is plaguing Singard Kilbreth.

River is sitting on the edge of the four-poster bed when I return to my room, tapping a sandaled foot against the floor. I smile sheepishly and mutter an apology for making her wait before I note the irony in that. Offering an atonement for making the Black Art's housekeeper wait before dolling me up in fashion Sin will approve of—disgraceful. She pulls a wooden chair tucked in the corner to the center of the room and motions for me to sit. I gather the hem of my skirts and take a seat, and River's hands begin unraveling my braid and combing my hair immediately.

"Why the glum face, dear? Are you not excited for your date tonight?" she asks, seemingly forgetting she was annoyed at me for my tardiness just minutes ago.

I meet her warm eyes in the mirror. "Tell me you're joking. I possess no desire to ever speak with Mr. Langston again, but Sin is making me go." I half expect her to question me on what business the Black Art has planned for me, but she doesn't. And for that, I am relieved, as my mood is sour enough without having to share *what* I am with her, if she hasn't already been informed.

"I know you likely don't want to hear this, but Singard isn't all bad, you know. The boy has had a tough life. Lost his mother young. His father—now you know I have the utmost respect for His Grace and his father, but... he can be a lot for a young boy to handle. Even for the young *man* he is now. Those two bicker constantly," she scolds, shaking her head as she works out a tangle with her fine-toothed comb.

The creases around her eyes tell me her concern is genuine. I don't need to read her collective to know she is pure light, through and through. I almost ask about his mother again but stop myself. She likely won't elaborate further, and it doesn't matter anyway. I lost my mother young too, but you don't see me walking around swinging my sword and offing people as I see fit. Not that I've actually seen Sin do that, but if His Grace's reputation precedes him, then it is only a matter of time before I do. I just hope he doesn't decide to turn his blade on me before I find a way out of my current predicament.

"He swore an oath to protect Aegidale, and that includes everyone. Transcendents live in fear every day because of the prejudices he and his father and Ephraim created. He shouldn't get to pick and choose who he deems *worthy* of his protection, and I simply don't see how you or anyone else can defend that."

"Sin is doing what he thinks is expected of him. His father can be very... *convincing*," she says, rolling her brown eyes once in the mirror. "I've been serving the kingdom for decades, and I've looked after Sin since he was quite young. He has a good heart but lacks the confidence to show it."

I huff with mock amusement at her comment. Nothing about my interactions with the Black Art suggests he possesses a heart at all, let alone a good one. And the smug grin permanently etched onto his mouth tells me he harbors a *sickening* amount of confidence.

"You can laugh, but it's true. Sin doesn't have what you do. You have a certain presence about you—something that suggests there is a whole storm brewing behind those pretty brown eyes. Sin walks into a room, and it goes still because they fear him. You, on the other hand, exude something far more dangerous than a sharp sword and the skill to use it. *Brains*. And, well, I think it's no surprise men tend to lack in that department."

I don't stifle my chuckle. "I appreciate your compliment, but he certainly has not struck me as the lacking confidence type. In fact, I'd say his arrogance is one of his most annoying attributes."

"He puts on a good show, I'll give you that."

I almost spew that his grip around my throat the night he threatened to rip it out felt far from a show, but I swallow the words. However reasonable River may seem, her judgment is clouded by her near familial relationship with my captor, and I'm not in the mood to listen to any more justifications for Sin's violent tendencies.

Likely lost in her own thoughts, she remains quiet as she continues working through the knots in my hair and brushing it into an obedient white blanket that drapes over my shoulders and tumbles down my back. Satisfied, River fumbles around in her basket, pulls out tiny pots of cosmetic powders and paints, and brushes them on my eyelids, cheeks, and lips. She opens the armoire and pulls out a dress the color of blue sapphires, and tosses it to me to put on. It is knee-length with long sleeves and a square bust line. Delicate silver ribbons crisscross down the front of the bodice, and River helps secure the dress at my back. She folds her hands under her chin, admiring her work for a moment before dropping them to gather her supplies.

"Well, if tonight is a complete bust and you find yourself miserable, you certainly won't look it. Come along, I'll walk you downstairs."

She escorts me from my room to the foyer where Ileana is waiting for me, her arms folded across her slender frame. Ileana gives me a quick once over and motions with her chin for me to follow her outside. I tail her to the south side of the castle where the castle's stables occupy a large portion of the rear facing courtyard. My eyes track her movement, the gentle sway of her hips graceful and poised, but something about the measured steps of her long, thin legs looks calculated, like she is unnaturally aware of her surroundings. I suppose after experiencing what she has, it makes sense she would be on constant alert for anything that feels wrong, out of place.

A part of me begs to call after her, convince her to stop walking and look at me, *really look at me,* as I lay my heart bare and beg her forgiveness for the role I played in her torment. If I could take it back, somehow reverse time and do it over again, I would. But the kingdom isn't the only one that doesn't offer second chances.

Scattered amongst the open lawn are rows upon rows of soldiers, paired up in sets and dueling. I ignore the tickle in my throat, the inevitable itch I feel when I see or hear or smell anything indicative of bloodshed. An image of curled finger-nails painted the color of murder flashes in my mind, those feminine nails tracing a line over my lips and down the column of my neck, to the base of my sternum, tempting me into having a taste of the blood drying on the tips of the grass. I've had a lifetime of practice masking the burn in my throat, and without so much as a flicker of emotion, I swallow the tempta-tion back down with the rest of *her*.

It would be impossible to miss the Black Art in the crowd, even if I wasn't scanning the horde of armored men for him. It isn't that I care to see him—I could very much do without ever seeing his face again—but not knowing where my enemies are is an amateurish mistake. The last time I let my guard down, I ended up in a subterranean cell, rotting as infection picked away at me like a swarm of vultures.

Sin's height is accentuated by the steel plate on his chest. He wears no shirt underneath the armor, the plate fitted directly against his deep copper skin, just enough metal to protect his most vital organs. He spars with another soldier, swinging their swords above their heads in a brutal dance of steel and sweat, and I use his distraction to assess him without his notice. The stretches of muscle in his arms bulge and pull tight as he thrusts and pivots with his partner, moving with lethal swiftness. Black trousers, fitted in his thighs, hang low on his waist. Sin's expression is one of immense concentration, assessing his partner's movements and twisting his body the exact way to avoid the incoming thrusts of his opponent's blade. And as a springtime squall tears through the courtyard, ripping his long black hair behind him, he looks almost *wild*.

With a final slice of his sword through the air, Sin disarms his partner, and the soldier falls to his knees, the tip of his blade inches from his mock foe's neck. My breath catches in my throat as his animated eyes flash to mine, his weapon still pointed at his partner. The tether, buried in the pit of my stomach, glows with perverse delight as I lock eyes with its creator, and I swear the spot on my hip, inked with the signature he found so amusing, warms at the sight of him. *I should have never called him that nickname.*

He knew I was watching. A glimmer of something downright disturbing gleams in his eyes as he watches understanding cross my face, the realization that he was aware of my watchful stare and was making a point—he is *stronger.* He knows I don't possess the strength to outmaneuver him without the help of the magic I keep locked up tight. And judging from the almost amused curvature of his mouth, he knows I have long forgotten where I stowed that key. Sin sheathes his sword into the holster slung on his low-rise trousers and extends his hand to his fallen partner, pulling him to his feet. I exhale sharply when he looks away and direct my attention back to Ileana.

We approach the stables, and a gray carriage linked to four black steeds waits expectantly out front. Ileana directs me to get into the coach, and a footman rushes to open the door and offers his hand as I climb inside. Three guards armed to the teeth with an assortment of swords and knives attached to their backs and waists step in next. Two sit on the red velvet couch parallel to mine, and the third plops down next to me.

I raise my eyebrows and look through the small square window to where Ileana still stands next to the ebony horses. She reads the question on my face. *Why the entourage?*

"Black Art's orders. The bloodwitch is to be protected. You didn't think you would be going alone, did you?" She spins on her heels, her mocking laughter still ringing in my ears long after she's out of sight.

The footman closes the door, and the carriage rocks

slightly as he climbs into the driver's seat. I know she meant to insinuate I was foolish for thinking the Black Art would allow me to travel alone, but it isn't her ridiculed tone that has my mind spinning as fast as the spokes beneath me, but rather, her word choice.

The bloodwitch is to be protected.

Sin may hate me for the power thrumming in my veins, but I am an asset to him, his kingdom, his claim to the throne. Aegidale won't respect a leader that doesn't put an end to the rebellion trashing their cities, their homes, rambling about self-proclaimed righteousness and destroying the same isle they claim they want to protect.

The Black Art wants to wield me as his not-so-secret weapon, more so than he is letting on. But he is foolish if he believes for a second my magic will ever exist to fulfill his desires. I am a bloodwitch—no, a blood *queen.*

And a queen bows for no one.

CHAPTER 13

"**K**eep your wits about you, miss. You never know where rebellion filth will wash up. We'll be here when you're ready to leave." The guard seated next to me extends his hand and helps me step out of the carriage.

The driver parked the horses outside the market center. If Blackreach's shopping square is anything like the one in Innodell, it is bustling with townsmen and traders during the day, and barren at night. Most vendors close their booths around midday, and as I step down the first cobblestone alleyway, it is clear this one operates no differently. Storefronts with colorful canvas awnings line both sides of the narrow street. Signs promising spices and furs and steel hang on their wooden doors, inviting those wealthy enough to afford them inside, and in Blackreach, it is likely such luxuries are a household staple. Small linen bags labeled with assorted spices, oregano and parsley and ginger, sit neatly arranged on a shelf visible through one of the glass windows of a spice shop.

A business like this would never survive in my modest hometown where residents don't earn enough to afford anything other than necessities and have to scour their cupboards for a single spice to cook with. Cosmina and I helped remedy our lack of coin for seasonings by drying and pestling herbs into blends and storing them in small jars. Cosmina was especially a fan of crushing up dried sumac berries and sprinkling the lemon tasting powder onto freshly caught game before we dried and cured the meat. If she were here now, she'd undoubtedly pop her head into the quaint shop to look for some herbs that don't grow in our neck of the woods. I would peruse the spices and tinctures alongside her and probably search for vanilla beans or extract. Vanilla was a rarity in our home as vanilla pods are incredibly expensive, but perhaps I could strike a deal with the shopkeeper, offer a trade of some kind. Eldridge, despite his burly outer appearance, enjoys sweets more than any of us, and the vanilla would be the perfect complement to sweeten his usual breakfast of corn-meal pudding.

I step away from the shop window. None of that matters anymore. As long as I am tethered to Sin like his obedient lap dog, thoughts of the ones I care about are dangerous distractions.

The narrow alley spills into a cobblestone ring where most vendors are likely to set up their traveling booths. In this evening hour, no salesmen spin tales of the effects of their potions, no apron cladded women whistle to pedestrians to take home a basket of produce or freshly baked breads. The market is empty, except for the wavy-haired lord sitting on the bench at the far side of the circle.

Bennett stands as I approach, flashing that toothy smile and quickly appraising my vivid blue dress with the less than modest hemline. He wears a fitted velvet coat of cobalt blue with silver threading embellishing the pockets and shoulders. I suddenly dislike the dress I wear, noting the similar color pattern between our attires, and force a return smile around clenched teeth, silently cursing the Black Art who undoubtedly intended for me to be dressed in what are apparently Langston's signature house colors.

He bows at the waist and reaches for my hand, brushing his lips across the backs of my knuckles. "It's lovely to see you again, Lady Wren."

I smile with forced warmness, knowing it doesn't meet my eyes.

"I brought us dinner. I admit I didn't make it, but I did request my favorite cook in our home prepare it, and I insisted she bake jam puffs. I will accept full credit for that." He picks up the woven basket from the bench and holds it up for my appraisal. "There's a spot just over there with a great view of the Malachite."

"Lead the way, my Lord," I say, angling myself in the direction he pointed.

During our meeting in the war room this morning, I learned the Langstons reside at Castle Summerswind, the second largest dwelling in Blackreach, next only to Scarwood. It is still strange for me to hear someone refer to something as magnificent as a castle as *home,* as if it were nothing out of the ordinary.

I follow Bennett down another alley, past the shops selling exuberant goods and rarities, to a wooden pergola with a slatted roof, vines entwined through the lattice top in a touch of decorative greenery. A vase filled with red roses and bay leaf branches sits on the center of the cloth covered table. As promised, the open vastness of the Malachite River is visible from the pergola, no storefronts or houses between us and where the flowing current brushes shoulders with the city.

"You didn't have to go to all this trouble," I say with mock enthusiasm, knowing damn well it was servants that clipped these roses and set up this space.

"You like it?" Bennett's eyes light up as if he is truly pleased with himself for doing the bare minimum.

"Of course. It is very sweet, thank you." *Did I just flutter my eyes?*

"Sit, sit," he ushers, pulling out the chair closest to us.

Smoothing my dress around my backside, I sit in the pulled-out chair, and Bennett begins unloading the contents of the basket. Thick slices of bread, still warm from the oven judging from the sweet, yeasty aroma coming off them, strips of salted meat, an assortment of freshly cut cheeses, cubes of fruit, decadent jam puffs, and a bottle of wine. He pours us each a glass of the red drink and drops a few berries from the spread of fruit into both our glasses.

"So, tell me about your family. What is it your folks do to earn their keep?"

I grab a slice of bread and layer it with some of the meat and cheeses. "My parents own an inn. Nothing much, but we live comfortably enough, for Innodell." The half-truth rolls off my tongue with rehearsed ease. Mentioning I am estranged from my parents would provoke too many questions, so best to fabricate that little detail.

"And is that what you do as well? Work at the inn?"

"Yes, I help them manage it. I quite enjoy it."

Bennett purses his lips as he skewers a piece of fruit with his fork, and for a moment, I wonder if he has ever visited Innodell, or if he thinks it too modest of a town for someone of his stature to be seen in.

"Such a pity," he says, popping the piece of melon into his mouth.

"Pardon?"

"I just don't think someone who has been blessed with such beauty should have to hide it behind an inn counter."

I know he intends for the comment to flatter me, but his condescension of working class turns the food to lead in my stomach. "I don't mind it one bit, actually."

He reaches a hand towards me and thumbs a strand of loose hair behind my ear. I will myself not to smack it away.

"You're very beautiful, Wren. You could use that to advantage yourself, you know?"

"What do you mean?"

Bennett shrugs his shoulders as if forcing casualness. "There are several lords looking to wed. Women with your... attributes... are heavily desired."

"Attributes?"

He laughs softly to himself and fixes me with his gaze, his blue eyes darkening as he leans forward, resting his elbows on the table. "Let's just say I don't think you'd have a lick of trouble finding a suitor. You'd never have to find yourself behind an inn counter again." Lines crease in his forehead as if even the image of it repulses him.

"I find pleasure in the work."

"Wed a lord and you'll find all sorts of pleasures, Lady Wren."

My name sounds foreign on his tongue, like it doesn't belong. He stands and slides his chair around the table so that he sits next to me. Slowly, he reaches out and traces little circles across my knee and down my calf with his index finger. *Oh, hell no.* I'll bat my eyelashes at the Langston boy and let him feed me my fill of jam puffs, but no one is touching me. Sin sent me here with strict orders to pry into Bennett's collective and search for any secrets the elite family may be hiding. He said nothing of having to get too *friendly* with him. Maybe only because he knows I would have refused, or maybe because the Black Art possesses some morals after all, but the reason doesn't matter. I clear my throat pointedly and cross my leg over the other one, pulling it from his reach.

I bring my glass to my lips and inhale its aroma—hints of cedar and something sweet like nectar—before taking a sip. "Anything new in business? I overheard Singard and his father speaking about Legion this morning. I don't understand all the jargon," I say, feigning a nervous laugh and peering up at him through my eyelashes. "Is there any news on that front?" I fling my collective out and latch onto his, a spider dropping onto its next meal. His mind collapses under the weight of mine like a crushed daisy turning to dust in my fist. Not an inkling of magic coats his veins, and his mind opens for me like a freshly bound book.

"The rebellion and their allies are nothing to worry about. Don't let thoughts of them frighten you."

"Do they have a lot of allies?" I ask, noting his word choice.

"Hard to say. If they have any *good* ones, we wouldn't know about them, now would we?"

I hold his collective steady, primed to rip any sense of manipulation from it, but it remains limp, unreactive. "Do you have any suspicions?"

A low laugh rumbles from his chest, and he smiles while looking at the table, pondering. "If you wished to continue discussing politics, why didn't I just invite you to my home?"

"My apologies. I just find it all so fascinating, and I can only imagine the stress you and your family are under with all the unknowns." The lie comes out as smooth as the velvety wine I pull another sip of.

"I assure you, if we learn of anyone betraying the Black Art, they will be promptly dealt with. The Langstons will not tolerate anyone jeopardizing His Grace's impending war."

"Impending war? The kingdom has been at war with Legion for years."

Bennett raises an eyebrow at me. "I'm not talking about Legion. War against those *things*."

"Transcendents? Sin is going to declare war against *all* transcendents?"

"He'll have our support of course, but Sin knows he needs to weed out any lurking enemies of the throne before making any official declaration. He doesn't like to be caught by surprise, and I don't blame him. Surprises lead to mistakes which lead to lost coin. As soon as he gathers everything he needs, the transcendent problem will be quickly eradicated."

I go rigid, my blood hardening into a cardinal sheet of ice, the wind nipping my skin suddenly too cold, the air swelling my lungs too dry. I knew—I *knew* this would happen. The kingdom has been dragging their feet, slowly building prejudice against the shifters little by little, biding their time so that as soon as their immediate threat was dealt with, they'd set their sights on their next target. Transcendents.

My family.

And the Black Art has me out here doing his bidding like some kind of humble mercenary. White spots cloud my vision, my fists tighten, my breaths short and labored. I resist the urge to bare my teeth.

"You don't need to be frightened," he whispers, misreading the sudden lack of color in my face.

The sudden shift in his energy snaps my attention back to Bennett. Before I can react, he presses his lips against mine, his hand finding my calf again and wrapping itself around it. He slides his palm up my leg and squeezes my thigh as he tries parting my lips with his.

I clamp my hand down on top of his.

Pulling my mouth away from Bennett's, I let my collective

snap back to its place behind my eye, not wanting to feel his *desire* a second longer.

"Was I—was I too forward?" he stammers.

"Yes. Don't do that again," I bark, not editing the hostility from my tone. "I should be getting back." I rise from my chair and tug the hem of my dress downward.

"I apologize if I alarmed you, my Lady. I suppose I thought your choice of dress was indicative of your interest in... in me. I clearly misread the air between us." He clears his throat loudly and looks away before continuing. "May I call on you again, Miss Wren?" *No. No you may not.*

"I think it's best you allow me to call on you should I be interested in your attentions again, Mr. Langston. Thank you for dinner." I dip into a quick curtsy out of obligation, though any respect I still harbored for Bennett before the date is long gone.

"I'll walk you back."

"No need, I made note of the way."

He nods. "Very well. Please send my regards to Sin and his lovely lady."

I incline my head in acknowledgment and carry myself back to the carriage, still parked where the driver let me out.

Against those things.

Sin sent me out here, having me believe I was vetting the Langstons for information that would allow the kingdom to close in on Legion, protecting my family. But it wasn't his war on Legion he was concerned with. He wanted to use me to gain information that would benefit his war on the transcendent race.

His war on my family.

I step into the carriage and stare at the black quilted walls of the coach, refusing to make eye contact with any of the guards sent with me to make sure no harm came to the Black Art's precious spy.

Red stains my sight. I am not a puppet, and Sin does *not* pull my strings. I learned a valuable lesson today—the kingdom will never offer protection to my family, no matter what bargains I strike with its leader. I think it's time the Black Art learns a lesson of his own tonight.

You do *not* pick a fight with a bloodwitch.

CHAPTER 14

Wrath stirs in my stomach like a venomous snake. It slithers up my chest, down my arms, curls into my hands—itching for the opportunity to strike. And for once, I don't shoo it back to its dark corner. I beckon to it with soft whispers—promises to let it feast—and a jolt of heat flies into my fingertips as it flicks its tongue in anticipation.

If I spill a drop of kingdom blood, I'll be forced to spill it all. The second I raise a hand to anyone, the temporary truce I have with the Black Art will be over. Guards will be on me immediately, leaving me with only two outcomes, one of them resulting in my sudden death. The second option would be a bit gorier.

I'd paint every godsdamned wall in that forsaken castle with their blood.

Sin thinks he has me pinned in a corner, that I won't fight back. If it was just me I was protecting—he is probably right. My life isn't worth the risk of unleashing *her*—the bloodwitch known for her insatiable appetite. But this isn't just about me anymore.

No one hurts my family.

I don't wait for the driver to help me out when he pulls the horses to a stop. I throw open the door, hop out of the carriage, and storm up to the looming double doors of the castle. The two guards posted at the entrance open the doors for me without question, and I march past them with as much assertiveness as if I was the Lady of the castle.

It is late, and likely the servants have retired to their quarters for the night, but that doesn't stop me from hollering into the empty foyer. "Singard!" I use his full name, partly because I am way too heated to be speaking something as casual as a nickname, and partly because it seemed to piss him off the last time I used it.

A dark head rounds the corner from the top of the stone staircase. Dusaro's chilling glare might have frozen me in place yesterday, but tonight, I melt it with my own fiery stare.

"What in the gods' names are you hollering about?" Dusaro asks with emphasized slowness.

"I need to speak with Singard."

"It is late, *girl*. He will speak with you tomorrow."

"I'm confident he'd prefer I inform him immediately of my findings with Mr. Langston. Take me to him."

It's not a complete lie. While my words to Dusaro suggest I have critical information to incriminate Bennett, the real reason for my urgency isn't any less valid. I'm sure His Grace would want to know I've spent the ride back to the castle imagining how lovely my fingernails would look painted in his blood.

His eyes narrow slightly, and he studies me for a beat before saying, "He's in the study." Dusaro turns his back to me and flicks his head for me to follow him.

Easy enough. I follow him to the floor with the war room but instead of veering left, we head into the right wing. When I passed through here this morning, I wondered if this was where Sin stored whips and other devices to make a person spill their secrets. Now, with every clack of my heeled shoes against the stone floor, I imagine it is bones snapping under *my* feet.

Dusaro leads us to the end of the long corridor and pushes open a plain wooden door without knocking. The study is larger than the war room with a desk carved from a deep red wood at its center. A few burgundy rugs are laid tastefully around the floor, and two oversized brown leather chairs sit on the left wall next to a tall, arching window. Potted plants are placed in the corners of the room, the green foliage a pop of color in the otherwise dark space. Sin sits behind an art easel in the far corner of the room, opposite the wall with the comfortable looking chairs.

He exhales loudly at our intrusion. "What is she doing here?" He drops whatever was in his hand to the small table next to him and looks at his father, not bothering to even acknowledge my presence other than to ask about me.

"I want to speak with you. Alone," I supply before Dusaro can answer for me.

I watch from my periphery as his father turns to look at me. "We don't take demands from prisoners."

"I think that's for the Black Art to decide," I snap. "And given Adelphia chose him and not you, you really needn't concern yourself with the matter, do you?"

Dusaro's eyes widen for a second, then sharpen into slits as he takes a step towards me, pointing his finger at my chest. "If you wish to live another day, girl, I strongly, *strongly*, beseech you learn to keep your mouth shut."

"I'll grant the request," Sin interjects, sounding almost bored.

Dusaro mashes his lips together into a thin line before turning and storming out of the room, the black cape attached to his coat billowing out behind him.

Sin rises from the stool behind the easel and prowls over to the desk. He leans against it, the desk at his hips, and folds his arms across his chest. The room is cast in shadows, the candles flickering in the wall sconces the only light in the study. Under different circumstances, I might find the space cozy. He fixes his heavy stare on me, and I take it as my cue to start talking.

"Langston is clean. Like I said."

Sin picks up a wine glass from the desk, takes a drink, then swishes the remaining liquid around in the cup. "What did he have to say about our friends?"

"He doesn't believe Legion has allies. But he also made the fair point that if their allies were any *good*, you wouldn't know about them, would you? I'm not saying you're wrong about Legion having a supplier, but the Langstons aren't it."

"What else?"

I cross the room, letting the heels of my shoes clack a little louder than necessary with each step, and gaze out the inlaid window. Not wanting to reveal my hand just yet, I say, "Nothing. But it was hard for him to say much else while trying to slip his tongue into my mouth."

I study his reflection in the glass window. An unamused smile crosses his face, and he runs a hand through his long hair. Someone with less experience reading others may have missed it, but the slight clench of his jaw does not escape my notice.

"If you have nothing useful to report, why are you in my study?"

I step away from the window and slowly walk towards him, not stopping until I'm about a foot from where he still leans against the desk. "What information do you have regarding my family? I upheld my half of the arrangement— it's only fair you now tell me what you know."

He rolls his head forward slightly and rests his bronzed

hands on the desk behind him. "I don't recall that being part of my bargain." His words are coated in that soft, disinterested tone he has perfected.

"Then release me so I may protect them myself."

"You know the law, little witch."

The one that states bloodwitches must be executed. But by Sin keeping me alive, he's already breaking his own precious law.

I take a step closer to him. Even in my heeled shoes, the Black Art is still taller than me. The warm glow of the candle light casts flickering shadows on his deep reddish-brown cheek, and I tilt my chin up when I whisper, "You are the law."

Sin stares down at me from under those dark eyebrows, his green eyes, darker in the dim lighting, searching both of mine.

I don't wait for him to respond before I say, in a voice soft as crushed velvet, "If you plan on keeping me alive to use me in your *genocide*, I suggest you plan again, Blackheart. I'd never cross my own family."

A smile positively disturbing crosses his face before he wipes it with another pull from his wine glass and sets the cup back down with more force than necessary. "I see Langston did have more to say, after all." Sin pushes off the desk, ascending to his full height, and takes a measured step towards me. Brushing his chest against my shoulder, he slowly circles me until he stands at my back.

I jump when his hands suddenly gather my unbound hair and move it so it falls in front of my shoulders. His breath warms the now bare skin where my shoulder meets my neck, and I can almost hear his head shaking as he tsks softly. "If you're not of any use to me alive, Wren, where do you think that leaves us?"

I steel my spine. "I'm afraid you'll have to kill me, Your Grace. Well... you can *try*."

The warmth on my neck vanishes as if he stopped breathing. And then it returns as he lazily traces two fingers down the side of my throat, and I nearly flinch from the contact. His low voice a caress in my ear, he asks, "Did you just threaten me?"

I will my pulse to stop thudding under his touch and fail miserably. "Yes."

His fingers invert so that he now brushes my neck with the backs of his knuckles. "Threatening your Black Art is punishable by death," he reminds me.

Don't lose your nerve now. "Are you going to punish me, Your Grace?"

He spins me around before I can react and grabs both my wrists, clamping them together inside one of his too-large hands. Sin yanks my viced arms above my head, and I flail wildly in his grip, a guttural sound promising vengeance ripping from my chest.

"You need to submit," he growls in my ear, his voice low and predatory.

Submit? *Submit!*

"I'm not your fucking pet."

"You are now. On your knees." He slams his other hand onto my shoulder, forcing me to kneel before him.

My words come out simmering with the same heat I send flying from my hands. "Get. Off. Of. Me."

He swears as the sudden rush of heat burns his palm, and he drops my wrists in recoil. I fall to my backside and throw my arms over my head, preparing for a blow that doesn't come. Instead, he grabs my arms and yanks me to my feet. Before I can get another rush of magic out, an invisible force sends me flying, and my back slams into the far wall, the impact sending books toppling out of the nearby bookcase. Sin, looking like darkness incarnate, stands in front of me, arms outstretched in front of him, keeping me pinned against the wall with his translucent wind.

Suddenly, I can't breathe.

His face betrays no signs of remorse as the air whooshes from my lungs and his magic constricts my airway. My hands claw at my throat, as if I could fight off the invisible attacker, and I fumble for my collective. The pressure on my windpipe increases, and my collective slips through my mental fingers. I reach for it again, and again, but I might as well be grasping at air. Black spots invade my vision, my head falls forward, the fight dissolving from me as my body goes limp, until I don't have the strength to reach for it again. My hands drop to my side as his magic chokes out the last of my resolve. His power... too strong... I'm going to die against this wall, my strangled breaths singing me to eternal sleep.

I fall to the floor.

As fast as it swept my feet out from under me, the phantom wind pinning me to the wall vanishes. My lungs croak as air swells them once more, and I press my hand to my chest as if touching it will allow me to suck in air faster. When my wheezing returns to normal breaths, I look up and find him leaning against the desk again, arms back to being folded tight across his black shirt. Sin's eyes are brighter now—a lighter green with flecks of yellow around the pupils, an effect of wielding magic. I'm sure mine are glowing vibrant gold now rather than their usual walnut brown.

"I told you, it would not pain me to punish you."

The sound of his voice sets my blood on fire. A growl tears from the back of my throat, something low and raw and primal, and I hurl a spinning orb of destruction towards him. He anticipates the blow and throws out a ward to halt my attack, stopping it in its tracks the same way I stopped the arrow.

The orb hovers between us, each of us willing it towards the other. If I was harboring any doubts about Sin's skill, they dissolve immediately as his magic pushes against my own in a wall of sheer power. If I kill him, consuming his collective would make me stronger, resilient, downright lethal. I wet my lips at the thought of his blood sweetening my tongue.

"Stop!" he yells over the hum of the vibrating orb hovering between us. "Lower your side, and I'll lower mine."

I hold his stare over the sphere, now glowing a brilliant blue with silver speckles glittering throughout. If I didn't know how much chaos was simmering in that shimmering ball, I'd almost want to touch it.

"Release it, witch, or one of us isn't leaving this room."

The heat coursing through me grows hotter, burns brighter, flows faster as I imagine him crumbling to his knees, his yellow-green eyes fearful for just a second before they go vacant. She whispers in my ears, drags a slender fingertip across my collarbone, encouraging me to bring the Black Art to his slaughter. *Our* slaughter.

"Lower it," Sin growls, flicking his head to the side like a wolf daring another one to challenge it.

Even if I wanted to, I can't extinguish the orb on my own now, not since he latched onto it with magic of his own, fueling it more.

"How do I know you won't turn it back on me if I let it go?"

"You don't. Now lower it." His eyes narrow, and his top lip curls up as he pushes against the orb harder, shoving it farther in my direction. He's trying to force me to drop it. I either lower my side or risk my magic weakening, taking the full blast of the destruction I created.

I can't scan his collective to know if he's planning on letting the magic crush me, not while I'm using mine to hold the orb against Sin's force. My options dart through my mind.

If neither of us relinquishes our hold, one of us *will* eventually tire faster than the other. And as much as I hate to admit it, I cannot overpower the Black Art so long as his magic is boosted with Adelphia's blessing. Not without unlocking the extent of my own power, and that lies in a scenario I'm not willing to act out.

"Why should I let go first?"

"Because I'm your Black Art and I'm demanding it. Let. It. Go."

With a look promising I'll haunt him forever should he double-cross me, I drop to my knees and slowly lower my side of the orb, my hold on it now at a disadvantaged angle.

The magic croons between us—a lethal lullaby begging to be unleashed, unfit to remain constrained indefinitely. Sin watches me carefully as he sinks to his own knees, lowering his side, his burning yellow-green eyes focused, intense... *sexy*.

Goddess above.

I shake away the image of those eyes beholding my bare skin, knowing it is the caster's high planting the provocative thoughts in my mind. It's been a long while since I've expelled this magnitude of magic in one setting; it's likely my resistance to its alluring effects have been reduced.

Sin nods to me, and with a silent prayer to an unnamed goddess, I release my hold. As soon as I sever the bond between the orb and I, he extinguishes it completely, allowing the chaos I conjured to return to the collective. The room is deafeningly silent without the hum of magic between us.

I rise to my feet, walk to the desk, and hoist myself onto it, crossing my legs and letting them hang over the edge. The room is a disaster. It was more than just books that toppled from their shelves—paintings lie scattered on the floor, the stool behind the easel lies on its side, and tiny glass fragments from Sin's cup glisten on the reddish rug like freshly fallen snow.

He regains his footing and sweeps a hand over his forehead and into his hair, before running that same hand across his jaw. His footsteps promise wrath as he crosses the room and stands in front of me, drilling a disapproving glower into my face. "Negotiate," he says, his voice low as if he's leashing his anger.

"Release me."

"That's a demand, not a negotiation."

"Fine. I want the tethering spell gone."

"No."

I exhale sharply. "Your eagerness for compromise is inspiring, Your Grace."

He folds his arms across his chest again, his expression suggesting I'm running out of time to strike a bargain.

"I'm more of a risk to you and others if I'm trapped here than if I just went home. I've never killed anyone... but I'm growing an appetite, and I suspect I have an affinity for pompous men with long hair." I smile warmly at him, letting my threat sink in.

"If I let you go, I have no way of knowing you won't end up in Legion hands again. That is not a risk I will take."

"Legion already tried forcing me to turn on you and failed. The whole *me surrendering and you locking me up thing*... don't tell me you've forgotten our good times already, Blackheart."

"They also didn't make a direct threat against your family last time. And as you just demonstrated, doing so turns you into something rather savage, *without* the bloodwitch power."

I throw my hands up. "So, then what, Singard? Are you just going to keep me here, dressing me up and sending me off to flirt with your allies in hopes I *may* discover some facet of information for you? Perhaps if you were a halfway decent person, you wouldn't have to worry about having so many enemies, Your Grace."

He stares at me quietly for an extended beat, contemplating, before sucking in his cheeks and blowing out a breath. "If I allowed you to return home so you may alert your family of your new arrangements, would you find that agreeable?"

"Agreeable for now," I answer slowly. And then as I consider his words, "Wait, you expect them to still be at home?" *That lying, selfish, arrogant piece of...* "You said you had information on their whereabouts, implying Legion had attacked them." I study his face as his jaw clenches slightly, and he shuffles his weight, but not so much as a glimmer of remorse touches his expression. "But you don't know anything about that at all, do you?" I laugh softly, shaking my head to myself as I acknowledge how foolish I was to have believed him. "Kindly go fuck yourself, *Your Grace,*" I say with a matching gesture.

"Careful, witch. You can accept my offer to allow you to temporarily return to your *den,* or don't, but make your decision quickly. By all means, refuse it. I have better things to be doing than keeping an eye on you anyway."

"Keeping an eye on me? You wouldn't be coming with—"

"Oh, yes I would," he interjects.

"I assure you I don't need a chaperone. It's not as if you have to worry I won't come back thanks to your little stalker spell."

"That's not what I'm worried about. If you even thought about running, I'd find you through that lovely mark on your hip and drag you back here by that pretty braid you fancy."

I mirror his pose by crossing my arms, tucking my hands underneath their opposite armpits. "Then why can't I go alone?"

"Because as I already said, I don't need Legion getting their hands on you and trying to pull another stunt with you at their mercy. Sure, you didn't cooperate with them last time, but unless my charming personality and wicked good looks have won you over, I'd rather my enemies not have a bloodwitch in their possession."

"I am *no one's* possession."

Sin drops his hands into his trouser pockets and takes a few steps towards me. His eyes drop to where the fabric of my dress clings to my hip. "My mark on your skin says otherwise."

Air hisses through my teeth, and I ball my fists to keep from slapping the smug curvature of his mouth from his face. "My family will not accept you. As soon as they see you, they'll immediately assume the worst and prepare to fight. I won't have them getting killed on my account."

"Your precious animal pack will be fine. They won't threaten me because they won't know who I am."

"They know who you are, Sin, they've seen you."

"Exactly. When they see a less handsome than myself guard at your side, they won't think anything other than I've sent an escort to protect you while Legion actively searches for the white-haired witch."

"I don't follow."

"Cassius is very advanced in potion crafting. I'll have him make us each a tonic that alters our physical appearances. You'll tell your family your identity is being disguised so Legion scouts don't spot you. They'll assume I'm just a guard sent to look after you."

I shake my head. "Transcendents are keen to illusive magic —they'll detect the cloak on you." Shifters of form, transcendents have an innate proficiency with transmutation magic. The second they get a whiff of Sin, they'll smell the masking spell.

"They'll note the spell, yes, but as long as they believe the magic is coming from only your disguise, they won't suspect my identity is also altered."

"That might work for a little while, but as soon as you're not around me, they'll notice the magic is coming from you as well."

He closes the remaining gap between us and tilts his head so that his lips hover just above my ear. "Then I guess you'll have to stay very close to me, little witch."

His proposal isn't a bad idea. Even if I went alone, my family's location isn't safe. I have no doubt Sin would use our tether to pinpoint my location once I returned home to our cabin in Autumnhelm. And if I want to keep Cosmina from coming after me and getting herself tangled up with Legion in the process, accepting the Black Art's attempt at a compromise is the best option.

I square my shoulders and straighten my back. "When do we leave?"

"Tomorrow. First light. And *Wren*," he growls my name, "enjoy your caster's high."

CHAPTER 15

The thick purple liquid shimmers in the vial like a sea of violet stars. I swirl it around, eyeing the thin film coating the sides of the bottle, and scrunch my nose. "What *is* this stuff?"

"I don't know, nor do I desire to learn. But Cassius said its effects are instantaneous. He also said it tastes like a horse's ass, so here—" Sin tosses an orange at me. "It will help dilute the flavor."

He continues raiding the large kitchen pantry and shoving provisions into his brown leather saddle bag. Mine sits already packed with several changes of clothes and some basic necessities on the long rectangular table in the center of the castle's oversized kitchen.

"How far into Autumnhelm is your dwelling?"

"If we leave soon, we can get there by nightfall," I answer, pulling back the bumpy peel of the fruit. And thank the goddess for that because the thought of camping with the Black Art again turns my morning breakfast of bannock and eggs to lead in my stomach. A servant had our morning meals already prepared and waiting for us in the kitchen when I came downstairs this morning. The generous helping of grains and protein will help fuel us for the long ride ahead, and the salted meats, array of breads, nuts and other jarred foods Sin shoves into the bag will hold us over until we arrive.

He buttons the saddle bag closed, kicks the pantry door shut behind him, and swipes the twin glass vial from the table. Popping the lid open with a thrust of his thumb, he brings it to his nose and inhales gingerly. "Mmm. I only hope it tastes as decadent as it smells," he says with a smile that is pure mischief.

I wasn't sure what his demeanor would be towards me this morning given our physical altercation last night, but he merely greeted me with a glance when I found myself in the kitchen, slid the potion across the table at me, and began raiding the oversized pantry. *As sunny as usual, then.*

Sin motions with his chin for me to pick up my matching tonic. I open the lid and dare a sniff, then immediately hold the bottle at arm's length as I turn my head over my shoulder, a shuddering cough shaking free. It smells earthy and foul, dirt and shit with a hint of something floral, but I can't place it. Like cheap perfume that was left sitting out in the stables on a balmy summer afternoon. "That is revolting," I say, turning back to eye the strange liquid.

"Bottoms up." He throws his head back, guzzling down the thick purple substance, and slams the vial onto the table. He points to the orange with a long finger and waves towards himself, his other hand a fist against his lips as if forcing himself to keep the contents down. I quickly hand the now peeled orange to him, and he bites into it, grimacing as he chews the sweet fruit. He wipes his mouth with the back of his hand and nods towards the bottle I still hold, swishing the purple potion around. "Down with it, then."

Pinching my nose closed with my thumb and finger, I bring the tonic to my lips and dump it down my throat. Immediately, I reach for the orange and sink my teeth into its juicy flesh, focusing only on the notes of sweet citrus on my tongue and not on the other heinous flavors coating my mouth. I look back to Sin who appears to have collected himself and wait a sec—

"I thought you said it was instantaneous," I say, noting his unaltered appearance.

"It is. I made sure Cassius crafted it so you and I keep our likeness to each other."

"You mean everyone else will see us differently now, except for us?"

"Precisely. Cassius is waiting for us at the stables to confirm it worked the way he intended, but I am willing to wager you and I look nothing like ourselves to the rest of the world."

I consider his words, holding out my arms in front of me, noting they don't look any different. I don't *feel* any different either. "Why did you instruct him to spell it that way?"

Sin slings his saddle bag over his shoulder, and grabbing my own, I follow him outside through a door in the back of the kitchen, likely a private entrance for the staff.

"I may not have known you for long, but long enough to learn the subtleties of your movements. Had your appearance changed, I'm not sure if that would have affected your facial expressions and body language."

I halt in the stone path leading to the stables. "You *what?*" It shouldn't surprise me he has been studying my movements. Sin has probably spent his entire life deciphering lies and weeding out enemies of the throne. Enemies of his father and Ephraim, and now his own. But still, the thought of him making notes of my patterns to use against me is unnerving.

He cuts his steps also and turns to face me. "Knowing your enemy is synonymous with survival. I wouldn't think I'd need to explain that to a bloodwitch."

I scowl and shake my head, my braid swinging side-to-side

down my back, though I'm not sure what my hair *really* looks like to everyone else. "Ever the strategist," I grumble.

"This way, should you tighten the lines of that pretty mouth again, I'll know you're about to strike me. Which I'll remind you, you've done three times now. May I suggest we not go for the fourth? I'm not sure how much longer I can cage my temper." He turns and continues walking towards the stables, and my black leather boots unglue themselves from the path a second later.

"Choking me against a wall is caging your temper?"

He ignores my question, and we walk the rest of the way to the stables in silence, the clacking of our leather soled riding boots against the ground the only sound between us. The faintest glow of daybreak warms the sky while the crisp morning air of early spring, still edged in winter's ice, nips at my cheeks.

Two horses, already fitted with saddles and bridles, neigh softly as we enter the dimly lit stables. One is a dapple-gray mare, its mane a vivid white with charcoal tips, and a matching tail braided in a similar style to my own. The other is a light tan, the shade of its velvety coat similar to that of the sandbars that stretch along the eastern border of Innodell. Its ebony mane rivals the mare's for beauty, and its long tail gently flicks behind it, unbound. I turn to Sin, my mouth falling open at the realization. *He didn't.*

"Did you have them styled in our image?"

"They are modeled after your true appearances, yes. His Grace has an affinity for dark humor."

I spin to face the voice behind me. Cassius emerges from a supply closet and slaps his hands together, as if ridding them of hay dust. I look back to Sin. "Really? You insist on tagging along, forcing us to drink those nasty tonics to disguise our identities, just to have our horses styled in our likeness?"

He shrugs and moves to secure his saddle bag to the large brown steed, but not before I glimpse the smirk on his mouth.

"I can't believe you would do something so risky and—"

"Enough. No one is going to make the realization." He reaches for the saddle bag looped over my arm, and I let him take it.

"You are insufferable, do you know that? For someone who acts like they've never laughed at a joke in their life, you sure have a twisted sense of humor."

Attaching my bag to the light-colored mare, Sin glances to Cassius still lingering just outside the closet. "How do we look?"

"Marvelous, Your Grace. You wouldn't suspect a thing."

I study Sin carefully, letting my eyes drift in and out of focus, searching for a weak spot in the glamour, but his image never falters. He looks as he always has, except he is dressed more casual today, given we are in for a full day's ride. He wears a fitted black shirt with silver threading along the chest pocket, dark trousers, and a twin set of swords strapped in an X pattern on his back. *So much for blending in...*

"What do we look like? We should know that right, so if we reference each other, we know what to describe?" I ask.

"Take out your braid," Cassius instructs.

"Why?"

"The magic alters your hair color, but the length and movement will be the same. Even in your disguise, your hair is braided, and given Legion knows you style your hair like that, you should take it out."

I reach for the ties securing my hair and unravel the braid, combing through it with my fingers.

"Better. His Grace's hair remains long but it is a golden blonde with a slight curl. His skin tone is a shade lighter as well, and his eyes are brown. You are brunette with blue eyes, and your complexion is a touch darker. Your heights and weights remain the same so your movements appear natural."

I stow the information away and approach the dapple-gray horse, letting her sniff my hand and patting her gently on the snout. Sin exchanges some final words with Cassius while I pet her side, and she snorts approvingly. I lift my foot into the stirrup and hoist myself onto her back, but I undershoot and grip the saddle horn as I begin to slide down her side. *Shit.*

Hands are on me immediately, one on my lower back to keep me from falling the rest of the way, and the other on my calf guiding it over the horse's rear. Warmth rushes to my cheeks in embarrassment, and I grip the reins a little too tightly, refusing to turn around and acknowledge the owner of those tan hands. I sit up straighter, priming my tongue to refute whatever insult regarding my inexperience he thrusts at me, but he returns to Cassius without a word as if the exchange never happened. With a nudge forward and a slap of the reins, I ease the mare into a walk, and she guides us through the wide opened doors.

Sin rides up next to me, the wind whipping his midnight hair behind him, mirroring the steed's tail that billows out at his rear. "Some ground rules before we take off. First, when we arrive at your... *den,* you need to stay close to me so your animal friends don't smell the glamour on me."

I don't turn to look at him, focusing on the sharp points of the gray watchtower in the distance instead. "Then it's a good thing we enjoy each other's company so much."

"Secondly, what is my name?"

"Excuse me?"

"Our ruse won't last long if you're calling me Sin, now will it? What is a name you will remember and not slip up and call me the wrong thing?"

I purse my lips. "Hm. Dickhead has a nice ring to it."

He exhales sharply.

"What, you don't like it?"

"We needn't bother disguising you as a lady because your mouth would surely allude to your status, or rather, lack thereof."

I shrug off the insult. "We can call you dick for short."

"Do you always bring up dicks when men speak of your mouth, little witch?"

I shoot him a glare that might have made a less stubborn man fall from their mount. "Keep talking like that, and you'll find yourself without one, Your Grace. Speaking of which, I should be armed in case we find ourselves in trouble." *In case you shoved iron in that bag when I wasn't looking.*

"Tell me, Wren, do you think demanding a blade in the same breath you threatened to remove my c—"

"Please don't finish that sentence," I interrupt, "but yes, I should have a means of defense that isn't my magic."

Sin pulls his horse to a stop, and I mirror him on my mare. He leans over and rummages through the bag hanging from the left side of his saddle. When he rights himself, a six-inch dagger with a black hilt and a holster are in his hands.

"If I give this to you—"

"I promise not to castrate you."

I reach for the knife, and he hands it to me hilt first. The handle is bumpy like fine gravel, allowing me to grip it easier, and the blade is honed to a lethal point. I weigh it in my palm, and he holds out the holster. Balancing myself on the horse, I fasten the twin black leather straps around my thigh and slide the dagger into the sheathe. Ideally, I'd prefer to have the weapon hidden, but given my attire of a white flowy tunic and black leggings, strapped over my pants will have to do. The holster is clearly designed for a woman's leg, and the Black Art isn't foolish enough to leave any weapon unsecured to his body, not where prying eyes might spot it. He already planned for this and intended on arming me. Why he made me ask for it, I don't know.

"If you won't let me have my first choice of names, I'll introduce you as Roarke." My gut clenches at the thought of lying to my family—deceiving them to believe the man at my side is an escort and not the hot-tempered leader plotting their extinction.

Sin raises an eyebrow at the name but doesn't dispute it. "Lead the way."

"Gladly. Oh, and Sin," I drop my eyes to his lips, then drag them slowly down his neck, "if this is a trap and you try to lay a finger on my family, I will slit your throat ear to ear." The smile I give him is as sweet as Bennett's jam puffs, and I take off in a gallop.

CHAPTER 16

I t was worth risking death to see the brief glimpse of shock on the Black Art's face as I rode off without a care, as if I didn't just threaten the most powerful man in Aegidale. He catches up to me a minute later, all traces of bemusement gone from his expression, his usual collected mask in its place.

Our horses pound the ground beneath their hooves, sending red dirt flying around us like powdered flames. The main road that winds through Aegidale is open and vast, only the fiery glow of the horizon for company and the occasional horses and carts of traveling tradesmen. If we follow the road right, it leads to Emberbourne, the city of steel and wealth. High lords and ladies and the wealthiest of merchants reside there, the city notorious for their production of kingdom steel. Their blacksmiths make most of the weapons and armor for the Black Art's armies.

We veer away from the smell of coal dust and iron and ride towards the dark green canopy of the Autumnhelm woods. Sin and I are mostly quiet as we ride parallel to the forest, the variety of greens and browns and the occasional pop of color from the local flora a stark contrast to the dusty red-tinged soil beneath us.

My heart pitter-patters in time with the clip-clopping of hooves as we gain distance towards the secluded cabin that has been my home for years. We pass a few more traders pulling wagons as they ride towards Emberbourne and her sister city to the west, Suncove—their carts likely loaded with an array of spices and furs to sell and barter with. Legion wouldn't dare travel a road so visible. They cling to seclusion—woods like Autumnhelm that better disguise their numbers, their assets. It was in those woods I met Ileana, and in those woods I left her.

⁂

It's a couple hours past dusk when we reach Innodell and finally cross into the forest. Our cabin isn't far from the perimeter—enough distance away from the city to remain secluded, but close enough we can ride in for work each morning. I nod to Sin when we come to the large red oak tree that marks the outskirts of our property. We dismount and lead our horses on foot the rest of the way in. With my altered appearance, whoever is home right now will already be alarmed by approaching strangers. No need to induce more panic by riding in on horseback.

Weaving our steeds around the thick trunks now spaced farther apart, we approach the quaint shelter I've called home for a little over a decade, my own small slice of comfort in this unforgiving world. Rising from the plush green clearing and surrounded by sky-hugging trees, the two-story log cabin welcomes me home. Animal pelts hang in the square windows, the furs offering protection from precipitation, or on nights like these, the chilled breeze that swooshes through the trees like a raptor diving for its prey. The high-pitched roof is a deep green and compliments the red tones of the cedar logs it shadows. A wooden porch wraps arounds the two visible sides of the cabin, a few white chairs and several plants in decorative pots adorning the space.

Home.

The front door cracks open, and a head of golden locks and brown eyes set deep in a boyish face peer out hesitantly from the threshold.

"Galen!"

He looks at me warily, and his mother appears behind him, clutching his shoulders and pulling him back in the house. Zorina steps onto the porch and closes the door behind her. "This is owned property," she says, eyeing Sin and me. Her hand subtly moves to the back of her waist, but I don't miss the movement, and I'm certain Sin doesn't either. I have no doubt she has a blade tucked into the waistband of her yellow pants.

"It's okay, Zorina. I know this sounds crazy, but it's me—it's Wren."

Her eyes widen slightly, and she angles herself as if trying to get a better look at me.

"I was captured by Legion and forced to surrender to the kingdom during an attack on one of their outposts. I made a bargain with..." I clear my throat, "with the Black Art, to return so I could let you know I'm okay, and to warn you. Legion is coming for you, Zorina, for all of you, because I refused to help them. This," I gesture towards myself, "is a glamour in case we crossed paths with any Legion soldiers."

Her tan skin blanches as she tries to make sense of my words. The arm at her back begins to relax but flexes again as her eyes shift to Sin. "Who is he, then?"

"This is Roarke," I answer without missing a beat. "The Black Art required I be escorted. It was part of our agreement."

Sin dips his head in greeting and offers a polite enough smile that he promptly wipes from his face the second she looks back to me.

"A glamour?" she repeats, lifting her chin slightly and looking down at me over her nose, her eyes still searching for a breach in the illusion.

I take a step closer, and Sin shuffles forward at the same time, keeping himself perfectly aligned with me. *He really is attuned to my movements.*

"Yes. You can ask me anything, and I'll answer it for you so you know it's me. Anything at—"

"What's going on?" the burly red-haired male asks, appearing behind Zorina, standing a foot taller than his sister.

She informs Eldridge of our exchange, and he fixes his light gray eyes on me. "Wren?" The ring of hope in the way he says my name shatters my heart, and I can't hold back the tears that rush from my eyes as I nod. Eldridge squeezes around his sister and barrels towards me, opening his huge muscular arms for me, and I dive into them, letting him lift me off the ground and spin me in a circle before setting me back on my feet. He holds me at arm's distance and assesses me for damage before leveling his stare with mine, all relief gone from his face.

"This is really you?"

I nod and wipe away the spilled tears with the back of my hand, too warmed by Eldridge's embrace to care that I showed weakness in front of Sin.

"Then whose guts am I spilling?"

A laugh escapes me despite him asking the question in earnest. I tug at the long red beard he keeps braided into a rope, hanging so low it almost grazes his navel. "No one's, not right now anyway."

He looks over his shoulder at Zorina and waves her forward. "It's alright, sister. I smell the magic on her. And even if I didn't, that smile can only belong to Wren," he says, turning back to me.

I steal a glance at Sin who's been silent at my side, and Eldridge tracks the movement. The smile vanishes from his face as he steps away from me and unknowingly squares up with the Black Art, their oversized chests almost touching. I've never met anyone as large as Eldridge before—his wide shoulders sit above a barrel chest, and his stocky build and muscular arms would have one thinking he threw mules around for sport. His gift of transcendence aside, Eldridge is pure *animal*. Where Eldridge's build is wide and brawny, Sin's is leaner and more athletic.

"So, you're the Black Art's *pet*?" he asks in a low breath.

Eldridge has always struggled to keep his temper leashed and is the main reason disguising Sin's identity was necessary. One look at the kingdom's leader at my side and Eldridge would have shifted and tried tearing Sin's heart from his chest. Attack first, ask questions later. But I suspect Sin isn't the type to offer second chances and would put my friend down without a second's hesitation. Which would be bad for two reasons: Eldridge is my best friend, and I would then have to assassinate the Black Art.

Sin doesn't so much as flinch from Eldridge's closeness but meets his eyes with a hardened stare of his own. "It is my privilege to serve His Grace. And as a member of the royal court, I suggest you watch your tongue." His tone is calm, but his arms are rigid at his sides like he's preparing to defend himself should Eldridge swing at him.

"Well, you carried out your mission, you can run back to your fancy castle now. Can you remove the glamour, Wren, or does he need to?" Eldridge diverts his eyes to me and jerks his chin in Sin's direction with the question.

"She's not staying," Sin interjects before I can answer.

Eldridge yanks his attention back to him. "What do you *mean*, she's not staying?"

"The witch is in kingdom custody now."

"The w— Who the *fuck* do you think you are?"

I put a hand on Eldridge's chest and push him back. He could have resisted my nudge if he wanted to, but he heeds my warning to back off and gives a half-step.

Zorina appears next to her brother and places a hand on his shoulder, attempting to calm him with her touch.

"I made a deal with Singard that I could come home for a few days to check on you all, but I have to return to the castle. And I can't remove the glamour. Only Singard has the reversal tonic."

"What business does the kingdom have with you that he's keeping you there?" Zorina asks.

I resist the urge to look at Sin to check his expression, but I *feel* the heat rolling off him. He's simply better at masking it than Eldridge. "The Black Art knows what I am. He knows... he knows I'm a bloodwitch."

Zorina hooks her fingers over her now opened mouth, and the panicked look in her hazel eyes matches the one in Eldridge's gray ones. "My gods," she sighs.

"I can explain everything, but I'd rather do it in front of everyone. Is Cosmina home, or is she at the inn still?"

My heart drops into my stomach as the panic on their faces twists into something darker, sadder. "What is it? Where's Cosmina? Where is she?" I ask, the words falling from my mouth quicker now.

"She left to go looking for you," Zorina finally answers. "A few weeks ago. But if you're here now and she's not with you..."

"Legion." Air hisses through my teeth. I turn to Sin without thinking and find him already watching me, assessing my reaction.

"Where were they when you last encountered them?" Eldridge asks.

"Just outside Blackreach. But I'm sure they're long gone now. Sin's armies took them out quickly."

Eldridge huffs. "Like I'm going to trust that cunt to take down Legion. Singard or Sin or whatever the fuck his name is —none of those kingdom cunts ever get anything done." He interlocks his fingers and stretches his hands out in front of him, rolling his neck as he does. "I'm not waiting around while they have a pissing contest. I'll leave tomorrow—I'll bring her back, and I'll roll a few heads doing it."

"Eldridge, stop it—you'll get yourself killed," I warn.

"I will not *stop it,* Wren. They took our godsdamned sister, for crying out loud. I haven't even said what I'm going to do to them for taking *you.*"

"All of you better stop it right now," Zorina yells over us. "Let's take this inside. Wren, your mother will be ecstatic to see you. We'll discuss the rest indoors. It's cold out here." She clutches her open sweater and pulls it across her body so the two seams meet and heads towards the cabin. I put my hand on Eldridge's arm and give a light squeeze, and we follow our sister to the front door, Sin trailing in behind us.

The smell of sun warmed wood and ash welcomes me as we pass through the worn-in door. There is no floor beneath our feet—merely beaten ground that is soft enough, and a few cones of moonlight shine in through the cut-out windows. Transcendents believe their magic is strongest with both feet on the crust, so most shifter homes are built without a foundation. White candles dripping with wax adorn every surface from the window ledges to the small kitchen table to the mantle of the fireplace in the center of the home. Rows of herbs

—clary sage, spearmint and parsley—hang to dry in front of the kitchen window, while sprigs of lavender are tucked in every corner of the house, dousing the whole place in an earthy sweet aroma.

My heart somersaults as I behold the place so near and dear to me, the home I was worried Legion had destroyed in my absence. Chairs with green and blue cushions occupy the living space to my left and vibrant overgrown plants splash the home with rich greens and yellows, a product of Morrinne's nurturing personality. Nestled in the back right corner are three beds, one for each of my brothers. A winding wooden staircase climbs to a smaller second story with four beds where my sisters and I slept.

The upper stairs creak, and I suck in a breath as Morrinne rounds the stairwell. Her deep brown eyes meet mine, dart to assess Sin at my side, then fixate on me again.

"Mom." My voice cracks a little as my mouth utters the word I feared I'd never get to say again.

"Mama, I know this is bizarre, but this is Wren. Eldridge and I already vetted her and—"

"I know who she is," Morrinne says, gripping the railing and descending the rest of the stairs. "You think I wouldn't know my own daughter when I saw her? Magic be damned."

I rush to her, throwing my arms around her slender body, and tuck her graying bun to my nose, inhaling the distinct scent of jasmine flowers permanently embedded into her hair. Morrinne is never without a piping cup of tea at her side, and the aroma of floral infused tea has become as much a part of her clothing as the buttons and seams. Galen bounds down the stairs and wraps his arms around my waist in a soul shattering hug, exclaiming my name. My heart leaps with joy as I scrunch my hands into his golden curls and crush him against me.

I fill all of them in immediately—from my time in the camp

to the tethering spell to what I learned from Bennett Langston —not leaving out the details of what I've learned of Sin's upcoming war. Sin is quiet while I explain. The only words he spoke since entering our home was to respectfully decline when Morrinne offered him a cup of tea. The five of us sit in the living space while he paces the other side of the cabin, occasionally stopping to eye the tonics and salves and canned jams Morrinne and I have made. I imagine our home is strange to him, having grown up in a state of luxury where everything has always been provided for him without the need to craft it.

"Tethering spell or not—you can't go back there," Morrinne says.

"I don't have a choice. If I don't return, Singard will track me with his ridiculous stalker spell, and I don't want him coming here." I resist the urge to glance over at him, knowing he is listening to every word between us.

"Let him come," Eldridge growls, his knuckles lengthening into claws.

"No. If he's already planning on committing genocide, we can't provoke him. He knows what you guys are. Right now, we need to worry about Legion and finding Cosmina. Everything else is secondary. *I* am secondary."

Eldridge scoffs. "If that Black Art bitch hurts you, I swear on my life, Wren, I will make sure the memory of your face is the last thing he sees before I rip him piece to fucking piece."

This time, I can't help glancing at Sin, now with his back to me as he studies a painting of a bundling of wildflowers on the kitchen wall, but I swear the fabric bunches at his shoulder blades. It's probably best I can't see his face, not wanting to see the thought of choking Eldridge with the same magic he used on me burning in his irises. I don't imagine many call the Black Art a *bitch* and live to tell the tale.

Morrinne reaches under the collar of her deep blue sweater

and unclasps a necklace. I recognize my sister's sapphire pendant immediately.

"Cosmina left it with me before she went after you. She said if you were to return without her, you could use the necklace to find her."

Cosmina is the only other mage in my adoptive family, so it makes sense she would have left something she wore against her skin every day to agitate the potency of a locator spell. Transcendents have magic in their blood, but a different kind. Natural healers and alchemists, they are proficient with restoration magics and resistant to more harmful destruction casts, but a locator spell... that is witches' territory.

I take the necklace and close my fist around it. "I can use this to track her, but I'll need to rest beforehand." There is no way my tired, aching body has enough stamina to hold the magical connection to her long enough for me to pinpoint her location, not without at least a few hours of sleep.

"Can I help somehow?" Zorina asks.

I nod. "If I can siphon a little of your magic while I do it, the spell should work more quickly."

I catch Sin turning to look at me from my periphery, no doubt considering the most obvious course of action. If I siphoned some of the Black Art's magic, I could find her in half the time, but given our current predicament, Zorina's will have to do. She agrees instantly.

"You all get some sleep, I'll take first watch," Morrinne says.

"Let me do it. You need to rest, you old broad," Eldridge huffs, but bumps her with a playful nudge of his elbow.

"You might as well get some shut eye, Eldridge, because I'm keeping watch either way. No way I'm closing my eyes with evil so close on Wren's tail."

I want to scold her for being stubborn, the darkness under

her eyes telling me she hasn't slept more than a few hours a night since I left, but I don't. If our positions were reversed, I'd be saying the same thing. The creases around my mother's eyelids are deep and worn in, her graying tawny hair now more silver than brown, and perhaps it is the time away that lets me see how quickly age is sneaking up on her. And if I wasn't so drained from the ride, I would be arguing to keep watch tonight too, but sleep is critical for me to restore my energy enough to perform the spell.

Zorina turns and looks at Sin still lingering in the kitchen. "Your...friend... can sleep in Theon's cot for now, but he'll be back later tonight and will probably want his bed back..."

"I'm not sleeping tonight. It's my duty to keep Wren safe, and I intend to do just that," Sin says, walking towards us and stopping a few feet away.

I lock eyes with him and nod once, playing along. Sleeping in Theon's bed isn't an option. As soon as there is distance between us, Eldridge will surely smell the glamour on Sin and do something stupid, like assault the Black Art in his sleep and get himself gutted in the process. I don't doubt Sin has more than just the twin swords on his back for weapons. Knowing him and his distrust of transcendents, I'm sure he has daggers stowed in every nook and cranny of his fitted pants.

"Fair enough. I won't turn down the extra set of eyes tonight, but don't think for a second I won't be keeping one on you too, mister," Morrinne warns.

I stifle a laugh at the thought of my fragile aging mother threatening the most powerful man on the isle and turn my head to hide the smile. Zorina tucks Galen into bed and then disappears upstairs to her own, while Morrinne fixes herself a fresh cup of tea and settles into one of the cushioned chairs with a leather-bound book, propping her feet up on the wicker footrest she constructed from plant material.

I head outside, and Sin falls into place behind me immediately. Neither of us speaks until we reach the horses and walk them into the clearing to tether them.

"Don't let Morrinne's age fool you—she's still sharp as a knife. She'll detect the magic on you if you stay up with her all night."

He pets his horse on the nose, pulls out two apples from the saddle bag, and offers one to each steed. "She won't notice because I won't be near her. I'm staying out here until morning."

"You're going to sleep outside all night?"

"And give your uncivilized friend the opportunity to slit my throat in my sleep? How naïve do you think I am?"

I walk around to the side of his horse and pull out a few of the remaining strips of salted meat. "It's not Eldridge you should be worried about. *I'm* much scarier," I say, tearing off a piece of the jerky with my teeth.

Sin stares down at me, his dark hair and reddish-brown skin blending with the night, but I still make out as his lips curl into a facetious grin. I close the saddle bag and turn on my heel, but not before I hear him mutter under his breath, "Yes you are, little witch. Yes you are."

CHAPTER 17

Honey beams of sunshine nudge me awake, their warm buttery rays shining in through the now uncovered windows. For a brief moment, when I open my eyes and stretch out against the lumpy mattress, it is just another day.

And then the memories of the past couple of months snap back into place, and the brief comfort I felt in those seconds vanishes completely. I pull on a pair of light-colored trousers and a faded purple tunic with white floral embroidery and follow the smell of smoking herbs and citrus beckoning me from outside.

Four sets of eyes snap to mine the second I step through the door. Everyone, excluding Sin and Eldridge, sits in a circle around the fire crackling and spitting in the center. Galen jumps up and sprints to crush me in another rib shattering hug, and his mother smiles warmly at me from behind him. Zorina's hazel eyes look brighter than they did last night, shadowed by her thick golden hair, locks that Galen surely inherited from her.

Theon rises from the sideways log he shares with his mother and opens his arms towards me. Theon is Morrinne's only biological child, but if our appearances didn't give it away, no one would suspect the rest of us weren't related by blood. I don't hesitate pulling him in tight, wrapping my arms around his lean body and inhaling the smell of moss and wood from his worn clothing. He pulls out of the hug to hold me at arm's distance, assessing me from head to toe.

"Gods, I've missed you, Wren. You okay?" he asks.

I shrug my shoulders. "I'm alive," I offer. "I'll be better once we find Cosmina."

He nods in agreement, his short wavy black hair bouncing with the movement.

"Eldridge?" I ask, noting his absence. Sleep found me quickly last night, but not before Eldridge slipped into Cosmina's bed next to mine.

"He took off this morning after most of us were awake and could keep an eye on you. He was rather... grumpy today," Zorina answers.

I don't blame him. If our positions were reversed, I would think he was a damn fool to return to Scarwood, to the Black Art that openly discriminates against both our kinds. I would think he was a coward for not holding his ground, to go back without a fight, and I would do everything I could to convince Eldridge to let us help him. I don't expect him to understand that I will not—I *cannot*—agree to fight for my life if it means jeopardizing theirs.

"Has anyone seen Roarke?" I ask, not comfortable with the thought of both Eldridge and Sin out in the woods alone where they may cross paths. Although if that had happened, I'm sure we would have *heard* the altercation.

As if he was watching and heard me, Sin steps out of the shadowed woods and saunters towards me, his eyes on mine and mine alone, seemingly unaware of the others now staring at him. The top few buttons of his shirt are unfastened, exposing the smooth, deeply tanned planes of his chest, and his black trousers hang low on his waist. His hair is tousled like he tried sleeping somewhere last night, but the tinge of purple under his eyes indicates he was unsuccessful.

Without a word, I abandon the plate of food Morrinne had handed me and rise to my feet. I motion with my head for Sin to follow and head back into the cabin, neither of us addressing the other until he closes the front door behind him. When the door clicks into place, I look over my shoulder at him.

"You need to eat. I can bring you a plate, but every crumb you spill in my bed is a clump of that pretty hair I'm yanking out of your head," I say, pointing to his inky locks with my chin.

"I don't require food."

I turn to face him, a hand finding my hip. "I guess it's different inside your fancy castle, but here, when someone offers you something to eat, you say thank you. We don't offer a meal out of obligation, we do it out of kindness."

He stares at me blankly, and I blow out a breath. Explaining kindness to the Black Art is like trying to start a fire with rain-soaked wood and no magic to conjure one. The stairs creak under my bare feet as I lead him to the second story and slap my hand on my bed, still unmade from last night's sleep. "I sleep here. You're welcome to use it—the others don't come up here during the day."

Sin reaches for the few remaining buttons on his shirt and begins undoing them, shrugging out of the clothing when the last one pops free. I divert my eyes, suddenly finding fascination in the dark blue sheets of my sister's bed.

"Get some rest, Blackheart. I'll make sure no one disembowels you while you sleep."

I leave him, only to return a few minutes later with a dinner plate I loaded with eggs, potatoes, and orange slices. Even though I directed him to use it, the sight of the Black Art in my bed unnerves me. He faces away from me, the creamy tan sheets tucked under his arm, his long, tangled hair splayed out around him on the pillow. His light snoring tells me he isn't pretending to be down, so I leave the plate on my bedside table for when he wakes and tiptoe back down the stairs.

"There's something off about your friend," Zorina says to me as I shovel breakfast into my mouth.

"He's not my friend. I'm being held captive, remember?" I say with forced lightness in my tone.

She shakes her head, her straw-colored hair bouncing with the movement. "I don't like the way he looks at you."

"Me either," Theon chimes in. "He watches you like... like he's waiting for something."

Waiting for me to try to flee, perhaps. Or maybe he took my threat to slit him ear-to-ear more seriously than I thought. Good. He should.

"I can handle him," I grumble.

"But can Eldridge?" Morrinne asks. "I can already see one more remark from that fair-haired friend of yours and your brother's temper is going to go flaring." She tsks quietly to herself. *Fair-haired. Glad to see the tonics are working as planned.*

"You can hardly blame him, Mama, with the Rut around the corner," Zorina defends.

The Rut. Has that much time really passed? Each spring, transcendents across Aegidale gather for an annual outdoor celebration to honor their heritage. It's common belief

149

amongst shifters that they all relate to Slaine, the first transcendent and the god of hunt and rebirth, in one way or another, believing it is he who chooses who to bestow the gift of transcendence upon. Legend claims the Rut marks the first day Slaine shifted, and the effect it has on transcendents is similar to that of deer in rutting season. They become agitated, irritable, and eager to hunt or fuck anything with a pulse.

"The Rut affects me too, child, and you don't see me storming off into the woods muttering about ripping people's heads off and pissing down their necks."

Lovely. I don't hate that I was asleep when Eldridge took off this morning, and apparently in quite a *mood*, it seems.

"That's not fair, Mama, and you know it."

Zorina is right. The Rut is known to affect males much stronger than their female companions. No wonder Eldridge's temper almost got the best of him being around a foreign male, let alone one exuding a sickening amount of arrogance and self-esteem. It isn't uncommon for Eldridge and Theon to bump heads around this time, and they've known each other longer than I've known either of them. Galen is too young to be affected, but once he matures, the Rut will come for him too.

Shoving the final bits of egg into my mouth, I share a pointed glance with Zorina and scramble to my feet. I head back inside and find the small woven basket Morrinne had made for me near the racks of dried herbs waiting to be pestled and made into seasonings, salves, and jellies. Reaching into the basket, tucked along the side where I had left it, is the cold, steel hilt of my athame.

I pull the sacrificial dagger from the basket and balance it in my palm. My magic stirs inside me, curling and weaving through every muscle and tendon until my very bones rattle with excitement. The ornate swirling pattern etched into the steel makes it look almost fragile—graceful even, but the sheer weight of it in my hand is nothing short of solid craftsmanship. I lift it to the window and turn it over in the beam of sunlight —one way then the other—marveling at the sparkling clarity of the sweeping crossguard, the designs there intricate enough to match the elaborate detailing of the hilt. Crafted into the handle is a nude, voluptuous woman with her arms raised above her head, dancing in tune with a silent melody.

Elysande. The goddess of war, vengeance, and femininity. The first bloodwitch.

Most mages worship the goddess of the arcane since it is Adelphia who strengthens the Black Art's power to protect the nation from those that would upset its balance. Cosmina had this athame forged for me specifically and gifted it to me a few months after we found each other. Elysande is often thought of as vengeful with an appetite equally as merciless, but her followers know legends have altered the truth.

The goddess feasts on men that harm women and devours mothers that bring pain to their children. Stories claim she went from house to house, ripping babes from their beds and fueling her power with their life forces, but her devoted know Elysande was the most nurturing of all the gods. She did go house to house, but it wasn't the younglings she sought—it was their wicked mothers and fathers that laid hands on innocent flesh. Elysande tore them to shreds, absorbed their lives to strengthen her power, and delivered the children to deserving women that would care for them.

I pledged my piety to Elysande the day my sister gifted me this athame, and while I can't be sure she is looking out for me, I survived being captured by Legion twice, and Sin hasn't slit my throat yet. Even though I've given him a neatly stacked pile of reasonable cause by now, starting with attacking him mere seconds after saving his life.

I pull one more thing from my basket—a hand drawn map

on parchment that details the major cities and woods of Aegidale—and head back to Zorina.

We sit cross-legged on the perimeter of the property, and taking Cosmina's necklace from my trouser pocket, I offer my opened palm to Zorina, closing my fingers around her dainty hand when she places it in mine. I take a few steadying breaths, focusing on that sensitive spot behind my eye, and dislodge my collective from its home. I will it away from me, attaching onto Zorina's collective almost immediately, and I grip her hand tighter, coaxing her magic to flow through her, down her arms and into her delicate hands. And just as I feel its slippery smooth finish tingling in my palm, I latch onto it like a ravenous viper. My chin lifts upward, exposing the underside of my neck as an offering of vulnerability to Elysande, and I squeeze my left hand around the blade.

That buried part of me—that raw, primal hunger—delights at the sticky warmth that pools into my hand. I conjure mental images of my sister—turning them over and over in my mind, studying the lines of her face, the soft curvature of her pale blue eyes, the cascade of her onyx hair rippling over her shoulders. I hold my bleeding palm over the parchment and utter words of intention, coaxing the blood to show me her location. Zorina's magic mingles with my own, our powers feeding into one another to birth a stronger, more potent blend that encourages the blood on the map to travel faster. I keep my eyes closed, rocking with the magical warmth crescendoing through my body, growing hotter and hotter until it's a white tipped flame in my wrists, my chest, my forehead.

I go blind with fury.

The burn becomes nearly tangible—tugging my body one way then the next—and I rock in its blazing storm as the rage coats all of me in its silken finish. My back arches and my shoulders shake as if caught in an uncontrollable wind, and I *feel* her. Cosmina.

Wounded. Angry.

Alive.

I fight to hold on to our connection, to cling to the scorching hate erupting from her, to see *something*. Anything. But no images flash behind my eyelids—no clues, no hints— and as quickly as the blistering heat surged through me, it vanishes.

Zorina calls my name. I turn to look at her, worry set deep in her green-brown eyes. "Wren, I don't think it worked."

I snap my attention to the map laid flat on the ground in front of us, and my blood clots in my veins. No. *No, no, no!* The blood I dribbled onto the parchment was meant to travel across the map and stop at Cosmina's location, but drawn on the map before me is not a path at all. Enveloping the entirety of the map are crimson branches climbing to each corner of the parchment, taunting, and revealing nothing.

"No, it worked," I croak. "It's a cloaking spell. Someone has her. Zorina, someone has Cosmina and is masking her location with magic. Someone that knew I would try to find her."

"Legion," she breathes, hooking her fingers over her mouth. "It must be them."

I shake my head, not wanting to believe it, but knowing she's right. Cosmina likely tracked Cathal for days, maybe weeks. But by the time she caught up with them, I would have already been inside Castle Scarwood. And when she didn't spot me with Legion, she would have looked closer. Close enough to get caught.

"They're masking her location which means they didn't take her to use as bait. If Legion wanted to bait me in, they'd be counting on me locating her with a spell and coming to find her, falling right into some trap they would have surely set. But hiding her location... this is different. They don't need me to come to them when they already know where I'm at."

"That sounds way more complicated."

"And way more deadly," I add. "They must be planning something. Something big. Legion knows I'm at Scarwood, so if they plan on bringing her to the castle, it's to force me to turn on Singard. To turn on all of them and bring the kingdom down in exchange for her life."

"But what do they expect to do with you afterwards? After..." she trails off.

"I become a bloodthirsty maniac," I fill in for her, and she smiles without warmth, a silent apology that I dismiss. She is right. "I don't know. They're either overestimating themselves or grossly underestimating me."

"What should we do?"

"I think I have to tell Singard," I say, not liking the sound of that at all.

"To hell with that. If he fears you, Wren, he won't let you anywhere near Legion when they come for you. He'll lock you away to rot with Cathal, or—and more likely—just kill you."

"I know."

"Then whatever you do, don't tell him!"

I debate my options silently. If I tell Sin that I suspect Legion intends to use my sister as a means to force my hand into turning on the kingdom, he might very well end my existence before I finish my sentence. But if I don't tell him and my suspicions prove true and Legion *does* march on the kingdom with Cosmina in their grasp, that leaves me in a precarious predicament. My first blow against the castle—soldier, guard, or the Black Art himself—will be met with immediate orders to put me down. To protect Cosmina, I would have to unleash myself on the kingdom, risking unleashing a blight far worse than the wrath of Sin and Cathal combined. End my soul for the salvation of hers, and I know if my sister was here, she would roar for me to do anything but that. To not ruin myself, my humanity, but in her heart, she would know her begging wouldn't change a thing.

I look back to Zorina, knowing there is only one option.

"I don't think I have a choice."

CHAPTER 18

The sky is streaked with shades of violet and orchid when Eldridge returns to camp. Our fire, still gleaming with brilliant shades of orange, cracks and spits between us. The others promptly excuse themselves soon after he plops himself on the sideways log across from mine, knowing the conversation between us isn't going to be pretty.

Neither of us speaks for a few minutes. Instead, we stare into the snapping flames, as if we could find the words to say hidden within them. When the silence becomes unbearable, I raise my eyes to his and force him to meet my gaze. His stone eyes, the color of the smoke rising above us, are set deep in his sun-kissed skin, framed by his long, tousled red hair. Eldridge is a mirror to the glowing embers in the pit—fiery and wild. His braided beard, the same red-orange as his hair, hangs all the way to below his chest. It's a rare sight to catch Eldridge not fighting to keep his temper on its leash, and judging by the tightness of his jaw, today is no different.

Zorina told him of our discovery earlier in the day—when she had left Galen with us and went to shift in the woods—no doubt to sniff out her brother and make sure his caged anger wasn't getting him into trouble.

"I wish there was another way," I finally say, needing to shatter the silence between my friend and me.

A quick burst of something like laughter erupts from him, and he rubs a large hand across his jaw, his stiff posture telling me he is anything but in a laughing mood. "It's my fault. I should have gone with her when she went looking for you."

"No, you shouldn't have. You did what you had to, what *I* would have wanted you to. You stayed here to protect the pack."

There is no doubt Eldridge is the strongest of us physically. Morrinne is aging, and her body does not move as fluidly as it once did. Zorina is the smallest of us all, not to mention her focus will always be on protecting Galen in any kind of altercation, as it should be. Theon is a skilled fighter. His slender body shifts into a lanky, sinewy beast—swift, but not as powerful as the sheer mass of Eldridge in his other form—the golden furred animal with a head and body as wide and muscled as a bear, and four legs as long and powerful as a draft horse. Eldridge *is* strength.

He runs his hand along the length of his beard. "I should have been there to protect you."

"*I* should have never gone hunting alone. I knew better, and I got cocky and did it anyway. What happened to Cosmina is my fault, and mine alone. But I *will* get her back." The truth of my words sinks into my bones, and I know that if the moment comes and I must choose, I *will* shed blood for her.

"You can't save her if you're dead. If that cowardly *bitch* kills you..." he stammers off, rage igniting in his stormy eyes.

I stand and erase the distance between us, sitting next to him on his log. He radiates as much heat as the popping fire in front of us, and I put a hand on his forearm, the cords of muscle there pulled tight, his fingers laced together between his knees. I've seen that anger in his eyes before—that glowing promise of something lethal and savage—the night Cosmina brought me home, and I told them what happened to me. What Cathal had done to me. I had to do nothing short of begging for days, pleading with him to not hunt them down and rip out their throats, one by one. Eldridge doesn't think clearly when his temper flares, and I have lost too many people to risk losing him too. My friend. My protector. And maybe something more if I hadn't been so broken my first several years here.

There is a connection between us—the rage we both fight —mine an innate struggle against my nature, and his a more raw hunger for those that would wrong us and dare to hurt us. That wrath he wrestles every day, every time someone darts a nasty, disapproving look in one of our directions, I feel that same violent desire every time I smell blood. If I hadn't been so damaged for years after I came here, our relationship may have developed into something more. But when I did finally choose to trust someone outside our pack, it ended with Cosmina bringing home a bloodied, beaten, used husk of a person, and no amount of Eldridge's softly spoken words of comfort could warm me on those nights I woke screaming, fighting off invisible enemies in the chilled air. I know my sanity was the only thing that stood between him and Cathal's intact throat.

"I will handle Singard. Nothing you do can help me now. What I want, what I *need*, is for you to stay and look after them. Keep them safe, *please*."

"How are you going to handle him? That whole lot of them has done nothing but hide behind castle walls their whole lives, killing anyone they don't like. There is only one way to handle a cunt like him," he spits.

"I don't know," I whisper. And the truth of *those* words quickens my heartbeat, each one now precious and numbered.

"If he hurts you, Wren—"

"Then what?" I cut him off. "You can't very well march on

the kingdom and cut them all down. They'll kill you without a second thought. They have iron arrows, weapons."

"Then I'd rather die fighting than sitting here and cowering while they continue to slaughter our kind."

Our kind. Transcendent and bloodwitch, but united by a singular enemy. We are the same in kingdom eyes—*the dead kind.*

"I will do what I must to get Cosmina back. I promise you that. But I cannot give you my word I won't go after that son of a bitch if he hurts you. He shows his face in the cities every now and again, winning their praises with his promises of protection against the enemy *he* created. I can wait. And when the moment is right, I'll rip his godsdamned heart out." The snarl in his voice is pure transcendent, pure predator.

I don't bother arguing with him. Nothing I say will cool the wrath coursing through him right now, so I resort to a miserable attempt at humor instead. "I'll make you a promise. I will try really hard not to die."

A slight smile tugs his lips upward, but it doesn't meet his cold, gray eyes. "Die, and I'll fucking kill you myself."

There is no escaping the Rut. The magic that simmers in their transcendent veins responds to it whether my family wants it to or not. Eldridge has been grumpier than usual, and earlier, he and Theon got into it over whose turn it was to bring in more wood for the stove. They won't hold it against each other —they both know where their renewed irritability is stemming from. The outdoor festival is tomorrow. It feels wrong to attend an event designed for blowing off steam while our sister is in peril, but if my brothers don't attend, they'll tear the cabin apart before nightfall. And while Eldridge would never try anything, his lingering glances in my direction don't escape my notice. He's horny, and I'm not ignorant to his feelings towards me, though he's never explicitly expressed them. He knows I'm not ready to return them.

I had no reason to attend the gathering every year other than that it was too dangerous for me to stay and be alone while a warmongering army with a proclivity for bloodwitches runs around. And while I'm likely the safest I've ever been with the Black Art at my side, staying would make my family suspicious of our ruse. Plus, I have limited time to see them, and I'll be damned if I waste a single second of it away from them.

I'm joining my family at the Rut, and I look forward to spending more time with them. Almost as much as I look forward to seeing the look on Sin's face when I tell him we'll be attending the event dedicated to shifters engaging in raw, primal activities.

CHAPTER 19

The Black Art is as keen on escorting me to the Rut as I am on informing him of my discovery with the locator spell. I haven't told him what I've learned yet, and I won't until we're heading back to the castle. I'm not going to risk Sin panicking and throwing me over the back of his horse like a sack of potatoes, insisting we return to Scarwood immediately. What the Black Art doesn't know won't kill him. At least not right now.

We left this morning, along with my brothers and Zorina, for White Hawk Meadow, the large expanse of plateaued land south of Innodell. Our mother stayed at home with Galen. Morrinne's older age and Galen's lack of maturity lessen the effects of the Rut's influence, making it not essential for them to attend. The Rut's night-long festivities, ranging from group hunting to group fucking, commence at dusk and endure until first light. I tend to keep to myself during the Rut, but this year, there is one man's stench I won't be able to hide from.

I eye Sin from my horse and almost wish I could read his thoughts, though I suspect his brazen disregard for transcendent life would leave me wishing I hadn't. The kingdom isn't ignorant to the annual shifter event, but sending an army into a pit of pissed-off transcendents fueled with otherworldly rage isn't exactly a recipe for success. So, the Black Art and his men remain in Blackreach, year after year, and pretend their enemies aren't dancing and drinking in the nude directly under their noses.

I have the immense satisfaction of witnessing the scowl of pure disgust cross Sin's face as we ride over the last of the grassy foothills and look down at White Hawk. The green carpeted meadow is crawling with men and women, laughing and chanting songs dedicated to Slaine, amber liquid sloshing from their drinks as they touch cups and throw their heads back in drunken amusement. The moon casts filtered light onto the clearing, the beams partly obstructed by the towering trees skirting the perimeter.

Eldridge lets out a howl of pure joy as he beholds the crowd before us, their cheers promising release from the Rut's influence. He turns to the rest of us from atop his horse and dips his head in a mock gesture. "If you need me before sunrise, you'll probably find me tongue deep in pussy, so try not to fucking need me," he grumbles before urging his horse down the final slope separating us from White Hawk.

My mouth falls open without my consent, and I promptly shut it, doing my best to wipe the surprise from my expression. Surprise and... something else. I'm not naïve to the fact Eldridge has taken lovers, as have I, but neither of us ever speaks about it in front of the other. It's a sort of an unspoken rule we have—don't come where you eat.

"That's disgusting," Zorina remarks from her horse. She shoots me a sideways look to gauge my reaction. I've never spoken about whatever feelings I may or may not have for her brother, but I doubt Eldridge's and my complicated relationship has gone unnoticed. I shake my head once but don't say anything, not trusting myself to not say something I'll later regret. Eldridge is allowed to do what he wants and *bed* who he pleases.

Feeling Sin's eyes burning a hole in my back, I urge my borrowed mare into a gallop and race down the hill.

"What part of 'you're not to leave my side' was lost in translation?"

I keep my eyes fixed on the makeshift stables ahead but feel the heat radiating off Sin. "Relax, Blackheart. I knew you'd be right behind me. You can't seem to stay away from me, after all."

He blows out a breath. "You're a glutton for punishment, aren't you?"

We dismount and tether our horses to the hitching posts. "You spend a lot of time threatening me, Your Grace, but I'm beginning to suspect you're all bark and no bite," I lie.

I jump as his lips suddenly brush my ear, not having heard him step around the horses as I finished securing mine to the post. A hand gathers my hair that had fallen over my left shoulder and moves it so it rests over my right, exposing my neck to his mouth.

"Would you like to feel just how hard I bite, little witch?"

His breath on my neck sends spiders skittering down my back, and my breath catches in my throat before I force myself to exhale, hoping he didn't notice the lapse. "There you go again making idle threats and—"

His teeth clamp down on the juncture of my shoulder and neck, and a strangled sound escapes my mouth as pain fills me. I jerk away from him, but his arm wraps around my waist like a steel band, pinning my back to his front.

"What the fuck are you doing—get off of me!" I tug at his arm, trying to pry it away from my waist, but it doesn't budge. I summon my magic to my hands and just as I'm about to press my blazing palms into him, his lips are at my ear again, this time tsking softly in it.

"I wouldn't do that," he murmurs. "Turn your magic on me one more time, and you'll see just how tame *that* bite was."

The promise in his voice is enough for my conjured flames to simmer out, and I slowly drop my hands to my sides, air blowing out of my nose like a pissed-off beast. His teeth find my punctured flesh again, biting down again for the briefest of moments—a warning—before he laps the blood with his tongue and mutters a word of intention under his breath. My flesh responds to his healing spell and closes instantly, while my clenched fists fly open.

Consequences be damned, I spin and smack the Black Art across the face.

I barely have time to glimpse the flicker of something feral in his eyes before he's grabbing both my arms and forcibly turning me so my back is pressed against his chest. He pushes forward, forcing me to stumble forward until my hips connect with the hitching post.

"I didn't use magic against you, Your Grace. You said nothing about smacking your ugly face."

I don't regret the insult. Sin is far from ugly—it's almost painful how beautiful he is—but his inflated self-image could stand to be poked at for once. His soft laughter, as if mocking my fruitless attempt to hurt him, turns my blood to fire.

I stiffen as he grasps both my hands in one of his and trails a callused palm down my side. Down, down until he's tracing over the curvature of my hip with his fingertips.

I could ignore his warning and burn him through my skin, but his grip on my hip has my thoughts clouded, breathing labored. Something tells me if I try burning him, he *will* bite me again. That thought disturbs me almost as much as the part of me that strangely yearns to feel his mouth on me again. It's wrong—I *know* it's wrong—but the presence he commands is intoxicating. And whether I wish to admit it or not, his touch sends a wave of heat through me that isn't entirely caused by the desire to hit him a second time.

I exhale as Sin's hand disappears from my hip, the fog clearing from my head, but nearly choke on my breath as he replaces his hand with the cool underside of his dagger. He applies just enough pressure to hold me still, but not enough to cut. Not yet.

"Listen carefully," he whispers in my ear, his voice low and deep and irritatingly confident. "I put this little heart on your hip to remind you of our special tether." Slowly, he drags the tip of his knife around to the inside of my hip where the small black heart marks my skin, leaving a fluttering sensation everywhere the blade teases my flesh through my thin leggings. Sin lowers his lips to the spot just beneath my ear and whispers against my neck. "Continue to disobey me, and I'll happily make it a permanent addition."

I don't so much as wince when he presses the dagger hard enough to nip my skin through my clothes, refusing to give him the satisfaction of seeing me in pain. My fitted leggings cling to the wetness now pooling just beneath my waistband, and I trace my top lip with my tongue, my rage bubbling out in the form of a humorless laugh. Looking over my shoulder, I spit at the Black Art's boots. "I can't decide if you're brave to threaten a bloodwitch, or just plain stupid."

I hear the smile as he takes a step away from me, still grasping my joined hands in one of his. "I'm going to let you go now, and when I do, you may run off and enjoy the party on your own. I have business of my own to attend to."

"You're going to leave my side while in a field swarming with people that will scent your disguise the second you're away from me?" Granted, they'll smell the magic on me too, but most of them will likely be too drunk to care or notice.

"I have no desire to be around the atrocities committed here tonight all in the name of some god they attribute their debauchery to."

"Are you worried no one will want to lie with you tonight, Your Grace? It wouldn't surprise me if you *get off* bedding the women you intend to wage war against," I spit.

"Do you think about me getting off often?"

The abruptness of his question floods my cheeks with warmth, and I'm thankful my back is still towards him. "Let go of me, Singard."

His thumb traces a quick circle on my wrist before he drops my hands. Immediately, I snatch them out of his reach and press them to my hip, healing the skin he barely opened.

"I suggest you get out of here, little witch. Unless you want me to lick that wound closed too," he says with a nod to my hip.

I shoot him a vulgar gesture with both hands before turning and heading towards the Rut.

CHAPTER 20

Whatever alcohol they're serving from the rustic barrels is cheap and poor quality. I grimace as the warm, amber liquid slides down my throat and burns my chest, its bitter aftertaste souring my mouth.

"This is putrid," Zorina says, choking down the remainder of her drink.

I smack my lips, then shoot down the rest. If I'm to bear witness to the activities present here tonight, I'm going to need it. I shrug my shoulders. "It's free."

I don't know what business Sin could possibly have to attend to this far south, or at this hour, but he disappeared as promised. Something tells me this many transcendents gathered together, let alone engaging in primal acts, makes the Black Art uncomfortable. Good.

Women scantily dressed, or some not dressed at all, sway their hips in circular motions in time with the beating drums. They dance through the clearing, taking in the admiring glances from onlookers, as they look for a suitable mate for the evening.

I remarked to Sin that it wouldn't surprise me if he bedded a woman here tonight that he planned on waging war against tomorrow, but I didn't actually believe my words. Sin isn't decent by any means, but I don't peg him as *that* kind of monster. And perhaps that is why he took off, so he wouldn't be approached by a horde of women interested in lying with him tonight. He would have no trouble finding many partners. At least not with his normal appearance, but not even Cassius's potion could disguise the sheer confidence that drips from Sin like rain from swollen clouds.

The Black Art is gorgeous and he knows it.

An image of Sin with a pair of women's legs wrapped around his bare hips flashes in my mind, and a blush creeps into my cheeks again. I blow out a breath. *Why am I thinking about this? I hate the man.* But the thought of him bedding another woman in these woods, pinning her between a tree and the sheer mass of his body, continues to plague my mind.

It must be the cheap whiskey.

Zorina and I make way through the mob of drunken, stumbling party-goers. My eyes sweep across the large group gathered at a log throwing station, half expecting—and hoping—to see Eldridge there. Chucking heavy pieces of wood around like they weigh no more than winter's decrepit leaves is one of his favorite activities, and my face falls slightly when I don't spy the giant, red-headed male in the group. A quick look tells me he's not amongst the group of men wrestling each other either, though I spy Theon going round and round with another large male around his size.

Ahead of us, teams line up on either side of a giant rope used for tug-of-war. Whichever team is pulled off their feet will find themselves spiraling into the cold mud. We stop and watch two teams of six try yanking the rope to their respective sides—

A symphony of howls jerks my attention to the right. Lining up along the perimeter of the clearing, their heads held high in triumph, are the transcendents that have shifted into their alternate forms for the night. Some black, others brown, and even a few sport white and sandy colored coats. A few of their heads resemble a wolf's, others more like a bear, and a few appear more feline than anything. Despite their varied head shapes, each possesses a set of lethal, pointed teeth, vivid glowing eyes, and stands as tall as a small horse.

"You can go ahead and shift," I tell Zorina, noticing she's started fidgeting since laying eyes on the pack.

She looks at me apologetically, despite having nothing to apologize for.

"I mean it, go on," I urge her. "I'll be fine. Maybe I'll go chuck a log or beat my fists against my chest. Who knows what trouble I'll get into—the options are endless." I wink at her and jerk my chin towards the transcendents at the perimeter of the clearing. Each year, those that wish to participate in the annual hunt line up along the edge of the woods, stretching their limbs and shaking out their coats as they wait for the boars to be released. "Go eat a pig or something."

She rolls her rounded eyes but begins unfastening the buttons of her sage tunic, and with a final glance in my direction to ensure I'm truly okay with us parting ways, she jogs towards the others. Leaving me alone. Minus the hundreds of too-large, sweating men and scantily clad women running their hands over the curves of their bodies as they embrace their peak femininity.

In transcendent culture, it is normal for the women to seek out a mate first. And I would be thick in the head to not recognize that is likely why Eldridge has only ever hinted at the feelings he may harbor towards me. Because I haven't told him how I feel first, and in his culture, that means I'm not interested.

But I'm *not* a transcendent. And *I* don't even know how I feel about him.

The only thing I'm certain about right now is that I need another drink.

I pour myself another two knuckles of the bad spirit and throw it down my gullet. And another.

A dense fog invades my mind, and my sour mood begins to sweeten as I join a group of dancing women. I make eye contact with a few of them that offer encouraging smiles, and I lean my head back, exposing my neck to the gods above and relishing in the faint mist now spritzing from the nighttime sky. My hips sway on their own, as if they think for themselves now, the cheap alcohol having severed the tie between my ability to think rationally and the need for something to fill the sudden emptiness between my thighs. Liquor always did leave me riddled with desire.

It was a bad idea to drink alone, but fuck it. Who knows how many days I have left in this life, and I refuse to spend them all chained to Sin with his stupid, invisible tether, and through the not so invisible heart inked on my hip.

My hand reaches up and caresses the spot he bit, the skin there now fully healed. I should have done a lot worse than slap him. *Arrogant bastard. Who goes around biting people, honestly?*

A bare-chested man with a head of golden hair and large brown eyes catches my attention from his perch next to the nearby fire pit. He watches me with approval, and judging by his tented pants, that glaze in his eyes is pure lust. Not really my type, but if Eldridge is off somewhere in those woods, tongue dee—

I refuse to finish the thought. I do not care where Eldridge is, or who he's with. Just as he shouldn't care that I'm now directing my full attention on the blonde man whose hand now openly rubs the crotch of his tightening pants while not breaking eye contact. Modesty has no place at the Rut. I suck in my bottom lip and bat my eyelashes in his direction—come and get it, mister beastly man.

An arm wraps around my waist and pulls me against a hard mass, shattering the drunken moment I was sharing with the less than handsome stranger. I whip towards the bearer of the mystery arm, ready to bark an obscenity, but the warning flashing in his stark green eyes halts the words deep in my throat.

"We need to go," Sin says to me. His tone is restrained, but the tightness of his jaw tells me he's holding back the urge to throw me over his shoulder and haul me out of here.

And being the drunken, stubborn ass that I am, I untangle myself from his arm and plant my feet. "I'm not going anywhere with you."

"I'm not asking, Wren." Angrier now.

"And I'm not leaving. In fact, you rudely interrupted me as I was about to approach that handsome gentleman over there and ask if he wanted to dance," I say matter-of-factly, lazily pointing in his direction.

Sin's eyes dart to the blonde man now staring at both of us for a brief second before dropping back to mine and narrowing. "How much have you had to drink?"

"Not enough," I say and then double over as laughter shakes my entire body.

I think I hear him swear under his breath, but I can't make it out over my chuckling.

He sighs deeply and runs a hand through his hair. He's so sexy when he does that. *Gah, stop it, Wren. Definitely too much to drink.*

"Now that I know you went and got yourself inebriated, we really need to get out of here."

"Why, so you can bite me some more? You sick fuck—is that why you ran off? So you could rub your cock while you thought about carving your initials into my forehead or something?"

I'm never drinking again. Especially not liquor meant for transcendents on their rowdiest night of the year. Sin arches an eyebrow, and for a second, I think I actually left him too stunned to speak before the reality of whatever situation we're apparently experiencing sinks back in and his usual scowl settles on his face. He reaches for my hand, but I yank it out of reach at the last second. I think I utter something about him being too slow, but then suddenly, my arm is being squeezed in his too-large hand, my reflexes severely hindered by the drink.

"Walk with me, or I'm carrying you out of here like a child," he warns, his voice low and threatening.

Before I can make some remark daring him to try it, a slow clapping behind me draws my attention. A man with a scruffy beard and a matching head of dark brown hair approaches, a woman with a long braid at his side. *Wait.*

I know her.

My eyes narrow into slits, and my fingernails dig into my palms.

Margalo.

I'd recognize that nasty woman anywhere, though she looks slightly different when she's not jerking me around by a collar. They won't recognize me or Sin thanks to Cassius's potion, which I am now hoping more than ever holds up. The clapping comes from the man at her side, and a small group of the transcendents who were partying just moments ago begin to close in on us. My eyes zero in on the Legion emblem pinned to his leather tunic, and by the pair's growing audience, the others noticed too.

He stops clapping and spreads his arms out in front of him, gesturing to the celebration.

"Quite the turn-out this year, friends." He smiles widely, and Margalo mirrors him, but her grin doesn't meet her wicked eyes.

"Legion are no friend of ours," a woman behind me spits in their direction.

The man's mouth falls open in an exaggerated "o," and he clasps his hands together in front of him. "Hey, hey, hey, we don't want any trouble, folks. We're simply here to burn off some steam like the rest of you. I'm Marcus—and this is Margalo." The edge to his words suggests trouble is *exactly* what they're looking for.

Legion may be supplemented with a large number of transcendents in their army, but they don't speak for the race as a whole. Most shifters despise Legion—believing they are to blame for the kingdom's growing prejudices against their kind. And they're probably not wrong to think that. Ephraim may have started the fight with shifter-kind, but Legion's response certainly escalated it. I have a never-ending list of choice words to label Legion as, but cowardly is not one of them. They are bold to show their faces at the Rut.

Or just plain stupid.

Sin's hand drops to my waist as if holding me in place at his side. This is why he wanted us out of here. He must have seen Legion approach from wherever he was off hiding. They couldn't have been here for very long given they're just now being noticed by the attendees, which means Sin must have had eyes on this place the entire time.

Eyes on me.

"Don't tell me you don't have room for a few more. Me and my friends back there," he jerks his thumb over his shoulder to the woods behind him, "would love to have a little fun tonight."

Maybe it's the alcohol in my system, or maybe it's the

unbridled rage of knowing they have my sister that compels my feet forward, but I take a step in their direction, crossing my arms over my chest. "Sorry, we don't mingle with abductors and rapists here. The only way either of you are having any fun tonight is if both of you go fuck yourselves." I squint my eyes in a smile that's all teeth.

Sin is at my side instantly, his hand on my back again, and this time, his fingers curl around my waist, pinning me in place. He squeezes my side in warning, reminding me we both have parts to play tonight.

Marcus's eyes drop to mine, his attention now wholly fixed on my altered face. And at this point, I don't even care if the illusion magic fails. I'd gladly let him see my face before I rip his to shreds.

"I see the Rut's affecting us all in stride this year," he says, licking his bottom lip as he drags his gaze down my neck and over my feminine curves. I swear I hear a faint growl from Sin's chest, but I tune him out, my attention solely on the Legion scum in front of me.

I slap my hand to my chest as I lean forward with laughter. "Or maybe I just don't like you."

Margalo squares her shoulders to mine, but a flicker of amusement flashes on the male's face. He thinks I'm challenging him.

"Oh, I bet we can change that by morning," Marcus says, his eyes dropping to my mouth for a moment before burning into my own again.

I feign a yawn as if the conversation now bores me. "I prefer to watch the stars without the company of pigs, thank you."

"Spend the night with me, and I'll have you seeing more than stars, honey."

My hand flies out in front of me, my index finger pointed at his leather clad chest, but I don't have time to spew my remark before Sin pushes me behind him, putting himself between me and Marcus.

"She's *claimed*," Sin growls the word, and I swear the temperature around us drops a few degrees.

No one *claims* me, but I can nearly feel the wrath emanating from the Black Art and decide to keep my mouth shut. Now is not the time to dispute him. Not in front of them.

Marcus takes a step towards him. Sin doesn't give an inch, but his hand curls into a fist at his side. He won't use magic here, not with his façade in place, but I don't doubt his hands are any less dangerous. I crane my neck to see around Sin's body. All trace of amusement has vanished from Marcus's face, and Margalo fixes Sin with the permanent scowl on her face.

Marcus licks his lips then wipes his mouth with the back of his hand. "Why don't we let the girl decide what she wants?"

"She is a *lady,* and you will treat her as such. And I think she's made it more than clear she's not interested in—"

"A lady? Is that what we're calling the whores now? I'll let you in on a secret, bud. Whores don't care who they're choking on so long as there's coin on the ta—"

Sin's fist connects with his face, an audible crunch, and Marcus's hand flies to cover his mouth and chin. When he lowers it, blood spritzes from his now crooked nose.

My mouth goes dry, desire blooming on my tongue, my eyes tracking the crimson rivulets dripping over his lips. I sink my feet into the ground, holding myself in place and biting back the urge to bury my teeth in Marcus's now red-stained neck.

Sin wraps a bronzed hand around his throat, and Margalo tries inserting herself between them, shouting threats at Sin and pushing against him, but it's useless. She might as well be chucking flower petals at Sin for all the harm she's doing to him. The others around us crowd in farther, preparing to fight should any of their Legion friends be watching from the trees.

I watch as Sin's grip tightens on his throat, almost lifting him off the ground, his next words laced with fury. "The only thing my lady will be choking on are your innards when I feed them to her."

He lets go of Marcus and takes a few steps back, shaking the blood from the hand he hit him with. Marcus presses his hand to his nose and pulls it away, noting the blood now coating his fingertips. Margalo clings to her friend, trying to force him to look at her, but he shoves her out of the way as he unknowingly approaches the Black Art. Never taking his eyes off them, Sin reaches behind himself and pushes me farther back. But unlike how Marcus thrusted Margalo away from him to get her out of his path, Sin shoves me to put distance between myself and the fight about to commence.

Thunder claps around us.

Except... it's not thunder. Eldridge, barreling through the crowd, tackles Marcus, taking them both to the ground. Margalo bares her teeth and pounds her small fists into Eldridge's back, inciting the other shifters to join in. One restrains Margalo with ease, while a few others work to separate Eldridge and the Legion fuckhead.

Blood sprays onto the grass, painting the tips the color of murder, and I wet my lips in instinct. The glamour may alter my appearance, but I don't know if it does anything to stop my faux blue irises from glowing as the sweet smell of their juices beckons for my darkness to come out and play.

Too focused on quelling the sudden thirst in my throat, I don't see as Sin turns and returns to my side until his lips are brushing the top of my ear through my hair. "Time to go, little witch."

The others are still struggling to pry Eldridge off Marcus,

whose face now appears as if he devoured a rhubarb pie with his hands bound behind his back. Eldridge can hold his own with ease, but my eyes dart to the darkened woods in the distance. The same forest Zorina disappeared into.

"I can't leave my sister. Not if there's a chance there's Legion soldiers out there."

"There's not. He only said that to prevent *that* from happening," Sin nods towards the pummeling taking place behind me.

"You're just saying that so I leave with y—Put. Me. Down."

Sin sweeps my legs out from under me and heaves me over his shoulder as if I was no more than a bag of flour.

I am *not* a bag of flour.

I smash my fists against his back like hammers, willing my magic to singe his skin, forcing him to drop me, but he continues walking, unphased. And then I feel it. The slight hum buzzing around him—he shrouded himself with a protective ward the second he picked me off the ground.

"I swear to the gods, you put me down right now or I am frying your ass the second you let me go."

Sin ignores my protests and acts as if my fists now wailing into his back are no more than drops of rain hitting his shirt, but I know that's not true. I may not be a large woman, but being punched repeatedly in the same spot has to hurt.

When we're back at the horses, he sets me on my feet and immediately holds up his hand as if to caution me from sending my fist flying into his face.

"There was blood being shed. I couldn't risk you losing control and giving away who you are. I needed to get you out of there."

My face twists into a scowl. "You listen to me. You don't know a damn thing about me or what I can and cannot control. I don't need you rushing in every time someone gets a damn papercut, and I *certainly* don't need you fighting my battles for me. That's not the first time a man has made a crude remark in my direction, and it won't be the last. But it *will* be the last time you ever stand between me and them like some godsdamned savior."

He throws his hand through his hair, sending it rippling out behind him and falling in uneven layers.

I take a step towards him and jab my finger into his stupid, hard chest. "And whatever nonsense you were spewing about *claiming me,* you can forget that too."

Sin grabs my hand and lowers it to my side, gently but with enough force I can't resist. "Whether you care to admit it to yourself or not, the second I put that heart on your pretty hip, you became mine. And I do not take kindly to others touching my things."

"I am not a thing, Singard."

"You are what I say you are," he spits, heat now flaring in his irises.

The sudden shift in his tone unsettles me, and I instantly forget whatever I was about to say. Tears burn in my eyes, and I look away. They're not tears of sadness, and I don't want him thinking his words have that effect on me. No. They're tears of rage. And as one leaps from my eye, I vow to myself that I will find a path to freedom. Never again will I be reduced to what someone else labels me as.

I untether my horse from the post and heave my leg over her as I settle into the saddle. Forcing myself to look back at Sin, I shake my head, and in a tone that could bring death to her knees, I say, "Wren. My name is Wren."

And with that, I urge my mare into a gallop, and we storm back up the hill.

He doesn't follow.

CHAPTER 21

I hate the Rut.

My temples pound like someone is beating on war drums inside my head, pieces of my knotted hair glued to my cheeks with sweat from riding home in the afternoon sun. I'm never drinking again.

The five of us have been mostly quiet—Eldridge too hungover, and Zorina and Theon too tired to be much for conversation. And I'm too pissed at Sin to even look in his direction. He hasn't uttered a single word to me all day as we make our trek back to the cabin.

As he shouldn't.

He knows I'll cut his godsdamned tongue out if he tries.

The Black Art and I are leaving at first light. Our saddle bags are packed, and I set out my clothes for tomorrow on the foot of my bed so I don't wake the others by rummaging around in my trunk. I've already said my goodbyes to my family. All except one.

I find Eldridge alone by the dying fire, watching as the final embers suffocate in the pit. He doesn't startle when I place my hand on his back. It's impossible to sneak up on any of my family with their advanced hearing.

I wrap both my arms around him from behind, my hands barely able to reach far enough to interlock my fingers against his stomach. Pressing my forehead to his back, I inhale his signature scent—worn-in leather and spice. He's tense under my touch, but after a moment, he blows out an exaggerated sigh and reaches up to hold my forearm against him. We stay like this for a long while, neither of us moving, neither of us speaking.

We don't need to.

We never have.

✤

"If we keep riding, we'll make it before the brunt of the storm," Sin says, eyes on the clouds now darkened and fattened with rain.

We're still a few hours out from Scarwood, and that's counting on us not stopping to relieve ourselves or our horses. And given we've only stopped one time several hours ago, and for a few minutes at that, we need to break.

"The horses are winded—we can stop at the next river."

"No time," he grumbles under his breath.

I run my hand along my mare's neck and give her a few gentle pats. She whinnies in response, but the sound is strained. "If we don't break them for water and rest, they'll collapse, and then none of us are making it back before the storm. We're stopping."

"They're bred for endurance—they'll be fine," he snips back as if empathy for the steeds is nothing but a nuisance.

"Your compassion for the comfort and lives of others is inspiring, Your Grace. Truly."

As if on cue, rushing water burbles in our ears from the woods at our right. I tug on the reins and steer the mare towards the running water, and she changes direction eagerly.

"Get back on the road, *witch.*"

I ignore him, and he curses under his breath behind me.

"If you are foolish enough to stop with that storm brewing on the horizon, I will not have an ounce of regret leaving you here to wilt in the woods."

"Likewise, Your Grace. Don't expect me to stop when I pass your sorry ass on the road next to your collapsed horse," I call over my shoulder.

A stream of obscenities chase after me, but I ignore them all, my mare and I ducking into the tree line.

She eagerly laps at the water as I rummage through the saddle bag and pull out some apples I stowed away for her. I scoop my canteen into the river, down the entire contents, then fill it again and tuck it away for later. Dropping to my knees, I lean forward and splash water onto my face and rub vigorous circles on my cheeks, ridding my skin of the collected dirt and sweat.

My lungs turn to ice.

I want to believe it's from the frigid water I dumped into my belly too quickly, but the hairs standing on the back of my neck warns me otherwise. I jump to my feet, swiping the dagger from my thigh and spinning around, ready to drive it into the gut of whoever pussyfoots behind me.

A hand vices around my wrist, halting the blade mid-swing.

"For someone who faults me for lacking compassion, you certainly have an affinity for violence, little witch." Sin releases my hand, apparently confident I'm not going to thrust it through his chest.

Foolish man.

I push past him, feed my horse the plump red apples, and pull out a few more for Sin's steed while he refills his canteen in the river.

"I was quite content to wilt alone, Blackheart." I scratch Sin's dark brown horse under his chin, and he nods his large head in approval.

"The only reason I came back was because you have demonstrated a pattern of luring in Legion soldiers, and I'm not in the mood to grind Legion skulls into dust today."

"Or feed me their innards?" I ask, throwing his words from the Rut back at him. I'm still furious with him for throwing himself between me and Marcus like I was a doll being played with too roughly. But I would be lying to myself if it didn't stoke a different feeling in me too—one more complicated and far more dangerous than fury—watching the Black Art threaten someone in my honor.

But I wouldn't dream of letting him know that.

"Keep defying orders, and it will be *your* innards I leave for the vultures."

I move to the side of his horse, offering a few pats and adjusting his saddle bag. "Charming as ever, Your Grace. Pray tell—do you engage all your prisoners in such meaningful conversation?"

He splashes water on his face and runs his wet hands through his long hair, the backs of his shoulders pulled tight under his fitted black shirt. *Does he have all his clothes tailored a size too small to show off his muscular physique?* Knowing the Black Art's taste for arrogance, it would not surprise me.

"I think we'd both be more content if you refrained from opening your mouth at all, little—"

Thunder claps above us like two boulders hurtling into one another. But even that's not loud enough to mask the breath that whooshes from my lips as Sin's horse plants a hoof into my rib cage. I'm on the ground a second later, my hand pressed to my left side, my ears barely recognizing the sound of both horses fleeing as the thunder quakes the ground and lightning strikes close by.

He's on me immediately, prying my hand away to assess the damage. At least that's what I think he's doing. Maybe he's using my vulnerability to shove his sword through my chest instead.

"Shh, Wren, it's okay. I have you, I have you."

For a second, I wonder why he's shushing me, and then I realize those strangled whimpers I'm hearing are falling from *my* lips. Sliding a hand under my knees and another under my shoulders, Sin lifts me off the ground in one gentle sweep. I don't protest. I couldn't if I wanted to.

The pain is blinding.

I turn my head inward so my forehead rests against the smooth planes of his chest. Oddly enough, the gentle rocking as he carries me through the woods is soothing. Or rather, it would be if the rain wasn't now pelting us with enough force to leave bruises.

"The horses. I'm sorry—I didn't mean for..."

"Don't talk, you'll only aggravate the break. The horses are trained to find their way back to the castle. It's only you we need to worry about right now."

I nod against his chest, unsure if he can see it but he'll feel my hair scratching against him with the vertical movement. Time eludes me. I'm not sure if it's been minutes or hours since Sin scooped me up as if I weighed no more than a sack of potatoes and traipsed through the tangled woods. Fire pokers prod at my side and I force myself to exhale in sharp pants through my lips, the pain too great to take anything more than shallow breaths. Tears sting my eyes and I bury my face farther into his chest, notes of cedar and peppercorn washing over me.

My eyes jolt open as Sin kneels and lowers me to a soft patch of grass.

He presses something cold and smooth to my lips. "Open up, love."

I don't know why—maybe I hit my head when I fell—but I part my lips without objection and let him pour a vile liquid down my throat. When the contents are empty, he pulls out a second bottle from his pocket and dumps it down his own gullet.

The potions. He's reverting our appearances.

He slides his hands under me, lifts me against his chest again, and continues on his way.

"I can walk," I mutter lazily, the bitter taste of the tonic clearing the fog in my head.

"We're almost there," he answers but doesn't slow to set me on my feet.

"Where are we going?"

"There's a military outpost not far from where the horses left us stranded. We'll commandeer a tent for the night and take one of their horses back in the morning."

Explains why he reverted our appearances. I doubt kingdom soldiers would give up a tent for anyone other than the Black Art himself.

"Does this mean I'm not a cute brunette anymore?" I ask with eyes closed, still focusing on taking steadying breaths to keep myself from hollering my way through the pain.

In no doubt an effort to distract me from the crushed bone that was once my rib, he lowers his lips to my ear and says, "I prefer blondes anyway."

The Black Art calls for wrapping tape and whiskey before ducking inside the military tent and laying me on the bed.

His hands are on the hem of my tunic immediately, grabbing the fabric and sliding it up my—

"Stop," I choke through the pain.

His hands halt immediately. "Wren, I need to look at it."

A man dressed in kingdom armor appears in the tent's entrance; tape, a bottle of amber liquid, and some balled up clothes in his hands. He sets them on the bedside table and waits for Sin to dismiss him, which he promptly does, his green eyes never leaving mine.

I push myself into a sitting position, dangling my legs over the side of the bed, and wince as I gingerly press my hand to my side.

"Your clothes are soaked—you need to get out of them anyway."

"And you think I'm just going to let you be the one to take them off?" I scoff.

He growls under his breath. "You must have hit your head harder than I thought if you think I'd ever have interest in *that* with *you*."

"Hmm. As far as I see it, only one of us is trying to strip the clothes off the other."

Exhaling sharply, he throws his hand through his hair and turns his back to me. I stand and face away from him, grabbing my shirt and—

"*Fuck,*" I wince, unable to bite back the pain that lashes through me as I try to lift my tunic.

He's at my rear a second later, hands balling the fabric at

the base of my tunic, his knuckles grazing my bare skin. He doesn't lift it, waiting a beat to see if I will refuse his help again. Shoving down my pride, I dip my chin in the slightest of nods, and Sin carefully slides my top the rest of the way up and over my head.

I suck in a breath as his fingers brush the ties of my bodice.

"I need it off," he says hurriedly, but his hands pause, waiting for my consent.

I nod again.

Sin undoes the ties of my bodice with impressive speed, and a wave of heat rushes to my face as I wonder how he became so practiced in the art of getting women out of their undergarments. The thin piece of clothing falls open, revealing my back to him.

Chilled air nips at my spine, and he yanks a blanket off the bed and drapes it over my shoulders before slowly lifting my left arm by the elbow. He presses the tips of his fingers where it looks like an ink pot spilled onto my side, and when they suddenly vanish from my skin, I shiver as the cold quickly rushes to settle where the warmth of his hands had been.

A loud ripping sound startles me from behind, and I look over my shoulder just as Sin tears off a length of the tape with his teeth. "I'll have Anika tend to you the minute we return. The rib is cracked. Wrapping it will help for now."

While mages possess the ability to heal wounds and injury —mending broken bones is best left to those trained in the art of healing and bone setting. This is a job for Anika—the castle's designated healer.

Sin presses the tape to my bruised side and carefully wraps it under my other arm and across the top of my waist. The backs of his knuckles graze the undersides of my breasts as he pulls the tape across my front with each wrap. I refuse to be embarrassed. I felt enough of that when his horse knocked me on my ass in front of him.

Desperate to distract myself from the situation at hand, I say, "This wouldn't have happened had you left me out there like you so boldly declared you were going to." After all, it was *his* horse that decided to paint a hoof-shaped bruise on my side.

"This wouldn't have happened if you hadn't insisted we dismount," he snaps. He tugs the tape a little harder but lets up when I wince at the pain.

"It was critical for the horses we did. I would trade a broken rib for a living horse any day, Your Grace."

He secures the remaining length of tape, and lowers my arms to my sides. I startle when he presses callused fingers to my back and traces the familiar jagged pattern that runs from my right shoulder blade to the left side of my lower back. It doesn't hurt—the wound is long scarred over—but something about the Black Art seeing the failure I wear on my back hardens my bones to diamond.

"What happened?" His voice is low, and I can't tell if that's genuine concern or mere curiosity in his tone.

"Cathal." I don't elaborate—I don't need to. I'm sure the Black Art is more than familiar with what the aftermath of a lashing looks like.

Sin is quiet for an extended beat, then drops his hand from my marred flesh. I'm certain the Black Art has earned more than his fair share of scars over the years, but kingdom healers can erase those kinds of marks with ease. With a family comprised of four adult transcendents and a fellow mage sister, we could have healed the scars on my back also, but I never wanted to. As soon as Cathal's whip bit into my skin, it birthed a memory that no amount of healing magic could erase. Removing the scarring only seemed like trying to cover up an experience I would never be able to unlive.

Sin clears his throat. "He is too valuable to kill right now, but he won't be forever. And when that time comes, Wren, it'll be in your name I rip out his callous heart."

His words stun me into silence for a moment, and I almost wonder if my ears betrayed me. Singard Kilbreth—reaper of souls and darkness incarnate—vowed to slaughter a blood-witch's enemy in her honor.

And I fucking hate my body for reacting the way it does to the sound of my name in his low, graveled voice.

I definitely hit my head.

"I'll heat you a bath. Your skin is freezing."

He calls for the large tub to be filled, and the soldier who escorted us to the tent begins bringing in buckets of water and pouring them in the basin. The tent definitely belongs to an officer as it is decently spacious and has an off-ground bed, private bath, and a couple small tables.

Sin returns to the bedside table and pulls his soaked shirt over his head, revealing a deep bronzed back, sculpted with muscle.

Nothing that lethal should be so beautiful.

The tips of his long hair brush the center of his spine, and he picks up the clean shirt provided, the layers of muscle flexing in his arms and shoulders as he pulls it over his head. He picks up the dry pair of trousers, and my breath catches in my throat.

As if thinking better of it, he slings them over his arm and walks to the bath, now filled with water. He places his hand to the side of the tub, and a moment later, steam rises in beckoning tendrils.

"I'll give you some privacy."

He takes a swig from the whiskey bottle, then ducks out of

the tent, and I don't waste time disrobing out of the rest of my sodden clothing and slipping into the bath. The water instantly floods relief to my chilled bones, and Sin's wrap job actually has reduced the pain in my side significantly.

He returns before I'm finished, now wearing the dry trousers, and merely shoots me a passing glance before he walks past, pulls off his shirt, and flops into the bed.

The *one* bed.

"Am I really meant to sleep on the floor?" I ask in disbelief. Just an hour ago, he promised to rip Cathal to pieces in my name, and now he expects me to sleep on the floor while he lies in comfort?

"There's plenty of room—I promise I don't bite. Well, actually..."

I *hear* the smile in his voice, and my hand instinctively caresses my collarbone where he had bitten me the night of the Rut.

"You honestly expect me to lie next to you?"

"You seemed to have no qualms sleeping with Eldridge at your side."

I scoff audibly at his suggestion.

"Though, I wonder if you would allow him into your bed as eagerly now that he has another woman's scent on his tongue," he muses.

"Do not speak on which you know so little about, *Your Grace*," I snip, muddling his title with condescension. Tears burn at my eyelids, and I quickly blink them away.

He doesn't respond, and when the last of the anger bleeds from my bones, I step out of the bath and dress in the dry clothes left out for me—a spare men's shirt and pants that swallow me in extra fabric. I eye Sin in the bed—the blankets tucked under his bare arms, his chest rising and falling in slow, steady breaths. He's asleep, or at least, he appears to be.

There really isn't another surface to sleep on; no spare chairs, or even a bedroll occupy the tent. And with my cracked rib, sleeping on the floor isn't a wise choice. Careful to not overextend my side, I lie on the bed, over the covers. There's not a chance in Hell I'm climbing *under* the blankets and risking waking up with our bodies tangled together in our sleep.

For a split second, his breathing pauses, and I'm certain he's aware I've slipped into bed next to him. I doubt anyone has ever managed to sneak up on the Black Art, even in sleep.

His breathing settles back into a rhythmic cadence, and just as I think I'll never be able to sleep next to my sworn enemy, all thought escapes me, and I fall into a slumber more peaceful than death.

CHAPTER 22

I t's well past first light when I wake in the empty bed.
Pain spears through the crack in my rib as I roll over,
sending the memory of yesterday's embarrassing incident to the front of my mind. I ease my legs over the side of the
bed and out from the warm blanket.

The blanket I distinctly remember sleeping on *top of* last
night.

I may live to see a million suns and still not understand the
Black Art. Threatening the very air I breathe one second and
sheltering me from the morning chill the next. And letting me
sleep hours past the time I'm sure he would have preferred to
leave, having seen his urgency to return to Scarwood
yesterday.

I find him outside the tent, shoving the rest of our dried
clothes into the saddle bag attached to a large ebony horse. Sin
scans me in a single glance, his eyes hovering on my side as if
he could assess the damage there through my loose-fitting
shirt.

Neither of us bother with forced pleasantries, but when he
waves me forward to lift me onto the horse, careful of my
broken rib, I don't object.

"Front or back?" he asks with a sly grin.

I shoot him a disapproving glower as I step up to the horse. "Back," I answer, not liking the thought of riding injured with him at my rear.

Sin lifts me to the back of the saddle, then hops onto the steed with the speed and grace one only achieves through experience. "You're full of surprises, little witch. I would have thought you'd prefer me behind you," he hums darkly.

"In your dreams, Blackheart."

Sin cracks the reins, and I wrap my hands around his waist as the horse he commandeered takes off in a violent gallop, his soft laughter lost in the thundering of hooves.

We're only a few hours out from the castle, having made it most of the way yesterday before the storm left us stranded in the downpour. The skies are calm this morning, but the wind on my face stings like a horde of bees. I press my cheek to his back, his large body a perfect barrier to the assaulting wind, and the smell of steel and cedar and sword oils wraps itself around me, tangling in my hair and flirting with my tongue. As much as I may hate to admit it, his scent is mouthwatering.

If Sin takes problem with my hands clutched around him, he doesn't vocalize it. He's probably too lost in his thoughts of who's next on his ever-growing hit list to even realize how tightly I'm forced to cling to him. And I can't help but wonder just how high my name is on that list.

Scarwood's southern courtyard is a tempest of armor and steel. Rows of soldiers speckle the open training grounds, sparring and running drills under the watchful eye of the moon. While I may have sneered at it before, tonight, satisfaction blooms in my gut as I watch them quickstep to their metallic songs. The better prepared Sin's armies, the higher my chances of rescuing Cosmina.

Ships of towering heights rear up from the castle's moat, the armored soldiers training in the shadow of their black and gray sails. Beyond the water barrier, my eyes barely make out the edge of Spiritwood, the woods that enclose the castle's east and connect to Autumnhelm at the bridge.

As promised, Sin escorted me to Anika as soon as we returned, and she quickly repaired the break. After a much-needed wash in the bathhouse and a hearty meal from the kitchen, I decided I could no longer delay the inevitable.

I scan for Sin across the training grounds and find him almost immediately. It isn't the long black hair or burnt umber skin that catches my eye. It's the darkness that hovers around him, moving as he does and making way as his sword slices through the night.

Even the shadows cower in his wake.

Aldred prowls between the rows, surveying the armies he commands and stopping to correct mistakes. Mistakes that could be the difference between killing and being killed on an unforgiving battlefield. He pauses next to Ileana where the Black Hand duels with a male partner much larger than herself, and they both lower their weapons at once. Aldred adjusts her stance, shifting the position of her hips and shoulders, then has her raise the sword in her slender hand once more.

My stare darts back to Sin as he extends a hand to his partner, heaving him off the ground and back to his feet. He wears the same steel plate over his bare chest and back, his long, sculpted arms exposed on either side. Molded to his thick thighs are black leather fighting pants—pants that leave little to the imagination of the powerful, muscled legs beneath them.

I call out his title, my voice falling from my lips softer than I meant and out of place amidst the tense surroundings. Even the air out here is a honed knife, sharp enough to cut through flesh should one take a careless step.

Even under the armored plate, I see the tensing of his shoulders when he hears my voice, and he rolls his neck once before turning to face me.

I swallow my gasp.

It has only been a few hours since we parted ways, but the chilling intensity of him clad in his silver armor nearly knocks me back a step. His eyes, bright as stars in the midnight sky, widen for a mere second before his usual hard stare slams down. He assesses me from head to toe, either checking me for lingering damage or scanning for new hidden weapons on my body.

"We need to speak. Privately," I add.

He shoots a quick glance around us. "How private?"

"Very."

His dark eyebrow threatens to touch his hairline, but after a quick read of the nerves surely written on my face, Sin nods and turns to dismiss his partner as he sheathes the weapon at his hip.

I follow him through the double doors of the southern entrance and up a winding staircase. My feet scramble to take twice as many steps as him to keep up with his long legs as he ventures down a long corridor that spills into the wing that contains his study.

Sin stops at a door with an arched threshold and presses his palm to the wood to unlock it before pushing it open and stepping inside. When I enter behind him, a sudden rush of heat floods my cheeks as I take in what room we now stand in.

His bedroom.

A massive bed with a towering head and footboard of black

stained wood juts from the wall to my left, a golden blanket draped over the red sheets. A couple armoires crafted from the same ebony wood line the opposite wall, and thick, pewter rugs are thrown tastefully about the polished stone flooring. A large chair made of what appears to be buttery soft black leather sits in the far corner, next to a decorative table with a decanter filled with a garnet-colored mead. The walls are devoid of art, merely painted with the same gray and silvery patterns as the rest of the castle's interior walls. A set of double doors on the far wall open to a balcony, and I glimpse a few plants adorned with simple, decorative pots dotting the outside space.

"You said we needed privacy, and I can't think of a more private place in the entire keep. They know not to disturb me here."

The ice in his words suggests a few may have made that mistake before and would surely never make it again. Sin leans against one of the armoires, this one having a wide mirror attached to the side of it, and crosses his arms. An invitation for me to begin.

Suddenly feeling awkward standing in the center of the room, now too aware of myself and not knowing what to do with my hands, I clasp them together and pin them against my waist.

"You never asked what I learned when I tried locating my sister back at the cabin."

He shrugs a rounded shoulder. "Why would it be of any importance to me where they're keeping her? It's not as if I was going to escort you to a Legion camp so you could entangle us both in your mess."

I scoff at his blatant disregard for my sister's predicament. "You needn't worry about that, Your Grace, because I do not know where she is, and even if I had been successful in locating her whereabouts, I would not require an escort, and surely not from the likes of *you*." The words spill from my mouth with frustrated haste.

"If you were unable to perform a simple locator spell, perhaps I've overestimated your power."

"I was perfectly able to, *you arrogant asshole,* but they're hiding her location with a cloaking spell."

He crosses the distance between us in one step of his long legs, his large hand cupping the entirety of my throat as he pushes my shoulders against the wall. I claw at his hands, and his grip tightens, restricting my airway almost completely.

"Such a filthy mouth you have. I'm beginning to think you enjoy my hands around your throat, little witch."

I swallow hard under his too-large hands, willing my pulse to stop pounding wildly under his fingers and failing.

He inhales deeply, his nostrils flaring as a gleam of what can only be described as pure sin flashes in his forested eyes. "It certainly smells like you do."

Lifting my foot up, I slam it down on his with as much force as I can muster through my now darkening vision. He chuckles softly like my assault was nothing more than a feather quill tickling his foot, but he releases me, taking a few steps back.

"You're an animal," I seethe, rubbing my neck as if I could massage away the imprint of Sin's callused fingertips, and sucking in a deep breath of air.

He smirks. "I've been called worse."

"*As I was saying,* they've hidden her with a cloaking spell which means they don't want me finding her. And if they don't want me coming to them, it must mean they intend to bring her to me."

"How convenient for them then, given they know precisely where you are."

"I suspect Legion plans on bringing Cosmina to Scarwood as leverage to try and persuade me to turn on you, on the kingdom. To offer me her life in exchange for the taking of yours."

His hands clench slightly where they grip his opposite elbows, his arms still folded tightly across his chest. "And what do you plan on doing if your suspicions are correct?"

Sin's stare is everywhere—my eyes, my mouth, my hands —watching every movement and burning holes in my flesh all the places he drags his heated gaze. Where I rely on my gift to detect when I'm being manipulated, Sin uses years of experience sniffing out traitors of the throne.

I blow out a deep breath, knowing now is not the time to let my pride get in the way. For once, speaking openly about who and *what* I am may be the best course of action to getting what I want. What I need.

"I have been hiding from Legion for *years*. Trying to prevent them from using me as a weapon and forcing me into becoming the monster I've never desired to be. I am telling you this... because I don't want to hurt anyone. But I will do what I must to keep my sister alive. She is not like me, she is *good*.

"And if they hurt her... I don't know that I can hold myself back from slaughtering every last one of them. I hesitated telling you because I feared you may have resorted to chaining me in iron and locking me back down there. I am asking for your help, Sin... help me help her. Whatever you must do with me afterwards... just let me save her first."

His eyes dart between both of mine, scanning for distrust I'm sure, though his expression reveals nothing of his thoughts. Sin's face is a calculating front, running through every possible scenario and outcome of what I have just suggested.

Tension rolls off him in such heaps, I can nearly taste it on my tongue. Keeping his eyes locked on mine, he asks, "With this new discovery, should I assume you are willing to swear fealty to me and fight alongside us?" A careful question.

I give an even more careful answer. "I will fight with you against Legion," I vow. "In order to free my sister and eradicate their army as Legion will always be a threat to my family because of me. I will not, however, fight alongside you if you go forward in waging war on transcendents."

A flicker of dark amusement tugs up the corner of his lips. "Will you fight *against* me then? If I do declare that war?"

I snatch my bottom lip with my teeth as I mull over my answer, choosing my words with care. "I will do what I must to protect the ones I love, and the ones who are helpless."

Sin's footsteps echo through the room as he takes purposeful steps to close the distance between us, his eyes never leaving mine. Holding as still as a deer caught in a wolf's sights, my feet flex inside my boots, ready to dodge if he decides I am not worth the risk and attempts to put me down. He stops when his body is mere inches from mine, the tips of his inky hair grazing the tops of my breasts.

"That's a bold statement to make to your Black Art," he purrs, no threat in his words, but his tone cold enough I don't risk moving just yet. I plant the soles of my boots against the stone floor as his fevered stare threatens to knock me backwards. And then with a note of indifference, he says, "You begin training tomorrow."

"Training? Do you doubt my capability?" I ask incredulously.

"Not with magic," he allows, "but how are you with a blade?"

I'm decent with knives and have sparred with swords before, but only in a casual setting with my adoptive siblings, and certainly not enough to hold my own on a battlefield. He swipes the answer written on my face with an arrogant smile.

"Your law says I should be killed because my magic is too powerful, and you're concerned I don't know how to wield a piece of metal?"

He inches a half step closer to me, shrinking the already too close distance between us. "The first rule of combat—physical or otherwise—" his arm cuts the air, and before I can track the movement, the unmistakable chill of metal grazes the underside of my chin. His dagger flirts with the delicate skin of my throat—the knife he pulled from somewhere hidden in those fighting leathers, "is to never rely on one weapon. Even magic," he murmurs, his voice a velvet whisper in the room.

I don't jerk away. I remain a statue as my body internally ignites with the surge of my collective, ready to weaponize myself at a moment's notice. The Black Art's lips part in a rapacious smile, his tongue gliding over the fronts of his top set of teeth, and he lowers his blade, returning it to its hidden holster with the same swiftness he had drawn it. I don't need to imagine the damage he could do with the *sword* that still hangs at his waist.

"You make your point," I spit.

He chuckles and runs a hand through his hair, sending the layers falling down his back, his mood seemingly lighter now.

"But I'm confused. Why are you so willing to let me fight with you? You're not worried at all I'll try to turn on you the moment they bring her here?"

"You underestimate me," he says, smoldering heat still simmering in his eyes.

"No. I think you underestimate *me*."

River had said Sin lacked confidence, that he could stand to learn some things from me, but I think it is precisely his overbearing arrogant attitude that has him dismissing the threat I pose so easily.

He shakes his head. "You're wrong. I have thought a great

deal of things about you, but dismissing your power has not been one of them. But if you were going to try to kill me, you would have done it already."

"I could say the same about you," I challenge. "I didn't know Legion was holding my sister captive before. How do you know that hasn't changed things for me?"

"You just gave me an unbeatable weapon to use against them. Perhaps that has changed things for me," he suggests with a smirk as wicked as it is devastating.

I command my body to move again, but pause at the door before leaving. I study his face as I sift through his collective with my own, feeling his immense pride and amusement blossoming in my gut. Amused that I have now willingly pledged to fight alongside him, ensuring a victory for the kingdom I loathe.

Bastard.

His mouth widens into a tight-lipped grin as if he plucks the thought right from my head.

"I don't trust you," I contend, mainly to try to snatch that smile straight from his lips. But it only widens farther, and a new trail of fear slithers around my bones when he answers.

"Good. Because you really, *really* shouldn't."

CHAPTER 23

I have never worn armor a day in my life, though I suppose the linen gambeson vest River brought me isn't exactly *armor*, but still a protective layer between myself and the weapons we will wield today. I turn in the mirror—to the left, then to the right—trying to find a stance I can rest in that doesn't make me feel completely ridiculous.

Convinced no such stance exists, I head to the dining room sporting the ridiculous navy linen covering and fix myself a plate from the breakfast options spread out on top of the long, elegant table. After gobbling down a generous portion of ham and porridge, I find Sin in the southern courtyard.

He's once again clad in nothing but a steel armor chest plate and leather swordsman's pants. I steal a glance at those pants, wondering what sort of hidden weapons he stashed in there this morning. The Black Art grabs an arrow from the quiver strapped to his back and nocks it against the bowstring with fluid grace. He takes a mere second to aim before releasing the tension on the string, sending the arrow hurtling to bury dead center into the cloth target.

"Knives, swords, arrows—do you actually enjoy being this vicious, or does it just come with the title?" I ask as I approach him.

Sin turns to me, an easy grin on his mouth, apparently finding comedy in the question I didn't fully ask half-heartedly. "Don't forget magic that can crush your insides." He winks and gives me a quick once over, assessing the fit of my vest.

I shuffle my arms uncomfortably. "Are you planning on cutting me in half if I make a mistake?" I ask, gesturing towards the protective covering I was told to put on this morning.

"One—I don't need a sword to split you in half. Two—it's not to protect you from *me*. It's to protect you from your own novice mistakes." He unslings his bow and quiver, dropping them to the grass, and picks up the broom laying at the target's base.

"I've used a sword before," I say.

It isn't a lie. We kept a few in the cabin to protect ourselves against outsiders. Any method of defense that didn't require my family members to shift skins to protect themselves was the better option. Should someone break in, a clean slice through the ribs would be the preferred method, although I know Eldridge would be itching to shift to use a more... predatory approach. Admittedly, the swords were too big for my stature and always felt cumbersome and unbalanced in my hand. I am significantly better with my bow or my knives, but nothing has ever compared to my magic.

"Wielding a sword and killing with one are not the same," he says, tossing me the broom.

I catch it and turn it over in my hand. It is a standard house broom with a long wooden shaft and a bundling of birch twigs at one end.

"Ah yes, the ol' *sweep them to death* maneuver. I can't wait to learn it."

Sin throws me a sideways glance and laughs—*actually*

laughs—before shaking it off and drawing his sword. His very *real* sword. "I would be a fool to trust you not to kill yourself with one before I've taught you a thing or two."

Sin positions himself next to me, a mere few inches of space between our shoulders, and demonstrates how to grip the hilt—or in my case, the broom handle. He models how to adjust my grip depending on the direction I'm swinging and shows me the basics of a half, full, and horizontal cut, and a thrust lunge. He is surprisingly patient as I struggle to swing and step at the same time, offering corrections and repositioning me.

"Loosen your grip," he tells me for what must be the hundredth time.

I shoot him an exasperated look, convinced I *am* holding it looser than before, and he shakes his head. Sin steps up behind me, pressing his chest against my back, and loops his arms under mine to grab my hand with his on the hilt. His proximity pricks the hairs on the back of my neck and has my hand clenching the sword *much* tighter now as he forcibly pries my fingers from the handle and repositions them so the weapon balances more evenly in my grip. Satisfied with my new stance, he backs away, and I exhale sharply.

The light practice I had done at home was recess compared to training under the Black Art's watchful stare—eyes that didn't miss a single mistake—and I make a lot. At some point, I forget to feel silly waving my broom around, too focused on coordinating my steps with my lunges and my hand positioning.

When he's confident I have learned the bare basics, Sin invites me to spar with him. He slows his pace down as much as he can without tripping himself, allowing me to get the feel of striking with the broom, and what it feels like to have those strikes deflected. I practice adjusting my approach as he blocks my thrusts, and maintaining my balance as I shift my weight between my feet.

Relief washes through me when he says we can stop, the moon having relieved the sun an hour ago. The broom must only weigh a fraction of his weapon's weight, but my arms burn at keeping it held out in front of me for so long. Sin wipes the back of his hand across his forehead, and I wonder if his muscled arms feel even a twinge of soreness.

"You did well," he offers, collecting his belongings.

"Bet you didn't know how deadly I was with a broom," I respond coolly, pulling another chuckle from him.

"Your body will ache tomorrow. Take a bath now to soak the muscles, and they won't hurt as bad when you wake up."

I nod, not wanting to admit my arms started burning hours ago.

"Meet me here tomorrow. We'll break from this and focus on casting."

"Good, because this has done a number to my confidence," I mumble, handing him back the broom, then turning to head towards the bathhouse.

"Little witch."

I pause and look over my shoulder, just as he motions with his chin for me to follow him. "This way."

My feet fall in line beside his, my eyebrow spiking when I look at him with a silent question.

"There's a collection of oils and herbs in the private bath. It's only ever occupied when guests are visiting, but as we have no visitors today, it's yours to use."

"Oh," I say, surprised at the Black Art's display of... kindness? Not quite, but almost.

Sin escorts me to a small structure with vining green plants climbing up the sides and across the slanted roof. He pushes open the door and heads to a large cabinet along the wall, while I take in the small steaming pool in the center of the bathhouse. "Undress and get in. I need to read these labels..." he says, his hands fumbling over the small glass jars of assorted herbs, flowers, and oils, each with handwritten scrawl on the side detailing their medicinal properties.

With his attention on the collection of jars in front of him, I disrobe and step into the bathing chamber large enough to fit a few bodies. The warmth wrings some of the soreness from my arms instantly, and a deep sigh falls from my lips.

"Do I *want* to know what you're moaning about back there; in quarters that are not your own I might add?"

"I was *not* moaning!" I snap. "The water just feels nice, alright? Not all of us have honed our bodies into... well, that," I say, glancing at where he stands, his bare abdomen visible on either side of the armored plate. "Us normal people actually feel pain, Blackheart."

"I would think you've come to resent that nickname now that it's been so adoringly marked on you."

I flash a vulgar gesture to his back, and his shoulders rise and fall ever so slightly, as if he felt the expression aimed at him. My eyes dart to the small black heart permanently inked into the skin of my hip, and bile coats my mouth.

"I understand why you marked me, Your Grace. If I had someone as wonderfully talented and powerful as myself in my company, I would wish to claim them as my own too. Now only if I knew someone as powerful as myself... hmm... maybe in the next life."

"You spill a lot of shit from that pretty mouth for someone who wouldn't survive fifteen seconds in combat without your magic. You made that perfectly clear today."

"And you're awfully arrogant for someone who doesn't know basic herbal properties. Am I going to have to wait for

205

you to finish reading every label in the cabinet, or can you just fetch the lavender and calendula on your left?"

His hands snatch the two jars from the cabinet, the one with the dried lavender for soothing muscles and the other with the rich orange tones of dried calendula petals, ideal for reducing swelling. Sin sprinkles a generous amount of the herbs into the water and finishes with a few drops of oil from a tiny, dark bottle.

"Thank you."

Keeping his eyes fixed on the water now clouded from the additions, he says, "Just wanted to make sure you didn't have any excuses when I knock you on your little round ass tomorrow."

I smack the water, assaulting him with a hundred tiny droplets that he sidesteps with a wave of his arm, the shadow of a smirk on his face.

"Sure, we'll see about that."

His eyes never wandering to where I sit naked in the steaming water, he heads for the door. "I don't make idle threats, love."

⁂

Alone in the private bath, my mind drifts to thoughts of tomorrow when we'll be dueling with magic in place of swords.

That will be interesting.

Enjoy your caster's high, Sin had said. He knew the effect expelling that amount of magic the night I confronted him would have on me—the purely physical reaction it would stir in me, and the heat it would send beelining straight to my thighs.

I dueled with Eldridge a lot. He practiced conjuring his shields around him, while I worked on my casting, never enough to shatter his shields completely, but enough to build up the muscle memory of grabbing my collective and willing it away from me, again and again. Naturally, the caster's high would follow, and if Eldridge hadn't seen me at my lowest point, maybe I would have acted on those instincts.

But he *had* seen me—when I was so weak, so feeble. And now I don't know if he could ever see me as something different, as *someone* different. Could he see me as the woman I wanted to be now?

A woman who was shatterproof.

My thoughts wander to the feelings I often felt when Eldridge and I would duel and the magic that would coerce my body into betraying me. I slip a hand under the water and find myself slick with the thought of him.

The anger that flashed in his eyes when someone dared to speak ill of me... the feel of his bulky arms wrapped around me on the coldest of nights. His possessiveness...

My mind drifts to the night of the Rut when Eldridge interfered after... after Sin decked a man for his crude suggestion. And then slung me over his shoulder as if I was nothing more than a belonging.

His belonging.

I slip a finger inside and this time, the sound that escapes my lips *is* a moan. And for the briefest of moments, before I come to my senses and vanish the thought completely, I wish the Black Art was around to hear it.

CHAPTER 24

The sage tunic and gray leggings I brought from home are far more comfortable than the gambeson vest I wore the day prior.

I don't need armor today. Not when the weapons we'll be wielding come from inside us, rather than from the steel sheathed at our hips. And perhaps the thought is foolish—*definitely* foolish—but something tells me the Black Art wouldn't actually hurt me. At least not so long as we're fighting on the same side. Once Legion is eradicated...

I braid my snowy blonde hair into a thick rope and head to the dining hall to nourish myself before what is likely to be another exhaustive day of training. The assortment of food does not disappoint, and I help myself to a serving of eggs, ham, and a few cubes of fruit before washing it down with a couple glasses of water. When I finish, I gather my dishes to drop them in the wash basin but pause when I hear hushed voices bickering from the kitchen.

"Do you feel it's the right thing to do?" River asks, her gentle voice pained with concern.

The low growl that responds is undeniably Sin's. "It doesn't matter how I feel about it."

An annoyed sigh—River's. "Ludicrous! It does matter. Your word is law—if you don't want to do something, then bloody say you aren't doing it. You're the Black Art, Singard, *you* were chosen. It's about time you start acting like it."

"That's exactly what I'm doing," he snaps. "I'm protecting my land."

A long pause passes between them, and I hold my breath, still clutching the dirty dishes in my hands.

"But are you protecting your people?" River finally asks, her tone rhetorical.

Sin lets out an exasperated sigh, and I can almost *hear* his hand running through his hair, a habit I've noticed the Black Art favors when stressed.

"We have company," he grumbles.

And now I feel it.

The pit of my stomach tightens like sodden clothing being wrung out to dry—the tethering spell reacting to the proximity of its creator. Sin feels it too then, the tugging, if he knew I was here despite my complete silence.

Swallowing my pride, I round the corner into the kitchen. Sin gives me a quick once over, his expression unreadable, before turning and leaving through the door at the back of the kitchen.

"Is everything alright?" I ask the castle's housekeeper.

River shakes her head and tosses her long, scarlet braid over her shoulder. "I'm not so sure it is. That boy—that *damned* boy—he wants to do the right thing, but he's as stubborn as his father. Maybe more so. And it makes me furious because he knows better. He *knows* what is right." She excuses herself and hurries out to the hall, leaving a trail of anger and annoyance behind with every thudding step.

Leaving through the same door as Sin, a private entrance

for the kitchen staff, I spill into the eastern courtyard. I scan the mass of uniformed men scattered around the barracks but find no sign of the dark warlord.

Fine. If I'm to be branded like property, I might as well use it to my advantage. I close my eyes and focus on the permanent knot tethered deep in the pits of my stomach—the anchor Sin cast there when he marked me with his signature black heart.

Angling my body one way then the next, I follow the tugging of the invisible rope to the edge of the Spiritwood Forest, the portion of the woods inside Scarwood's impressive barrier walls. I find him facing a small pond, the water a glass mirror reflecting a kaleidoscope of forest colors.

I cross my arms. "Avoiding me already, and I haven't even dueled you into embarrassment yet."

He doesn't flinch at my voice, as if he already sensed my arrival. "Just testing your ability to find me through that tether is all."

I don't need to read his collective to hear the lie in his words. Whatever he and River were discussing earlier has clearly upset him. "I apologize for overhearing earlier. It was not my intention to eavesdrop."

The Black Art shakes his head as if to dismiss it altogether. "There was nothing more to be said anyway."

I've always felt it a violation of privacy to tap into one's collective, but curiosity consumes the better part of me, and I scrape a mental finger across his mind, digging in a nail just deep enough to peek in.

I nearly vomit as my gut suddenly twists itself inside out.

Claws rake down the lining of my stomach, threatening to disembowel me, and just as I'm certain my insides are about to spill from my gut, his voice snaps me back to the present.

"Get out of my head," he snarls.

I snatch my collective back at once. "I'm sorry," I blurt out.

Sin runs a hand through his dark hair, sending the layers falling unevenly over his white flowy shirt. The stark color of his top accentuates his deep bronzed skin and bright emerald eyes, and his fitted black trousers hug his trim waist. He turns to face me, and with a sharp exhale and a clap of his hands, he says, "Let's get started."

"Should I grab a twig and start practicing how to wave my wrists the correct way, Your Grace?"

He tosses his head back in laughter—*real* laughter—and I smile to myself, hoping the joke will help ease the suffering of the burning man inside of him, even if for just a few moments.

Ever consumed with the feelings of others. *I am a terrible bloodwitch.*

"It was for your own safety," he says, grinning at what I'm sure is a mental image of me waving the broom around like a lunatic.

"Maybe today I need to use pretend magic for *your* safety," I taunt.

"If you're going to be talking like that, you better be prepared to show up."

I dip my knees in a mock curtsy. "I will go easy on you, Your Grace."

"I was thinking we could warm up by channeling our magics together—get a feel of each other before we begin."

Shutting my eyes, I raise my arms in front of me, my elbows slightly bent and my palms facing him. I roll my shoulders a few times, ordering my body to relax. Focusing on my feet, I sink my sandals into the grass, grounding myself with the soil. I breathe in and out through closed lips, stilling my mind, and as if on cue, my forearms begin to warm.

The heat spreads to my wrists, pooling into my

outstretched palms, and shoots into my fingertips. I curve my hands towards my chest, holding the magic close to me for a moment and then push it away to merge with his. My power mulls over Sin's, tasting it, flirting with it. Our collectives take turns dipping into one another and exploring all the pockets of the other's source.

Sin's magic is cold—a blanket of snow on my chest, the nip of winter's wind on my cheeks—and the starkness of fresh mint coats my tongue. When I open my eyes and find his already watching me intently, I force my face to remain expressionless.

It was only the week prior we were flexing our magics and trying to overpower the other, before we had to cease fire, avoiding an explosion bigger than anything his magic or mine could accomplish alone.

An eruption that would have surely resulted in one of our deaths.

My warmer power skates around his, curious of its icy slopes, and scratches at its boundary. Our collectives flirt across the seam dividing his from mine, and suddenly, that line erupts into a white-hot flame, sending a lick of desire straight to my thighs. With a shared look, we drop our collectives and lower our hands, the magic sizzling out from both our fingertips.

"That was something," he murmurs, the sound breathless.

"That was... something," I agree, not having a better word to describe the surge of power we both felt when our magics tangled like new lovers lost in silken sheets.

Legion doesn't stand a chance.

"Let's duel. You wield, I'll shield," he says.

I back up several steps, creating an appropriate distance between us. Sin lowers into a defensive stance, bending at the knee slightly, and nods for me to begin. My collective bends to my will eagerly now, having been warmed up with our exercise. I weigh the magic in my hands, ensuring it is restrained—not strong enough to inflict any real damage if he somehow fails to block my assault—but strong enough for him to test his shields. Confident I'm in control, I take a steadying breath and push off a golden orb.

Sin catches it with his ward immediately, his barrier stretched in the space between his palms, and my orb bounces off it and disintegrates into nothing. Dragging his tongue across the fronts of his teeth, he flashes a devastating grin and motions with two fingers for me to continue.

You want more, Blackheart?

I chuck another, and another, and another at him, each one hurtling towards him with more speed than the last, and each one disintegrating as it collides with his conjured ward. We continue this for a while longer before reversing roles. Sin's magic comes in rapid spurts, its surface slick with ice, and slams into my resistance again and again, coating my ward in layers of frost and peppery sweetness.

He casts from both sides of his body, and sometimes across it, forcing me to leap back and forth to concentrate my shield where his magic is about to hit. When he finally lowers his hands, my back is slick where rivulets of sweat bead across my neck and down my shoulder blades.

"Wield again. But this time, stop holding out on me," he barks, wiping his own sweat from his brow with the back of his arm.

I shake out my arms that are now rigid from casting and shoot him a stern look. "You know I have to."

"Says who?"

"*Says who?* Says you and your stupid law!" My blood begins to heat again, but this time, it's not in anticipation of dueling.

"I'm not asking you to kill anyone. I'm only asking you to embrace your power, and not this weakened version of it."

"And what if you miss the block and I hurt you? I lose control and don't stop?"

The Black Art's stare strips me bare, and dropping his voice, he asks, "Do you think that will happen? Say you accidentally hurt me... do *you* think you would spiral out of control and kill me, and kill the entire godsdamned kingdom while you're at it?"

A loose breath rattles out of me, and I shake my head, not in answer but in disbelief he is asking at all. "It has never mattered to you or your kingdom before," I spit. "You have *only* ever assumed for us, and insisted on our extinction on the basis of legends and lies. So don't ask me today, *Your Grace,* if I think I can control it." My words drip with venom—heavy, furious, and positively lethal.

Sin looks at me for a long moment, a calm expression on his face, but his jaw taut and his lips thinned. And then with predatory swiftness, he slinks back into a crouch, raising his arms as if preparing to take me on hand-to-hand. All traces of pleasantry vanish from his voice when he orders, "All of it. I can handle your power, even if it does come from a filthy bloodwitch."

Chaos explodes inside me.

My fingertips fade into golden wisps of pure, raw power. Pouring all my focus and intention into each thrust, I send waves of destruction rippling towards him, smashing into his walls again and again, each one denting them a little farther.

I'm barely aware of Sin, my power swelling up inside me like a raging tsunami, drowning out all thoughts of reason. He dashes left and right, reinforcing his shield, trying to hold it steady against my wrathful wake.

A steady roar pierces my ears as my fury rams into his

barrier again, and it crumbles beneath my collective. I pull it back, and with the ferocity of the Howling Sea and my own ringing cry of anguish and resentment and vengeance, I hurl myself at his defense again. My blood thickens when I hear it snap, and the screaming—*my* screaming—drowns out his own holler of pain, Sin's face contorting with the impact of my rage.

I double over with the sudden surge of him.

CHAPTER 25

I am so, so thirsty.

A crippling dryness scratches my throat, and I wonder if this is what the trees felt the day Lostgarde burned. When the kingdom scorched the land that borders The Feral Vale to ensure that whatever creatures lurked within those dense woods couldn't creep out.

Creatures like me.

White hot claws rake down my throat, begging for me to drink—not water, but... *him*. I raise my head to look at Sin, his body splayed out on the grass floor, and I dare a step closer.

The fire burns brighter.

Another step.

Hotter.

Another.

I swallow hard, willing the saliva to be enough to quench my thirst, my insatiable thirst, and take another step. I stoop to my knees and lean an ear towards his chest. His eyes fly open before I can listen for his heartbeat, and in his near reflective yellow-green eyes, I glimpse my own glimmering amber ones, brought to life from the dueling.

Sin, digging his elbows into the ground to prop himself up, pulls himself away from me slowly, his yellow-tinged eyes never leaving mine as he rests his back against a nearby tree. I rise to my feet and walk over to him, each step slow and controlled and steady. I scan for damage, but it is all internal. My final blast of magic shattered his wall.

Shattered a few ribs.

He reaches a hand inside his trouser pocket, and when he pulls it back out, a knife with a glistening sharp, beak-shaped blade is cupped in his palm. For a second, my heart sinks watching him prepare to defend himself, readying his knife to thrust into my chest should I lunge for him. But it isn't fear swirling in the depths of his eyes as he beholds me.

I sink to my knees in front of him.

Before I register what he's doing, Sin flips his hand over and presses the blade into his callused palm. Blood rushes from the long incision, his entire palm stained like a cardinal's wing and spilling over the edge of his hand.

Drip. Drip. Drip.

Each drop soaking the grass is deafening, beckoning me to dip my head and suck it from the lush green blades.

I go deadly still.

Sin, holding my stare very, *very* carefully, slides closer to me and slowly raises his bloodied hand to my mouth.

Why is he doing this? All the torment I have felt buried deep within him—can he endure it no longer? Does he wish for me to end his suffering?

My tongue is as dry as the red-tinged dirt. If only I could taste, just for a moment, the sweet juice oozing from his hand. He is still as stone, as if the slightest twitch of muscle will trigger my need to chase.

"You can control it," he whispers, reaching out his good hand and brushing the backs of his knuckles along the column of my neck. His words are soft as moonlight on velvet, his glowing eyes vibrant against his dark skin, his beautiful black hair, and I want... I want to *taste* him. To suck his vital fluid straight from its bleeding source.

I also want to grab that knife and bury it in his gut—for the insatiable rush of power it would give me. And to punish him for doing this to me.

"You can control it," he murmurs again, his words brushing the space between us as if I projected my own ward around me, to try to block that sweet, sweet smell of him. "Listen to me," he purrs. "Listen to my voice. You are Wren. You are *good*. And you can control it."

I push her down, down, down. Down to the pit of my stomach, as deep as I can bury *her*—I push her down where I can't hear her voice, feel her hunger, see through her eyes. She who would undo me, laugh as I slaughtered my friends, my family, and relished in lapping up their blood as their life force filled me, stretching every organ wide with their fragrant, red liquid.

I am Wren. I am good. I can control it.

Sin raises his stained hand so that it hovers just beneath my nose, an inch from my pointed, lethal teeth, and I force myself to raise my eyes from the bloody meal he offers me to his entrancing stare. A feline smile tugs at his lips as he drops his hand from my neck and wraps it around my arm, pulling me towards him. He presses the cold hilt of the dagger into my palm and wraps my hand closed around it. His own hand comes down on top of mine—guiding me, leading me—to his exposed forearm, inches from his other gaping wound, and I shake my head.

I shake and shake and shake.

I want to—*so badly* I want to—to slice into him and hold his arm above my head to drip into my open, waiting mouth. But I won't.

I am Wren. I am good. I can control it.

I can control it.

Sin pushes down on my hand, and I bury the knife into his arm. His beautiful red sap leaks out of him, and the smell—the sweet, almost floral scent of him like hyacinths in rain—wafts into my nose, and I *burn* for him. I inch closer and slap my palms to his chest, against that white shirt separating my teeth from his pounding, fleshy heart, and hoist myself onto his lap, gentle of his ribs that may or may not be broken. My lips pull back, and I eye the side of his throat, the blood that flows just beneath that thin layer of skin, so easily bitten into.

"Go on then, love. *Take a bite.*"

The sound of his voice ignites something ancient in me, and I arch my back, my hips inadvertently grinding into his. He's calling my bluff, but when I look down into his eyes, I want to *devour* him, bones and blood and all.

He tilts his head back to look up at me, his beaming eyes now smoldering with his own caster's high, and the sight of him beneath me, bloodied and broken but *wanting*, undoes me. Tendrils of sopping hyacinths weave into my nose and to the back of my throat, the smell of his blood encasing me in a euphoric shroud. A moan spills from my lips at the thought of drinking him dry, and a sound of approval rattles from the Black Art's chest.

I can control it.

"I have to get out of here." Air hisses through my teeth.

I make it exactly three steps before I collapse into a deep, unyielding sleep.

CHAPTER 26

Panic licks at my nerves when I wake. I'm curled up in the grass like a newborn babe, the ground freezing and unforgiving beneath my spine. My entire body goes rigid as soon as I gain awareness, knowing something isn't right and trying to decode how I've ended up here. I was dueling with Sin and... the memory of the events lashes behind my eyelids like a crack of a riding crop.

Sin had been arguing with me about not holding myself back. Called me a *filthy bloodwitch*... antagonized me.

He *wanted* this to happen.

The Black Art's power is strengthened with Adelphia's blessing—his shield wouldn't have broken that quickly—not with the goddess of the arcane on his side.

"And the dead awakes," he murmurs behind me.

The sound of his voice melts the frozen casings on my limbs as I remember the smell of his spilt blood—and my desire to taste him. I wanted to *consume* him so badly. I almost did.

But I didn't.

I tried to *run away*.

I would have had he not hit me with the sleep spell. No doubt Sin knocked me out so I would sleep off the blood high before barging back into the castle. Warmth brushes my cheeks at the memory of how I acted—how *wild* I felt. But it is quickly replaced with rage at his trickery.

"You deceived me."

"Are you furious with me?" he asks in a low voice.

"Why? Why would you do such a *stupid* thing?"

An extended beat passes before he answers. "You can't help me win this war if you won't fight."

I spin to face him. He's still sitting against the tree I left him at, but he healed the wounds he—*we*—inflicted on his hand and arm. The dried blood staining his flowy white shirt is the only evidence the embarrassing incident occurred at all, but he should pay Anika a visit to assess internal damage.

"And I suppose you didn't care if I failed your ridiculous experiment and tried to kill you? Of course not, because if you *had* managed to fight me off, it would have provided you cause to kill me. And if you *couldn't* stop me, and I took your life right there against that tree, you still win because then you wouldn't have to wake up and look at your pathetic self in the mirror another day."

"You will watch your tongue in my presence," he snarls, clenching his hands draped over his bent knees. The air between us thickens as tension rolls off him, and I know not to push him further. Not right now.

"It wasn't just your life you risked, Singard. If you kill me after we take out Legion, at least I'll die knowing I was protecting the innocent. You could have taken that away from me today. If I lost control, if I had hurt you... hurt others, then I'd be no better than you and your father who would rather kill my family for simply being what they are."

"There will never be peace so long as their kind continues to wreak havoc in the cities," he says, calmer now. The bored king.

"Most of Legion's soldiers aren't even transcendents! They're just people who don't want to be controlled, who don't want to worry that they, or their loved ones, are the kingdom's next target."

"You say that like you support them."

I shake my head. "No. I say that because humans are more monstrous than any transcendent I've ever met. The shifters that are fighting with Legion... they're *scared*. They have a right to live in peace, just as I do. Your kingdom is cruel," I say, drawing out my final word.

"How can you say that after what they did to you? They stole you, chained you up like a fucking *pet,* and you dare point a finger at *me* when all I did was show you that you have the means to put an end to them."

"If you have to justify your actions against those of Cathal's, what do you think that makes of you?" I spit back at him.

"If I hadn't done that—hadn't shown you that maybe, *just maybe*, you shedding blood won't turn you into some horrendous monster, you would never fight how I *need* you to fight."

"You are sadly mistaken if you think I won't give up my life for my sister's freedom and my family's safety without a second thought. When the time comes, I *will* kill for them, even if doing so does turn me into some legendary beast because I'm certain you hadn't planned on letting me live long after the war anyway. Isn't that right, *Your Grace?*"

"You're a fast learner, little witch."

I swear the temperature around us drops a few degrees as his stare turns razor-sharp. If looks could kill...

Rising to my feet, I slap my hands against my tunic to send the dirt flying off it. I want to storm far away from here, from him, but I linger for a moment, looking at him over my shoulder. "Should I send a healer?"

I hate myself for asking, for showing that there is a part of me that still feels guilty for hurting him, even if he did weaken his shield on purpose.

"No. I can walk back."

Nodding, I leave him and head towards the castle, unable to stop myself from imagining the kind of power the Black Art spoke of. A power without limits, restrictions... without fear. I *had* shown control earlier, and I can't help but wonder just how far that control can stretch.

CHAPTER 27

The morning after I nearly ate the Black Art, Aldred reported to my room and explained he'd been assigned to lead my training. The commander offered no explanation as to why the sudden switch in my training partner, and I didn't bother to ask. Though I suppose licking my lips at the sight of his open wounds would be enough to prompt the bravest of warriors to take a step back.

Aldred and I have been sparring the past week, mostly with swords but with some hand-to-hand combat sprinkled in too. Occasionally, I spot Sin making his rounds through the courtyard, overseeing his armies and stepping in as needed, but never veering too close to where we trained.

He must have paid Anika a visit the night of our altercation because he prowls the grounds with no signs of injury, as if the incident never happened at all. His eyes never even glance our direction when he comes near, perhaps because he trusts his commander enough to leave us alone, or maybe he simply doesn't want to be close to me. Either way, I'm content to be rid of his ever so sunny disposition.

Aldred is pleasant enough. He doesn't bore me with small talk and lets me take short breaks when I need to. Additionally, he doesn't seem to mind training with a bloodwitch. The commander has never brought up what I am, and I suppose I respect him for that reason alone.

With the castle at my rear, I don't see him approach. And my mind is too focused on perfecting the elbow-to-chin strike Aldred showed me to hear his footsteps. It isn't until Aldred suddenly snaps to attention and jerks his hand to his brow in a salute that I sense him behind me, courtesy of the tugging on the phantom tether between us.

"How is our favorite bloodwitch performing, Commander?" Sin asks from behind me. Though I can't see him, I *feel* his eyes burning into the back of my head, like a deer knowing a wolf lurks just out of sight. Watching.

Always watching.

Aldred drops his arm to his side as he rattles off a report of the techniques we've covered, what we are currently working on, and my overall progress. I laugh once without humor and tug my bottom lip between my teeth as they talk *about* me, like I'm a child being handed over to her nanny.

Sin moves so he stands perpendicular to me, the side of my shoulder nearly brushing against his chest. "Learn any new tricks?" he asks, the smugness in his tone sending my fingers curling into my palms.

Desperate to swipe that infuriating smirk from his face, I whirl towards him, my right hand slipping into the waist of my trousers and grabbing the athame I tucked inside my pants. I halt the blade an inch from the underside of his chin.

"I learned to never rely on one weapon. First rule of combat, Blackheart." I tilt my head to the side, flashing him a smile as sweet as iced violet tea.

Sin's mouth widens into a wicked smile as I spew his earlier words back at him. The distinct sound of a sword being pulled from its leather holster licks at my ears, and Sin throws a hand out towards Aldred, a silent order for him to back down.

The Black Art drags his tongue against the fronts of his teeth in a movement that is pure predator, and looks down at me from under those dark brows, absolute amusement gleaming in his vivid green eyes. He wraps a hand around mine and lowers the knife between us before uncurling my fingers from the dagger and prying it from my hands. Turning it over in his hand, Sin studies the athame from hilt to blade.

"Elysande?" he asks with a note of surprise.

I nod. "Is there a problem with that?"

He shrugs. "A little unusual, but I suppose a bloodwitch *would* worship the goddess of war."

I can't tell if he intends the comment as an insult or not, but I scrunch my face in an exaggerated smirk and hold my hand out expectantly. He strokes a bronzed finger over the carving of the dancing goddess before placing it in my waiting palm, curling my fingers back around the handle and lowering my hand to my side.

"I'll let you two get back to it, then. Glad to see you listen, little witch," he says over his shoulder as he strides off towards the next row of sparring partners.

Aldred shoots me a disapproving look, which I meet with a shrug and sink back into my fighting stance.

I attempt another locator spell in the evening, drawing a map on a spare sheet of parchment, but it yields the same crimson vines climbing to each corner of the paper. I crumple the map and fling it into the wastebasket, then heal the incision I made to perform the spell.

I barely finish healing my wounded palm when River taps on the door twice. She hurries in and places a tea tray on the bedside table.

"Evening, dear. I've come to inform you that His Grace has requested your presence on an upcoming trip."

"*Requested?*" I repeat, calling out the lie, though I'm certain she didn't mean it as such.

She scoffs, but it doesn't touch her eyes. "You leave tomorrow morning. Best pack your things tonight and be ready by sunrise. His Grace is very particular about leaving at first light."

"Where are we going?"

"Isn't for me to know, dear. The tea is chamomile," she adds matter-of-factly. "It will help you sleep, and I suggest you drink up because you're likely in for a long day tomorrow, wherever you're going. You'll want your rest."

I nod and mutter a thank you, accepting it isn't River that has my nerves bundled so tightly. Heeding her advice, I shove a few clean sets of clothes into a satchel. I don't know how long we'll be gone, but if the number of days is more than the number of outfits I bring, Sin can deal with the smell.

Exhaustion seeps into my bones, and I slip into bed without drinking the tea.

CHAPTER 28

Rapid pounding on the bedchamber door sends my pulse leaping from my neck and my legs tumbling out of bed.

Fuck. I rub my hand across my nape, rolling my shoulders forward and back, having strained it during my violent jolt awake.

"Be outside in five. Make it six, and I'm throwing you over my shoulder again and hauling your ass out of there."

"Uh-huh," I call just loud enough for Sin to hear the annoyance in my tone.

I pull on a tunic the color of a cream dipped persimmon and off-white leggings, and secure a tan leather bodice over my clothing. My fingers make haste to secure my hair into its mohawk braid, and a quick glance at my reflection confirms I look as exhausted as I feel. The nightly terrors plaguing my sleep are taking its toll on my body—the undersides of my eyes darkened with iris shadows like day old cosmetics.

Slinging my satchel over my shoulder, I trudge downstairs and plow through the heavy set of double doors at the castle's entrance. Two ebony horses saddled and ready for riders fidget at the bottom of the stairs, while the Black Art tsks softly to the one nearest him, scratching the underside of its chin.

I stuff my satchel into one of the saddle bags and ignore Sin's outstretched hand as I grip the horn of the saddle and heave my leg over the horse. Sin mounts the other with impressive speed, and we make our way past the watchtowers that I note are as heavily guarded in this hour as they are during times of peak traffic.

We ride through Blackreach and find ourselves on the single road that leads to the bridge. Neither of us speaks until we're nearly at the Malachite, him apparently accepting I am not going to be the one to initiate conversation after the ridiculous stunt he pulled a few days prior.

"You aren't going to ask where we're going?" he prods, breaking the silence.

Not missing a beat, I say, "I didn't think a *filthy bloodwitch* would have the right to know."

Sin shoots me a lingering glance. "Still mad about that, are you?"

I don't bother turning my head to look at him and instead, ignore him entirely. I see him purse his lips in my periphery, obviously deliberating with himself, and then his shoulders rise and fall in a quick shrug as if he answered some unspoken question he had asked himself.

"I spoke ill of you to rile you up, and surely you know that. Now whether you're too stubborn to admit it or not, my plan *did* work. You demonstrated great capacity for control. Think about that, Wren. You could wipe out every one of those pricks that imprisoned you with half a thought if you let yourself have it."

I shift in my saddle and sweep my eyes to his. "Careful, or you'll make an argument against yourself, Blackheart."

If he's right and I truly possess enough control to wield my magic and render Legion extinct, what is to stop me from blowing the kingdom to smithereens when I'm done?

He clicks his tongue against the roof of his mouth. "I don't know how bloodwitches do it, but in the *civilized* world, we don't thank our allies by killing them."

"Right, because in the civilized world, you just slaughter *everyone*. An impartial killer—quite admirable really, Your Grace."

The glare he shoots me is sharp enough to slice through bone as if it were a heap of melted butter.

Brushing off his look, I continue, "And is that what we are —allies?"

He doesn't answer for a while, leaving me to tune in to the crunching of red ochre dirt beneath hooves and delighting in the spring wind grazing my flushed cheeks. By the time Sin does speak again, I've forgotten I was waiting for an answer at all.

"There are much worse things we could be, little witch."

His tone is softer, and for a fleeting moment, it almost dislodges an agreement out of me before I think better of it. I press my knees into the horse, and we take off in a thunderous gallop, the beating of its mighty hooves against the dirt drowning out the voices arguing amongst themselves in my head.

We stop to rest in the outskirts of Emberbourne and snack on some of the dried meat and large, round blood oranges he packed in his saddle bag. After watering ourselves and our horses, we continue riding south as the sun blooms into golden petals that stretch across the afternoon sky, and eventually fade into a deeper, harmonious blend of orange and scarlet as the last hours of daylight hovers around us. The rolling peaks of The Red Tops rear up in the distance, their sky-punching tips disappearing behind the clouds.

We ride closer to the mountains, their namesake peaks impossibly tall above our heads. The Red Tops are a natural border separating the wealthier cities of Aegidale from the dry, famished pits that are Baregrove and Lostgarde. Legends say Lostgarde was once lovely, vibrant with tangled trees and blooming flora, before the kingdom scorched the city. Because bordering Lostgarde is the heavily forested abyss known as The Feral Vale, home to another type of magic it's believed the kingdom fears.

The inhabitants of the vale can't emerge in sunlight, so the kingdom burned everything outside of its verdant borders, forcing the monsters to stay hidden beyond the woods. Lostgarde suffered the heaviest loss of infrastructure, but the western parts of Baregrove were also devastated, leaving once thriving cities to despair in the wake of the kingdom's destruction.

Curiosity piques my interest as to what business the Black Art has this far south, and why he wanted my company for the trip. The towering, craggy peaks grow taller as we near them, their red tips staining the clouds with their blood-soaked teeth.

And then I see it.

Settled on an outcropping of rock is a comically small temple. And carved into its front-facing surface, her chiseled features partially shadowed beneath the setting sun, is Elysande.

⁂

The temple is square shaped with four walls constructed entirely of red sandstone and brick. Carvings of sentries wrap around the three visible sides, protecting their idol from those brave or dumb enough to try to harm the goddess of war and vengeance.

Sin and I dismount at the base of the temple and tether our horses to nearby trees before hiking the remaining way up to Elysande's tiny house of worship. There is no opening in the front, the walls solidly constructed of russet stone shimmering in the final beams of daylight—stone that has been made smooth with wear.

I press my palm to one of the sentries—a winged woman with a drawn bow—and drag my hand across her dress, the chiseled beading of her bodice bumpy and textured under my fingers. Next to her, an overgrown man stands with a sword raised high above his head, both of his disproportionately sized hands clenched around the hilt. More sentries adorn the east and western sides, and I'm pleased at the number of female soldiers carved into the stone, so unlike the all-male army the kingdom has at its disposal.

And above them all, watching over her quaint dwelling, is Elysande. Long hair with waves like the ocean coil around her bare, feminine frame. Elysande stands with her arms above her head, her left hip slightly higher than her right, as if the artist carved her mid ceremonial dance. Tentatively, I reach a hand towards her, and I can't quite explain it, but a part of me swears there is life inside those smooth, vermilion stone eyes.

I glance behind myself and find Sin watching me closely, seemingly more interested in my reaction than in the temple itself. I almost ask him why he has brought me here but tuck the question away for now, too mesmerized by the beauty of the temple to disrupt the moment.

I walk to the rear side of the construct. The fourth wall is mostly open—an invitation for those brave enough to enter. The room is small, big enough to pack six bodies in at most, and only three comfortably. And standing against the most interior wall, taking up much of the space, is a statue of the idol herself. Elysande's stone hands are neatly folded against her skirt, her head tilted down as if ready to hear the prayers of those who have come to pay their respects.

I glance back at Sin again, who hovers just outside the temple. I'm not sure if he is trying to give me space, or if the goddess of war really does make him uncomfortable, as he alluded to yesterday. I raise my eyebrows, daring him to answer the silent question on my face.

"It is part of my duties to oversee the upkeep of the shrines. This is certainly the smallest of them." He hesitates for a moment, then continues, "I thought you might feel closer to her here, to your patron, if you wanted to pray and ask for strength in controlling your... abilities."

A kind gesture. One likely made out of remorse for deceiving me into hurting him. I turn back towards Elysande, vowing to consider the Black Art's attempt at an apology later, refusing to let it spoil this moment with her.

I kneel on the ground and lean my head against my left shoulder, exposing my neck to the goddess, a shared symbol of respect amongst many of the deities. After a moment, I right my head and tuck my chin towards my chest, and when Sin excuses himself, I begin to pray.

I ask Elysande to protect Cosmina and grant her strength to endure what she must until I can save her. Thoughts of Eldridge roll in like storm clouds, and I pray for my friend to find comfort as he struggles to tame his own demons, and to provide him clarity in times of stress. I ask her to protect the rest of my family—Zorina, Morrinne, Theon, and baby Galen —from all harm. To keep them safe if I should meet an untimely end.

And lastly, I think about my parents, allowing myself to relive the memory I keep locked up tight. The night my mother shooed me from our home upon learning what I was, like I was a wild animal riddled with disease. I cried—no, I *begged*—her to let me stay, to allow me the chance to prove I would never harm anyone. My begging only strengthened her shoves until my backside landed in a sludge of wet mud. She slammed the front door shut behind me, and the sound of that slam still jostles me awake some nights.

Tears prick my eyes, and for once, it feels good to *feel*. I unsheathe the athame at my thigh, the carving on the hilt now less impressive compared to the grand statue looming above me.

I dig the blade into my expecting palm and let the blood pool into the nestling of her skirts where they brush against the stone flooring. Leaning forward, I rest my forehead against the ground and ask the goddess of war, vengeance, and femininity to grant me strength. To grant me control of my power so I may call on it when I need it most. So that I may wield it for *good*.

When the tears have dried from my eyes and my breathing steadied, I heal the wound on my hand and ignite the blood on her skirts with a wave of magic, the smoke escorting my offering to the heavens. Paying her a final farewell, I exit the temple, leaving no trace I was there except for the weight of the promise I bid to her.

CHAPTER 29

W e set up camp just beyond the tree line in the small nestling of woods between The Red Tops and Emberbourne. Sin gathers a bushel of dry plant material and small, broken sticks to sustain the fire I brought to life with magic. Keeping the flames roaring with magic would be hardly a drain of energy, but Sin prepares the kindling regardless, and I'm beginning to think he just enjoys working with his hands. I watched as he birthed a fire from scratch the night he hunted me down after I stopped that arrow from piercing his heart, as if he didn't possess magic at all, which is certainly *not* the case.

Both of us too tired to hunt, we eat more of the salted meat and bread he packed in his bag. I study Sin as he tears off chunks of the dried meat with his teeth, his black shirt pulling tight across his chest and arms each time he raises his hand to his mouth.

I imagine it is exhaustion that has him so quiet—preparing his armies for their final stand against Legion surely has left his mind and body in need of rest. My temples throb at the mere thought of what it must be like dealing with Dusaro every day.

"Thank you for bringing me there." I hadn't been able to

235

voice my appreciation before, but it feels wrong to not extend some sort of acknowledgment.

His slender eyes flash to mine, and he wipes the back of his hand across his face. "I would like you to answer something for me."

I blow out a breath and look at him pointedly. *Of course he wants something in return.* "What?"

"You mentioned before that your parents tossed you out when you were young... after they learned what you were."

"Are," I correct.

"How did they find out?" he continues.

The smell of blood, it... appeals to me, I told him the night he interrogated me in the cell. I swallow hard. I *hate* talking about them, why is he asking this now? Perhaps he noted my tear-stained cheeks when I brushed past him outside the temple and suspected I had seen more than just Elysande inside those walls.

"My mother... is a cruel woman. She was very heavy handed, and to put it lightly, a complete and utter bitch. She punished me with great severity even when I had done nothing wrong." I tear my eyes away and stare into the flames before continuing, not wanting him to see the tears pricking the corners.

"But I was an only child and lonely, and despite hating her, I craved her attention still. I sometimes misbehaved just to get her to notice me. In hindsight, I think I struggled regulating my emotions because no one knew what I was, what I was capable of. I had all these urges and violent desires bottled up inside me, and I didn't know how to handle them, or channel them in a healthy way.

"One day, I was so upset about something she said to me—so *mad*—that I didn't even think about the consequences of my actions. I grabbed her arm and shredded it with my nails. I don't know why I did it. I just... in that moment... I *wanted* to. I was furious and wanted to hurt her. But then she started bleeding and... I had never made someone bleed before that day. The smell was intoxicating. I couldn't think right, see right, nothing... It was like I became a different person when I smelled the blood. Everything about it drew me in—the color, the smell... I wanted to taste it. Something came alive in me at that moment."

I wipe the tears from my face with the back of my hand, hating myself for presenting the breaches in my armor to him on a silver platter, but also not caring. If I'm going to die anyway, what's the harm in one more person knowing my story?

"It was that moment she knew what I was, and that moment, she cast me out of her house and out of her life."

I dare a sideways glance in his direction and find him absentmindedly running a hand across his jaw as he watches the fire hissing and popping between us. "What of your father?" Sin asks quietly.

I shrug my shoulders. "My father was a decent enough man I suppose, though he never protected me from her. He loved me in his own way... I think... but I wouldn't say he was a good father. If he had found someone other than my mother to share his life with, then I think maybe he could have been. But she ruined him, and he allowed her to."

When I glance back at him again, this time I find him watching me, his bronzed hands clasped together and dangling over his bent knees.

He clears his throat. "I'm sorry for the pain you endured at their hands. Say what you want about the kingdom, Ephraim, me... but when I hurt someone, it's strategy. It's *war*. But parents beating on their own young is something reserved for the lowest of monsters."

"It seems we may have one shared belief after all, Your Grace."

"When Legion captured you the first time—the time your sister found you—you and Cathal were... involved." Not exactly a question, but his face burns with curiosity.

"For a while, yes. He came into the inn I helped run. This was before they were ever known as Legion, when no one even knew what they were planning. I'm not too proud to admit I acted out of loneliness back then and soaked up the attention he was all too willing to give me. Cathal was the only other person I shared my secret with, apart from my family. My *other* family," I clarify. "I trusted him, and it was a mistake. One I won't make again."

"Tell me about it."

I raise an eyebrow and shoot him a dubious look to which he raises a dark brow of his own and mirrors my expression. "What, do you have somewhere else to be?" He motions around us to drive home his point that we're both stuck in the woods for the remainder of the night.

A short laugh falls out of me—okay, *fine*. "Cathal came for me the same night I confided in him. He brought a few others with him, and they bound me in iron and threw me on a horse. Dragged me to the other side of Autumnhelm where they had camps set up for their expanding army. Legion was actively recruiting then, in secrecy of course. I didn't know what was going on, or who the people were. And then... and then they threw me off the horse and—" I trail off, remembering the stench of their worn boots as they took turns kicking me in the gut.

"And what?" he prompts.

"And they did bad things to me." My voice is void of emotion, as if saying it out loud would be too painful, so my mind pretends I'm speaking about someone else.

"The same bad things they did to Ileana?" he asks.

I pull my knees to my chin and wrap my arms around my legs. I don't know if I'm more surprised that Ileana shared her experience with the Black Art or that she *trusted* him enough to be so vulnerable.

"Yes... but just once. That first night. After that, they kept me chained to a tree away from where they all slept. But I would have chosen that over what Ileana went through. They forced her most nights. I... I could usually hear it." My arms wind tighter around my legs as I hug them to my chest.

A glint of something other than the crackling fire flares in his eyes, but it's not directed towards me. "*Fuck*, Wren. Where's a godsdamned drink when you need one?"

I flash him a dangerous smile. "I have a feeling our taste in drink differs, Your Grace." My eyes drop to the long lines of his tanned neck.

His slivered eyes widen for a brief moment and then a smirk that is pure devastating pulls up the corner of his lips. "Still thinking about what I taste like, love? I said you could take a bite."

"If I'm remembering correctly, Blackheart, only one of us has bitten the other."

His expression twists into something darker, feral even, as he parts his lips and drags the tip of his tongue across the fronts of his teeth. "And if I'm remembering correctly, you tasted divine."

I capture my bottom lip between my teeth as I mull over his words, distracted by that look he gives me. The one he's giving me right fucking now.

He's toying with me. Trying to lighten the mood after I darkened it with my confessions. Fine. I could use a distraction.

"It's not often I let men that speak of what I taste like live, Your Grace."

He shrugs a shoulder as if I didn't just threaten him, facetious or not. "Me either."

"Excuse me?"

Sin leans forward, his green eyes burning with as much heat as the fire between us, locked on mine. "I also don't intend to let men live that would dare speak of your... exquisite flavor."

The warmth on my face isn't entirely from the flames now, but I don't dare look away first. I refuse to let him think he's embarrassed me, even if internally, every part of me is itching to sink into the ground and never reemerge.

"It's a bit of a stretch to refer to a single bite as tasting me. I'd prefer you didn't."

"Didn't taste you?"

He's *definitely* toying with me. "You know what I meant. But yes, that too."

He licks his lips. "Liar." His mouth rounds around the word.

"I beg your pardon?" I scoff.

His eyes flicker between both of mine. "I don't think you minded it at all. In fact, I'd say the scent coming off you right now indicates the opposite."

I *feel* my eyes widen as I cross my arms across my chest and curl my legs off to the side. I don't know if he's merely teasing me, or if his boosted magic actually has heightened his sense of smell, just as mine is attuned to blood.

Sin laughs softly, then relaxes, leaning back and resting his arms behind his head. I mirror him from across the fire, and a twinge of loneliness pangs in my chest at the sight of the nighttime sky. Cosmina and I lay under the stars so many nights as we chatted about our days and our hopes for the next. A part of me wonders if she's looking up at the sky now too, wherever she is, and if she thinks of me when she does.

I'm coming for you, sister. Perhaps she will feel my message as she gazes upon the stars shimmering with the vibrancy of a thousand suns.

"Has she told you why she hates me?" I whisper.

He doesn't need me to specify who. "Ileana said you left without her."

"I did."

"Would you have been able to free her with them keeping her so heavily guarded?"

"Not while I was weak from the iron, and there were too many for Cosmina to handle on her own—way too many. With the iron in my blood, I wouldn't have been able to control the magic well enough to restrain it to wound and not kill. I was too much of a coward to risk it. Cosmina did what she came to do—she rescued me. I don't blame *her* for it at all. I could have gone to Ephraim to report what I knew, but I was afraid he'd be suspicious as to why Legion had taken me in the first place, and I was scared he'd piece it together and learn what I am. Ileana suffered because of *my* fears. She has every right to hate me."

"Ileana is strong though. She freed herself and fled before they could catch up to her. And knowing my Black Hand, I don't think she would have been content allowing someone else to rescue her anyway."

I smile to myself. Ileana is many things, but a coward is not one of them. I envy the fire inside her. "How did she end up at Scarwood?"

"After her escape, she sought refuge at the castle. She didn't have a home—not one she wanted to return to anyway —and she reported everything to Ephraim and my father who was his Hand at the time. Ephraim offered to shelter her while she recovered. She never left the keep—she barely left the castle—probably too afraid they'd somehow be out there. It really shook her up when Ephraim was killed in Suncove.

"We all assumed my father would be the one to take his place, but as you know, he was refused at the Rite. I performed it next out of obligation. I never thought in a million moons I'd be chosen, but when I began the ritual... it was like my body didn't belong to me anymore. I could feel my magic getting stronger by the second, it was like my blood was being set on fire. And when I thought it would never stop, it did. In a blink of an eye, I was chosen.

"I would have appointed my father as Hand, but since our law forbids familial ties, I allowed him to choose. He wanted Ileana. I think he just liked that she hated Legion as much as he did, and since she is mundane, it made sense for her to serve as emissary to a mostly mundane land. I wasn't sure she'd accept, but to my surprise, she was thrilled and accepted immediately. She never mentioned a bloodwitch when we told her to tell us everything she knew about Legion."

It takes me a moment to make sense of everything he shares. I suppose Ileana wouldn't have the same reasons to hate the kingdom that I did, but to serve as the *Black Hand*.

And then it hits me.

Ileana can use her position to *make sure* Legion pays for their crimes. She may not have magic in her veins, but being the Black Hand gives her an entirely different kind of power to wield.

Ileana didn't hide that she knew who and what I was the night in the ballroom. Sin knows she didn't disclose that sensitive information. He could have executed her for treason. But he didn't.

"Are you two betrothed?" Perhaps the rumors circulating

the ballroom held some truth after all. It would explain why he spared her if she is his intended.

He pauses for a beat and then chuckles to himself. "My father would like that very much, but no, we are not. Even if I was interested, I... I don't think I could pursue her, at least not for a while. Ileana is still very nervous around men. She won't be alone with them in a room. Even when she's alone with me, she is... easily startled. If I courted her, she would feel pressured to accept my advances due to my position, and that isn't right. She is learning to trust me, and I respect her too much to jeopardize that."

Sin may have inherited some of the wickedness of his father, but he isn't *that* kind of monster. I roll onto my side and prop my head up with my hand. "Did you fight in the war with Baelliarah?"

"Yes." His tone is clipped.

"You would have been young," I say, noting that Sin can't be much older than me.

"Yes."

I study his expression that has turned somber, and wonder if he regrets the feud between the two lands, when our transcendents fled to our closest neighbor, seeking refuge from Ephraim's tyrannical reign. It wasn't that Ephraim cared about his people that fled—he just didn't want to risk them forming an army across the sea. Innocent blood was shed in that war, of both transcendent and the mundane that tried to protect them. And Sin had been one of the soldiers that crossed the sea to retrieve what was never theirs in the first place.

"Thank you for taking care of her," I whisper. Despite my hatred for the kingdom, I'm not ignorant enough to not realize there were far worse fates for my friend.

"I will make you another deal, Wren."

I prop myself up fully now, noting this is the second time

he's used my actual name tonight. Sin sits up and meets my stare with an expression more serious than I've seen on him in a while.

"Fight with me—give *all* of yourself to me—and we wipe out Legion permanently. Do that, and I vow to release you."

My gut clenches as my organs perform a series of somersaults inside my stomach. "When you say *all* of me, you mean I would have to kill them?"

He nods slowly. "If it comes to that, which it likely will, yes."

"You aren't worried I'll lose control?"

The Black Art leans towards me, his eyes sweeping both of mine as if searching for a reason not to trust me. "Are you?"

My breath catches. Just this morning, I scolded him for asking me that same thing when neither he nor his predecessors ever bothered to ask before. But now he presents the question laced with compromise.

I rack my brain for the right words to respond with, but it's as if every thought I ever had, and every argument I rehearsed in my head for this very moment, has vanished. I close my eyes and inhale through my nose, steadying my breath and my thoughts.

"I damn well owe it to myself to try. And even if I lose control and you have to put me down after the war is won, it's worth it if it means freeing my sister."

He nods in understanding, and with the moon above as witness, I make a deal with a devil.

CHAPTER 30

His fur is oily beneath my fingertips. I rake my fingers through his sandy coat again and again, wondering what happened to the usual plush blanket he once adorned.

And then I feel the wetness, a warm liquid pooling from his side, and my hand freezes over the thudding pulse of the wound. I try to pull my hand away, but it doesn't budge. I pull and pull, but my hand is too heavy, stuck in a viscous glove of vital fluid and blood, and then I hear her.

A night splitting scream echoes around us, and I yank my hand from his side, to cover my ears and shut out the sound of her shrieks, but the smell of my palm snags my attention. I turn my hand over in front of me, admiring the thick carmine clots speckling my skin, and the shrilling screams grow louder.

I plunge my fingers between my lips and suck. I suck and suck and suck until my lips screech against my skin, and I slide my fingers out, dipping the point of my tongue into the underside of my finger-nail. I look up and find Eldridge watching me, whimpering from the wounds I caused, hurt and betrayal fresh in his storm-colored eyes. Gently, he shakes his magnificent sized head, pleading with me to stop, to remember.

I throw my head back and caterwaul at the memory of who she used to be.

⁂

A hand clamps over my mouth and nose, but before I can throw my elbows into the attacker's chest, a pair of lips find my ear.

"Don't move." Sin's whisper is barely loud enough to hear. He's covering me entirely with his body pressed firmly against mine, his palm hugging my mouth and the tips of his hair splayed over my arms like garden snakes. "Don't make a sound."

The clip clopping of hooves along the road turns my blood to ice. No one would be traversing the road at this hour. No one but Legion soldiers.

Our eyes lock, and I nod under his hand. The energy of the dome-like shield he projected around us pricks at my own magic like a static charge. It'll serve to bounce off any incoming arrows should one of them hear us on the other side of the thin layer of trees separating us from the road. We let the fire burn out last night, and the remainder of the smoke has cleared—as long as we stay still, there is no reason for them to notice us.

Sin slides his hand off my mouth and sets it on the ground next to my head. It would make too much noise for him to slide off me completely, so he hovers above me, supporting most of his weight between his arms that act like prison bars on either side of me. The clacking on the road grows louder until the group is directly parallel to us, hidden by the tall veil of trees.

"How much longer until the next pick-up?" a male voice asks.

"Shouldn't be more than a few days. They'll send word when they're ready for us," a woman replies.

"I'm fucking starving. Let's just go now."

A horse whinnies as the sharp ring of a *slap* pierces the air, and the male voice swears.

"We go when they tell us it's safe, and not a minute sooner. Do you understand?" the woman asks, not a drop of patience in her tone.

"Yeah, yeah, whatever. I just wish they didn't take so fucking long."

The line of trotting horses moves past us, the hushed whisperings of their riders fading with them. When the sound of them quiets completely, Sin slides off me, and the crisp air assaults my skin where his body had been trapping our heat between us. I search for his eyes in the night, but it's too dark to distinguish more than the silhouette of his body.

The body that was just pinning me to the ground and protecting me with an invisible shield.

"What pick-up are they talking about?" I ask.

"I *knew* they had a supplier," he growls, more to himself than me.

"But you don't know who it is."

The laugh that comes from his chest is pure animal. "For now. But hunting is my favorite pastime."

My mouth dries at his words, knowing it is *people* he prefers to hunt.

"Should we follow them?"

"No. When we return tomorrow, I'll send men back here to pick up their trail and tail them. For now, go back to sleep."

Hoping he doesn't hear the fear in my voice, I say, "I'm not sleeping knowing they're that close to us."

"I'll stay awake and keep an ear out. It's fine—you can sleep."

I push up to a sitting position. "I'll stay up with you. It's better if we're both alert."

"No one is getting past me, Wren. If I hear anything, you'll be the first to know. I won't... nothing is going to happen to you if you sleep."

I don't say anything for a moment, wondering what he was about to say before he corrected himself. He *did* shelter me as soon as he heard Legion approaching. I have no reason to believe he wouldn't do it again.

"Fine," I agree, my tone clipped. "But if you hear *anything* —wake me immediately."

"Deal." He blows out an exasperated sigh. "You may call me many things, little witch, but I'm not daft. Only a fool would break a promise to a bloodwitch."

I can't tell if he means the comment to be sarcastic or not, so I merely shake my head knowing he can't see it and lie back down. And despite the adrenaline still pounding through my veins like stampeding horses, I find myself drifting in and out of sleep as exhaustion eventually weighs me down. At some point in the night, I fall over the edge completely, Sin's voice echoing in my head as the words he left unspoken now ring with the clarity of church bells.

I won't let something happen to you.

CHAPTER 31

I t isn't the thudding of the sideways rain against the window that dampens my mood this morning—it's the *noise*. A mass of collective energy stings my own like a horde of furious bees. I throw on a clean sage dress with flowy sleeves and hurry from my bedchambers, not bothering to braid my hair.

It's been a few days since the Black Art and I returned to the castle from our visit to the goddess's temple. As he said, he sent a small group back to pick up Legion's tracks, but I haven't heard if they found anything yet. In fact, I haven't seen much of Sin at all since we've returned.

The foyer is empty—the shadows cast by the room's towering archways the only company in the lonely entrance. I find River in the kitchen, hammering a rolling pin against a sheet of pink fillets, a tad too aggressively to be casual. She doesn't look up when I enter, but rather keeps her attention fixed on the meat before her, definitely hitting them harder now.

"Is there another event here today? I sense a crowd." It's too early in the day for a ball, but perhaps the Black Art has prepared a speech to deliver.

"Not an event. An execution," River answers with forced calmness. She straightens and folds her hands against the divots of her waist. "That boy... oh, that *boy*. Let me tell you, he is really messing it up big this time," she says, shaking her head.

My spine steels. "Who is being executed?"

"A damn kid. Well not a kid-kid, but they're all kids to me," she sighs, tracing a finger along her eye where a single tear jumps out.

"What was the crime?"

"Nothing worthy of this," she says with a shake of her head and resumes beating the poor cutlets into submission.

I don't bother returning to my chambers for a cape before I'm bolting out into the rain. The guards at the gate point me in the direction of the execution, and I sprint out of the keep, my gut groaning as the phantom tether there cinches down tight. Or perhaps it's just queasiness from what I fear is about to happen.

Please Elysande, don't let this be what I think it is.

It doesn't take me long to find the crowd of busy bodied villagers huddled around a raised platform. I push through them, shoving at their bulky cloaks and coats, ignoring their sneers and grumblings that if I wanted a better view, I should have arrived sooner. Heaving my shoulders into their sides, I make my way to the front of the crowd.

Kneeling on the wooden deck, his wrists bound to his ankles in long iron shackles, is a young man. He appears to be a few years my younger with a head of golden hair and ivory skin, and judging from his iron restraints, not entirely human.

A transcendent.

Sin appears from behind the platform and approaches the young man with slow, calculated footsteps. Dusaro and Ileana appear and take their places on opposite corners of the stage.

Ileana's expression is reserved, while Dusaro waves to the crowd, encouraging their cheery applause and whistles of approval.

The Black Art stares at his feet, not even bothering to look at the pleading transcendent before him until the crowd quiets down. And when their rousing hollers finally do fade, there is nothing about Sin's expression that suggests he is in the mood to reconsider.

The crowd goes deadly quiet when he speaks, his booming voice rivaling the thunder in the attention it demands. "Thatcher Alderman, you are hereby accused of inflicting injury to another while in a state of transcendence. Due to the nature of this crime—I, Singard Kilbreth, Black Art of Aegidale —sentence you to death."

Thatcher cranes his neck back to look up at Sin, shaking his head as pleas for mercy fall from his mouth. There is no softness in the Black Art's all-consuming glare as he closes the small gap between him and the prisoner at his leather clad feet.

"Sin!" I call his name.

His head snaps up at the sound of my voice, and he quickly scans the crowd to find me. I continue as soon as our eyes lock. "Sin—*Your Grace*—please reconsider your sentencing."

"The decision is final," he growls, strands of wet black hair sticking to the sides of his face like sodden branches.

I ignore Dusaro's warning glare burning a hole in my face. "There must be another way. He can serve the kingdom, work in the castle. For as long as you see fit, a lifetime even. I'm sure you could always use more hands around the—"

"This is not the time for negotiations, *girl*," Dusaro drawls, cutting me off.

My stare doesn't waver from Sin's, and something close to

remorse crinkles around his eyes before promptly fading away. His jaw tics with a steadfast decision.

"I beg you, Your Grace. *Please*." I am not beneath groveling when a life is at stake.

The rain pelts us harder as if hurrying his decision, and the crowd shifts uncomfortably, muttering annoyances at the delay. Thatcher begs for reconsideration, pledging fealty as his tears mix with the rivulets of rain droplets streaming down his cheeks.

"They came at me first. I was only defending myself! But I'll never shift again, just don't kill me. Please don't kill me. Please, Your Grace, I beg for mercy."

Thunder claps overhead as if even the storm clouds sensed a decision has been made. Sin shifts his gaze to my right and summons a guard with a wave of two fingers. Hands clamp down around the tops of my arms and yank me backwards, but I dig my feet into the ground and thrash myself free.

"Let me stay! Clearly you enjoy an audience," I say, gesturing to the gathered townsfolk, "so go on then. Show us what happens to those born differently than the precious Black Art." I spit the words up at him.

Sin's slivered eyes narrow farther, but he nods once to the guard who then takes a step away from me. I shift my focus to Thatcher and make a silent vow to remember him. I take note of the roundness of his cheeks, his wavy blonde hair, his aquamarine eyes and pretend not to notice his resemblance to Galen. This could very well be my nephew's future.

No. No, it *can't* be.

I hold back the tears, refusing to allow a single remaining memory of Thatcher's short life be clouded through bleary eyes.

Please let it be quick.

It isn't.

Sin swoops down with the speed of a raptor and grabs Thatcher by his shoulders. As if he was struck by the storm's lightning, Thatcher writhes in the Black Art's grip, his body jerking forward and back in rapid succession. Tendrils of blue magic emanate from Sin's fingertips, but his hold never loosens, even with Thatcher's violent convulsions.

The transcendent throws his head back in a blood-curdling scream, and the chains connecting his hands and feet begin to rattle. His body twists and contorts at inhuman angles, no longer belonging to himself, and his face begins to widen.

Sin is forcing him to shift.

He didn't bind Thatcher in iron to protect himself. No, it was for show; to prove a point to the high lords he knew would gather here to witness the turpitude unfolding before us.

That even iron has its limits.

They won't question that the most powerful mage of Aegidale had to flood the transcendent's veins with magic to force his body to shift under the iron. They will only watch as Thatcher morphs into something foreign, something monstrous, and cheer as their almighty Black Art slaughters it before them.

Slayer of beasts, they will call him.

Thatcher's face begins to blur as his features stretch and elongate. With a metallic ring, his chains break at the ankles as his legs widen and shift into thick, muscular stumps. He stands on his new hind legs, his shirt ripping across his chest that now emerges broad and covered in a yellow-tan coat.

The shifter tilts his huge, furred head back in an ear-splitting howl, and when he lowers it again, his light eyes are now set in a face of golden fur, his snout long and rectangular. His second skin is a mix of something canine and bear, and the size of a small horse. His ears are short and pointed, and now lowered as he bares his razor-sharp teeth at Sin, emitting a low guttural growl.

This is what Sin wanted. Because the scene unfolding is all these people will go home remembering about today: that the accused transcendent shifted under iron and threatened the Black Art.

Sin unsheathes the long sword at his hip and that sound—the sliding of steel against leather—will haunt my dreams, waking and not, until my final breath.

I don't wince as his sword connects with Thatcher's broad neck. I don't wet my lips at the innocent blood that sprays onto the wood and speckles Sin's dark surcoat, his face. I don't hear the celebration at my back.

But I see *him.*

Bloodied and severed and erased at the Black Art's shoes. How soon after defeating Legion will Sin declare war on all transcendents? How soon after I help him stop Legion will he turn on me and send his men to hunt down my family like rabid dogs? Just when I thought that *maybe* Sin wasn't a complete monster, he reminded me why so many in Aegidale cower at the mere mention of his name.

I can't make an escape and find Cosmina on my own. At least not flee with her afterwards so long as the tethering spell binds me to him. Sin would hunt me down. No matter how far we ran, or how deep into the woods we hid, he would find me.

He will always find me.

But if I slip away just long enough to find her—rescue her—I could accept my demise when Sin inevitably comes for me if it means freeing my sister on my own. It hadn't occurred to me before, but the longer Legion remains a threat to the kingdom, the more time my family has to form a plan before war is declared on their kind. Finding Cosmina on my own is my family's safest option. She could return to the others and together, they could hunker down in a new location.

But for this plan to work, I need to be as fast as the lightning striking overhead. I need to know Cosmina's precise location.

And there's only one person who can tell me.

CHAPTER 32

Cathal looks terrible. He's slumped against the wall of his cell, his dark hair tousled and overgrown, matched by the unkempt beard swallowing half his face. He doesn't look up as I approach, likely assuming my footsteps belong to the guard responsible for coming down here and tending to him. Judging from Cathal's disheveled appearance, I assume Sin gave orders to not tend too generously.

"They don't know I'm here," I say, announcing my presence in the dank, subterranean dungeon. I don't have long before Sin and the others return to the castle after bidding their farewells to those in attendance. The stench of rotting food and urine assaults my nose as I step up to the cell containing the man who once abused me.

Cathal rolls his head up lazily to look at me. The skin around his eyes is swollen and purple, and his once straight nose now hangs crooked. His lips are cracked, and his dark brown tunic is torn and riddled with blood stains. "Come to let me out, sweetheart?" His voice is heavy and sluggish, dehydration and malnourishment rotting him from the inside out like diseased fruit.

My soft laughter has a hint of hysteria around the edges. "I'm onto your little plan, Cathal."

"Pray tell sweetheart, which little plan is this?"

"The one where you expect me to hand myself over to Legion in exchange for Cosmina's life. If you ever bothered to listen to a damn thing I told you, you'd know my sister would rather die than to let me work for the likes of you."

He licks his lips and shuffles so he sits up a little straighter, resting his hands over his knees. Iron shackles connect his wrists with only about six inches of space between them, and an identical set binds his ankles. "Or maybe I listened to you so well, sweetheart, I knew you'd do anything for that gorgeous sister of yours. Even if it means marching that sweet ass of yours into hellfire."

I slam my hands against the cell, magic pooling into my fingertips and begging to be released. "You listen to me, you ignorant prick. I will never make a deal with Legion, but I *will* fight alongside the kingdom to destroy your entire gods-damned army if you don't tell me where she is. Where is Cosmina?!"

His laughter quickly turns into a deep coughing fit as Cathal hacks into the side of his closed fist. When he finishes retching up one of his lungs, he looks at me with a half amused, half delirious glint in his eyes. "I never thought I'd see the day where Wren, the ever-self-righteous queen of gods-damned placation, has threatened me. I think we both know you haven't got the *gall*."

I lower onto one knee and curl my fingers towards myself, admiring my fingernails as if I just buffed them with a pumice stone. In a voice that sounds almost bored, I say, "I will rip the hearts out of every single one of your men and *feast* on them. My only regret will be if I kill them too quickly and deprive myself the pleasure of hearing them beg for their lives before I do. I bet they'll sing real fucking pretty with my blade at their cocks, don't you?"

Cathal's cracked lips twist into a hideous smirk. "Still thinking about their cocks, sweetheart?"

The cell door groans as it slides open between us. I jump back, startled. *Goddess above, how did that—*

Sin steps up beside me, rain dripping from the tips of his raven hair and down his long-sleeved black leather surcoat. The Black Art hovers above his prisoner, staring down at Cathal with a look that is downright frightening, casting him in shadow.

"Here to ruin our fun, Sire? Wren here was just telling me how she couldn't stop thinking about our c—"

Chaos explodes next to me.

Sin grabs a fistful of Cathal's weathered tunic and yanks him to his feet. Cathal gets one protest out of his foul mouth before Sin slams his back against the wall and drives his knee into his stomach. Once. Twice. A third time.

Cathal rolls his head back to look at Sin, coughing as his lungs are compressed with the impact of the blows. "All this over a fucking bloodwitch. I should have just killed her when I had the chance, and now you're too much of a fucking pussy to d—"

Sin's fist connects with his jaw before Cathal can rattle off the rest of his sentence. Again. And again. Blood spurts from his nose, his mouth, dripping onto his tattered tunic. His scent pets my tongue with a honeyed sweetness reminiscent of freshly dried figs, but my mouth doesn't water at the smell of the Legion commander's spilled blood. A wine connoisseur has no interest in a bottle that has been brewed with rotten grapes.

I startle when Sin slams his palms against Cathal's chest, golden magic seeping out from his hands.

Cathal's hollers of pain nearly split the dungeon in two.

I watch in horror as Sin heals him. Healing him so he may continue to break him.

Cathal twists and cries out as his ribs are poorly mended, and his jaw and nose snap back into alignment. As soon as the magic vanishes from his palms, Sin grabs a fistful of the fabric at Cathal's chest and throws him to the ground. He steps over him, and with a sound that can only be described as pure, masculine rage, the Black Art pounds his fist into Cathal's face, now leaking blood from all orifices, losing all sense of self to blinding fury.

The caster's high.

Sin would have had to use a tremendous amount of magic to force a transcendent to shift under iron. Mages are vulnerable to emotion after expelling great amounts of magic —commonly lust—but in more extreme circumstances, it can invoke bouts of serious wrath. With Sin's power influenced with that of the goddess, it surely takes a lot more casting to invoke the caster's high, like how a drunkard needs to ingest more brandy to fall into a stupor. Flooding Thatcher with enough power to break the magical binding of a purifying element has broken the seal on the Black Art's control.

In different circumstances, I could watch him gut Cathal and not blink an eye. But the Legion commander may be the only connection I have to finding my sister. I need him. And judging by the increasing speed of Sin's punches, I don't think he's stopping to heal him again.

No one else is dying today.

"Stop," I say, my voice quiet but firm.

Sin's fist halts inches above Cathal's broken jaw as if frozen in place. He stays there for an extended beat, as if he had forgotten I was present at all, before uncurling his bloodied fingers from his tunic, and Cathal's limp body falls to the ground with a thud. Unconscious, but alive.

Probably alive.

Sin turns his head just enough for me to glimpse most of his profile and note the muscles feathering in his jaw. "You have *seconds* to tell me why you're down here." He moves to face me fully now, his head dipped slightly as he approaches, making him look all the more predatory.

But I am not prey.

"I asked him where Cosmina is." I will my voice to hold steady as I stare into his eyes now glowing yellow-green from the use of magic.

He stops approaching when there's only a few feet of distance remaining between us. "And what did he tell you?"

He is an ocean caught in its own storm, waves of anger rolling off him and threatening to knock me back with their wake.

I lift my chin a little higher. "He wouldn't," I admit.

"Coming down here to get answers on your own—trying to get out of our arrangement, little witch? I offered you a deal. Sneak behind my back again, and I'll easily find a different purpose for you," he drawls, his voice sharp as the athame strapped beneath my dress. Sin's stare strips me bare as he scans my face, looking more beast than man. He takes another step forward—a challenge. "Never come down here again," he whispers, his words weighted and heavy.

"And what if I do? Will you kill me too, *Your Grace?* Since that seems to be the only way you're capable of solving problems."

He erases the remaining distance between us in one step, his hand forming a collar around my throat. My shoulders slam into the wall behind me as he pins me between it and his body. My pulse thrums wildly in my neck as my veins swell with the rush of magic. I prepare to scald that hand the second his grip tightens any farther.

"Let go of me," I warn through clenched teeth.

Air huffs from his nose, and I swear my flesh burns away to bone as he slowly drags his eyes up my body before settling on mine. My heart flutters like a hummingbird's wings, and I only hope he can't hear it. Though if his boosted magic has enhanced his sense of smell as he *suggested,* I can only imagine what it's done for his hearing as well.

I go deadly still as he leans in and presses his forehead against mine. "*Never...* sneak behind my back again, Wren."

This time when he speaks my name, it isn't to show respect, but rather to assert dominance. He keeps us here for another breath, his large hand wrapped around my neck and his forehead pressed to mine.

When he finally drops his arm, I resist the urge to rub my throat. I stand tall, showing him he does not intimidate me, despite the icy tendrils skittering down my spine like spider legs.

Sin walks back to the cell, and the door slams closed as he magically locks it with a wave of his hand, Cathal's body still limp and unresponsive inside. He leans against the door, looping both arms through the bars and grabbing his wrist with his other hand. I push my collective out and envelop his, but this time, I don't recoil as his rage and anxiety courses through me. But I don't need to read him to see just how deep his personal torment has settled.

I push off the wall and linger behind him. The tension rolling off him charges the air between us as if his body was a thundercloud about to erupt.

"Your heart is sad. It will hurt more when you finally face all that pain you've buried so deep inside yourself. A lot more. But it's got to be better than this," I whisper.

The door to the dungeon slams shut behind me, and I head towards the stone staircase off the foyer. Dusaro barges through the entrance, and his face morphs into pure fury when he spots me at the foot of the stairs and beelines towards me.

I expect him to spew a nasty string of insults when he approaches. I don't expect the open-handed slap as he strikes me across the face.

Stumbling backwards, my hand immediately flies to my cheek.

"How dare you question his authority in front of a crowd?" he bellows.

Lowering my hand, I say, "I tried to prevent him from making a humongous mistake. One I have no doubt *you* highly encouraged!"

Dusaro pulls his arm back to hit me again, this time with a clenched fist, but I dart out of his path. When I spin back to face him, I hold a ward taut between my palms. If he tries to hit me again, the ward will deflect the blow.

"Your prejudices are sickening. There was no need to—"

He swipes my legs out from under me, and I go tumbling forwards. My hands absorb the brunt of my fall, stopping my face from colliding with the floor. Dusaro's weight crashes onto my back, sending my stomach flush against the stone. He pins my body between two muscular thighs and yanks my head back by a fistful of my unbound hair.

"You like making us look like fools, do you? How's this for looking like a godsdamned fool?" Dusaro slams the side of my head into the floor, but before he can hurl it to the ground for a second time, I set myself on fire.

Phantom flames ignite my skin and erupt into a golden ring around me, the quivering tips of the blaze sneering at him as Dusaro scrambles off me, muttering a string of swears. His arms cover his head instinctively, the lapels of his black jacket smoldering as I rise to my feet once more, leaving an outline of my silhouette scorched into the floor.

I prowl around him, a facetious smile teasing my lips as I display my power, a firestorm careening through my plump, swollen veins. Dusaro glowers at me with nothing shy of ferocity beaming out from within his dark eyes. My defense is ready when he sheathes his arm in an icy blue ward and pulls his fist back to hit me again, but halts mid-swing.

Sin's bronzed hand wraps around his father's knuckles and forcibly lowers Dusaro's arm to his side. He steps between us, putting me at his back as he faces his father.

"She embarrassed us in front of half of Blackreach. The bloodwitch publicly questioned your authority, and you didn't have her arrested! What kind of Black Art would allow something so *filthy* to question him like that?!"

"Kind of like how you're questioning my authority right now, Father?"

"I wouldn't have to question you so much if you could make a decent decision just once in your life! But you can't, and it is an embarrassment to our family's name. You always were weak. Just like your *mother*," he chastises.

"That is enough!" I shout, throwing my arms down to my sides. "You both should be ashamed of the atrocity that happened out there today. I am disgusted by the cruelty of you both. I can think of a thousand different things I would like to see happen to him," I shove a finger in Sin's direction, "but having you as a father isn't one of them. You are an embarrassment to Aegidale and a disgrace for a father."

Dusaro heads straight for me, aiming a finger at my chest. "If you don't do something about her, Singard, I will. And that's a godsdamned promise."

In one swift maneuver, Sin pulls his father against his chest and wraps an arm of corded muscle around his neck, holding him snug in a headlock. I've never seen the Black Art be physical with Dusaro, but I've also never seen him this high on magic either.

"You're not going to touch a hair on her pretty little head," Sin murmurs. "You know what happens when people try to touch what is *mine*."

Dusaro snickers, but his reddish-brown skin pales beneath his son's grip. "Don't tell me you have feelings for the bloodwitch."

"Don't think so low of me, Father," he growls. Sin drops his hold and steps away from him, but remains between us, not trusting Dusaro to not lunge for me again.

Dusaro straightens and shoots me a disgusted look before turning back to Sin. "I have sent word to Sterling about what has happened here today. We are expecting the Langstons tomorrow evening."

"You're just telling me this now?" Sin huffs with annoyance.

"I shouldn't have to. You should have alerted them the minute that *thing* was brought here. But to no surprise, you failed to do so, so I stepped in to do what needed to be done. And *you*," he spits, turning his attention back to me, "will be with the Langston boy tomorrow evening. Get him to invite you to Castle Summerswind. I want that entire castle interrogated with your..." he makes a circling motion around his head to imply my ability. "Now that we have proof someone is helping them, I want you around Lady Langston, their daughters, and every servant in their ranks. I hear Sterling's eldest son will be returning soon as well, and when he does, you can infiltrate his mind too. Your work isn't done, girl," he finishes, sneering down at me over his slender nose.

I spit at his feet. "You make me sick."

"Get out of my sight."

Hurtling myself up the stairs and into my room, I slam my door shut and lock it with magic. It won't be enough to keep Sin out if he decides he wants in, but it will keep the hand-maidens out. I throw myself onto the bed and wonder if any of Thatcher's family was watching from that crowd today.

CHAPTER 33

I am left with two options. I could sneak down to Cathal's cell again and offer him a little violent... *persuasion* of my own, but the risk of Sin finding out is too high, too dangerous. He'll have someone watching his cell at every hour now, I'm sure. Which leaves me with the second option: I play along while I look for another way out.

Tonight, the Black Art is hosting a dinner with Sterling and his son to ensure they are in agreement about the kingdom's very public execution yesterday morning. Locking in an alliance with the overseers of trade means gaining their troops, and ultimately, a faster elimination of Legion, and victory in the war Sin plans on declaring soon after their demise. Thatcher's death will likely motivate Legion to attack sooner—Cathal's stand-in leaders no doubt using the event as means to fearmonger their soldiers into fighting before they're appropriately equipped and ready.

My dress is a pale shade of blue, its color reminiscent of hydrangea flowers, with a ruched waist and flowy bell sleeves that hang off my shoulders. River added a swash of gold to my eyelids and painted my lips the color of blood. Fitting for the occasion, I suppose. She left my long hair unbound to fall freely down my back in soft waves.

266

I clear my mind of thoughts of Thatcher and my family and how they'll be reduced to pawns in the kingdom's fight for civil domination. Right now, my focus needs to be on finding Cosmina and securing her freedom. If fighting alongside the kingdom is the only way to free her, I'll help earn the Langston's support now and strap on the armor as I charge into battle.

I wipe my tears, smearing them into nothingness, and walk downstairs in the pretty dress.

* * *

Wide stretched smiles erupt across the table as two servants dressed in matching linen smocks place generously loaded plates in front of each of us. Sin sits at the head of the long dining table, wearing a burgundy coat of weathered print with a flared hem and laced-up chest. His usual free-flowing hair is tied back with a small leather tie.

Sterling sits across from Sin at the opposite end of the table. Bennett's father appears close in age to Dusaro, but his graying hair and creased forehead indicate a life spent in negotiation and settling disputes. He wears a navy-blue tailcoat with the letter *L* woven into the chest pocket in fine silver thread.

Bennett sits across from me, dressed in a similar blue jacket with silver embroidery as his father's. Dusaro sits to Sin's left next to Bennett, and on my side of the table, Aldred sits between Ileana and me. Sin briefed me before the meal on the role I am to play tonight. He told the Langstons I have family that have been caught in Legion cross hairs, and am aiding the kingdom with my proficient, yet nothing extraordinary, mage abilities. And being an old friend of the Black Art, I am trusted to be present during the dinner while they discuss strategies of war.

The first half of the meal is an exchange of casual conversation concerning family and mutual friends. Bennett occasionally asks me about my life in Innodell, to which I lie through my teeth, not willing to share anything personal with someone of his virtues. I keep my attention on the Langstons, ignoring the heated stare Sin gives me every time Bennett speaks to me directly, monitoring my responses like a hawk circling a plump rabbit.

The conversation shifts political after the servants bring in dessert—sweetened egg custard with currants and slivered nuts.

Sin swirls the mead in his glass, then takes a deep pull of the amber drink. "It won't be long now. They're impulsive. But what they don't know is there will be no retreat for them this time. We'll evacuate the city and meet them head on in Black-reach. We'll create chokepoints in the city and cut off their points of retreatment. Once they barge through the gates of Blackreach, expecting us to be waiting for them at Scarwood, we'll lock down the city and move in. And when we're done, the only thing remaining of Legion will be their ghosts."

"It's a good plan, Mr. Langston," Dusaro chimes. "I've fought against Legion many times—their turnover is high, so they're ghastly inexperienced and flightier than sparrows. We'll have the element of surprise on them, and as soon as they realize the trap they've walked into, they'll panic. Picking them off will be easy, especially if we have the Langston battalion at our side."

The Black Art's father looks polished in a fine black tailcoat and white shirt underneath, his dark hair smooth and shiny, and the few braids in his hair don't have a strand out of place. *Goddess above,* the resemblance between Sin and his father is striking, their dark skin equally as smooth, their noses both long and slender, and their narrowed eyes both downturned at the corners.

I corral what remains of my pudding with my spoon while I push my collective away from me and latch onto Sterling's. His body may display signs of age, but his mind is sharp and calculated, and I don't sense any nervousness or traces of deceit.

"It's always an honor to do our part in serving, Your Grace," Sterling says, wiping his chin with a decorative cloth napkin. "The cost, however, will be extravagant. Is fighting them in the city really the best option when we have open land that isn't bordered by homes and shops that will surely be destroyed and need to be rebuilt?"

"My Lord, if I may interject," Aldred addresses Sterling, "Legion is most familiar with fighting on open land. They aren't accustomed to the cities because they can't traverse them during the day. They'll be in uncharted territory to begin with, and I've already been compiling plans to stake traps and chokeholds throughout Blackreach. The devastation will be great, but the devastation if we do not do this will be far greater. I'll see that the residents are relocated to shelters and outposts we have set up. There won't be civilian casualties, and if we have your support, there will be few casualties of our own."

Sin thanks his commander for his input, and Dusaro offers Aldred a nod of approval. As the conversation continues to thicken with political jargon, Bennett speaks to me less, and I note hardly anyone asks Ileana to weigh in her opinion. Apparently being mundane makes her opinion less valid than Sin's. Or perhaps it is simply because she's a woman that they don't ask her thoughts.

When the servants return to collect our dishes, I lean across the table towards Bennett and flash him a sweet smile.

"Would you accompany me for an evening stroll, my Lord?"

Bennett grins, revealing a set of white teeth. "It would be my pleasure, my Lady." Rising from the table, he shoots a sideways glance to a smirking Dusaro. I glance to Sin and find him now entirely focused on Bennett, apparently also noting the exchanged glance between him and his father. Bennett doesn't seem to notice the warning glare on Sin's face—a glare I'm not sure how to interpret. Sin shifts his stare to me and sweeps his eyes down my body—his gaze lingering an extra second on my breasts, my waist, my legs—and drags his tongue over his teeth as if he finds me disapproving.

Is there something wrong with how I look?

When I looked in the mirror, I thought my appearance could mistake me for a lady of high stature, but the Black Art's lingering stare has me questioning if my taste in attire is perhaps not suitable at all.

"*Careful* with my Wren, Mr. Langston," Sin says, swishing the remainder of the mead around in his glass.

I arch an eyebrow, but Sin doesn't look away from Bennett, his eyes dropping to the hand he places on the small of my back as he guides us out of the dining hall.

My Wren. I'd like to shove *my* fist up his ass.

We head outside to the northern courtyard and walk along the stone path through the castle's gardens. The hedge's pink and purple flowers have a faint shimmer to them as the droplets from the afternoon rain reflect the silvery beams of moonlight. Bennett glances up at the sky, the faint light casting shadow on one side of his golden-brown hair.

"I assume you are staying the evening and riding home tomorrow?" I ask.

"Yes. His Grace has generously offered to put us and our driver up for the evening. I dare say we'll be seeing more of each other if our troops are to be drilling on castle grounds."

"Do you think this will escalate Legion's next attack?"

"Most definitely. I hope it has them furious. It's always more fun to kill them when they're all stirred up about something." He winks as if what he just said would somehow be a turn on for me.

I feign a laugh. "You're confident your men are able and ready for this fight?" I sink my claws into his collective before he has time to respond.

He shrugs. "Men are ready for anything when you pay them well enough. There is a reason my family has stayed in power for so many generations."

I comb through his mind with invisible fingers and resist the urge to gag as I sift through layers of pride and lust. Nothing to indicate he says anything other than what he believes to be true. As I told Sin before, the Langston boy is honest. Pompous, arrogant, and irritating—but honest.

We step into the Spiritwood trees, and I lead us to the small pond where Sin and I dueled with magic. "Speaking of your family—will you be taking your father's place when that time comes?"

I sit on a worn-down rock near the edge of the water, and Bennett relaxes on a nearby tree stump.

"Yes, unless Cornelius decides he wants to be a part of the family again."

"Cornelius?"

"My elder brother. My father and him had a bit of a falling out a while ago, but he has sent word he intends to return to Blackreach soon. I'm not sure about his reasoning, but I would be surprised if it wasn't because he found trouble and doesn't have the coin to get himself out of it."

A brisk wind rips my hair forward and chills the back of my neck. As the breeze settles, it leaves an eerie silence in its wake as if the birds and evening critters sensed the darkness within me and scattered.

"I hope your reunion goes smoothly, my Lord."

"Sin says you're going to be fighting alongside us?" He poses his words as a question.

My shoulders pull back when I look at him head on. "Yes. I'm willing to do what I can to help stop those... *dogs*," I mutter, the insult bitter and unflattering on my tongue.

He lets out a sound of approval from his chest and moves to sit at my feet. "I think a woman willing to fight for what she believes in is very, *very* sexy," he whispers, slipping a hand onto my knee. "You're very beautiful, Wren."

"You're too kind, my Lord, but perhaps you've had a touch too much mead at dinner," I laugh without humor, attempting to dismiss the compliment.

He pushes up to his knees and tilts his head so his mouth hovers near my neck, his breath hot and unsettling against my skin. "I don't need a drink to know you look absolutely... tantalizing," he murmurs and presses his lips to the side of my neck.

I lean away, but his hand races to grab the other side of my neck, and he pins me in place, while his other hand finds the slit in my dress and slides up to my thigh.

"Bennett, n—"

He presses his mouth to mine and forces his tongue between my lips. As quickly as he invaded my mouth, I slide my hands up between our chests and shove him back.

"This is making me uncomfortable. Let go of me."

He pulls his head back to look at me and cradles my face in his hands, brushing his thumb across my cheek. "There's no reason to be uncomfortable, darling," he says quietly and dips his mouth to my collarbone. One of his hands grabs my thigh again, and his fingertips stroke the fabric of my underwear. This time, I grab both his shoulders and push him back harder.

"I want you to stop," I say, now louder and firmer.

"You won't want to stop once we start, I promise," he breathes against my skin. In one swift motion, he stands, hoists me off the rock by my bottom, and lays me back in the tall grass. He covers me with his body, his mouth crushing mine as his fingers begin undoing the buttons on his coat.

I slam my palms into his chest. "Bennett, I said *no*. Get. Off. Of. Me."

He shushes me and drops his hands to his waist belt, unfastening it with impressive speed. "Let's just try—you'll love it. Come now, you're not going to say no to a Langston, right?"

"I just did," I say, sliding out from under him and yanking my dress down that slid up in the entanglement.

Bennett looks at me with his mouth slightly dropped and arms splayed out in front of him as if he truly can't comprehend I'm telling him no. "Are you being serious right now? Come now, Wren, don't be a fucking idiot."

"Don't be a fucking asshole. I'm leaving." I turn and take a step away from him when he grabs my elbow and jerks me back towards him.

"You're not going anywhere," he growls, all friendliness gone from his eyes. "Not until I release you."

"No one *releases* me. Not even a pompous Langston prick," I spit.

Rage twists his face into something monstrous, and he strikes me with the back of his hand. I grab my cheek instinctively, and when I lower it, I'm certain my face more than matches the anger on his.

"How dare you speak to a lord like that. It seems you needed to be reminded of your *place*. A low-born girl from

Innodell *refusing* a Langston? I can't say I've experienced it before, but I can certainly think of a punishment on the spot."

I don't hesitate. I let the heat tunnel through my veins as it rushes from the valve I keep tightly sealed and into my palms. With a feral yell, I throw my hands against his chest and burn him in the process. He topples backwards, letting out a few curses unfit for a lady's ears.

But I'm not a lady, and he's certainly not a godsdamned man.

Bennett regains his footing and saunters towards me, licking his lips and sliding a hand into his now unfastened pants. "You're going to regret that now, bitch."

I ready myself with another surge of magic, ready to blast him harder and farther into the woods this time, restraint be damned. *No one touches me. Especially not a mundane asshole on a power trip.*

He lets out a low, dark chuckle. "I would have made sure you enjoyed yourself. But now... now I think I'll make you scream for other reasons. Don't even think of trying that again if you ever want to see the outside of a cell again."

A loud roar splits the night, and a symphony of snapping branches crescendos towards us. Bennett instinctively reaches for the sword absent from his formal wear, fear molding his face as his hand swipes for his phantom weapon. I throw my hands out with a defensive ward sprung between them just as the final bushes between us and *it* part, and the sound rattling from its chest heightens to a high-pitched wail.

The transcendent leaps from between two trees, its powerful paws stampeding into Bennett's chest, and tackles him to the ground in one experienced maneuver. Bennett rakes his fingers through the mud as he scurries himself backwards, eyes wide and panicked, staring into the face of the snarling beast. It paces before him, never taking its eyes off Bennett, never turning to acknowledge me.

The animal is long and sinewy with four muscled legs and fur the color of midnight. It holds its large head low as it prowls towards Bennett, who now spews promises to leave transcendents alone, a desperate attempt for mercy as he finds himself weaponless and too spineless to face death. Its ears are short and slightly rounded at the tips, and the shape of its skeleton is almost feline. Bennett looks at me with eyes wide as small dinner plates, then looks between the transcendent and me.

He's gauging the distance.

While the black furred beast slowly closes the gap between them, Bennett is debating turning tail and running. Hoping it will go for the easier prey—the woman who hasn't yet run away while its back is turned.

He doesn't know I'm the deadliest creature in these woods.

Bennett scrambles to his feet and slowly bends at the waist, sliding his hand under his pant leg and pulling out a knife with a six-inch blade. The feline flicks its head with a rattled growl, daring him to pull the weapon on him. Bennett looks to me again, and for a moment, I think he is going to toss me the knife, to give me some means to defend myself before he flees.

I was wrong.

While I may be the deadliest predator in these trees, Bennett is the weakest—of mind, heart, and soul—and he darts through the woods like a freshly sprung arrow.

The Langstons don't view transcendents as people, but rather as inhumane monsters who rely on instinct alone, so surely it will turn and attack the easier prey, the one just standing here out in the open.

But I know better.

Bennett takes off running without so much as bidding me a second glance. I make no move to stop the transcendent as it pulls its lips back in a snarl and leaps after him, burying its impressive claws into Bennett's back. He hits the ground face first, rolls onto his back, and comes face-to-face with the beast. Saliva drips from its jowls, and its lips quiver as the transcendent lets out a low, guttural growl.

Bennett buries the knife into its side, and the raven-furred animal yowls when it makes contact but doesn't take so much as a step backwards. Instead, it opens its jaws in an ear-splitting roar.

I don't wince as it sinks its teeth into Bennett's neck and shakes with lethal ferocity. When Bennett goes limp, lying crumpled in a pool of crimson regret, the predator drops its prey and huffs over its kill. It still doesn't turn to look at me, but it knows I'm here. I lower into a crouch with my magic still simmering in my hands, waiting to see how it reacts now that its first target is dealt with. This isn't just a transcendent—it's a transcendent that managed to get inside the castle gates of its most hated enemy.

This kill was personal.

I eye the knife protruding from its side and can't help but wonder if Bennett would have tried to threaten me with it had I kept fighting him. The wound will be easy enough for the transcendent to heal in its human state, but shifting back around the knife will be incredibly painful. I take one measured step towards it. Its ears flicker at my movement.

"Are you alright?" I ask, my voice coming out breathier than I intended.

Its hunched shoulders seem to tighten farther at my voice, but it still doesn't turn to look at me.

I take a second careful step. "I can pull it out. It'll hurt, but it will be worse if you try to shift around the blade."

I wait for some sign of acknowledgment, but not a muscle twitches along its long, muscular body. I reach towards its unwounded side, willing my hand not to shake, and gently press my fingertips against its short, sleek coat. When it doesn't recoil at my touch, I press my palm into its black fur, noting the deep shades of blue illuminated in the moonlight. Very carefully, I slide my palm across its side.

The beast shudders at my caress.

I move to its wounded side and grab the leather-bound hilt, bracing my other hand against its stomach for leverage, and rip the knife free. It lets out a sharp howl of pain, and blood pours from the wound, blood that it's losing too quickly if it doesn't shift back and heal, blood that... that smells so familiar.

Like hyacinths in the rain.

The knife falls from my hand, and I gasp as I inhale the scent of its blood. Its ears flicker at the sound, noting the realization on my breath, hearing the thrumming of my pounding heart.

No. It can't be.

The smell of him flares my nostrils wide, and my mouth waters at the scent it never got to taste. He finally turns and faces me, his large, powerful paws inches from my leather sandals, and raises its head so it stands at full height before me. His face more closely resembles a cat's than the canine likeness Eldridge and Thatcher shared, and set deep in its angled face are two brilliant eyes staring back at me.

Familiar, yellow-green eyes.

His eyes.

And then I feel it. The tugging in my stomach—the phantom tether buzzing with excitement at the proximity of its creator. The magic in my gut doesn't lie. The smell of his blood in my nose, on my tongue, doesn't lie.

277

My heart fractures with truth.

Sin slowly retreats into the brush behind him, the silhouette of his body disappearing within the trees, leaving only the eternal spring of his eyes visible through the woods, until those too, disappear.

CHAPTER 34

H e doesn't knock before charging into my room, throwing the door open hard enough it slams into the wall, and his face, twisted into a mask of fury, envelops the threshold.

Dusaro.

I rise from my perch on the red cushioned seat in front of the vanity, ready to face the wrath festering in his deep brown eyes. I knew he would come.

"What. Happened?" he asks, spit nearly flying from his lips as he shouts the question at me.

"What?" I feign a recoil to suggest his intrusion was not one I stayed awake waiting for all night.

"Don't play with me, girl. What happened with Bennett last night?"

I didn't utter a peep to anyone when I left Bennett's limp body in the woods last night, content to let his cold, lifeless corpse be a meal for the vultures and flies. And even that seemed too merciful for a predator of his kind. I barely slept a wink last night.

I waited for *him*.

Wondering if Sin would come to my room after he shifted and healed, but the door I left unlocked never cracked open. A hundred questions plagued my mind through the night, followed by a thousand accusations and names I wanted to scream at him, but I won't dare mention a word of it to Dusaro before I have a chance to speak with his son.

How can Sin be one of them? And why did he intervene if it meant risking I would discover his secret?

Sin appears in the doorway behind Dusaro, no sound of his footfalls preceding him. The weight of his stare is heavy, but I don't drag my eyes away from his father. Not yet.

"Bennett and I went for a walk through the gardens, and we spoke for a while. His mind was clean, like I've said a hundred times before. He invited me to Summerswind, and I later excused myself to bed. He escorted me to the entrance, but said he was going to stay out for a little longer to enjoy some fresh air before retiring to his chambers," I lie smoothly. "Why are you asking?"

"Bennett's body was found this morning outside the keep."

Outside the keep. He must have circled back and moved him after shifting, to hide that Bennett's death happened inside the kingdom's gates.

"Goddess above," I whisper, hooking my finger over my mouth. "What happened to him?"

"Throat ripped out by one of those godsdamned monsters!" Dusaro hollers.

I dare a glance at Sin who watches me intently, his jaw clenched, but I swear the smallest hint of relief flashes in his eyes. "Retaliation, you think? For Thatcher?" I ask.

"Possibly. Unless it was one of our own," Dusaro drawls.

I furrow my brow. "You just said it was a transcendent."

"It would appear so, but I also know some of us have a taste for... *showmanship.*" He folds both arms across the lapels of his black coat. "I'm going to ask again, and this time, think very carefully. Did either of you," he glances to Sin then back to me, "have anything to do with the Langston boy?"

Looking square into Dusaro's dark eyes, I say, "Of course not." I sink claws into Sin's collective, waiting for his own answer.

He keeps his attention on me a moment longer, surely feeling my talons dragging their jagged nails across his mind, before looking at his father. "No." The word rolls off his tongue with ease, but his mind quivers as if it can't quite support the crushing weight of his lie.

Dusaro studies each of us for a minute then blows out a sharp breath. "Sterling left this morning to be with his family. This is a warning from Legion then—their way of saying they're coming. Keep your wits about you," Dusaro grunts to neither of us in particular. He turns and leaves the room, his long, straight hair swishing well past his shoulders.

The room grows heavier as soon as the door clicks shut behind him. I clear my throat and shift my attention to Sin. His irises have faded to their normal shade of green, no longer glowing with their yellow-green hue, and no longer encased in a face of raven black fur. A hundred questions threaten to tear out of me, but I read the unspoken word on his lips—*later*. I nod once in acknowledgment, and he follows his father out of the room.

Aldred intercepts me in the hallway on my way to the southern courtyard for sparring to fit me for armor. He has me try on a steel cuirass plate that covers my chest and stomach, with black winged pauldrons and matching gauntlets for my forearms. My thighs and shins are protected by plates of blackened steel but don't restrict me from moving freely enough to cast.

I spend the day wielding both magic and a sword in the armor, getting accustomed to the feeling of moving within the casing. Aldred spends the better portion of the day fine tuning my stance and lunges and correcting me firmly. The better prepared I am to fight, the lower the risk of causality for all of us. I don't take his gruff demeanor as anything other than him wanting to protect his people.

The distraction is welcome. Sparring with Aldred keeps my attention on the commander and his very lethal sword which he wields with alarming accuracy, and not on the Black Art and the gigantic secret I've unveiled. Or rather... the one he let me see.

When we part ways at sundown, I scarf down two bowls of lamb stew and head to the bathhouse, eager to scrub away any lingering smell of Bennett on my skin. I feel no remorse for him as I wash my thighs where his hands had grabbed me, and scrub at my sides where his legs had pinned me.

His face flashes in my mind.

Not Bennett's. Cathal's and his treacherous smirk as he watched his friends beat and berate me. I remember hearing his laughter off to the side as they took turns claiming my body for their own, when I was too young and ignorant to know how to defend myself. I would have killed Bennett before I let him repeat what others had done to me before. I would have accepted the consequences of his blood on my hands, would have truly tested my ability to control *her*. If I had failed, Cosmina would rather die than know I had to lie down for another monster.

I brush out my hair and slip into a jade night dress and matching silk robe. It is hours past sunset, but I need to see him.

I tap the back of my knuckle on his door twice, not that I have any doubt his transcendent hearing heard my footsteps approaching his bedchambers. The lock clicks free, and the door creaks opens.

Sin stands on the balcony with his back to me, looking out over the castle's grounds with his shoulders slumped forward and his hands perched wide on the ledge. A half-drank glass of amber liquid sits next to him on the railing. He unlatched the door with magic then, likely waiting for me, knowing I would come looking for him here.

I step into his chambers. The space is as I remember it—the large four-poster bed draped in blankets, the dark wood armoires along the walls, plush gray rugs laid across the floor, the buttery soft leather chair in the corner. I cross the room and pause at the open doors leading onto the balcony. He doesn't turn around but picks up his glass and takes a deep pull.

"You moved the body," I say, shattering the heavy silence in the room.

"Had to."

"You were afraid they'd blame you?"

Sin shakes his head lazily, teetering the glass between his thumb and forefinger. "No. They would have blamed you," he says softly.

His words send a shiver down my spine. He is right. Even if Dusaro knew for certain Bennett died at the hands of his son, he would have pinned it on me. I would have been sentenced to death, and not a soul would've questioned it.

"How did you move him outside the gate without the guards seeing?"

"There are... passageways," he answers carefully. *Hidden tunnels.*

"But no one would have seen him leave. Surely Dusaro is questioning the guards posted at the gate last night."

"Already taken care of. I spoke with the men on watch last night. They'll remember seeing him now," he replies, his tone almost disinterested.

My head nods in understanding, even though his back is to me and can't see it. I walk to the small table on my right and pour myself a glass of mead from the crystal decanter. The sweet, honeyed beverage is cut with distinct notes of clove and nutmeg. I savor the flavors while I gather my thoughts, thinking of how to phrase the questions that have been stewing in the back of my mind since last night.

"How?" is all I manage to choke out.

"Persuasion is a skill of mine, little witch," he drawls, not understanding I'm not asking about the guards anymore.

"No. I mean... *how*? How are you doing this? Fighting against the very people you belong with."

"I do *not* belong with them," he snarls, turning to look at me over his shoulder.

"You're a transcendent."

His only response is a low rumble from somewhere deep in his chest.

"Is your father also?"

He turns around to face me fully now. "No." His black shirt is unbuttoned, and I scan his bare skin for injury, but there's not a mark on him, no sign the incident ever even happened.

I take a step towards him. "You could end this, Sin. This stupid prejudice. You could unite everyone, I just don't under—"

"It's not that simple, Wren," he cuts me off. "Do you really think I can show up in the cities and shift in front of everyone? After everything the kingdom and I have done to them... showing them what I am would inspire a war far deadlier than what I'm planning. I just killed one of them for attacking a mundane, and a day later, *I* killed someone while in transition. That is not something they'll forgive."

"So you would rather slaughter innocent people than accept the mistakes of your own? *That* is what is unforgivable. You wouldn't have to show anyone what you are if you didn't want to—you could just *stop* the fighting."

"And do you understand how suspicious that would be? If after decades of the kingdom pushing against them, I just stopped. If anyone ever discovered what I was, I'd be dead before the next sunrise."

I shoot him an incredulous look. "You're the Black Art, Singard."

"That doesn't make me invincible!" he roars, slamming his glass down on the ledge behind him and then running that hand through his hair.

"I don't understand how you are—"

"It's not something I'd expect a *bloodwitch* to understand," he snaps. "Don't pretend your problems are worthy of being compared to mine."

Heat burns in my cheeks like a fire ignited in my throat, choking out my words before I can spit them. *How dare he? The Black Art that hides behind his throne while wearing a crown of lies dares to insult my character?*

My hand flies open before I can think better of it, and I slap him across the face.

A small part of me regrets it as I lower my now stinging palm, but a much larger part of me almost wants to hit him again.

A humorless smile widens his lips, and he flicks his tongue across his teeth as he rights his head to look at me again. Wrath emanates from him, juxtaposing the chilled air sweeping across my chest.

"Go," he orders, his voice low and tone clipped, but he makes no move to strike me back.

I turn my back on the man that keeps his emotions buried so deep inside himself that I'm not sure even he remembers where to find them, and storm out the door.

CHAPTER 35

I am not ignorant to the giant target plastered on my forehead. The Black Art does not trust me, as he shouldn't, and I now possess information that has the potential to incite riots unlike ones Aegidale has ever seen.

I am not safe. Not that I ever have been, but I certainly find myself peering over my shoulder a lot more since learning of Sin's secret. I've spent the past few days training from the burning red sky at dawn to the pink tourmaline clouds at dusk, with only one of those days spent with Aldred. The Black Art's commander has taken to integrating the Langston troops with the kingdom's armies, ensuring every soldier has a placement.

I've caught glimpses of Sin as he makes his rounds through the courtyards each day, and while we've never made direct eye contact, as soon as my back is turned, I feel him watching me. Perhaps he's debating if the strength I add to his army outweighs the risk of keeping a bloodwitch's lungs filling with air. Sin promised my freedom in exchange for my alliance—a temporary truce that would hold until Legion was eradicated. But now that I'm in possession of such sensitive knowledge, I would be a fool to not be on my guard. *Will the Black Art really let me leave his castle and risk me exposing his truth?*

After dinner and a bath, I head to my quarters for the night.

I haven't been sleeping well, unable to turn off the thoughts that pick at my brain like some kind of incurable blight. I've been so furious with him. Angry at him for shoving my title down my throat as if the word *bloodwitch* was some sort of poison, and angry at myself for letting it bother me so much. *Why do I even care what he thinks?*

I clutch the bed sheets to my chin, and in the privacy of my room, I let the tears spill without restraint. The scarred over wound my parents left behind splits open inside me, and it feels like a thousand tiny fragments of shattered glass embed into my heart. They could not love *what* I am—and they will never know how that influenced *who* I became.

The balcony doors fly open.

I kick my legs over the bed and grab my athame from beneath my pillow. There's no roar of a storm outside, no howling of wind that could have blown open the doors. Gripping my dagger, I step onto the balcony and dare a glance over the ledge. I scan the gardens beneath me, but the flowered hedges and ivy terraces stare back at me with the stillness of a mural. Just as I wipe the wetness from my cheeks, movement from the tree line jerks my attention.

Peering out from the dark woods like lanterns above the nighttime sea, are two glowing yellow-green eyes.

He blew open the balcony doors, apparently still able to manipulate the collective while in his other skin. I can barely make out the form of his dark, feline body against the night, but I watch as Sin dips his large head in a subtle summons— no, a request. If he insisted on speaking with me, he'd have simply forced himself into my room. He is giving me the choice.

I hold his stare for an extended beat, then rush to pull on a robe over my black nightgown and quickly fluff my unbound hair with my hands. I hurry from my room, down the spiral staircase, and to the part of the woods where I had seen him. My lower belly tingles as I draw near, the tether sensing his presence, even though he's slipped back into the trees by the time I reach them.

Goddess above, don't let this be a trap.

Sin stands in his human form—tall and bronzed and shirtless. His sculpted shoulders and chest a giveaway to years of backbreaking work, his defined obliques peeking out from the pale linen trousers slung low on his waist, a nod to his years of swordsmanship. He says nothing as I approach, and I note the primal stillness of his stance. I've seen it on Eldridge enough times over the years that I'm surprised I didn't make the connection with Sin sooner. I should have known, and I didn't.

I stop a few feet away from him and clasp my hands behind my back. "I suppose I neglected to thank you for intervening that night," I say. Despite his demeanor when we spoke after, he *had* protected me in the moment, risking everything to do so.

"You don't need to thank me," he murmurs. "Besides, you seemed to have it handled."

"Were you following us?"

"I overheard my father and Bennett talking about you before the dinner—talking about... *things.* I knew if he tried to put hands on you, you wouldn't have it, and I worried what would happen when you didn't. Bennett carried a reputation for being aggressive with women he deemed entitled to him. I knew him for almost my entire life. You kept fighting him every step, and I knew he would see it as a game, a chase. And if I know anything about you, it's that you would never let yourself be caught.

"So, I tailed you both after you left. I was following just close enough to hear you, in case he was stupid enough to try anything. I was planning on intervening so you wouldn't reveal the extent of your power and risk him learning what you were. Not shifting back before getting to you... that wasn't planned." He folds his arms across his bare, coppered chest, his slivered eyes narrowing farther as he relives the event from his own memories.

"Why didn't you shift back?"

His hands slowly curl at his side, and he closes his eyes for a brief moment, as if he needs to keep his wrath in check. When he reopens them, he says, "I heard what he said to you. I was trying to get to you as fast as I could and was going to change at the last minute, but then he... he *hit* you, and it was like I couldn't think clearly anymore. In that moment, when he put his hands on you, I didn't want to change back. I wanted to *feel* him die in my jaws."

He steps towards me, close enough I feel the heat coming off his body and filling mine with his warmth. I drop my eyes to my feet and hope the moon's light isn't bright enough for him to see the flush in my cheeks.

"Wren, you can't tell anyone about this."

"I need some answers, Sin. You can't be talking of war on shifters in one breath, then telling me you *are* one in the next."

He blows out a long breath, then runs a hand through his long hair and moves to lean against a nearby tree.

"One might say I am quite good at keeping secrets," I say, gesturing towards my body to summarize my point.

He rubs a large hand across his jaw, then drops them both to the waist of his trousers, hooking his thumbs into the band. "My mother was a transcendent. My father... he loved her despite what she was. He loved her so much that he kept her identity hidden from everyone, especially Ephraim who was obsessed with plotting how to exterminate their kind altogether. She left when I was young—a boy still. She wished to see her family, so my father arranged for her to meet with them in secret. He told Ephraim he was sending her to scout out locations for healing temples in Baregrove," he says, his eyes not quite meeting mine as he speaks. "She never returned. They killed her. Murdered her for treason against their kind. They couldn't accept that she married the Black Hand who was assisting Ephraim in his plans to eradicate transcendents. It did not matter to them that she loved him. My father went mad when he discovered what they had done. He became worse than Ephraim. Escalated action against their kind, hence the restrictions that later became law."

"Sin..." I trail off, thoughts eluding me as I make sense of his words.

He shifts his weight and kicks one foot up to rest on the trunk behind him. "I didn't develop it until a few years after she was gone. My father was sure I didn't inherit the ability because even at a young age, I was wielding destruction magic better than most transcendents ever can. I was terrified to tell him the first time I shifted. He was... so angry. Ashamed that his son was carrying the blood of *their* kind in his veins. I thought he was going to kill me. And I think maybe the only reason he didn't was because of her. He loved her too much to do that to her only child.

"So, he forced me to keep it a secret, and we told no one. Neither of us ever anticipated I would perform the Rite. When Ephraim died, everyone was certain Adelphia would bless my father, and when she denied him, I know it gutted him—way more than he ever showed to the public eye. The council suggested I perform it next, and it would have been suspicious if he tried to refuse that. I thought for sure Adelphia would have denied me as soon as she sensed I held both the magics in my blood, but she bound a fraction of her power to mine instead. Everyone was thrilled I was chosen—except him, of course. I knew instantly he hated me even more for it, furious that the goddess would have chosen a *transcendent* over him.

"I inherited the responsibility of defeating Legion, and I already held a reputation on the battlefield. They knew me to be ruthless, cold—I killed many of them during the war with Baelliarah, and even more in Legion strikes. I suppose I can't blame him for hating me, not after what transcendents did to my mother."

Tiny cracks split my heart as I listen to Sin's truth. In all the times I read his collective, I never detected this secret. In hindsight, the overwhelming shame and loneliness I felt each time I peeked in must have been pointing to this all along.

Sin isn't a monster—he is a transcendent oppressed by his own father, taught to hate his body for the magic that flows through it, and conditioned to despise his own people that reacted to the crimes of his father. Sin's wickedness doesn't stem from some royal blooded corruptness; it comes from a lifetime of abuse.

"I'm so sorry about your mother. But never, *never* suggest again that your father had any right to do what he did to you. No one deserves to feel they are not worthy of love simply for being as you were created to be."

"I killed Bennett right in front of you," he blurts out. "I ripped his throat out with my own *teeth*, and you just looked at me standing over his body and asked if *I* was alright," he says, chuckling once without humor.

"Because I don't distrust your kind, Sin. Transcendents took me in when I had no one. When my own mother threw me from my home, *they* were the ones to take me in. Protected me. Taught me how to fight, how to hunt, how to take care of myself. And Cosmina... while she isn't a transcendent, I trust her judgment more than anyone's, and she trusted them. That was good enough for me. I know what it's like to live with the fear that if the world knew what you really were, they'd kill you in the same breath they accused you with. They don't understand that just because we have the power to hurt others, that doesn't mean we will."

"I killed Thatcher," he whispers, closing his eyes and resting his head against the tree. Regret casts his face in shadow.

"Nothing can be done to bring him back now, but you *can* revert the laws that threaten them, and you *can* work to clear the prejudices. Adelphia chose *you*. Maybe it's time to start considering why."

Sin opens his eyes and cocks his head to the side, his hair fanning out across the tree like black vines. "Aegidale will riot against me if they know what I really am."

"You can convince them otherwise. Show them it is possible for us all to coexist in peace." I step up to him and square my shoulders to his, forcing him to level with my gaze. "I will keep your secret, Sin. *So long* as you don't start a war with them afterwards."

An ultimatum. I will safeguard his secret on the condition he does not declare war on transcendent-kind. He says nothing, but nods slowly.

He clears his throat. "I never apologized for my behavior when I found you with Cathal. I shouldn't have lost my temper, and I should have never," his eyes drop to my neck, "... touched you. Forgive me."

"I know how strong a caster's high can be. I almost bit your throat out after you let my magic pummel you like a gods-damned fool."

He chuckles softly and slips his hands into his trouser pockets. "And I shouldn't have said what I did the other night. I didn't mean it," he adds.

"I shouldn't have slapped you."

"You're right—you should have done a lot worse." He shoots me a half-hearted wink, and my stomach does a somersault in response.

He is dangerously attractive.

I throw up my hand. "Wait a second."

He furrows his brows.

"The Rut... that would have affected you."

A slow smile spreads across his mouth.

"That's why you bit me." I nod, more to myself than him, as I make sense of his aggressive behavior the night I made him accompany my family and me to the annual shifter event.

His lips part as he sweeps his tongue across the front of his teeth. "That was fucking torture. The Rut affects me the same as any other transcendent, whether I want it to or not. Being that pent up with the need to shift and... engage in *other* activities and not being able to was driving me mad. It's why I didn't hang around. I needed distance from the others. And from you," he adds darkly.

"From me?"

Sin pushes off the tree, ascending to his full height and towering over me. "You can hardly fault Eldridge for his comment at the Rut. Your scent was driving him wild with need, and he couldn't have you. He may have chosen another mate that night, but it was you he was thinking about."

"How could you possibly know that?"

"Because I almost did the same thing."

My breath catches, and his eyes flash to my mouth, his advanced hearing missing nothing.

Goddess above.

I am suddenly all too aware of him. The closeness of his bare chest nearly brushing against mine, his eyes tracking every movement of my body, the devastating smirk on his face...

Seriously. It should be a crime for something so wicked to be this beautiful.

I swallow hard, burying embarrassment in the pit of my stomach. If he's bold enough to drop a comment like that, I refuse to let it go unaddressed.

"You almost did what?" I ask.

"Take a lover," he answers, not missing a beat. "Just to be rid of my thoughts of you, even if it would have been temporary."

"Then why didn't you?"

"Because I feared it would have only made me more ravenous for what I truly crave."

I would trade away my magic for the ability to slow my pulse in a heartbeat, embarrassment rising from the depths I shoved it in and coloring my cheeks.

Tilting his head towards me, he grabs my chin and drags his nose from the base of my ear to the curvature of my jaw. "I haven't been able to get the scent of you out of my mind."

Every fiber of my being screams for me to place my hands against his chest, to feel his bare skin against mine, but I don't move. For the first time in my life, I feel powerless. As if this man, looking like darkness incarnate, has the ability to strip me of all sense of rationality and bend my will to his.

I do *not* like this feeling. Like I'm not in control. This is wrong. Very wrong.

But the wetness pooling between my thighs seems to disagree with me.

"Would you like to know what you smell like, little witch?" He pulls back just enough to search my face, and when I nod weakly, a soul shattering smile blooms across his. "Like the sea. When you're angry, your scent shifts sweeter, like the calm before the storm." He inhales deeply and lets go of my chin. His fingernails lengthen into claws, and his eyes brighten to a vivid green with that yellow ring around his pupils.

Standing before me, partially shifted into his other form... he's *magnificent*. Extraordinary.

Sin reaches towards me again and slowly drags the back of one of his long nails across my cheek and down my neck. Not deep enough to draw blood, but enough to sting. In the best way possible. When he reaches the base of my throat, he loops his nail under the bodice ties of my nightgown. "And when you're aroused," his eyes flash to mine with a smirk that is pure sinful, "you smell like fucking starlight."

That's it. I slam my palms against his chest, desperate to feel all that bare skin, and the second I reach for him, he whirls us around, pinning me between him and the tree. His arms form a prison on either side of me, and he rolls his bottom lip between his teeth as a low growl rumbles from his chest. And as quickly as he spun us around, he drops an arm to my lower back and arches me towards him, dipping his head to skim his lips across my chest.

"What are we doing? I hate you. You hate me," I choke through bated breath.

"Does it feel like I hate you?" He grinds his hips against mine, and it takes every ounce of self-control I have left to keep my eyes front and center, and not spiraling to the back of my head. Because pressed against my most sensitive place, I feel *just* how much he craves me.

He laughs quietly between my breasts, only the thin black silk of my nightgown separating them from his mouth. "Fucking starlight."

This time, embarrassment doesn't rush to my cheeks. Only the warm pang of desire courses through me and settles low in my stomach.

"Sin. Stop." I *need* him to stop. Because if his mouth drifts an inch to the side, or his hand drops any lower, I'm going to lose myself to him completely.

He smiles against my chest as if he knew I would stop him, then raises his lips to my jaw for a fleeting second before taking a step away from me and dropping his arms.

"See—I said you have more control than you give yourself credit for."

Bastard.

I give him a knowing smirk and adjust the ties of my nightgown. "Careful, Blackheart. I will rip out every last one of their hearts myself if I have to, including yours. And with that kind of power, I could bring armies to their knees."

"Then it's in your best interest to feast on my heart last, love."

"And why is that?"

"I fight much better on my feet. And if you bring me to my knees before you, little witch, I dare say you'll be in no mind to let me off them."

I can't stop the stupid grin from betraying my reaction to his words. "Goodnight, Your Grace." Clutching my robe closed, I turn my back to him and head for the castle.

"Oh, and starlight," he calls after me. *Please don't let this be my new nickname.* "Try to keep your moaning down when you pleasure yourself tonight, dearest. I need my beauty sleep."

Without turning around, I flash him a vulgar gesture above my head. When I'm out of the woods, I swear I still hear his dark chuckle on the wind.

CHAPTER 36

"How little do you think of me, honestly? You expect me to sit back and kick my feet up while I watch the *men* head into battle?" Ileana asks, slamming her palms onto the rectangular table in the center of the war room.

"Not little at all, my Lady," Cassius placates. "But think of what you represent to Aegidale. You were a Legion prisoner, and now you command the greatest army in the realm. You are a token of strength, resilience. If you go and get yourself offed by the very people that imprisoned you, think of the devastating message that would send to your people."

Your people. I suppose they are her people now.

Ileana is mundane, but she more than makes up for what she lacks in magical ability with sheer tenacity. I can't fathom a single person having more of a reason to want to witness Legion bleed for their crimes than the Black Hand herself. And I'll be damned if any of these arrogant fools who have never had to endure the perversions of men try to take that from her.

"How do men even see from so high up on that pedestal that they place themselves upon? It would be an affront to prevent the Black Hand from defending her own people," I argue to the council.

I've hardly spoken since we've gathered this morning to discuss strategy. Scouts reported sightings of Legion troops laying low in the valley outside Baregrove. It won't be long now before they stampede into Blackreach expecting to lay siege to the castle, only to meet the Black Art's army *outside* the keep for the first time.

"Remind me again, Your Grace, how you know your friend?" Sterling drawls, laying the weight of his stare on me.

I had wondered if I would feel guilty being in the same room as Bennett's father—shame at not confessing the real cause of his son's death—but I feel nothing. Except maybe regret that I wasn't the last thing Bennett saw before he choked on his own bubbling blood spilling from his mouth as I wedged my blade deep in his gut.

"Wren has lost friends to Legion's scintillating recruitment tactics," Sin answers smoothly, waving a hand as if to dismiss the brunt of my insult. "She is advanced with her magic. She'll make a great asset," he adds casually.

Sterling scratches the side of his face with one long finger. "I see. You must have had some excellent mentors along the way, Miss—?"

"Just Wren." I dropped my surname the same day my parents tossed me from their lives like I was nothing more than spoiled meat. "And indeed, my Lord. I have been most fortunate." I offer him a smile, hoping he doesn't notice the clenched teeth behind it.

"I must agree with the mage though," he continues, waving a hand towards Cassius. "I think it'd be outrageous to have the Black Hand on the battlefield."

Dusaro mumbles an agreement from inside the steaming mug of tea he brought to his mouth. Aldred remains stoic as if he's more focused on debating the tactical advantages and disadvantages in his own head than with those less experienced in the art of war than himself. Sin leans back in his chair making a tent with his fingertips as if the topic bores him altogether. Anika hasn't uttered a word since the meeting began, and Ileana's face is nothing short of furious.

"Sin will be fighting," I challenge. "So surely it can't be a matter of jeopardizing our assets, my Lord."

"Singard is also our supreme ruler, not to mention incredibly adept at his art. Not being present would be an insult to his people. Ileana, on the contrary, must be protected at all costs."

"If Ileana had a cock, would she be worthy of your confidence then, my Lord?"

Dusaro sucks in a sharp breath as if appalled at my question, but Sin's eyes flare with amusement, and a lopsided grin pulls up the corner of his lips. The same full lips that were pressed between my breasts the night prior, and Goddess help me, I haven't been able to stop thinking about that.

"Maker help them if I did," Ileana murmurs to me.

"It's His Grace's decision," Aldred says, directing his attention to Sin who drops his hands and sits forward, resting his elbows on the table.

"Ileana is more than aware of the risks. She deserves to make them bleed their own blood."

"Singard," Dusaro interjects.

"My word is final," he says, his sharp tone implying it is not up for negotiation.

I shoot Ileana a sideways smirk, and she mirrors me with one of her own.

"Ensure the last of the evacuations are complete by end of day tomorrow," Sin addresses his armies' commander. "I'm riding into the city this afternoon and you," he shifts his attention to me, "are coming with me."

For a city that's nearly evacuated, a tempest of chaos blows through Blackreach. Several sets of hooves pitter patter across cobblestone roads, distant shouts ring out as soldiers call to each other from post to post, and doors and windows snap shut with audible thumps. What remains of the elite city is closing down, and only the gods know how much damage it'll endure once the fighting commences.

But it doesn't matter. The city could be blown to bits, and the kingdom would see to its full reconstruction before ever throwing a crumb to more impoverished regions. Places like Innodell where families work their hands to the bone, all while wearing threadbare clothing and sustaining themselves on bland, spiceless food. But a city like Blackreach that houses high-ranking lords and ladies will never reap the effects of poverty, no matter how badly it is devastated in the wake of battle.

I ride next to Sin on a chestnut-colored horse, Dusaro trotting along on the back of an all-white steed on the other side of his son. We veer right onto a long street flanked on either side by small shops with vivid awnings and flowers arranged in large decorative pots by the doors. Above our heads, large cauldrons are hoisted to the rooftops, later to be filled with boiling water infused with iron shavings.

"A ballista will be set up outside the keep should any of them make it that far," Dusaro says, pointing with his chin towards the castle's towers rearing up in the distance like the city's personal backdrop.

"They won't make it that far. None of them are making it through this," Sin says quietly with a shake of his head.

In an alley to my left, a small group rigs up torn bags of flour to trip wires, and another ballista is posted at the far end. And as if anyone could dodge that kind of attack in such tight quarters, the roofs on either side are stacked with quivers and arrows.

A high-pitched shriek has the three of us turning towards a woman in a deep blue cloak with a small girl no older than five clutched to her side. Two armored soldiers loop their arms around her elbows and drag her backwards, her daughter's knuckles white from clinging to her mother's loose-fitting cloak.

She kicks her legs out in front of her, desperate to gain leverage to stand her ground. "You cannot do this to us! When this city burns, some of us are left with nothing!" she shouts, seemingly to no one in particular.

Sin and Dusaro take off towards them while I hang behind, still in ear shot, but not close enough to be in the way.

"She's one of them, Your Grace. Don't know about the kid," one of the guards says, prying the young girl's hand from her mother.

"DO NOT touch her," she yells, flailing her legs out to try and kick the one who grabbed her daughter.

"She's one of what?" Sin asks.

"Legion. We found her tampering around with some traps, trying to disarm them. When we approached her, she tried slashing us with nails that weren't human."

"The sentence for treason is death," Dusaro spits from his horse's back.

"Go to Hell," she snaps back at him.

Sin hops off his horse, his black riding cloak billowing out behind him, and approaches the woman. My hands grip the reins tighter.

"Stay away from her," the woman yells, trying to put her body between the girl and Sin.

He pauses a few feet away from them. "Why were you tampering with our traps?"

She scoffs, and her mouth twists into a scowl. "Because if you're willing to destroy the only homes some of us have, your people deserve to die along with us. I have no dealings with Legion, *Your Grace,* but that doesn't mean I despise you any less."

"We have safe houses set up for the entire city. You would be protected," Sin placates.

"And what of after? Sure, you can rebuild our homes with your fancy tools and all that coin, but some of us don't have the means to get back what we must leave behind. I've been out of work for months because no one will pay me because of what I am. Because of the prejudices *your* people created," she says, yanking one of her arms free and jabbing a finger at Sin.

"Enough of this—lock her away until we have time to deal with her *appropriately,*" Dusaro says with a dismissive wave of his hand.

"What skills do you possess?" Sin asks, unphased by the woman's spiteful tongue and ignoring his father's remark.

"I'm a healer. I owned an apothecary, but once everything went to Hell, folks stopped coming around, and I lost the business. Ironic, isn't it? I have enough herbs and tonics in my home to heal an entire army, and you're going to let them go up in smoke as your men bleed in the name of vengeance."

"The healing temple can always use more skilled hands. Temporary medic tents have been set up outside the city for now—take her there and ensure she's properly paid for her labor. Make sure the child has something to eat upon arrival," Sin says to the guards. Turning his attention back to the woman, he adds, "The kingdom sponsors all supplies for those on the payroll."

She clicks her tongue. "You're delusional if you think they won't oust me as soon as they find out what I am."

"Are you going to tell them?"

She looks at him with a dazed look and in her hesitation, Sin addresses the guards at her side again. "Tell them nothing more than she's a skilled healer and is being placed at the temple by special assignment of the Black Art. They don't need to know where her magic comes from or what activities she partakes in in her own time. Is that understood?"

They nod, and each mirror a salute before escorting the woman away, her scowl now melting into disbelief. When Sin turns his back to her and mounts his steed, relief colors her cheeks, and she scoops up her daughter, now walking with the kingdom guards willingly.

As Sin settles back in the saddle, Dusaro tsks with a shake of his head, his long braids bouncing with the movement. "You're too soft, boy."

With a slap of the reins, I catch up to them and fall in line next to Sin. I study his profile and note the hard set of his jaw as if he's trying really hard *not* to look at me. I don't know if he spared the woman out of mercy, or because he feared I would make good on my vow to expose him should he continue feuding with transcendent-kind. But it doesn't matter.

The right choice was made.

CHAPTER 37

I'm not asleep when I hear the light knocking on the other side of my door. It's been two days since evacuations finished in Blackreach and scouts reported Legion is lingering in Autumnhelm, just beyond the bridge. If they stay on target, they'll make their move tomorrow, so retiring to my chambers a couple hours before the sun set fully seemed responsible, though I haven't been able to sleep.

Snapping my fingers to light the candles seated in the wall sconces, I sit up and tuck the sheets in around my legs. One downward glance, and I regret not having closed the balcony doors before lying down, my charcoal nightdress clinging to my nipples that have hardened into tight points from the cool breeze blowing into the room. I unlock the door with my magic, and it groans as it swings inward.

Sin envelops the threshold. The fire crackling softly in the sconces provides just enough light for me to get a good look at him. He wears a loose-fitting white shirt with a deep neckline, exposing the smooth, sculpted planes of his tan chest. Fitted black pants hug his powerful thighs, and his shoulders nearly brush the doorway on either side of him. He closes the door behind him, and his eyes instantly take in my attire, lingering a few seconds longer where my nipples threaten to tear through my nightdress. *Stupid kingdom silk.*

Sin tears his ogling stare away from my chest to meet my own and crosses the room, the floor creaking softly under the weight of his black boots. He sits on the foot of the bed. "I wanted to give you something before tomorrow."

He slips a hand into his trouser pocket and pulls out a small black vial. Its scent invades my nose immediately, and my mouth goes dry as the damp floral aroma caresses my lips, my tongue, my throat. He grabs my hand and slips the bottle into my palm, wrapping my fingers closed around it.

"Your blood," I breathe. I open my hand and run a thumb along the vial's surface. There is a braided rope he cinched around it, making it fit to be worn as a necklace.

"I know it isn't the same as shedding it yourself, but it's still a fresh source of goddess-blessed blood should you find yourself in need of more power tomorrow."

I stare at him wide-eyed. "Do you know how dangerous it is to give a bloodwitch something like this?" Having but a drop of someone's blood grants me power over them, a direct link to their collective, and the Black Art has just given me a *bottle* of his.

His eyes dart between both of mine. "I trust you... Wren," he whispers, and my heartbeat quickens at the sound of my name on his tongue.

I thumb the vial and resist the urge to pop its lid and inhale deeply. Inhale *him*. The mere thought of it heightens my arousal, and I clench my thighs together in reflex. If he was serious about being able to smell my...

Goddess save me from this embarrassment.

Did he just smirk? Sin stands, a wicked grin on his mouth, and his hands move to the waist of his trousers. "I have something else for you too."

He unsheathes a sword from his hip I don't recognize as one of his own. It's smaller than the ones I've seen him spar with, its hilt designed for a slighter hand, but its blade honed to the same lethal perfection as any of his. He holds it out to me, pommel first. I accept it eagerly and study the intricate swirling pattern carved into it. It rests snugly in my hand—a perfect fit.

"It's beautiful," I say with awe in my tone.

"I had my best smith on it. I would have made it myself, but I haven't had the time."

"You forge?"

He shrugs his shoulders. "A hobby. When my mind is spinning, I like to keep my hands moving."

I noticed he had a habit of doing tasks the mundane way instead of willing them complete with magic. The Black Art of Aegidale. The warlord known for being able to bring a man to his knees without lifting a finger but *chooses* to blacken his hands with steel and ash.

I rip the blankets off me and step out of bed, all too aware of the scantily clad nightgown clinging to my body. "Stand," I tell him.

He raises a dark eyebrow but obeys, *towering* over me.

I kneel before him.

Resting my hands on the crossguard, I present myself and my sword to the Black Art. "I pledge to serve you in the battle to come, Your Grace. So long as Legion remains a threat to us, I am your arm to wield."

It's a formality, of course. Sin and I have already made our compromise, but nonetheless, it feels right to pledge it verbally.

Sin stares down at me for a long moment, a mix of respect and... something else on his face. "I accept your pledge and in return, I swear to protect you in the face of battle tomorrow.

Now get off the floor—you don't belong there." He wraps a large hand around my bicep and pulls me against his chest. My breath catches as he leans forward to brush his lips against my ear. "But if you're fond of kneeling, I can find a better purpose for it."

He brushes past me, heading for the door, and I wonder if his transcendent ears hear the lapse in my breath. I should let him go. Walk out the door so we can both get some rest before tomorrow, and then I can pack my things and leave after the war is won. Because something tells me if I call after him, it will break the seal holding in the carnal desires we've both been stifling.

That would be very, *very* dangerous.

But I've always had an affinity for playing with fire.

"Do you enjoy the sight of me kneeling before you, Your Grace?"

Sin freezes, his back towards me, and I could choke on the tension filling the space between us. Slowly, he turns to face me again, and he walks back towards me, this time not stopping until his chest is flush against mine and his hips are pressed against my waist. He reaches up to cup my jaw. "If you're asking if I've spilt seed thinking about this pretty little mouth," he runs his thumb over the swells of my lips, "the answer is yes."

I capture my bottom lip between my teeth, and he growls at the sight of it. He inhales deeply, his nostrils flaring. "Does that thought arouse you, love?" he asks, already knowing the answer. *Smelling* it from between the thighs I clench together as if I could hold back the wetness now pooling there.

"When?" I ask.

He arches a dark brow at my question.

"You said you pleasured yourself thinking about me. I want

to know when." I straighten my spine, willing my lips not to tremble under his touch.

Sin drops his hands to grip my waist and pushes us both back onto the balcony until my ass bumps against the railing. He dips his head and presses his full lips along the column of my neck.

"The night we shared a bed, when I left so you could bathe," he whispers against my skin. "I didn't have release at the Rut, and I barely made it to the woods before I was fisting my cock and coming in my hand, wishing it was your gods-damned throat."

I grab the railing behind me as his mouth moves lower and his fingers ball up the fabric of my nightgown around my thighs. He drags his lips across my collarbone.

"This is wrong. Sin—Singard, this is... wrong," my words trail off as he bites down on the juncture of my neck and shoulder, and a small moan falls from my lips, inciting his own growl of approval.

"Is it wrong that you're dripping at the thought of me—of us? You know I can smell it," he says, then licks the spot he bit. He slides my dress up, and his hands grip my full thighs. My heart thrums erratically in my ears. I can't think straight, my mind consumed with his hands on my skin, the heat coming off him, the smell of his blood from the vial now sitting on the bedside table. *This is wrong. But why is it wrong? I can't remember now.*

I gasp as his fingers lightly brush against my underwear.

"Can I touch you here, love?"

It isn't logic. And it certainly isn't *right*. But my thoughts are clouded with his hand so damn close to where I *ache* to feel his touch, and I nod. "Yes," I whisper, hating and loving myself for giving him permission to touch me where I need to feel him most.

He hooks two fingers into my panties and pulls them to the side, baring me to him. His eyes drop to my cunt, now throbbing in anticipation, and his eyes glaze with lust.

My head falls back as he slips a finger inside me.

"Oh, little witch," he murmurs, feeling my wetness there.

I arch my back as he begins to slide his finger in and out of me, breathy pants falling from my mouth as he does. Sin wraps his other arm around my waist, supporting me against the balcony railing as he fucks me with his finger, then two. I grind against his hand, desperate for release, but also terrified to let this man make me come. The man that held me captive. Threatened my life. Choked the very breath out of me.

But somehow it all makes me burn hotter for him, as if the wrongness of it makes it feel that much fucking better.

I cry out when he withdraws his fingers. "What are you—"

"Turn around," he orders.

Dazed and a little confused, I spin and prop my elbows against the rail. A couple stories down, a few guards patrol outside the castle.

Sin nudges the inside of my ankle with his boot. "Widen your stance."

I obey, walking my feet out so I'm spread a little farther. "Someone could hear us," I say, looking at the guards chortling with each other as they make their rounds beneath us.

"Good, then they'll know *you're mine*. Wren—what a pretty name. Let's see if you sing like one too."

His fingers plunge back into me, and I can't stifle the moan that rips from my chest as he fills my emptiness. He reaches underneath me and palms my aching breast with his other hand, and I call out as he squeezes it, my head falling back to rest against his shoulder, his own sounds of approval vibrating in my ear. I arch my back, grinding my hips against his, feeling his arousal jutting into me as he thrusts his fingers in and out of me in a rhythmic cadence. I press my ass against him harder, surely soaking the front of his pants with my wetness, and a sound of approval rattles from his chest.

"That's it, take your pleasure. Fuck my fingers."

Goddess above, I'll come to his voice alone if he keeps talking like that. He curls his fingers up to hit that spot and oh—OH!

"Just like that, love. That's a good fucking girl," he growls in my ear. "Lean back and sing for me, Wren."

Fuck. *Fuck!*

I clench around him as the rush of pleasure shatters me and I come undone in a thousand pieces, Sin's name falling from my lips as I ride out my release. And when the euphoria finally fades, I right myself and my nightgown, letting it swish back over my thighs. Sin holds his hand up, admiring my cum glistening and stretching between his fingers, and then takes them both into his mouth. He sucks me off his fingers with a sound of approval, his lips making a loud *pop* when he slides them from his mouth.

"If you taste like this every time you come, you're going to be a very addictive problem, little witch."

Fucking hell. I reach to unfasten his pants, but he pins my hand under his.

"No," he snarls, frustrated.

My brows furrow, but before I can ask why, he says, "I can't let you do that so long as I have you tethered to me. It's not..." he lets out a long groan, "it's not fucking right."

"But I want to," I insist. And judging from the huge bulge straining against his pants, he wants it too.

Sin leans forward and rests his forehead against mine, blowing out a long breath. "There is nothing I want more than to make you scream my name until you're hoarse in the throat, but regardless of what you want right now, you're here against your will. I won't go further until you can make that choice fully of your own volition."

I drop my hands back to my sides. "You're serious? So where does that leave us now?"

He lifts his head and bites his lip, and the sight of that alone could probably make me orgasm again. "It leaves *you* crawling that sweet ass back into bed and getting your rest so you keep us all from dying tomorrow. And it leaves *me* returning to my chambers so I can take my own release with the taste of you still in my mouth."

He cocks his head and brushes his lips across the corner of my mouth without actually kissing me there, we *still* have not kissed on the mouth, and then turns and heads for the door. Like he did earlier when I should have let him leave. Not call after him and especially not consent to doing what we just did.

But I'm really glad I did because *Goddess help me,* I haven't come like that in... well... ever.

Sin hovers in the doorway before leaving and bids me a final glance over his shoulder. "Who knew the stars tasted so fucking sweet?"

And with that, he closes the door behind him, and I swipe the vial off the table and inhale it as I slip my own fingers back inside my depth.

CHAPTER 38

I always knew I might find myself at war with the kingdom one day. That eventually the day would come where I would have to stop running, stop hiding, and fight. But I never expected to be fighting *with* the kingdom, and certainly not with the Black Art at my side.

We are the epicenter of his army.

Sin and I stand side by side, half of his army spread through the city at our front and the other at our backs. My cuirass with the black winged pauldrons is fitted snugly against my core, steel plates protect my legs, and matching winged gauntlets hug my forearms. The sword Sin had forged for me hangs in anticipation at my waist, my dagger tucked into its holster, and my magic hissing in my palms like a viper that has just been stepped on. I look over at him and find him already staring at me.

"Ever think you'd find yourself trusting a bloodwitch in battle?" I taunt, hoping to ease both our nerves.

Sin maintains a calm, stoic appearance, but his collective rumbles with unease and restlessness. "Probably about as much as you thought you could trust someone in *our* uniform."

"I see you put on real armor today," I tease, looking pointedly at where he usually wears nothing but a steel plate over his bare chest. Sin is fitted in his own suit of blackened plated armor with twin swords strapped across his back. His long hair is secured into a loose bun at the nape of his neck, a few loose hairs framing the sides of his face.

"I had to cover up a little today, didn't want you getting your head lopped off because you were distracted."

I smirk and look away before he can see the blush on my cheeks. As much as I may hate to admit it, his appearance *is* a distraction. Suited up in armor, his eyes burning with intense focus and his hands clenching at his sides as if he's itching to reach for his sword, he *looks* like the reaper Aegidale and its neighbors have come to fear.

The ground rumbles beneath our feet as the distinct shrill of Legion battle cries pierce the air, and the galloping of their armored horses stampede towards us.

A storm of arrows hurl above our heads towards them, knocking a few soldiers off their horses, but the majority of them lodge into their poorly crafted shields. The first sendoff of arrows is our agreed upon cue, so Sin and I jump into action. We conjure a wall of fire before us and stretch it into a line that extends far off in either direction, through the side streets and alleys, creating a flame barrier between our first and second armies. Legion's mundane won't be able to cross the fiery blockade, forcing their transcendents to separate from the rest and dividing their numbers. The shifters will be able to cross the fire, but it will temporarily weaken their defense. It takes a lot of magic to wound a transcendent, but a sharp sword can slice through their skins as easily as any human's.

Ahead of us, the sound of metal against metal cleaves the air, signaling the fighting has commenced. And as predicted, a wall of transcendents come barreling towards our fire barricade. I plant my feet, opening and closing my hands as the magic warms there and simmers in anticipation. Our second army moves in around us with weapons drawn as the pounding of the transcendents' monstrous paws grows louder. And as soon as the Legion shifters are in range, Sin and I unleash a wave of destruction magic towards the charging beasts.

It hits the six shifters in the center the hardest, sending them stumbling sideways for a brief moment, while the others break off to cross the barrier from farther away. The ones in front regain their footing and lower their shoulders as they near the flames, hurtling themselves through the blazing wall like rabid, overgrown wolves.

Sin and I retreat a few steps as they tear through, their coats littered with ash and their bared teeth glistening with saliva as they growl and dip their heads. We reposition to stand back-to-back, covering the blind spot of the other as we surround ourselves with a ward. The transcendents separate and charge into the second army, while three of them stay and circle around us, snapping their heads to the side and licking their snouts as they let out low, guttural snarls. Two of them are reddish colored and the third a dark blonde, each with sharp pointed ears, long rectangular snouts, and golden eyes set deep in their canine faces.

Our ward is too strong for them to get much closer, so long as we can maintain its potency. The weight of Sin's back pressed against mine keeps me focused, grounded, as I pour my intention into the ward protecting us.

I swear to protect you in the face of battle tomorrow, he promised last night. And right now, with our bodies pinned together at the shoulders, I trust the Black Art with my life.

The flames that were ravenous with hunger a moment before vanish into a thick gray fog.

They extinguished the barrier.

We knew it wouldn't hold for long against a species known

for their advanced abjuration magic, but we did underestimate how many of them would still be standing before the wall came down.

The ground shakes beneath my feet, and I strain to see through the barricade that has been reduced to a smoldering curtain, but the smoke is too thick. My knees buckle as whatever is approaching draws nearer, making the city streets quiver beneath my boots and—

"Sin!" I call over my shoulder as a second surge of transcendents come rushing through what remains of the smoking wall.

This lot of them appear diseased, patches of skin blistering beneath their charred furs like a bubbling stew. Our men must have rained the boiling, iron-infused water on their backs before they breached the defense. Kingdom soldiers move in and surround us, lunging and hacking at the beasts while the three surrounding us snap at and test the boundaries of our barrier—a barrier that won't hold against this many of them.

"We need to put them down!" Sin yells over his shoulder. "Give me your hands!"

I reach behind me, and as soon as his white clenched knuckles lock on top of mine, my spine arches as he bleeds the magic from my body. I don't fight him as he rips the collective from my blood and siphons the magic right from my veins. My arms convulse and shudder in his grip, my body teetering on collapsing as Sin drains me from the inside. And suddenly my head is too heavy, and my neck falls limp against his shoulder, my knees threatening to give out next.

"Hang on," he growls under his breath, his hands tightening unbearably around my own. With a feral shout, Sin releases a wave of destruction strengthened with the magic he tapped straight from my own source, and the symphony of howls that follows in its wake snaps me back to alertness. I open my eyes and watch as the furred legs of the three imme-diately surrounding us wobble under their weight, and they crash to the ground, limp and broken and bleeding.

Sin spins me to face him, demanding to know if I'm alright, and violently shakes me when I don't answer. But I can barely see him through the red haze clouding my vision, and I struggle to hear his voice over the whispers in my head.

Her whispers.

My eyes narrow in on the fallen beasts, on their torn sides and dripping wounds, and I...

I *smell* them.

I inhale the scent of their suffering, hints of mulled wine and citrus petting my tongue, and I lick my teeth at the sight of them. Sin grabs my chin and jerks my head forward, forcing me to meet his eyes, and I bare my teeth at him instinctively.

"Remember who you are," he says, his words coming out hurried but gentle. "You are stronger than her."

I am stronger than her.

She who would rush to their fallen, crumpled bodies and snap their necks without a second thought; she who would lap the blood pouring from their wounds; she who would laugh as they begged for mercy.

Remember who you are.

High-pitched chants sung from the lips of Legion soldiers dance across the dense, smoking wall moments before they emerge in the flesh, weapons held above their heads. Swords, hammers, battle axes of varying sizes and quality stampede towards us, and I nod to Sin as I spin towards them, drawing my sword from my hip.

He pulls his own weapon from his back, and side-by-side, we stare down the flood of monsters storming towards us with the force of a raging tsunami. My agility surprises me, the cast-er's high pumping my body with adrenaline, allowing me to move faster, sharper. I jab and thrust and lunge with more swiftness than I could muster in training while my magic replenishes itself.

I quickly infer that an order was given to protect me at all costs as I am never alone. Sin's men flank me on all sides, letting me beat down my opponent but always stepping in to deliver the fatal blow once they've fallen before me. We hack through them one by one, our kingdom steel easily finding the holes in their makeshift armors and overpowering their pieced together weapons. The smell of bloodshed invades my senses, encasing my very bones in a euphoric glaze as I allow their affliction to fuel my power. I pivot to my right as a screaming woman charges me with a raised hammer, and dodging to the side, I spin and plant my foot into her backside, sending her stumbling into one of our soldiers who puts her down a second time—permanently.

Now facing the other direction, I catch sight of Sin through the blanket of smoke. Five transcendents slowly circle him, forcing him to resort to magic before it's regained its full potency. But even he knows five shifters is too much for the Black Art to take on with steel alone. Goddess-blessed magic doesn't make his human skin any less vulnerable to jagged canine teeth.

It only takes one well-placed bite.

I channel a defensive ward around me, strong enough to deflect any incoming swords or arrows without draining too much of my replenishing magic. Pirouetting around the horde of bodies dripping with sweat and blood, and leaping over the fallen at my feet, I dart towards Sin. I almost reach him when I hear the scream. My lungs turn to ice as recognition of those throaty shrills seeps in.

Ileana.

I whip towards the sound and find her behind Sin on his

left, shrieking and howling as she hacks at the men who have hurt her in so many ways, and quickly drawing attention to herself with the sounds of her fury. Now sprinting towards Sin, I thrust what remains of my own magic into his ward, strengthening it. It expands outward, forcing them to put more distance between each other, and I dive through the protective barrier before the two nearest me even notice I'm here. They lower their shoulders and hurl themselves against it, searching for a weak point in our protective casing. We feed our power into the circle, and a few of them wince as the perimeter of our ward singes their fur everywhere it brushes against them. The ward is strong, but not strong enough to put them down on its own when it's divided between five of them actively shoving against it. Sweat rushes down my face, my neck, and my very bones grow heavier as exhaustion seeps into my every fiber, turning my marrow to sludge.

Sin whips to look behind himself, and I follow his stare to see what his transcendent ears heard that I could not. Behind us, Ileana is quickly becoming more surrounded as her cries of anguish baited them to her like hunters to a wounded wolf. Ileana has never been a predator, but even a lone wolf will attack a few humans if it's pissed-off and hungry enough. And she is fucking ravenous.

Worry corrupts Sin's face. He needs to move to her side, break the chokehold they've trapped her in, but if he drops his hold on the ward, the weight of the transcendents pushing against it will be too much for me to hold alone. His eyes flicker between us and her, judging how long it would take him to cut down the men around her and be back at my side.

Too long. And he knows it.

It's her or me. And he's not moving.

Ileana's vicious screaming grows louder as she swings her sword almost carelessly now, blinded with unbridled wrath.

She stops a blade from piercing her left side with her own, her weapon sliding off his with a blood tingling screech, and she pivots to face the weapon's handler, ignorant to the bearded man rushing at her from behind. He raises his hammer above him, the Black Hand's blood glistening in his eyes like midnight stars.

I cannot fail her again.

The memory of Ileana's pain surges through me as I remember all she endured night after bitterly cold night. I allow that agony to shred me to pieces and consume them all as I rip off the veil separating me from *her*. And with a wailing yowl I don't recognize, she leaps from my very being and sinks her daggered claws into his chest. His hammer clatters to the ground as he arches forward, and I rake mental talons down the front of his leather skins, imprinting the shape of my fingernails swirled in his blood. He heaves over, blood gurgling from his mouth, and he collapses with a thud behind her as his final breath falls from his chest.

My veins swell with the rush of his collective, my blood thickening with power and adrenaline and wrath. His scent flares my nostrils wide, and I lick my lips as I look at the Legion soldiers still surrounding her, their eyes wide with panic now focused entirely on me. I hear that eldritch shriek again, the wild one coming from *my* lungs, enveloping the air around us as if it might grow spindly limbs of its own and suck the ichor from every pulsing wound. One by one, the men around her contort into unnatural angles with the snapping of bones, falling to their knees and fading from their bodies as I absorb them into mine. My head falls back in laughter as the chaos rushes through my chest, my stomach, my thighs. Ileana spins on her heel to see who is responsible for their deaths, and I lower my glowing eyes into her deep brown ones—eyes I never want to see riddled with fear again.

Behind me, a rumbling orchestra of growls rips from somewhere deep in the five shifters' throats as they threaten to overwhelm an already exhausted Sin. I reach a hand towards the bearded man now dead at her feet and wrap a phantom fist around his collective. I pull and pull and pull— willing his blood to obey me, forcing it to serve me as its master—and with one final tug, a long spear, created and dripping with his crimson juice, materializes in my palm. I hear as one of them rears up at Sin and snaps at him, its pointed teeth clacking together. They're breaking down the barrier, each trying to land a bite, and each attempt boiling my blood hotter.

No one touches my Black Art.

Without a second's hesitation, I turn and hurl the blood spear into the face of the transcendent closest to Sin. A wicked smile too wide for my face stretches my mouth as it whimpers and slumps to the ground, fresh blood pouring from its face. I restrain myself from pouncing on the dying animal and lapping at the cardinal stream spewing from the hole my spear carved into its giant head.

The four others shift their focus to me, and as if they share a mental thought, they charge me at the same time, promises of death staring me down from within their inhuman, golden eyes. I widen my stance, and with a delicate wave of my hand, I rip the dead transcendent's blood from its body and send it spiraling into the others like daggered rain. It pelts into three of them, sending them tumbling over as the essence of their fallen friend bleeds their lives from their skins.

I kneel in front of the one closest to me, its fur as white as my hair, and its glowing yellow eyes reflecting my own. I grab its blood-soaked chin, swipe my athame from my side, and slit its furred throat, relishing in the cardinal droplets splattering my face. The fourth one charges at my rear, and gripping the dagger in my hand, I spin around, ready to drive the blade into its fleshy heart.

The beast vomits blood on me as Sin plunges his sword into its gut, its juice sputtering from its mouth as it crashes to the ground before me. He yanks his weapon from the shifter's side, his blade coated in its thick, scarlet syrup. Sin meets my eyes with his yellow-green ones, so vivid from the magic expulsion, and extends his hand to me.

The last of my control I've been clinging to rushes out of me at the sight of him. His hair is slick with sweat and blood, loose pieces stuck to his copper cheeks, concern for me apparent in his brightened eyes.

I *want* him.

With every nerve in my body and every breath in my lungs, I want him. I want to let the caster's high consume me, ravage me, as we give in to the carnal desires we've both been fighting. Resisting because what would it mean if the man sworn to protect the realm from my kind *wanted* me? And worst—what would it say of me if I wanted him back? The man who threatened my family, my freedom, my life...

But tapped into this part of myself, the visceral hunger I've buried so deep in my core, I can admit what I've known to be true for a while now. A part of me, some raw, primal piece of myself, is falling in love with the Black Art.

It's wrong to want him. I know that. He is poison. A tonic promising tangled sheets and stolen kisses and everything *wrong* in the world. Maybe it isn't love. Maybe it's but a primal need, as much a part of me as the bones in my flesh, but try as I might, I can't stop drinking him.

And I don't think I want to.

I grab his hand and let him pull me to my feet. His eyes sweep over me, assessing me for damage, and my core blooms with desire at the sight of his concern. I act without thought...

logic has no place mingling with feelings like these. Sin is poison, and I'm going to willingly swallow him whole, even if it kills me.

Slamming my chest into his, I wrap both hands around his neck and pull his mouth to mine. For a moment, as I press my lips to his, he goes rigid beneath me. His mouth has greedily tasted my neck, my shoulders, even the skin between my breasts, but never my lips. Because sharing a kiss is beyond just acting out of carnal need... a kiss is intimate. Deep. Soulful.

Just the night before, I widened my stance and bared myself to him so he could pleasure me at my very core. And even then I didn't feel as... connected... to him as I do with his mouth against mine. Sweet, delicious poison.

I part his lips with mine, and his body comes alive beneath me, like the taste of me stokes the flames inside him. His hands drop to my waist and pull me against him, our armor awkward and in the way, but it doesn't stop his mouth from devouring mine, his tongue relishing in the taste of my own. I nibble his bottom lip as I pull away and lick the blood smeared on the corner of his mouth. I hold his stare as I back away, tucking the hungry look on his face away in my memories, then turn and run through the sea of the injured and dying.

I scale a ladder leaning against the side of a storefront and hop onto the roof, throwing out a ward around me to deflect any incoming arrows. I use the height to survey the fighting beneath me, noting how much we outnumber them now. It won't be much longer until Sin and his men finish picking them off like starving dogs, but from this vantage point, I can accelerate our victory.

With a wave of my hands, I birth fire onto the road beneath me. Leaping from rooftop to rooftop, I feed it through the streets and alleys, creating partitions and boxing the soldiers into groups. Ensuring each group contains more of our men than theirs, squashing any chance they had of inflicting more casualties on our side and hastening their demise.

I find Sin through the smoke and ash, taking on three men on his own in the city's center. The scent of blood is heavy in the air, some of it metallic, some of it sweet, all of it absolutely mouthwatering. Power washes through me like a live current, thickening my skin as if it were impenetrable, fueling my magic with sparks of chaos and drowning my thighs in the arousal from it all.

Sin is hunched slightly forward, his weight light on his feet, and I wonder how I never noticed how *beastly* he is, as if he can't fully hide the animal lurking within him. He bests the three of them with ease, but exhaustion is apparent on his face. With no more enemies to cut down in the ring of fire I strung around him, his eyes find me on the rooftop. His breathing is heavy, and I note the blood seeping through the cracks in his armor. I reach for the small vial tucked under my chest plate and pop the lid open with my thumb. His lips part slightly as he watches me dip my nose to it and inhale deeply, inviting him inside of me. Not breaking our stare, I dip the pointed tip of my tongue into the bottle, tasting him.

Pleasure rocks through me.

He goes unnaturally still as he feels my power surround him, and gently, I cradle his collective with my own and deluge him with healing magic. He doesn't wince as his wounds close over under his armor. He's too focused on me, his own caster's high nudging forth the same feelings thrumming inside me. He wets his lips, and it takes every ounce of self-control I have left to not jump off this roof and devour him right there in the city street, listening to the cries of the rebellion as they fight for their final breaths.

I force myself to tear my gaze away from him to check on the others, and pleasure sweeps through me again as I watch us slaughter the men that once thought they could enslave me. And as our side finishes them off one by one, zone by zone, I inhale the fire magic back into my lungs.

Sin orders for our injured to be tended to immediately and to begin retreating. I watch with admiration—at the very presence he commands—and if it was possible for me to become more aroused, I do as he wipes the red from his face and runs a hand through his long hair now damp with rebellion blood. He watched as I slaughtered his enemies without mercy, crushed their bones with the force of my will alone, and witnessed their energy flooding my core. He didn't so much as blink as he beheld my transformation, or scoff as I grew slick with more than just their blood. He *wanted* me.

And I am going to have him.

CHAPTER 39

The deep rumbles of victory drums possess my body, the music gripping my hips and dancing behind me as if we are one. I throw my head back and cherish the rhythm moving through me with each beat of the war instruments. Each strike of the drums a body that fell at my feet, the memory of their anguished cries singing in my blood like colorful songbirds. My pulse quickens and slows in sync with the tempo. I don't remember a single time in my life I have felt this *good*. Limitless. Like my body belongs to me and me alone.

It must be the wee hours of morning by now, but none of us have slept since returning to the castle. Bonfires have erupted across the grounds, men dancing and drinking merrily around them, laughing as they pound their wooden cups together in celebration. Some of the maids and servants even find themselves amongst the crowd, cheering with the others and swaying to the music.

I dance through it all. High on luscious chaos, the remnants of blood magic guide my hips in slow, rhythmic circles, and I dance, and I dance, and I dance. Sin doesn't hide his staring. Maybe it's his own soaring caster's high that grants him the confidence to not shield his watchful gaze for once. He mingles through the courtyard—playing their games and sharing their drinks—more carefree than I've ever seen him. But his eyes never drift far from me. And when his soldiers take turns dancing beside me, *behind* me, his glowing irises darken with indignation, sending a jolt of heat between my thighs every time. I wave the men towards me, one after the other, just to glimpse that fury in his eyes and relish in the pleasure each tic of his jaw sends through me as his need to possess my body like his beating war drums deepens.

Maybe he's keeping tabs on me to make sure I don't suddenly snap with the swell of blood magic and decide to take out half his army before they can blink. Or maybe he just likes the clothes I changed into when we returned—a deep purple dress with twin straps that tie behind my neck, the neckline plunging between my breasts. The hem is longer in the back; the front short enough to glimpse the cuffs of the thin stockings fitted around my thighs underneath. And judging from the Black Art's wandering eyes, I'm betting on the dress.

I wonder if he's thinking about how deeply I kissed him, surrounded by his enemy's limp corpses, and how rebellion blood tasted on my mouth. Our eyes lock across the courtyard again, and I tilt my head back and slowly, *slowly*, drag my tongue across the fronts of my teeth, reminding him how just hours ago, it was my tongue on *his* teeth.

Caressing my hand across the bare skin between my breasts, I hold his stare for a beat longer, then turn and head for the castle. *Come and get me, Blackheart.* I open the door to his study with magic, mine now able to overpower the locking spell he used, and leave it ajar as I hop onto his desk. Facing the threshold, I spread my legs, the skirt of my dress bunching at my waist, and slip my hand between my thighs.

I smell him when he's on the stairs, his cedar and peppercorn scent alone enough to dampen me under my fingertips. It takes all I have not to moan at the sight of him when he steps through the door, his eyes instantly glued to where I touch myself. I lean back and spread my legs wider, my cunt crying at the sight of the pulse thrumming in his neck. Pushing off the desk, my wrist flicks to the side, and the door slams shut behind him. Sealing him in here with me. Sealing our fate. Because something tells me we're not walking out of this room the same as we entered it. And eyeing the bulge straining against Sin's pants, I'm not certain I'll be doing much walking at all anymore.

I trace my tongue across my upper lip, thinking of all the places I want to taste him under his clean black shirt, and all the spots I *need* him to taste me. His chest rises and falls in rapid succession, his feet still planted on the ground, but his eyes glazing over with lust. Ever the strategist... the warlord of Aegidale knows if we give in tonight, it changes the game forever. I may not be familiar with battle tactics, but I'm quite certain fucking the enemy on your work desk isn't recommended. I raise one eyebrow at him as I swirl a finger in my wetness, daring him to make his choice.

The action breaks him.

Sin rushes me, grabs my waist with both his hands, and pushes me back until my ass presses against the desk. My fingers curl in the loose fabric of his shirt, and his mouth crashes into mine with hunger, like he can't get enough of me fast enough.

More—I need more. Desperate to feel his skin against mine, I unfasten the buttons of his shirt and rip it down over his muscular arms. Something feral breaks free in me as I behold the sight of his bare, sculpted chest, his obliques like chiseled stone from a lifetime of swordsmanship. Sin's not just beautiful.

He's devastating.

His hands find the laces along the back of my dress and without care, he drags a now lengthened claw down them, and the bodice busts free. I untie the straps behind my neck, and he yanks the top of the dress down, baring my full, swollen breasts to him. Sin slides a callused hand down the side of my stomach, the tips of his shifted claws digging into my skin, and he cups my breast with the other. He devours me with his mouth, kissing everywhere he can put his lips—my neck, collarbone, chest—and I bury my hands in his unbound hair. Need burns through me like a raging fever, his mouth a soothing balm to the inferno scorching within me.

I cry out as he flicks his tongue over my nipple, and moan deeply when he takes it into his mouth and bites down. Not hard, but enough to send my toes curling inside my shoes. And then he grabs me under my thighs and lifts me onto the desk, the balls of my feet curling over the sides. He steps between my spread legs and presses his lips to the shell of my ear as he strokes a finger across my slit.

A growl of approval rattles from deep in his chest. "So wet for me, little witch."

He retracts his claws, then plunges a finger inside me, both of us unleashing rhapsodic sighs as he begins to pump in and out of me. My hands tangle in his hair, and when he hooks a second finger inside, my head falls back as waves of pleasure wash through me.

"Sin..." I pant, unable to finish my sentence as he presses his palm against my clit, sending a tidal wave rippling through my core.

I rock against his hand, completely at his mercy as he curls his fingers up to hit the spot I need him to and... and... *Goddess above*. No. Not yet.

"Sin—stop!" I call out.

He stops immediately, and I almost whimper when he slides his fingers out of me, leaving me painfully empty. His breathing is labored when he presses his forehead to mine. "Did I mistake your intentions, love?"

I shake my head against his. "No, it's not that. There's just something I need to do first."

I force myself to pry my hands from his hair and place them on either side of his face, tilting his head down to look at me.

"I am not here with you right now because of any spell. I'm here because I want to be. Something about you sets my soul on fire, Singard, and I'm ready to burn."

He leans in and captures my mouth with his again, but gentler this time. Softer. Letting his lips and tongue say what his heart isn't ready to.

My hands trail down the cut planes of his chest, tracing arcane lines into his skin. I pause with one hand pressed to his stomach and the other on mine. He knows what's coming and watches carefully but makes no move to try to stop me. Sin promised my freedom, and I don't doubt he would have released me himself before we left this room, but I am done being freed at the will of others.

I grab onto the phantom rope linking us and shred at it with mental talons. It buckles beneath me, trying to resist my will, but I grip it harder, willing all my intention to its extinction.

My lips skim across his chest and up the column of his neck as the tether begins to split and fracture. I drag my tongue along the underside of his jaw before leaning up on my toes and planting my mouth at the base of his ear. "I release us from this bond."

His arms snake around my waist and pull me against him, my mouth drying as I inhale his peppery scent, my tongue yearning to lap at his essence like cream.

The tether snaps between us.

I inhale deeply as my lungs swell with newfound autonomy, the last of the Black Art's control bleeding from my body.

Leaving me unbound.

Feral.

Starving.

Slamming my palms against his hard chest, I shove Sin away from me. He stumbles backwards, just far enough for me to slip around him and push him against the desk. *My fucking turn.*

I leave no part of him untouched, starting with soft bites along his neck, nibbling his collarbone, licking his chest. When I finish swirling my tongue across his abdominals, my fingers move to unfasten the buttons of his trousers. His hands clamp down on top of mine, and he tilts my chin up with one finger, forcing me to meet his eyes, their irises still a smoldering yellow-green.

"You're high, love," he murmurs.

"So are you," I whisper back, ripping my hands out from beneath his.

He groans in frustrated delight and dips his head to gently tug the crown of my ear between his teeth. "Which is exactly why I can only restrain myself long enough to ask you this once," he says, nibbling my lobe again. "Are you sure?"

Not tearing my eyes from his, I sink to my knees before him. "I haven't been able to stop thinking about what your cock tastes like."

How's that for an answer, Your Grace?

A growl rips from his chest, and I yank his trousers down. His cock springs free, and I *feel* my eyes widen to the size of small dinner plates.

It's the most mouthwatering thing I've ever seen.

And definitely the Black Art's deadliest weapon.

If the magic high wasn't fueling my confidence, I may have hesitated at the *sheer size* of him. But instead, I lick my lips and wrap my mouth around his swollen cock, staring up at him as I do. He swears under his breath as I take him farther into my mouth, but only half of him fits before he's hitting the back of my throat and I gag around him.

Sin stares down at me like the sight of my hollowed cheeks sliding up and down his dick is the most beautiful piece of art he's ever laid eyes on. He reaches for my head and twists his fingers in my hair as I swirl my tongue over his length and devour him as if I was a starved woman. Grunts of pure masculine pleasure tear from his chest, and I suck him faster, letting his cock touch the back of mouth again and again. His other hand finds the back of my neck and grips me around the nape—wanting me, *needing* me —as his nails lengthen into claws again and pierce my skin. The smell of my own blood on his fingers sends pleasure rocking through me harder, and I drag my tongue up the underside of his shaft, watching as he fights to keep himself from shifting.

With a frustrated growl, he pulls himself out from between my lips and lifts me off my feet, setting me back down on the desk and ripping my knees apart so I'm bare before him. He leans forward, the ends of his hair brushing over my nipples, and he kisses the underside of my jaw. His cock throbs against my thigh, wetness already beading at the tip. I arch my back, desperate to feel him against me, against my pussy now sobbing for him.

Sin raises his lips to mine and murmurs against them. "I'm going to fuck you now, love. Is that okay?"

Goddess, yes.

I nod, inching forward to grind against him.

A low snarl in my ear. "*Use your words,* little witch. Tell me you want it."

"I want it. Please fuck me, Your Grace. Now..."

His breath so hot on my neck, his hands digging into my thighs splayed open around him... I've never wanted anything more in my life than to feel him fill me to capacity.

I cry out as he slides himself inside of me. Sin moves slowly, giving me time to adjust to his size, to *stretch* around him. He swallows my moan with his mouth, entwining his tongue with mine as he pulls out of me.

The Black Art isn't gentle the second time.

He thrusts back into me, this time seating himself all the way to the hilt, his cock hard and thick inside of me. A strangled scream rasps from my throat, and he moans at the sound. His hands tighten around my ass as he pumps in and out of me, his cock stretching me around him easier as I grow wetter with each deep-seated plunge.

My head falls behind my shoulders as he fucks me, and I grind my hips against his, sheathing him in my warmth. I feel no embarrassment as I call out his name, moans falling from my lips as the sound of his sex slaps against mine. And when he leans forward and takes my nipple between his teeth, chaos explodes inside me, and I fall over the edge, unable to stifle the screams that follow. Sin buries his face against my neck as he finds his own release, and if it's possible for me to get any wetter, I do as his cock pulses inside me, and he spills his seed deep in my cunt.

My back collapses to the desk, and I pull him against my chest, his nose in the hollow of my collarbone. I comb my fingers through his hair as we lie here, holding each other, our breath slowly returning to normal.

Sin props himself up and presses his lips to mine once more, this time much gentler, sweeter. When he stands, he pulls me with him so I'm sitting upright, and he tucks my hair behind my ear. "You are so beautiful," he whispers, his voice more raw than I've ever heard it.

He leans forward and kisses the spot on my hip where his black heart once adorned. "I'd be lying if I said I wasn't going to miss seeing my mark on you. But I've found more enjoyable ways to claim you," he says, his eyes taking in his seed now running down my thighs.

"I take the tonic," I say. The concoction of herbs that prevent pregnancy. "I packed it in my bag when we visited my family."

"I know," he responds smugly.

I raise an eyebrow at him, and he grins.

"I saw it on your table when I visited your chambers last night. Certainly planted images in my head. And if I dare say, you live up to your namesake. You sing so pretty, little Wren."

I smile with mock sweetness and tie the straps of my dress behind my neck while he steps back into his trousers and pulls his shirt back on. He motions for me to turn around so he can lace my dress again.

"No need. I'm heading to my chambers. I'm officially wiped out."

He frowns, and then murmurs, "Stay with me tonight."

"Not done with me yet, Your Grace? I'm already going to be thinking of you every time I try to walk tomorrow."

He laughs softly, but it doesn't touch his eyes. "Sleep in my chambers tonight. There are about a thousand men out there wondering where you slipped away to right now, and I don't want them tracking you down." His tone is lighthearted but weighted with genuine concern. Concern that I have no doubt would turn into something much... *messier,* should anyone actually try anything.

"What kind of woman do you take me for?" I jest.

He leans forward and whispers against my lips, "A very... *very* desirable one."

"Then it's a *very* good thing I'm quite capable of looking after myself."

He chuckles. "You have made that abundantly clear."

I step away from him and dip my knees in a mock curtsy. "Goodnight, Your Grace."

When I turn into my room, I lock the door with the bolt only, knowing he will come by later and spell it closed. And for some reason I don't fully understand, I want him to be the one to seal the others out.

CHAPTER 40

Cosmina kneels on her pinkish bare knees, her neck tilted towards the sky, her dark hair cascading over her shoulders like a subterranean waterfall. Blue veins vine around her neck like vicious necklaces, and her breath turns labored and shallow. A twig snaps from somewhere in the forest around her, and she jerks her attention towards the sound just as a large, black mist appears within the trees. Her eyes go wide, but her knees remain planted in the mossy ground. She bares her teeth in a threatening snarl. As if it were sentient, the mist rears up in response and rushes towards her like a storm about to swallow her whole.

I fly upright, ripping the sweat-drenched blankets off my body.

Cosmina.

She wasn't there.

After the battle, the blood magic left me in a drunken high, crazed and... and distracted. My cheeks warm with the memory of last night's events—or early this morning's, I suppose—realizing I have no idea how long I've been asleep. But the high seems to have faded with sleep and an unknown number of hours, and I am thinking clearly now.

She was supposed to be there.

That was our plan, our arrangement. We would overwhelm

Legion, free Cosmina, and my sister and I would be allowed to leave Scarwood unscathed.

Legion was massacred. Blood magic had been coursing through me, sent me flying into a frenzied version of myself that was consumed with... *him*. Sin overwhelmed my senses—his smell, his appearance, his... the way he *looked* at me. When he drained the magic from my veins to protect us both, he panicked trying to get me to respond, to make sure I was okay. In the heat of battle, he didn't need a spell to keep me near him. His concern for my wellbeing was enough to bind my will to his.

The Black Art watched as I slaughtered his enemies without remorse and licked their blood from my lips. He wasn't frightened of me, disgusted by me, or thought any less of me.

He *wanted* me.

It all comes back to me with clarity now. I remember his face—the bearded man that nearly delivered a fatal blow to the back of Ileana's skull. She was outnumbered, too gone with rage to pace herself, and she wouldn't have survived the night.

I killed him.

And I controlled *her*.

But the rush of power that followed silenced all thoughts of Cosmina—drowned out anything that wasn't blood or war or him. Sin was high too. I kissed him while the city was being shredded around us, teased him in the courtyard celebration, baited him to his study. I *pursued* him.

Does he regret what we did? The Black Art sleeping with a bloodwitch violates more laws than I care to consider, but he knew what he was doing. His actions may have been influenced by his own caster's high, but he *chose* to kiss me back, and he certainly acted on his own free will in the study. And as much as I may hate to admit it, I'd do it all over again.

What we did this morning felt right.

He felt right.

I hurry to the bathhouse and scrub all remnants of yesterday from my skin—the faded red stains on my hands and face, the dirt in my nails, the scent of cedar and peppercorn still lingering on my skin. My lungs inhale deeply, swelling with freedom and opportunity. And for once, my gut doesn't clench with the weight of Sin's binding spell. No black heart marks my hip.

I am no longer tethered to the Black Art.

If I leave Scarwood now, he'd have no magical rope to track me down with. But I'm not going anywhere without my sister. Sin and I made a deal, and I intend on making sure he upholds his end of the agreement.

River is waiting in my room when I return; no doubt Sin asked her to keep an eye on me to make sure I'm now acting with some inkling of sanity. She informs me Sin has been occupied in the Great Hall for much of the afternoon, meeting with lords and shopkeepers of Blackreach to discuss plans for the city's reconstruction.

I put on a knee length black dress with a fitted waist and slight flare to the skirts, and braid my hair down my back. Fumbling through the tiny tins and pots of cosmetics River left, I dab some powder to my cheeks and eyelids, and when I'm thoroughly convinced no amount of powder can cover up the anxiety on my face, I give up the cause and leave my room.

The doors to the Great Hall span the length of the wall from the stone floor to the arched ceilings with large golden handles. The guard posted outside opens one of the doors for me, and I step inside. The room is large but predominantly empty aside from the rows of wooden desks and chairs seated in the center—likely seating for the council—and the oversized throne occupying the dais along the far wall. And seated in the towering gold throne with crimson velvet cushions, dressed in the black leather surcoat he wore the night I met him, is Aegidale's Black Art.

His eyes are on me the moment I enter the room, as if he'd been waiting for me, knowing I'd come find him here. An older man dressed in a dark tailcoat—a lord—stands at the foot of the dais. I curtsy out of respect for them both and quickly divert my eyes to the other end of the Hall where Sterling stands with a man I don't recognize. The head Langston waves me over to them, and I hurry to his side, grateful for the excuse to be out of Sin's direct line of sight.

I curtsy again before Sterling and the tall man dressed in a dark blue coat with silver threading at his side. Another Langston then, judging by his attire. "Son, this is Wren—an old friend of His Grace. She fought in the city with them yesterday, and Singard tells me she was an excellent asset. Wren, this is my eldest son, Cornelius."

As soon as he drops the name, the resemblance hits me with such obviousness, I'm not sure how I missed it. Cornelius is taller than his brother was, and Bennett's chilling blue eyes are replaced with warm honey ones, but he has the same thick, wavy brown hair, angled jaw, and thin, wide lips as his late sibling.

"Pleasure to make your acquaintance, my Lord," I say.

"Pleasure is mine, my Lady." He smiles, revealing a set of remarkably straight white teeth. Dusaro and Bennett had both mentioned the eldest Langston son planned to return, but his brother also hinted that his family held strong reservations towards him. I wonder what prompted him to leave Blackreach, and why he has chosen to return now.

"My condolences for your brother," I say with forced apology in my tone. I don't mean it, but it may appear strange if I don't offer them.

"Thank you. While it won't bring my brother back, I am glad justice was served, nonetheless. I appreciate your part in helping to avenge him and the countless others lost to Legion's fruitless cause."

"We wish it was under better circumstances, but Lady Langston and I are most pleased Cornelius has returned to us," Sterling says, sizing up his son with pride, and not the distaste Bennett suggested was the norm.

"It was time to take my place in the family business—didn't want to let this one screw it up too badly," he jests, elbowing his father in the ribs.

I dare a glance over my shoulder to see if Sin is still occupied with the visitor and find him still engaged in conversation, but the tapping of his nails on the throne arm and the slight bounce of his leg suggests he is readying to send the man away.

Sterling follows my gaze. "Stellar idea of him to host the ball."

"Ball?" I ask, turning my attention back to the Langstons.

"A token of appreciation for the city's residents being so flexible... a celebratory ball you could say. Invites will be going out tomorrow to all of Blackreach as most families will be able to return to their homes given most of the fighting stayed away from the residential areas."

"Stellar idea indeed, my Lord. Quite generous of His Grace to offer a distraction while the city's center is rebuilt."

Cornelius clasps his hands together in front of himself. "Miss Wren, I hope it is not too forward of me to ask, but would you accompany me to this ball? I'm afraid I've been away from home for quite some time and haven't had the opportunity to rekindle old acquaintances just yet."

"Me?" I blurt out, tucking away a loose strand of hair behind my ear.

"I'll admit I'm not much of a dancer," he says, putting his hands up in mock defense, "but I've been told I'm quite the mediocre conversationalist."

The last time I danced with a Langston, it didn't end well for either of us. I steal a glance over my shoulder again, noting the conversation behind me is coming to a close. Perhaps attending the dance with Cornelius will send a message to Sin—one that clearly states I don't expect our relationship to change as a result of what transpired between us. Surely the Black Art will want our... indiscretion... to remain between us. He needn't worry I have any intention to illuminate the pleasures we shared in the shadows. Plus, if Cornelius turns out to be anything like his late brother, I'm happy to reunite them.

"I would be delighted, Mr. Langston," I say, fanning out my dress and dipping my knees.

"Cornelius," he corrects. "Excellent. It seems my return to Blackreach won't be so miserable after all, even if I have to deal with this old man," he chastises his father with a half-hearted grin and a bump of his elbow.

Behind us, the visitor bids his farewell, and a servant escorts him out, the heavy door of the Hall groaning shut behind them.

"I look forward to your company, Cornelius. Now if you two will excuse me, I must see if I can steal a moment of His Grace's time."

Hoping my throat doesn't bob as I gulp down my anxiety, I turn and walk to the foot of the dais, feeling Sin's eyes glued to me with every step. He sits far back in the cushioned throne with his legs spread wide and his hands clasped together at the fingertips in his lap, the embodiment of casual, but his expression is anything but relaxed.

I slip into a deep curtsy. "Your Grace. I know you are quite

341

busy with arrangements, but I request a moment of your time. In private."

He straightens in his seat and rests his elbows on the arms of his throne. "Gentlemen," Sin calls to the Langstons who still linger in earshot. "Leave us for a moment."

They each bow and make a swift exit without a word, and the few servants lining the walls follow after them without being asked. When the room is vacant aside from us, he turns his attention back to me, his eyes now back to their usual shade of green and smoldering with curiosity. He's sitting taller now, but his legs are still splayed apart in front of him. A facetious smirk blooms across his face as if he knows it's taking all I have to not drop my eyes and drink in the sight of him.

I resist the urge to scowl and instead straighten my spine and look him dead in the eye. "I am elated for the kingdom's victory, but also disheartened events did not go as we predicted and planned for. I saw no sign of my sister yesterday, and now with Legion's devastation, I am very worried what is to become of her."

Lines split his forehead, and he rubs a hand across the bottom of his jaw. "Do you have any leads on where she may be?" he asks carefully.

"I'm certain they have her. I don't know what long game they're playing, but if someone is masking her location, that can only mean they don't want me finding her before they're ready. There *must* be more of them still, there has to be."

Because if there isn't... I'm not willing to acknowledge the possibility Legion disposed of my sister somewhere, her body spelled with magic to never be found.

"I want to see Cathal. He must know where she is, and if he won't talk to you, let me speak with him. I have learned how to control abilities I think might be most... *persuasive.*" Like shoving my dagger into his chest and slurping the blood from his thumping heart.

"I can assure you I have a surplus of tricks up my sleeve too. But with Legion gone, I have no use wasting resources to keep him alive anymore. Other than for my own personal gratification in watching him suffer," he adds darkly.

"No! Please... no. Not as long as Cosmina is missing. We need to find her first, then I don't care what you do with him. But he may be the only person alive that knows where she is."

He exhales sharply and idly scratches the underside of his chin. "Wren..."

"I pledged to fight alongside you, and I upheld that promise. And now I'm *asking* you to help me find her. As soon as I do, we'll leave, and you can be rid of me for good."

His lips turn down at that comment, but he doesn't respond.

"Please, Singard. Don't make me beg."

"As much as I'd like to see you kneeling before me again, love, I wouldn't want you to mess up that pretty little dress. Give me a few days. I leave for the city in the morning to oversee preparations, but I'll be back at the end of the week to host a celebratory ball here. We will convene then."

"I worry we don't have that kind of time," I press.

"The end of the week," he repeats, sharper now.

"*Fine.* End of the bloody week."

"You're welcome to attend the ball, of course. I promise I won't force you to dance with anyone this time, except maybe me. That is, if you're feeling up to walking by then." He raises an eyebrow at me, accentuating that lazy, feral grin he's perfected, and I *hate* the burn it instills low in my stomach. My body betraying me.

"I'll see if Cornelius is willing to let go of me long enough to spare you a dance," I say in a tone as bitter as it is sweet.

The smirk vanishes from his mouth, and I can't help my cheeks from swelling with amusement as the muscles along his jawline feather slightly.

And as quickly as it appeared, I wipe the smug smile from my face. "I look forward to our continued arrangement, Your Grace. But if you cannot offer me an agreeable plan by the end of the week, then I'm afraid I'll have to take my leave. Though, I do think it is in your best interest to keep the kingdom in my good graces."

He chuckles with dark amusement. "Tell me, little witch, do you intend on killing all your enemies now, or just the ones I ask you to?"

I lick my lips. "Only the ones I take to bed, Your Grace."

I turn and head for the doors, but not before I glimpse the *ravenous* look on Sin's face, like my comment incited some kind of hunger as wild and raw as his heart. A heart I will eagerly rip from his chest and devour if he doesn't make good on his word.

CHAPTER 41

River dropped off a pouch of coin in my room the morning Sin left, insisting the Black Art left it for me to purchase a gown from the modiste's shop in town. I accepted it, easily reading the unwritten message inscribed on the leather bag. Sin wants to buy me a gown to show just how little he cares that I've agreed to attend the celebration with Cornelius. And judging from the number of silvers I found in the bag, he doesn't want me skimping on quality.

He *shouldn't* care that I bring a date. Not when the Black Art and I have nothing between us except a night of unbridled lust that was a natural consequence of our magic expulsion. I've reminded myself several times since our night in the study that we acted on impulse and nothing more. Singard Kilbreth and I do *not* belong together—nor will we ever. The only thing preventing him from riding city to city slaughtering every transcendent in his path is the agreement we made: I keep his secret undisclosed, and he doesn't brutally murder my family. Only a monster could fall in love with someone like that.

And speaking of monsters, I look downright *malevolent*.

A long red dress made from crushed velvet hugs every single one of my curves, the neckline plunging deep between my breasts, the vertex almost at my navel. Gloves of the matching color adorn my arms to the elbow, and I wear a pair of strappy golden heels. River helped style my hair into a thick crown braid and placed a crystal leaf comb along the side, and I admire how it catches the light when I turn my head in the mirror.

Knock, knock. "I have a delivery for you, my Lady," a servant calls from the other side of the door. I let her in, and she hands me a long, rectangular box with a small envelope stuck to the top of it. As soon as she leaves, I rip open the envelope and pull out a piece of decorative stationary with a note penned in excellent script.

So our guests know where you lie.
-S

I crumple the paper, toss it aside, and open the slender box, my eyes threatening to pop from their sockets when I behold the treasure inside. A golden necklace, seated inside a protective velvet cutout, stares back at me, the fine shimmering metal as radiant as the summer sun. A teardrop pendant hangs from its center, a large garnet inlaid in a gold setting.

I swipe the paper from the floor, smooth it open, and reread Sin's note.

Where you lie.

I nearly ignite the parchment with sparks at my fingertips. There is no doubt in my mind of the double meaning in his words—clearly, a necklace of this value could only come from the kingdom's wealth. The Black Art wants me to wear the necklace like some sort of kingdom trophy, while also suggesting I am off limits to the lords in attendance tonight.

Off limits to Cornelius.

As if Sin has any ownership of me.

I slam the box shut, toss it onto the bed, and strut out of the room, holding my chin high to accentuate my very bare neck.

Cornelius is striking in a deep blue coat with matching trousers, his wavy hair freshly combed and plastered to his head with some kind of holding agent. He's waiting for me at the bottom of the stairwell and takes my gloved hand in his when I reach the bottom step.

"You look exquisite, Lady Wren."

With my hand clutched in his, I dip into a deep curtsy. "As do you, my Lord. Shall we go stir up some trouble?" I shoot him a playful wink and motion towards the long corridor that leads to the castle's ballroom.

I allow Cornelius to keep my hand as we make our entrance. The space is the definition of elegance, from the golden chandeliers with dripping crystal accents to the fine lace tablecloths draped over the long tables pushed against the walls. Bouquets of flowers picked fresh from the garden spring from decorative vases, their petals rivaling the elaborate gowns twirling around the room for vibrancy. Green garland with colorful berries poking through the leaves wrap around the tall white pillars, the smell of pine penetrating the room with its earthy aroma.

I slam down a wall between my energy and the swarming horde of collectives in the room, refusing to allow it to overwhelm me tonight. With my sister's fate unbeknownst to either of us, I need a distraction. And right now, Cornelius is looking mighty distracting.

Silver clinks against glass, and Dusaro gathers the attention of the room from the dais at the far end. The sight of Sin's father alone has my hand itching for the dagger I strapped to my thigh, so I place it on Cornelius's arm instead. The room erupts into a thunderous applause as Sin and Ileana enter from the far door and make their way to the dais.

Sin wears a black tailcoat tailored to perfection with a crisp white shirt beneath his jacket, and dark trousers that conform to his legs in all the right places. Ileana walks a few steps behind him dressed in a strappy silver gown that compliments her dark complexion, her black curly hair cascading down her back. Never is Ileana without beauty, but tonight, she is nothing shy of perfection.

I scan the room, noting how everyone's eyes fixate on Sin immediately, as if his presence alone demands their attention. He delivers a short welcome with rehearsed grace, the kingdom's responsibility in the city's destruction instantly forgiven with a single speech from their charming leader. As soon as he dismisses the crowd to enjoy their evenings, they are both surrounded by townsmen and their wives eager to share their appreciation for Legion's recent devastation.

Cornelius is well-mannered and refined, and introduces me to many of the old acquaintances he knew from his past. We sample some of the pastries with fruit filling and share a large slice of a mouthwatering tart, rich with the earthy flavors of mushrooms and caramelized onions. And as promised, he steers far away from the dance floor during group dances, which is why it surprises me when he asks me to join him for the partner dance.

I notice Sin hasn't participated in any of the group dances either. He's been swarmed with people talking his ear off on all sides, and I'm not sure if he's even noticed my presence here tonight at all. Which is a shame, as I really want him to see I have chosen not to wear his stupid, possessive necklace. I also notice the goblet of mead that hasn't left his hand all night, apparently *his* date for the evening.

Cornelius leads me to an open space on the floor as the musicians begin to play their stringed instruments. He places his hands on either side of my waist, remarking on the softness of my dress, and we step in time with the harmonized music.

"You're decent on your feet for someone who acts like the dance floor might attack them, my Lord."

"I said I didn't *like* dancing, not that I couldn't," Cornelius says, pulling me closer to him and flashing me a dangerous grin.

"Well, dancing looks rather good on you. Perhaps you should engage in the activity more often," I tease, giving his arms a slight squeeze.

Am I flirting with him?

"Apparently *war* looks good on you. My father mentioned you fought in the city. How does a woman of your stature find herself tangled up with the lot of Singard's men anyway?"

"Please, I have no stature," I dismiss. "They abducted my sister, and I've been trying to find her since."

"Trying to? As in, you have still been unsuccessful after our victory?"

I nod. "We have been unable to locate her, but I *will* find her. Somehow."

"It was certainly brave of you to be in the city. Fighting transcendents is no easy feat."

"I fought against *Legion*," I amend.

Cornelius raises an eyebrow at my correction. "Are you a sympathizer?" he asks, lines splitting his forehead.

"If you're asking if I believe it's wrong to fault someone for simply existing as they were born, then yes. We should be judged by the identities we create for ourselves, not for the ones assigned to us at birth, my Lord."

"And what identity have you created for yourself, Lady

Wren?" Before I can answer, Cornelius spins me away, and I twirl directly into his sight.

The heat in Sin's eyes nearly melts my dress from my flesh. He stands next to a garland wrapped pillar, swirling a glass of amber mead in his hand. He drags his gaze down my attire, the sharpness in his stare threatening to shred my gown to ribbons. When he finishes perusing over my dress, he looks pointedly at my neck and takes a deep pull of his drink.

I spin back to Cornelius before Sin sees the smug grin bloom across my face. "I... I haven't decided yet," I say, almost forgetting what he had asked me. "But I fear if I don't find Cosmina—my sister—it may not be worth me creating an identity at all, Mr. Langston."

The music simmers to a close, and we each bow at the waist. When we both right ourselves, his eyes shift to somewhere behind me. "I think someone wants your attention," he says.

I spin on my heel and find Ileana staring at me expectedly. My knees dip in a deep curtsy before her, the action feeling strange in her presence. "My Lady," I greet.

Her eyes sweep my dress, and she folds her arms across her slender waist. "As the Black Art's Hand, it is my responsibility to check in with everyone after battle," she says disinterestedly, lifting a hand and admiring her nails. "How are you feeling?"

"I'm fine," I dismiss. "How are you recovering, my Lady? You look well."

"I'm not ignorant to what you did for me out there," she blurts out, ignoring my question. "You took a grave risk, and you saved my life in doing so. Thank you," she adds bitingly, the gratitude not quite touching her eyes.

Oh. "It was my honor. Ileana... you will never know how sorry I am for that night. I acted out of fear, and while I know it doesn't do a damn thing to change what you went through, I want you to know I've pledged to never be that person again. The kind of person that was able to leave you there. I... I'm sorry. I'm just so sorry."

She adjusts her stance but keeps her arms folded tightly across herself. "There were a lot of them, even for someone with your... gifts. It was selfish of me to have expected that from you. And as His Grace has already chewed my ass out about it, I'm aware I need to work on controlling my... impulses," she says, half rolling her eyes as she remembers a private conversation between them.

I can't help but chuckle at her expression. "Men—what do they know?"

Her lips twitch, and she meets my eyes again. "He's not as bad as he may seem. Between us, I'd plant a knife in Dusaro's eye without an ounce of guilt, but Singard... he's alright."

I blink away my surprise. I may have only known Ileana for a short time, but long enough to know *alright* is a generous compliment for her.

"Though if I have to continue listening to his self-righteous grumblings every time Langston looks at your ass, I might actually find myself preferring his father's company," she says with a mock shudder.

I offer her half a smile and excuse myself to go find Cornelius again. I'm halfway across the room when a hand smoothly winds around the small of my back. I turn to apologize for disappearing on him and—

Goddess help me.

"Did you not like my gift, or do you simply enjoy refusing me?"

I crane my neck up to look at the Black Art, always surprised at how much he *towers* over me up close. "The necklace was beautiful. It was your complete and utter lack of respect for me that I did not wear it."

He furrows his brows. "What do you mean?"

"So our guests know where you lie," I scoff, shaking my head as if I could shake off the sting of his words. "I am not some whore you call on when you're bored so that you may decorate me with jewelry and flaunt me as your toy."

Sin tilts his head to the side and his brows scrunch closer together. He remains quiet for a moment, and I do my best to not display the hurt on my face, but the downward curve of his mouth suggests I failed. "It was not my intention to make you feel anything less than valued. I admit I selfishly wished to make a statement to Langston and every other male in here that can't seem to take their eyes off you, but not at the expense of hurting you. Forgive me."

His apology feels sincere, and he steps next to me so his shoulder brushes mine as we face opposite directions. He tilts his head down and whispers for my ears alone, "No one would be looking at the necklace anyway. You are stunning, love."

I step away from him without a word and continue looking for Cornelius, who I find conversing with a small group. I tuck the Black Art's apology away to process later and link my arm through Cornelius's when the musicians announce it is time for the final dance of the evening. We join the other couples on the floor, and when we conclude the dance with a bow, Cornelius offers to escort me to my room.

"I'm going to wash up before turning in for the night, but thank you for a lovely evening, Mr. Langston."

"Then I shall bid you farewell, my Lady."

With a polite smile, I turn to leave but stop when he calls after me.

Wearing an expression more serious than I'd seen all night,

he says, "Keep your ears open, Wren. You never know what threats are lurking just beneath your nose."

Puzzled by his words and vowing to attempt to make sense of them tomorrow when I am more clear-headed, I acknowledge his warning before turning and leaving the ballroom.

CHAPTER 42

I *should* wash up and head straight to my chambers, but I can't shake the nagging thought that I should go find Sin. It's possible I overreacted to his note, and his apology did seem genuine, but it doesn't excuse his behavior. He insinuated I *belong* to him, and nothing could be further from the truth.

I made sure of that when I snapped the tether.

The ballroom was beginning to clear out when I left, and I didn't see Sin lingering about anywhere. I head down the corridor towards the staircase, expecting he may have returned to his room. He may be less than thrilled if I invite myself to his quarters, but I need to talk to—

"Little witch."

My stomach somersaults at the sound of his voice. The massive doors of the Great Hall are propped open on my left, and Sin sits in his high-backed throne, a cup of mead in his hand and a bottle on the dais next to him. Firelight from the wall sconces casts deep shadows across the room, across his face. He watches every step I take towards him with scrutiny, a lone wolf assessing its next meal. His wrist flicks lazily to the side, and the doors slam shut behind me, the locks audibly clicking into place.

"Is sitting in the dark while you drink yourself to death and conjure up new ways to torture people a frequent hobby of yours, Your Grace?"

He smiles around the glass he brings to his lips. "Not all people—only the beautiful women who refuse my gifts."

"Would you like to talk your way out of the scintillating note you left some more?"

Sin cocks his head in a movement almost feral. "Is that all *he* wanted to do with you? *Talk?*"

Incredulous laughter falls from my lips, and I fiddle with the comb in my hair. "Cornelius was a lovely conversationalist, actually. Why—jealous, Blackheart?"

"Why did you come with him?"

"He asked me," I retort, as if the answer should be obvious.

With a final pull of his drink that empties his glass, he sets it on the floor next to him and rises from his throne, his height accentuated by the raised platform. "Do I need to remind you what happened the last time you found yourself alone with a Langston?"

"I wasn't alone with him, and perhaps I need to remind you that the only reason I was in that situation with Bennett in the first place was because *you* forced me to spend time with him."

"It was war, Wren," he drawls my name. "It was strategy."

"You would have let me lie down for him if you thought for a *second* I wasn't going to kill him, risking your precious strategy. Since apparently, as your note suggested, I am only worthy when I'm warming someone's bed."

"That's not true," he snarls, stepping off the dais.

My hands ball into fists at my sides, my magic licking my veins as rage floods through them. "You were only there to keep me from exposing your little scheme."

"I wouldn't have cared if you killed him, Wren."

"Then why didn't you let me?"

"Because *I* wanted to kill him!" Sin roars. He's directly in front of me now, his shadow casting me in darkness. When he takes one last step towards me, closing the gap between us, the torrid heat simmering in his eyes is enough to plant a fever deep inside me. "I was never going to let him even *touch* you. And when he tried, there wasn't a force in the realm that could have caged that anger. He was dead the same second he even *thought* about you that way."

"You tethered me to you against my will," I remind him, tilting my chin up.

"Are you going to fault me for a spell you were able to break yourself?" he asks, reaching to adjust the comb I twiddled loose.

"I broke it with blood magic! Magic I gained fighting for *you.*"

"And I seem to recall you liking the rush it gave you," Sin whispers, dipping his head lower and grazing his teeth across the crown of my ear. "Fighting for me, fighting *with* me."

It consumes all my self-control to not tremble beneath his touch, to hold my ground. "You shouldn't have put me in that position."

"Then what position should I put you in, little witch?" He cups the side of my face in his hand and drags his lips across my cheek, to the corner of my mouth. Pausing, seeing if I will refuse him.

You're drunk," I say, smelling the honey mead on his breath.

He chuckles once. "Hardly. Just enough to forget that I shouldn't be feeling this way about you." Still firmly holding my jaw with one hand, his knuckles lengthen into claws, and he trails a long nail down my bare sternum.

I should run. Shove him away and run far from this place, far from him, but heat feeds my center like timber to a fire.

Sin hooks a nail into the deep neckline at my navel. "I've been wanting to rip this off you all night. Consumed with thoughts of what I wanted to do to you after I shredded it from your body."

I gasp when his hands suddenly collar my neck, tilting my head back as he kisses my throat.

"I haven't been able to stop thinking about how pretty you'd sing with my tongue inside you," he murmurs against my jugular.

His words send a storm barreling between my thighs, and even now, with the smell of spiced wine hovering between us, he waits for me to make the next move—to give him some small sign I want this.

Ignoring every instinct screaming for me to bolt out of here, I grab a fistful of his silky hair and yank his head back. "Prove it."

Faster than I can blink, we're entwined in a maze of limbs and tongues, my dress hiked up to my hips and my legs wrapped around his waist. My hands act of their own volition, tearing his clothes from his body until only his trousers remain between us. And then he does the unthinkable.

Sin sits me on the velvet cushion of his throne, spreads my knees, and kneels between them.

His lengthened claws dig into the backs of my thighs, his hand just above the dagger still strapped to one of them, and slowly, he swirls his tongue through my wetness. I shove my hands into his hair as he tastes me in long strokes, and a strangled cry falls from my lips when he slips his tongue inside. Wicked pleasure rocks through me, sending my thighs quivering around him as I watch as the Black Art laps at my cunt.

Seated in his throne.

One strappy heeled shoe hooked over his shoulder.

Where Sin struggles with words, he more than makes up for it with his actions. And if thrusting his tongue inside me while he kneels at my feet is his way of apologizing, I'd let the man drive a stake through my heart.

My moans threaten to shatter the windows behind us as he consumes every inch of my neediness, drinking me in like my pussy is the sweetest wine he's ever tasted. I twist my fingers in his hair, his dark head bobbing between my thighs, his long nails still firmly gripping the undersides of my legs. "Sin," I choke out, desperately aware of how *empty* I am.

He pulls back enough to raise his eyes to mine, a feral smile crossing his lips. In lightning speed, Sin swipes the dagger from my thigh. He flips the blade in his hand and presses the handle against my opening, his irises burning with unbridled need. "Do you want more, love?" he asks, swirling the hilt around my center.

My legs jerk closed in reflex, pinning his arm between them. Sin has placed a blade to my throat before, but *this* is different. The thought of him fucking me with the hilt of my own knife paralyzes me with fear, my thighs going rigid as if the brush of the cool hilt electrocuted me into permanent stillness.

And my pussy weeps in response.

"Spread your legs. *Now,*" he adds when I hesitate.

Swallowing my fear, I allow my knees to slowly fall apart.

"Such a good girl," he breathes against my delicate skin. "Now listen very carefully, Wren. I'm going to fuck you with your dagger so that the next time you think of pulling it on me, you'll remember how I made you come all over it."

Fucking hell.

"Tell me to stop if that's not what you want, love," he

murmurs, dragging his nose across my thigh, his light scruff pricking my skin.

Absolutely not. Tell him to stop. Goddess above, tell him!

Fuck.

I tilt my hips towards him and barely glimpse the ravenous look on his face before he plunges the hilt inside me, and my eyes roll deep in my head. The sounds of my wetness rival my moans as he begins to move it in and out of me, the hilt becoming slicker as my pussy invites it inside like an old friend.

"Just like that, Wren. *Fuck,* you're taking it so well."

He pumps the dagger inside me faster, and with his other hand, strokes my clit in small circles, sending a pleasure as dark and ancient as the gods pulsing through me.

"Look at me." His voice cuts through my howls of rapture. "Look at me while I make you come."

I force my eyes to open and lower them to where Sin watches me intently, his erection straining against his pants as he brings me to orgasm with my own weapon. The last of my restraint shatters as ecstasy washes through me, and I allow the Black Art to claim me again. Sin slides the blade through my slick folds once more, letting me ride out my release until the very end, and then slowly pulls the handle out and sucks my cream from the hilt.

When he's finished cleaning the knife with his mouth, he pulls me to my feet, his chest pressed to mine and his cock throbbing against my belly. He curves his hand under my jaw and parts my lips with his, letting me taste myself on his tongue, desire licking at my thighs all over again at the flavor in my mouth. My hands trace across his chest and around his muscular arms, arriving at the waist of his trousers where my fingers promptly work to unfasten them.

A guttural moan escapes his lips when I take him into my

hand and curl my fingers around his girth. His head falls back to look at the ceiling as I stroke him, again and again, delighting in the impossible swelling of his cock as it beads and pulses in my palm.

Sin's hand catches mine, and he spins me around so my back is towards him, his lips at my ear. "Grab my throne. And I suggest you hold on tight, little witch."

I lean forward and grip the arms of the chair as he yanks my dress up so my full ass is exposed, rubbing against me and—

Pain thrashes through me as my pussy *stretches* around his hardness, my fingers curling over the armrests and a deep moan spilling out of me. He doesn't wait for me to adjust to the size of him before he's pulling out and slamming into me a second time. Again.

And again.

Whatever animosity I was still harboring towards him, Sin fucks the last of it out of me, claiming me with each merciless thrust. I give it right back, grinding my ass against his hips, pulling his own grunts of pleasure from his lips, one after the other.

I whimper as he suddenly pulls out of me and look over my shoulder, but he snaps my head forward. A moment later, something clatters to the floor behind me, and I almost look when the smell of him invades my senses.

Sin's blood, as fragrant as the hyacinths of early spring, permeates my nose, my tongue, my throat. I nearly go cross-eyed when he brings his arm to my mouth, blood pouring from the fresh wound on his forearm.

He sliced himself with the dagger.

"Drink," he demands, his voice low and full of need.

My lips part over his arm now sobbing crimson rivulets,

and my cunt throbs with the need to consume him, my chin going taut as I strain to keep my mouth off him.

"I want you to taste me while I fuck you. So be a good little bloodwitch and fucking *drink*," he orders again.

Sin roars as I latch onto him and buries himself deep inside my warmth. I drink and drink and drink, moaning as his blood crawls down the back of my throat, coating it with his essence, and I grow wetter with each slurp as if his juice drips all the way to my pussy. I let him control me like this, allow him to show me just how much he hates and needs me at the same time, and with the taste of his blood sticky and sweet in my mouth, I soar to new heights.

The sound of my climax hurls the Black Art into his own release, and his cock spits into my core, flooding me with his warm cum. My head falls back to rest on his chest, and he wraps both arms around my front, our breath rapid and uneven.

I don't know the exact moment it happened, but somewhere along the way, sparks ignited between us. As Sin buries his face into my shoulder, they rear up in an all-consuming fire, setting my heart ablaze and filling my body with ash.

And the worst part about loving him isn't his need for control or violence. It's knowing that no matter what he does, or who he hurts, my heart will still burn for him.

CHAPTER 43

Water beads across his shoulders as I twist and wring out the cloth, tiny rivulets streaming down his beautiful, bare back. I knead my palms into his shoulder blades, my hands working tirelessly to loosen the knots twisted deep in his muscles.

Sin's private bathhouse is lavish, the floor and tub both crafted of smooth stone, and benches inlaid into the walls for seating and dressing. A large cabinet with its doors propped open reveals a wide variety of oils and soaps, and a stack of neatly folded drying linens. Hints of rose and grapefruit rise from the steaming water, bleeding into our skin.

"You're tense," I murmur, digging my knuckles into a particularly deep knot beneath his right shoulder.

Sin sighs in agreement, and when I finish working the soreness from his body the best I can, I lean back and pull him with me so he rests against my chest. He's been strangely quiet since we snuck away from our entanglement in the Great Hall to wash up in his bath. Perhaps the same thoughts plague him that nip away at my own mind like diseased vultures. Twice now, we've given ourselves over to carnal lust. Three times if you count the late-night debauchery on my balcony.

But if it's only lust between us, why does it feel like I *need* him? Like it's no longer my beating heart keeping me here —it's his.

"Would you like to talk about what's bothering you?" I ask, pressing the side of my face against his, my fingers drawing lazy circles across his chest.

His hands come down on top of mine, pinning them against his chest, his body a rock beneath me. Unmoving. Unfeeling. Exhaling sharply, he sits forward, escaping my arm prisons holding him against me.

"What's wrong?" I ask again, this time with more force. Because the Black Art's lack of words is beginning to frighten me, especially after what transpired between us less than an hour ago. I expected nothing less than his usual smug teasing once we fled from the castle in a fit of hushed laughter and darted through the light sprinkling of rain to his bath quarters.

With his back still towards me, he rubs both hands across his face and cradles his head in his hands for an extended beat. "You didn't deserve any of this, Wren. None of it was fair to you. What I did to you..." he trails off, dragging his fingers down his cheeks before his hands plop into the water.

"No. It wasn't. And neither was the way you were treated by those closest to you. That wasn't fair to you either, and I think... I think maybe you're seeing that people can and *will* care about you if you let them. *I* care about you, Sin," I whisper, the words feeling strange in my mouth now that I'm saying them out loud. "Maybe it's wrong and maybe I shouldn't, *but I do.*"

He shakes his head. "Don't make excuses for me. I could have chosen differently. Done things differently. And I didn't, and it's too late, and I'm *sorry*, Wren." His voice cracks around my name, and my chest aches at the sound of his pain.

I scoot towards him and wrap my arms around his stomach again. "I know."

Gently, but with enough force to pull my hands away, he turns sideways and steps out of the bath. He doesn't bother drying himself with the linen before he's pulling his trousers back on and reaching for his white shirt.

I lean my elbows onto the side of the stone and watch him dress, confused by his words but giving him room to make sense of his own thoughts.

"You have to live your life hiding who you are every day because *my kingdom* fears what you are. If someone had dropped you on our doorstep a few months ago, boasting about how they trapped a bloodwitch, I would have taken the final breath from your lungs and not paid you a second thought. And that..." he pops his shirt out, then begins fastening the buttons. "For that, I hate myself."

"But you didn't. You had the chance to kill me and you didn't," I say softly, now really hating the sudden switch in his tone.

"So that I could use you! I forced you at my side with threats of what I would do should you not serve me. What you may feel for me now does not change what I did to you. And it never should."

I motion towards the stack of linens behind him, and he tosses me a length. Wrapping it under my arms and around myself, I step out of the bath, my wet hair plastered to the sides of my face. "Why—why are you saying this now?"

When he turns to face me, I almost don't recognize him. The heat in Sin's eyes is gone, in its place a stark coolness that encases my heart in ice, swells my lungs with air cold enough to chill them in place, never to expand with breath again.

Sin takes a step towards me, which is also a step closer to the door. "Because everything about you lures me in, Wren. When I'm around you, it feels like I'm *starving*. Like if I don't consume you in *every* possible way, I'll be torn apart, never to be whole again. I will not—I cannot—allow myself to do that to you anymore. Which is why you need to leave," he adds darkly. His voice is low, cold, penetrating my chest, shattering my soul.

Which is why you need to leave.

"I'm not going anywhere," I say, crossing my arms and hating the fragility in my tone. "Not without my sister. You said we'd come up with a plan, you... you promised we'd—"

"I can't help you find her," he interrupts me. "I'm sorry, but I can't."

"We made a deal, Singard, you don't just get to walk away from that. I will not allow you to walk away from *me* like that."

He looks at my feet but remains quiet, his silence only fueling my rage now simmering to a lethal heat.

"Why are you acting like this? One minute you're holding me captive, the next you're fucking me on your precious throne! You took what you wanted from me so I'm no longer worthy of your time, is that it?"

My nails dig into my palms at my sides, every hair on my body primed as if I'm about to sprint into combat. Because in a way, I am. He does not get to hurt me like this.

Sin bores his eyes into mine. "You know that's not true."

"Then what is true? Tell me! I fought in your gods-damned war. I brought your enemies to your feet, and I slaughtered them before you. One by one, I ripped their souls from their flesh in your name, a line I vowed to never cross. So, tell me, *Your Grace*, why the fuck you think you get to walk away from me now?" I demand, not a trace of fragility left in my tone.

"Because if you knew who I really was, Wren, what I'm truly capable of, you wouldn't want me anywhere near your sister."

I throw my arms up and charge towards him. "That's bullshit! I deserve the truth—you owe that to me! I don't believe you."

He halts me in my tracks by grabbing my chin and tilting my head back to look at him. "You should. And soon, you will."

My body stills under his touch, and he lightly presses his lips to mine and whispers against them, "Just know how sorry I am when you do."

Sin drops my chin and storms out, leaving me naked and shivering with only my wrath to warm me.

CHAPTER 44

I should have left hours ago. Thrown my few belongings into a bag, taken a horse, and rode through the night. As if I would be able to pull a few hours of rest before morning with the Black Art's words lingering in my mind, hanging on my heart.

I wrestled with my feelings for Sin—hated myself for growing attached to a man capable of such heinous acts. But never did I mistake him for something he wasn't. The warmth of Sin's touch did not blind me to the coldness of his heart. And I wanted every piece of his frigid black soul anyway, smugness and swords and all.

What a stupid girl.

I was naïve to think Sin wouldn't hurt me the second he had the opportunity. He even *warned* me—told me not to trust him. And foolishly, I ignored his cautions, lit my heart on fire and chucked it at him to do with as he pleased.

He is no better than Cathal.

At least Cathal didn't pretend there was anything between us after he learned what I was. He didn't take me to bed, whisper sweet affirmations in my ear, crush my heart with his godsdamned bloody fists.

The Black Art's wickedness runs deeper than Cathal's prejudices.

Sin's very blood is as dark as his heart.

And I wanted to consume it all until my battered lips were swollen with need and my tongue dripping with raven regret.

Stupid, stupid girl.

The floor quivers with a deep rumbling, the pitcher of water careening off my bedside table, the frames encasing paintings of sweeping landscapes swinging wildly against the wall like a broken pendulum. I'm out of bed, dressed in a tunic and pants, dagger strapped to my thigh in less than a minute.

An explosion.

Another thunderous boom shakes the castle, and my hands break my fall as I tumble sideways on the stairwell. The ceiling creaks as more are roused from their beds, vases topple over on the foyer tables, and flickers of orange lick at the arched windows.

What is happening?

Now flying down the stairs, I barrel through the double doors of the castle's entrance but skid to a screeching stop when I behold the horror before me.

The barracks are on fire.

Blazing curtains of orange and red shroud the quarters as soldiers rush from their beds, clad in nothing but their night wear. Several rush to try to drown the flames with well water, casting bucket after bucket onto the fiery storm. I scan the area —no enemies within the keep, no arrows flying over the wall.

No sign of an attack—perhaps a terrible accident.

The well water does nothing to calm the flames' fury and they climb higher, sneering down at the sweating, frantic men chucking water into their enveloping swells. I'm across the courtyard in a blink, lifting my palms to the rearing wall, willing the fire to bow before me. The flames buckle beneath my magic but don't shrink, refusing to surrender to my will.

I push against them harder. Perspiration beads across my brows, and my lungs cough in protest, but still, I command the inferno to die.

A hand grabs my arm mid-air, and Sin yanks me back a few steps, putting distance between us and the burning buildings.

"It won't go out!" I shout over the barracks now cracking, wood splitting as interior walls begin to fall, smoke filling every open space inside.

He grabs my hand with his, and we channel our magic together, sending our now joined collectives spiraling into the torrid heat.

The flames burn and burn and burn. Unwavering. Unyielding.

Glass shatters at our rear, and I turn in time to see the windows of the castle's western wing blow out as fire now claims that too. We abandon the barracks, running for the castle, and connect our magics again as soon as we halt at the foot of the fire.

"Get everyone out—everyone out now!" Sin bellows to a horde of men now rushing inside, pulling the thin fabric of their nightshirts up over their mouths and noses.

"Why isn't it working?" My body trembles with the force of my power and his, Sin's magic bleeding into my own as we unite against the fire trying to claim our home.

His home.

The reminder of Sin's dismissal lashes through me, but I

bury it deep. Shoving him into the conflagration won't erase the pain and will only put others still inside at risk. They need his power.

His power that, right now, might as well be nonexistent against the incandescent flames wrecking his stronghold.

Another window shatters outward, this one from the ground level, the fire taking another part of the castle as its own. Dusaro appears at my left and grabs my other hand with his. I try not to recoil as he binds his own inky magic to ours.

"Alchemist fire," he spits as the flames continue to burn and smolder and claim.

Alchemist fire.

Fire birthed from a sacred ritual, and very, *very* difficult to conjure. Impossible to extinguish with hands other than its creator's. Whoever gave life to these flames didn't do it on a whim—this attack was orchestrated.

We're not putting these flames out. At best, the three of us can hold it here, prevent it from spreading, but our magic has limits. Even Sin, whose collective was blessed by the goddess of the arcane, will falter eventually. I whip towards him to demand a plan and find him tracking the fire's path with his eyes, his mouth silently muttering to himself as he holds his arms out in front of him. He looks over my head at his father, Dusaro's face cast in a hazy red shadow as his lips twist into a smirk at his son's panicked expression.

"Get her out," Sin orders with a slight curl to his lip.

Dusaro chuckles without humor, his eyes creasing in the corners as he shakes his head. "No time, Singard."

"I have to hold it," he snarls, the veins in his forearms bulging as he exerts all his energy into holding the flames steady.

My own arms turn to lead as exhaustion seeps into them,

but I hold fast. We can't drop our hold until everyone has been evacuated.

"Get. Her. Out," Sin growls again, his tone rivaling the flames for wrath.

"I told you it would catch up with you," Dusaro drawls. "I'm not going to risk our home crumbling to the ground to take care of your *pet*. Let her burn," he spits, cold indifference wet on his tongue.

Fury rips across the Black Art's face, his eyes narrowing into slits. Sin's hand clenches around mine as he bares his teeth at his father.

I look between them both, confused and irritated they're choosing now to have a pissing contest while someone is trapped. "Who needs out? Ileana? Where is she?" I demand, panic rising in my voice. If Dusaro won't risk getting her out, I will.

Sin doesn't answer me, no sign he even heard me on his face as he continues to stare down his father, his expression threatening something much worse than alchemist fire.

"SINGARD!" I shout, and his eyes finally drop to mine. "Tell me where she is—I will get her!"

"The gate! Your Grace—the gate has been breached!" Aldred warns from behind us.

From over my shoulder, a small group of about fifteen steps out from a cloud of smoke and ash. Behind them, Sin's guards lay strewn across a now blood-soaked lawn, though no one in the group has their weapons drawn. A woman of small stature stands in front of the rest, clearly their leader, and raises her hand above her head. The air turns rouge as she recalls the fire into her palm, leaving the castle smoking and ruined and bare.

The mother of the flames.

"That's not possible," Dusaro breathes next to me, dropping my hand as we release our joined magics.

371

"Stand down!" Sin calls to the soldiers now charging the group. None of their hands even flinch towards their weapons, though if they managed to create alchemist fire, I doubt they intend on fighting with steel at all.

Sin and Dusaro rush forward to meet the infiltrators where they stand. The woman in front, the one who commanded the flames, is short in stature with dark wavy hair that falls to her shoulders. A labyrinth of lines and circles drawn in black and white paint is smeared across her rounded face. Behind her, the others all wear similar masks of painted-on geometric shapes slathered across their cheeks and forehead, and again under their eyes. They wear no armor, and the swords and knives hanging from their sides appear well-crafted. This is not Legion.

"Sera," Dusaro murmurs, his voice a mix of awe and disbelief.

"You haven't changed a bit, Dusaro," the woman replies. Her voice is lower than I expected, juxtaposed by the roundness of her cheeks and the feminine slope of her shoulders. Her pine green eyes sweep across Dusaro and rest on Sin who hasn't moved a muscle since calling off his men.

"Singard," she whispers, her deep voice softening around his name. "I've missed you so much."

"Mother," he utters, almost a question, as if he doesn't trust his eyes not to deceive him.

Mother? His mother was murdered, labeled a traitor for marrying Dusaro—a betrayal that was punished with her permanent silence. Judging by the surprise in both Sin's and his father's voices, they believed that to be true.

But now that I study her, I see the resemblance. Her green eyes are a darker shade and rounder than her son's, and her pale skin a stark contrast to the deep umber brown Sin shares with his father. But it's there—in the straightness of her nose and the curve of her lips—she is undeniably Sin's mother.

"How are you here? How... They killed you... they..." Dusaro stammers off, shaking his head as if he could rearrange the thoughts in his mind until they make sense.

"I left, Dusaro. I had a duty to protect my people."

"Protect your people—protect them from *what?*"

"From you," she drawls, double edged sharpness in her tone.

"I don't understand. We nearly started a war with transcendents because we thought you were dead. We slaughtered an entire army that was formed in response to our actions against them. You *allowed* us to think that. How could that have helped your people, Sera?"

Never have I heard Dusaro speak with such uncertainty. He stares at—*at his wife*—as if he hardly recognizes her at all. If it weren't for her apparent disdain towards him, I'd have written her off as being as vile as the rest of them.

"Did you expect I'd be content to stand by and watch as you and Ephraim spread your lies and your hate for my kind? Teaching people to fear us, as if we were the ones inciting violence. Motivating them to kill us before we killed their wives, their children." Sera shakes her head and tsks softly to herself.

"I would have protected you. I always protected you," Dusaro responds, confusion in his tone and his usual sneer replaced with tenderness.

"By hiding me! You stowed me away like some treasure you didn't want to share. That's not protecting me, Dusaro. I was a prisoner." Sera takes a step forward, and every guard around us mirrors her with one of their own.

"And you thought running away, *abandoning your son,* was

better than the life I could have provided you? That's beneath you, Sera, even for one of *them*," he spits back at her.

She ignores his comment but shifts her attention to Sin. "Son, I wanted to take you with me so badly. Leaving you was the worst part—it's why it took me so long to leave at all. But I knew if I took you, if I let him think they killed both of us, your father would have never stopped coming for them. You had to stay to give your father a reason to use caution. Please understand that, Singard."

"*Oh*—save your breath, Sera," Dusaro chastises.

I dare another glance to Sin whose face remains expressionless, stoic as he stares at his mother, considering her words and processing this new truth. Legion was birthed in response to the kingdom's prejudices against transcendents. Prejudices that greatly accelerated when it was believed they were responsible for Sera's death. How many people did Sin and his father slay in response to a betrayal that never happened?

"You killed him, didn't you, husband? Did you ever tell our son that?" Sera asks with forced humor in her tone. "That Ephraim wasn't as obsessed with the extinction of my people as you? But you... you were so foolishly blind with rage, you needed to get him out of the way so you could manipulate the crown to do your own bidding? Blaming the assassination on Legion—tsk, tsk, now that's beneath *you*, Dusaro. My only regret is not seeing your face when Adelphia denied you at the Rite."

Dusaro scoffs and jabs a finger towards her chest, now taking a few steps of his own towards her. "Ephraim was killed by the rebellion," he barks.

"*I am the rebellion!*" Sera roars back.

Wrath colors Dusaro's face a deep shade of red, while Sin's bronzed face blanches as he makes sense of her words. I fight back the urge to grab his hand, to give him a tiny squeeze to remind him he's not in this alone. But the Black Art made it perfectly clear he needs my comforts no longer when he broke his promise to me, so I pin my hands firmly at my sides.

"What have you done?" Dusaro whispers, rage lowering his voice to a deep, controlled tone.

"*What have I done?* I spent the last decade and a half building an army. Seeking out those that will fight alongside us, fight for the land we are rightfully owed. We deserve to be free, to run without consequence. Did you really think that little show in the city was a victory? That was a *distraction*—a necessary sacrifice Cathal and I agreed to long ago, to give us time to slip some of our own inside your keep. And you all were so desperate to lap up Legion blood you ran right at them. They are no longer your concern—*I am.*" Sera is small, but she is a beacon of strength as she addresses the two most powerful men in the realm without an ounce of fear. She is also minutes from having her throat ripped out as her words click in my mind. Legion didn't show up with Cosmina in tow because they never had her.

This bitch did. My eyes zero in on her pulse ticking away in her neck.

"What exactly are you asking of us?" Sin finally speaks, his throat bobbing as he struggles to keep the seal on his emotions in check.

Her face softens again at his voice, and she directs her full attention to her son now. "To release transcendents from your restrictions, your prejudices, your lies. Grant us land to form our own place in Aegidale, to self-govern as we please. We keep to our business and you to yours. We have ideas for treaty lines and trade routes and—"

"That is rich, Sera," Dusaro cuts her off, his light chuckling crescendoing to a deep laughter, and he claps out his amusement.

"If you deny us this, it will mean war. Not the carrying on you've done with Legion over the years—*real* war. Singard, nothing would cause me greater pain than watching you meet your end early, and certainly not next to him on the battlefield," she says, jerking her chin to motion towards Dusaro. "But I will not protect someone who kills my kind for the sake of running their blood through their hands, even if they are my kin."

My kind.

She doesn't know. His mother doesn't know Sin inherited her transcendence after she left.

"I grew up believing you were murdered in cold blood," Sin says. "I made decisions—I did unspeakable things, *Mother*—because I believed that." His mask slips as he addresses the woman that left him to be raised by Dusaro. Fled to protect shifters while inadvertently abandoning her own transcendent child to be brought up by the man who hates them most. Every life Sin reaped in her name was a lie. As if he wasn't already struggling to tame that darkness within himself, this truth erases any sense of morality he may have found in his choices.

"I didn't have another option," she responds calmly, but the corners of her eyes fold into creases.

"You could have just left! You *chose* to manipulate us. To let me think my own mother was brutally killed."

"What choice did I have? You were so young then, Singard, you don't remember. It wasn't safe. Even with your father there to protect me, he was only one person. If Ephraim discovered we were lying beneath his nose, he would have killed both of us for treason. And worse, he wouldn't have taken a chance to see if you inherited the gift. I chose life. Not just for me, but for you. And I'd do it all over again because that's what a mother does—she protects her child!" A tear springs from her eye, and she quickly wipes it away.

"You invade my home, kill my guards, *set fire to my castle*, and you dare make demands of me?" Sin's hands ball into fists as fury rolls off him in waves thick enough to choke the life from anyone standing too close. And yet, all I want to do is run to him. Throw my arms around his waist and tell him that he is loved.

I dig my feet into the ground.

"We needed the advantage. You wouldn't have listened to us any other way. I did what I had to do," Sera speaks calmly, steeling her spine.

"I ripped people apart in your name. I will do it again," Sin warns, his voice as cold and promising as death itself.

He's taken countless lives in exchange for the loss of his mother's, and now, he vows to reap the souls from their bodies because she *lives*.

Sera shifts her attention to where I lurk behind them. "I heard rumor there was a bloodwitch in your ranks."

A guttural growl rumbles in Sin's chest.

"Wren, is it? My name is Seraphine. A friend of mine informed me you might be interested in joining us, and I certainly wouldn't refuse someone with your power."

Now it is my throat that releases a warning growl. "Give me my sister, and I'll consider not drinking the blood of your friends from your *skull*."

A smile stretches across her rounded face. "Now I *really* wouldn't refuse you an offer," she says with approval. "Legion nor I ever touched your sister. I am surprised actually that someone with your abilities has been manipulated so easily. Perhaps you should have searched a little closer to home while looking for her."

"Leave now," Sin warns, his top lip curling over his teeth.

"Where is she?" I demand, taking a step towards her, magic flowing to my arms instinctually. Sin's mother or not, I will rip the blood from her body, ounce by ounce, until she tells me.

"I wouldn't expect you to believe me. Ask her yourself," she says, waving a hand to the opened gate behind her.

Appearing in the portcullis tunnel, her arm draped over Cornelius's shoulder, Cosmina limps towards us.

Goddess above.

"You traitorous cunt," Dusaro seethes, watching the eldest Langston son help my sister into the keep.

"Give her to me," I snap, rushing towards her.

"We recovered her a few hours ago. After mentioning to Cornelius you believed Legion was hiding your sister, he confirmed with me and what remains of Legion that we didn't have her, nor did we ever. Putting the pieces together was really quite simple if you had just thought about it. But sometimes we don't want to see what's right in front of us."

"This is your final warning. Get. Out. Now." Sin's voice is pure lethal, but Sera doesn't so much as flinch.

"You raise a hand to me and I have enough alchemist fire to burn your entire kingdom to ash," she threatens.

"Try. It," Sin dares between clenched teeth.

"Enough!" I shout. I shove Cornelius out of the way, sling Cosmina's arm over my shoulder, and hoist her weight onto my hip. I bare my teeth at him as I step away, and Cornelius merely gives me a nod as if understanding and expecting my reaction.

"It's okay, sweetie. I have you. You're okay. You're safe— you're safe," I whisper against her head, burying my face in the side of her tangled, black hair that reeks of natural oils and filth. Cosmina's usual fair skin is now a ghastly shade of translucent white, too thin, and pulled tight across her hollowed cheeks. Vibrant shades of plum and garnet strangle her wrists—bracelets I recognize.

She's been shackled in iron, weakening her to the point she can barely walk, just as she found me many years ago in a Legion camp. My sister twists slowly in my arms, turning to look at me, her sky-blue eyes frightened and confused.

"Where have you been?" I ask softly, brushing the hair from her eyes.

She raises a bone white arm and, with a trembling finger, points behind me. "With the Black Art."

CHAPTER 45

When I was younger and learning to hunt, Theon taught me to claim my kill immediately, never to leave it in the woods where predators might smell it and take it as their own. I would have done well to heed his advice here at Scarwood. I should have left the same second I snapped Sin's tether, returned home and looked for Cosmina with the help of my family. But instead, I clung to a seed of hope after seeing the faintest glimmer of something gentle tucked away deep inside him. Somewhere along the way, I dropped my heart and left it for the lurking wolf to claim.

And he fucking devoured it.

Cosmina lowers her arm, and I search both of her eyes with my own. Fear glitters in her light blue irises, even now, with my arms wrapped around her tight and our bodies pressed together. Her body trembles, her limbs adjusting to being without the iron turning her blood to lead.

He did this.

While I was risking everything for the sake of Sin's war, wrestling with my own conflicting feelings towards him, he was holding my sister captive.

Not Legion.

Not Sera.

Him.

Everything goes still. My bones harden as if they've been petrified in place, my limbs stiffening like thick spring bark, and I wish I could sprout roots from my feet and bury myself in the organic material. Sin calls my name from behind me, but I barely hear him over the chattering of every moment we spent together replaying in my head, over and over.

"What happened?" I ask Cosmina, my voice barely audible.

She coughs to clear her throat, the sound strangled as her poor lungs are as weak as the rest of her. "I went looking for you when you disappeared. By the time I caught up with Legion, they had just attacked a kingdom outpost. I came to Scarwood to report your disappearance because I knew Legion had taken you—I had no idea you were already here. When I told the Black Art who I was looking for, he had me locked up. They... they did things to me to give them information on you... kept saying you were a Legion spy. They thought I was too. Eventually, they grew tired of asking and left me chained in the cell. *Fucking pig*," Cosmina spits at the ground, and when she raises her eyes behind me, I know whom she's boring her menacing stare into.

I crush her against me, tears falling into her hair as images of the torment she must have endured flash in my mind. She suffered trying to rescue me. All the while I was dancing in elegant ball gowns with her captor. Dancing and... other unspeakable things.

Shame burns through me.

Cornelius walks forward and hovers a few feet away from us. "After you told me you fought Legion because they were holding your sister, I confirmed with Seraphine we didn't have her. We've been working with Legion for a while, and I never knew of any plan about sisters. If we didn't have her, it only made sense that our enemy did. I found her in a cell beneath the castle, hidden with illusive magic. I got her out before we unleashed the alchemist fire," Cornelius explains.

"How did you find her? You're a transcendent?" I ask. Naturally proficient with illusive magic, a transcendent could have sniffed out her location easily enough, as long as they were searching in the right place.

"No. There's a... a bit more to us than that. Come with us, and you'll see for yourself."

I should have known.

All the time I spent sifting through the complicated mix of emotions rooted in Sin's collective, and I still didn't see it. He let me think he was doing me a *favor* by allowing me to return home, all the while knowing I would find Cosmina missing, springing his plan into action. He knew I'd offer my aid when I suspected Legion took her—that's why he accepted my offer to fight alongside him so quickly. And *that's* why he didn't want me rummaging around in his head, because he feared if I looked hard enough, I'd uncover the betrayal he'd stowed away in there.

"Please let me explain, Wren."

Sin's voice shatters the last of my resolve, and I slowly turn to face him. "Is it true?"

He doesn't move for a long moment, and then in a voice softer than I've ever heard from him, he answers, "Yes."

I knew it was true. I didn't need to ask, but I wanted him to look me in the eye and admit what he had done. Tears sting my eyes as they dribble down my cheeks, and I turn my back to him.

"It is time for us to take our leave. Will you be joining us, Wren?" Sera asks.

"Lead the way."

Cosmina steps out from under my arm, and we follow after Sera's group now leaving through the tunnels.

"No. Wren, no—stop!" Sin says, grabbing my arm and pulling me to a halt.

I spin on my heel and shove my hands into his chest as I push him away. "Every. Single. Day. Every day you let me worry myself sick, imagining what terrible things Legion must be doing to her. And every time you looked at me, you knew she was rotting away beneath our feet. There is nothing you can say to me, Singard. *Nothing!*" I shout the last word.

Cosmina stops in the gate and turns to look at me. I nod for her to go ahead, and she disappears in the tunnel with the rest of the group. Sin's soldiers scatter back towards the castle, beginning to clean up the debris and tend to those injured in the attack, leaving Sin and me staring at each other in the middle of the courtyard.

"I didn't want this to happen," he placates.

"Is that so? Pray tell, when exactly did you decide you didn't want this to happen? Was it before or after you tortured my sister and lied to my face? Before or after you convinced me to slaughter an army for you? Before or after you used me for a *good fuck,* Singard?"

"It wasn't like that. Wren, I *swear* to you, it was never like that," he says, putting his hands up as if to caution my anger.

"You're a godsdamned monster," I choke through the tears falling faster now.

"Your sister came here right after you did. I thought you were both working with Legion, so yes, I... questioned her."

"Tortured her," I correct.

He sighs but doesn't deny it. "I made a horrible mistake. When Cathal told me what you were, your secrecy made sense, and I realized Cosmina had been telling the truth when she said you had nothing to do with Legion. But I still didn't trust you. I had no idea who you were or what you were planning. All I knew was I wanted you on our side when we met Legion head on. You were an asset I wasn't willing to lose, and I didn't tell you about your sister because she was leverage if I needed to force your hand. I *wanted* to tell you. The night after we went to the temple, I wanted to tell you so badly, but I knew you'd be furious, and you wouldn't have fought the same if you didn't think they had her. You didn't hesitate killing them because you thought you were doing it for *her*."

I capture my bottom lip between my teeth and shake my head. If it was possible to hurt more, I do as his words pierce my chest as if they could carve out my heart and plop it on a silver platter.

An asset.

"Do you bed all your assets, Your Grace?" I ask, resting my hands in the divots of my waist.

Sin takes another step towards me but halts when I fling my hand towards him, my own fire magic simmering in my palm. I lower it when he nods in acknowledgment and backs off.

"What happened between us after the war... that was never a part of the plan. When I followed you into my study, I felt a... a hunger I never have before, and it wasn't just the caster's high. It was like the high kept me from hiding how I felt about you. How I've *always* felt about you."

"Save it," I say, no longer meeting his eyes, unable to stomach looking at him for a second longer.

"I didn't know how to let you go," he continues. "I didn't *want* to. I knew when I released your sister and you learned what I'd done... I couldn't bear the thought of losing you like that. I planned on sending you away when I returned from the city, but seeing you at the ball... there it was again. This feeling like if I let you leave, I wouldn't be able to breathe. It was selfish and wrong, but I couldn't let you go. But after we... again..." he waves his hand to imply our coupling in the throne room, "I was so furious with myself, and I knew I *needed* to let you go. That's why I was sending you away, because when you were safe and home, I was going to release her and make sure she was returned safely. I just couldn't bear seeing your face when you learned what I'd done."

I try to fight back the tears, but they rush down my cheeks. I run my hands through my hair, gripping the roots too hard as if feeling the pain in my scalp will lessen the ache in my chest. "You know what the worst part is, Singard? It isn't the lies or the betrayal... no. It's that I didn't even see it coming. I read your collective so many times, and I couldn't see the manipulation through all the *guilt* you feel about yourself. I actually felt bad for you—I wanted to take that pain from you. If I could have, I would have, to spare you from that hurt, and now I don't know which one of us that makes more pathetic."

"Wren," his voice cracks around my name.

"I TRUSTED YOU!" The words fall out before I can stop them. "I brought your enemies to their knees before you, and I would have turned them to dust had you simply asked me to. You watched as I ripped their blood from their skins and as I fought to hold onto my humanity. And all the while you stood there, KNOWING it was for NOTHING!"

"You'll never know how sorry I am. For all of it," he whispers, lines creasing his forehead. "Don't leave with them. Leave me, leave this place, but don't join them, Wren."

"Why not? Are you worried I'll expose your little secret? Imagine how your own mother will feel when she learns her son is killing his own kind."

"Because we're going to *war* with them," he growls.

A humorless laugh rattles from my chest. "Scared?"

"Yes. But not for the reason you're thinking."

"So, *not* because you're worried they'll finally tear your godsforsaken kingdom down, piece by piece and limb by limb, with me on their side?"

He shakes his head softly. "Because they won't win, Wren. And I don't want you on their side when the fighting begins. I cannot protect you if you're on enemy lines."

"Protect me? You forced me into servitude, and *now* you're worried about me getting hurt?"

"It's different now. *We* are different now."

"We are nothing," I spit.

He's against me in a blink, his chest brushing mine and his hand cradling my cheek. "I have *never* felt this way about anyone. And I know you feel it too. I would burn the realm to ash to keep you safe, but if you join them, you are making a direct threat against the kingdom. I know you're furious with me, but don't... don't do this, love."

When I rise onto my tiptoes and crush my mouth to his, heat explodes between our bodies like a million stars raining down on us.

And I know our fate is as sealed as our lips.

With a final tug of his hair between my fingers, I pull away, eyeing the fire now feasting inside the turrets behind him. It's only destruction magic, nothing he won't be able to put out quickly, but my intent is as palpable as the flames licking the castle's guts.

Turning my back on him, I dart through the open portcullis, Cosmina pausing when she hears my racing foot-falls. My sister gives me a knowing look, noting the tears staining my flushed cheeks, my reaction to the Black Art's betrayal too visceral to stem from anger alone. When she opens her arms to me, I throw myself against her, tucking my head against her bony chest, and she wraps her frail arms around me.

An unearthly yowl pierces the caliginous night, the sound of Sin's torment sinking into the cracks of my fracturing heart. I slam my hand to my chest as if I could stop myself from shattering completely, but his pain bleeds through my fingers and seeps through every splintered nerve until I can no longer separate his suffering from my own.

Smoke swells into the sky as the remains of the fire I birthed in the castle rises to the heavens, carrying my message along with it.

War is coming.

To be continued...

Wren and Sin's story will continue in The Bonds That Break Us.

ACKNOWLEDGMENTS

I am convinced it is easier to write an entire novel than to express the gratitude in my heart for everyone that has helped bring my debut to life. I will begin where it makes most sense.

To my lovely readers: your support means the world to me. There is no combination of words that exists to describe just how deeply I appreciate you all. None of this would be possible without you. From the deepest, darkest pits of my bursting heart, thank you.

To Brittany Weisrock: you will never know just how grateful I am for you. Thank you for taking a chance on me and believing in my work. Your guidance is unmatched, and I am so thankful for your enthusiasm and dedication in turning my manuscript into a real-life book. I will never forget how I felt when I read your email that changed my life.

To my lovely cover designer, Emily: thank you for delivering all the dark romantic vibes and designing the cover of my dreams. Your eye for design is incredible.

To Jon and Jeanette: you have always believed in me, even when I didn't myself. Thank you for being a constant in my life, and lending an ear all those times I needed to vent. Jeanette, if you haven't guessed by now, Morrinne's character is heavily inspired by you. Thank you for being the mom that I needed.

To Richelle: your drive and motivation is infectious. For as long as I can remember, I always wanted to be just like my big sis, which in hindsight, I'm sure was incredibly annoying to have your little sister copying your every move. Thanks for putting up with me anyways, and for being the best role model. You deserve all great things.

To my incredibly talented writing friends and beta readers: I am eternally grateful for your encouragement when I needed that extra boost of serotonin. Thank you all for the time you spent reading this book, offering suggestions, and helping shape this book into the version it is now. You know who you are.

To Bryan and the entire team at Lake Country Press: thank you for giving Sin and Wren the best possible home. You never fail to go above and beyond in all that you do, and I am honored to be counted amongst your authors.

Lastly, to my incredible husband, Ian: you have never doubted me. Ever. Even on my darkest days, you have been a light in my world. I am convinced this book would not have come full circle if not for your encouragement, reminders to rest when I need to, and your warm hugs. Thank you for loving me, our son, and most of all: thank you for teaching me to love myself.

About the Author

Erin is a lover of all things fantasy and more than a little obsessed with morally gray characters. She holds a degree in Film and Media Studies but has shifted her focus to her one true love: writing novels set in fantastical places with dark, twisty romance. A self-proclaimed iced coffee enthusiast, you can often find Erin writing in local cafes, poorly singing along to the radio in a Starbucks drive-through, or rewatching The Vampire Diaries with a cold brew in tow. An avid traveler, Erin has lived all over the country, but Alaska and the Pacific Northwest has a special place in her heart. The Blood That Binds Us is her debut novel, and she looks forward to writing more stories where the "villain" gets the girl.

Milton Keynes UK
Ingram Content Group UK Ltd.
UKHW030651090924
448088UK00004B/375